Let It Be Me

I0846804

Let It Be Me

KELLY HENNELLY

2026

Let It Be Me
Copyright © 2026 Kelly Hennelly
All rights reserved.

No part of this book may be reproduced, distributed, or transmitted in any form or by any means, including photocopying, recording, or other electronic or mechanical methods, without the prior written permission of the author, except in the case of brief quotations embodied in critical reviews and certain other noncommercial uses permitted by copyright law. For permission requests, write to the author at: AuthorKellyHennelly@gmail.com.

This is a work of fiction. Names, characters, businesses, places, events, and incidents are either the products of the author's imagination or used in a fictitious manner. Any resemblance to actual persons, living or dead, or actual events is purely coincidental.

Illustration and Book Design by Alissa DeGregorio
ISBN: 979-8-218-87643-2
Self-published by Kelly Hennelly
Printed in the United States of America

First Edition: 2026

For Dad

You may not always think you got it right, but I'm living proof you did.

Thanks for never giving up—on yourself, or on me.

CHAPTER ONE

Tally

If hangovers could kill, I'd have been taken out by a sniper.

One bullet after another had come flying through the window—cheap wine, a failed situationship, and the creeping dread that I was once again making a mess of my life.

See, I could have done what I'd always done. I could have packed it all up and headed for the hills, or another country altogether, and pretended a change of scenery was the answer to all those dead-end prayers I kept sending skyward, forever unanswered.

Without fail, my life tended to spiral back to that same, chaotic choice. Stay and sort the wreckage, or duck out and hope it all looks better from somewhere else. And I was an expert at running. New cities, new jobs, new men—none of it had to stick if I told myself it was temporary. Reversible. Forgettable. Pencil marks I could erase later.

Running was easy. Running let me believe the problem was the place, not me. Staying meant I'd have to face the possibility that I was the common denominator in every failed attempt at a life.

So I kept moving. Hunting for the perfect moment, the perfect city, the perfect man—as if perfection itself would show up with a neon sign that said, *Congratulations, you've arrived at adulthood!*

Instead, all I'd managed to rack up was a pile of frequent flier miles and a nagging suspicion I was running in circles.

What I really wanted wasn't perfection at all. I wanted somewhere to land. Somewhere that felt like home.

Which, for me, wasn't a house, an address, or a name on a lease. Home was that weightless, fleeting feeling I'd yet to discover—but knew would let me finally exhale. Somewhere I didn't have to hustle, apologize, or explain myself. Somewhere I could let the tension in my shoulders soften and, maybe, just maybe, believe I was allowed to stay.

I'd never had that. Certainly not growing up in Newnan, Georgia, where my mother made sure I unfailingly knew I was an accessory to her carefully curated life, not the main event. Not in any of the cities I'd dipped in and out of like a girl trying on lives in a dressing room. Certainly not in New York, though I'd tried like hell.

That's how I ended up in a clawfoot bathtub in Brooklyn, dry-heaving into a plastic shopping bag, while my poodle, Nancy Reagan, stared at me like she was debating calling animal control.

I'd spent twelve years chasing that idea of perfection as if it were hiding in another zip code. Paris in the rain. A noodle shop in Tokyo during a thunderstorm. A tent under the Northern Lights with a man still saved in my phone as "???"

And yet, somehow, every detour brought me back to New York. The city was my toxic ex—I knew better, but I still couldn't quit it, no matter how hard I'd tried.

Three boroughs. Six apartments. One closet-sized storage unit I paid for and never opened. And unsurprisingly, I'd landed in a sweltering fourth-floor walk-up with a broken A/C and a dog who deserved better.

Nancy gave a half-hearted huff and did her usual slow spin before collapsing on the tile beside me.

"I know," I mumbled, wiping my forehead with the hem of my t-shirt. "This is not our finest moment."

She let out a sigh that sounded a whole lot like *speak for yourself.*

There was, of course, the possibility that I'd been searching so long that I forgot what I was actually looking for. I thought if I kept moving, kept chasing, I'd eventually stumble into a place where I fit. Somewhere I belonged. Or into a person who made me feel like I'd mattered all along. Or even just into myself, without all the judgment and guilt I carried around like luggage I couldn't unpack.

So instead, I took pictures of the kind of lives I wanted—ones with string lights, soup bowls, and hands reaching for each other across tables. I captured the joy of strangers because it was safer than asking why I hadn't found any of that tangible happiness of my own. Why I'd never been the girl worth staying for, or the one someone asked to stay. Why I inevitably seemed to end up right back where I started, heart cracked, bank account empty, pretending the loneliness of it all didn't feel like an open, gaping wound.

I wanted a life that felt still. That felt like it was all mine. And someone who wanted nothing more than to share that stillness with me.

But all I had was a plastic bodega bag full of nausea and a foreboding feeling that everything was about to change.

And God help me, I think I wanted it to.

In New York, I'd tried turning my camera into a livelihood. Weddings, engagement shoots, the occasional overpriced Bumble date session where some guy named Chad wanted to look casually windswept in Central Park. But the Big Apple didn't exactly roll out the red carpet for a girl with a Canon and a talent for spiraling.

My phone buzzed against the tile. I squinted at the screen.

VENMO REQUEST: $847.23 - SUBLEASE RENT (OVERDUE) Jess says: Hey girl! No pressure but my landlord is asking…

I turned the phone face down.

I thought that this time, I could finally make it here. I honestly believed it, in that stubborn, starry-eyed way people do when they've seen too many movies about wide-eyed dreamers and Broadway musicals where someone's big break is right around the corner.

I'd arrived in the city once again with an unpacked suitcase full of half-baked dreams and a portfolio of shots from around the world, full of what I was sure were world-changing images. Ones I thought could stop people in their tracks and make them *feel* something. I figured New York would take another look and scoop me off the sidewalk, a long-lost prodigy they'd be searching for all this time. That I'd land the dream job. The cover shoot. The Life.

Another buzz.

BANK ALERT: Your account balance is $23.18

Nancy looked from my phone to my face, her expression pitying.

"Don't," I warned her.

But the truth was quieter and grittier than that; I discovered, as most of us do when our dreams face reality head-on, that I was just another ordinary person, holding on to a tiny spark of ambition that flickered in the dark where only I could see it.

I hadn't booked anything even close to bill-payable in months. The gigs had dried up, the emails had slowed to a trickle, and the dream I'd stitched together out of hope and hustle was unraveling one late rent notice at a time.

I twisted the faucet and stuck my forehead under it, hoping the water might cool the heat creeping up my neck, the kind that had nothing to do with the hangover. Or at least erase the last few years of my life, if we were being ambitious.

This wasn't a rock bottom I could fix with a night out on the town or a new therapist. This was the kind where you're staring down a hole you dug yourself and still wondering if there's treasure at the bottom. Spoiler alert: there wasn't. Just a bag full of last night's bodega wine and a pile of receipts I hadn't dared to look at.

One, I knew, was from the bar where Nick worked—my latest failed attempt at human connection, the one I somehow kept "missing" every time I stopped in, including the night before. Another went toward wine and my usual lineup of emotional support snacks, grabbed after he dodged me yet again. The rest? Who even knew? All completely unnecessary. All painfully, unmistakably overdraft adjacent.

But maybe it wasn't *that* horrible. Maybe Nick really had been busy. Perhaps the job at the thrift store would turn into a steady gig if I just… showed up more. Maybe I could make rent *and* buy toilet paper this month.

And right as I was beginning to convince myself that things were not, indeed, as bad as my post-hangover anxiety was trying to convince me they were, my phone rang.

My voice came out raspy, coated in a film of last night's bottle of Cabernet and panic. "I don't have time for this, Doyle. I'm dying."

Doyle Aden—professional golden child, my younger brother by a whopping 18 months, and current holder of the World's Most Disappointed Sigh—was not feeling merciful.

"So, I listened to the five-minute podcast you left me last night—sorry, voicemail—and I'm confused," he said. "Are you pregnant?"

I froze, my head jerking up only to slam against the faucet. My stomach twisted as fragments of memory flickered across my brain, fractured and jerky, like a projector with a broken reel. Several phone calls, a string of texts, a blurry selfie, and far too much giggling to myself—every little piece looping through my mind, unrelenting.

"Excuse me?!" I squeaked, my voice higher than intended, hands flying to my forehead as if I could press the echoes of last night back into some neat, manageable box.

Doyle laughed, which felt deeply rude considering the circumstances.

"Girl, come on. You called me seven times. And on the final one, you left… a journey. It started with singing. Then there was a rant about a one-night stand giving you the wrong number and, I quote, his '*oily fat head*.'"

A fresh wave of nausea hit me.

"You told me about the size of his—"

"Oh my God, Doyle, stop."

"—which I could've gone my whole life without knowing. Then you realized your period was late. And after some very loud breathing, I got to experience the soundtrack of you taking a pregnancy test. Again. Not something I needed."

I slapped a hand over my mouth.

"You snored for a while. Then the timer went off. And then I was treated to: 'Oh shit. Ohhhh shit. Ohhhhhhhhh my God. Doyle! Doyle, pick up the phone! Congratulations, you're gonna be an uncle!'"

My stomach lurched, a full-on flip that left me breathless. Nancy caught the vibe and started barking like the apartment was under siege. I scrambled out of the tub, nearly faceplanting on the tile, and muttered, "This cannot be happening." My hand dove into the trash, fishing out the test as if it were radioactive. One word glared back at me.

Pregnant.

I whispered it to myself again, hoping the sound might make it go away. "This can't be right."

"Well," Doyle said, way too calm for the moment, "take another one."

I yanked the second test from the box under the sink and slammed him on speaker.

"I do not want to listen to another urine stream, Tally," Doyle groaned.

"Too bad!" I shot back, voice high, bouncing on the balls of my feet. Nancy yapped like a tiny tornado, her crusty paws slipping as she tried to climb the porcelain tub.

I set the timer and collapsed onto the closed toilet, rocking slightly, clutching my phone in one hand and the stick in the other, performing some sort of bizarre fertility ritual gone wrong. When the timer buzzed, I flipped the test over—and my stomach did another somersault. Positive. Again.

I shrieked, high-pitched and unhinged, a sound so jarring it made Nancy pause mid-yap before she skidded across the floor, bodega snacks flying, plastic bags scattering, the bathmat crumpling under her chaos. Then she hurled herself into my lap, eyes narrowed, delivering the canine equivalent of *Get it together, woman.*

My phone slipped off the sink and thudded into the bathroom trash.

"Hello? Tally River?" Doyle's voice echoed up, tinny and distorted from the bottom of the bin. "Are you okay?"

I clutched Nancy to my chest and leaned over the trash can, shouting down into it. "No, Doyle! Nancy isn't going to be an only child for much longer!"

A long, exasperated sigh drifted up through the speaker. Then silence.

I knew he'd hung up. He needed a minute to breathe, to recover, to Google whether adult sibling swaps were legal in Georgia.

I don't know how long I stayed slumped on the bathroom floor—long enough to scroll through my phone and confirm that, yes, I had called and texted the fake number Nick gave me at least six times. Certainly long enough to search Instagram for every variation of "Nick + bartender + Brooklyn" my sleep-deprived brain could dream up.

No hits. Just a dozen Brooklyn Nicks who were definitely not my Nick, and a handful of unanswered texts I wished I could unsend.

The apartment was still spinning when a knock thundered against the front door.

Nancy yipped.

"Maybe it's Nick," I whispered to myself. "Maybe he brought bagels and an apology for ghosting me, and we'll co-parent this baby over brunch."

I tried to shove down the memory of how I'd sat at his bar for months, telling him my life story over dirty martinis. How he remembered I liked extra pickles. How he managed to look completely smitten when I ugly-cried during karaoke—even when it wasn't my turn. How I'd convinced myself that remembering someone's drink order was basically the same as love. And how I managed to, stupidly, mistake convenience for interest when he finally asked me to come back to his place.

So he could nail that order too.

I laughed it off, but under all the sarcasm lived a quieter thought—one I let take up space in my heart—that I could bring him home to my momma one day, and she'd see I'd finally gotten it right. That I'd finally found someone who shared my hunger for the world, for chasing dreams. Someone who loved me for me.

I opened the door to find Jordan, my brother-in-law and Doyle's husband, wearing a face that said he deeply regretted answering his phone that morning.

Behind him came a throat-clearing sound. Dig, my best friend and emergency contact, stood in the dim cavern of the stairwell holding a grease-splattered bag of bagels. He stepped into view as if he'd been lurking in the shadows for hours, waiting for the perfect moment to make his dramatic entrance.

"A little birdie told me you needed a new life plan," Dig said, stepping over a pile of laundry as if it was totally normal to find leggings draped over a toaster on the floor. His gaze swept over me with the reverence usually reserved for saints and pop stars who died young. I looked like I'd been hit by a city bus and emotionally backed over again, but he still somehow managed to beam at me like the sun shone directly out of my ass.

Jordan dropped a tray of coffees and a paper bag on the counter with surgical precision, desperate not to touch any of the surfaces. "Eat. I thought this was just a hangover gone wrong. I see now that it was wildly optimistic of me to assume."

He scanned the apartment, keeping his face carefully neutral. The place was clean-ish, though heavily cluttered. Organized chaos. I needed to see all my things to know they existed. How the hell was I supposed to find anything if it was hidden in a drawer?

"Doyle called me," Jordan finally said, sighing. "I was in town for a sommelier conference, and apparently the closest adult with a working credit card and the means to get you through this crisis. He told me to check on you. I told him I don't do surprise interventions without caffeine, so I stopped for coffee. And then he insisted I call Dig."

Dig gave a little wave. "I dropped everything. And I mean everything. I was in the middle of a potential date-slash-revenge flirtation with this guy I met in the line at L'Industrie last night. He had a boat, Tally."

I shoved a massive bite of an everything bagel into my mouth, salt and seeds raining onto the floor, cream cheese spilling down my fingers. I might've been on the verge of tossing my cookies, but nothing came between me and a proper New York City bagel.

"It's, like, ten in the morning," I mumbled around the carbs. "Where did you even find someone with a boat—ya know what, never mind."

Jordan cringed at my less-than-ladylike attack on breakfast. "Anyway, we all thought this was another episode of *Tally TV*. A hangover, perhaps. Or some weird social experiment. Or you missing us since your brother and I haven't really seen you since you got back from Australia. But definitely not… whatever this is."

If I had my camera right then, I could've framed the shot: Dig holding the bagels like an offering to the gods, Jordan looking as if he'd been sent into a war zone without a helmet, me mid-bagel bite, damp hair sticking to my sweaty forehead like a wave had trampled me. Not exactly Pinterest-worthy, but still—chaotic, ridiculous, possibly even a little beautiful. It was life, in its most raw form.

Dig set his bagel down and crossed the room slowly, eyes narrowing in mock suspicion. Then, without warning, he reached out and laid a single, dramatic hand across my stomach.

"Is it true?" he whispered, eyes wide and fake-serious.

I smacked his hand away with a yelp. He gasped and retaliated with a slap to my arm, which I met with an open-palmed swipe to his shoulder. Within seconds, we were tangled in a full-on slap fight in the middle of the kitchen, Nancy barking at our feet like a referee on speed.

"For the love of God, people, stop it," Jordan snapped, stepping between us. "You're grown adults. Allegedly."

I collapsed onto the couch, breathless and laughing and still somewhat nauseous. Dig flopped down beside me, completely unfazed.

"God, I missed you," Dig said, brushing a crumb off my shoulder like I was a Renaissance painting and not someone who'd spent her morning yakking into a bag. "Even though I saw you two days ago, my life is truly not complete until I am by your side, watching you make the next poor decision in what will likely be a string of even more poor decisions."

Then he slid closer to the spot beside me, gently placed a hand on my knee, and in his most solemn, theater-kid tone said, "It would be my absolute honor to help escort you to Savannah."

I stared at him and blinked, tilting my head. Had I had a stroke on top of everything else that had gone wrong this morning?

"I'm sorry—*what?*"

Dig nodded, sincere and wildly unhelpful. "We'll pack up what matters most, hop in a rental, and head south. You'll start fresh. Like a glamorous pioneer. But with A/C and better eyebrows."

"No," I blurted, flinging my arms toward the disaster around me. "No, no, no. I can't just go to Savannah! My *life* is here!"

Jordan made a quiet noise in the back of his throat. Not a laugh. Not a cough. A noise nestled somewhere between pity and a sigh of spiritual defeat.

"Your brother's worried," he said, setting his coffee down. "He thinks being somewhere calmer might help you figure out your next move. Somewhere with… family."

Dig gasped. "Wow. Just gonna erase me like that?"

"I'm not moving to Savannah," I snapped. "That's where Doyle ran off to when he ditched me and our plans to travel the world together. To marry you!" I pointed at Jordan and furrowed my brow. "You stole him."

Jordan didn't flinch. "He offered himself freely."

"I can't abandon my life—"

His eyes swept the apartment—the futon Dig refused to fold the last time he stayed the night, the prints taped to walls because I couldn't afford frames, the camera gear scattered like evidence of a crime scene. He didn't need to say more. But he sure as hell did.

"What life, hun?"

Ouch.

"You don't have to say it like that," I muttered.

"You're currently working at a thrift store, and your dreams of becoming the next Annie Leibovitz crashed into reality three unpaid gigs ago. Also, need I remind you, you're likely six weeks pregnant with a guy who ghosted you after giving you a fake number."

I crossed my arms. "Why do you hate me?"

"I don't hate you," Jordan said, sitting beside me with a sigh. "I just don't understand you. But I love you anyway. And Doyle and I wouldn't be able to live with ourselves if we didn't try to help. Come to Savannah. Stay with us for a little bit while you figure out your next move. It's not a trap."

It's not a trap. Meaning, they hadn't yet, and wouldn't be telling my mother at this moment in time. Meaning that I was safe from the wrath I knew was eventually hurtling my way. But at least this bought me some time to try and figure it all out.

The panic in my chest didn't vanish, but it started to shift and morph into something else entirely—something resembling surrender.

"What would I even do in Savannah?"

Dig grinned. "I don't know. Start over. Take pictures of Spanish moss and strangers in love. You're always chasing that next moment anyway—might as well do it somewhere the backdrop doesn't smell like hot garbage."

I opened my mouth to argue. To list all the reasons this was my home, my life, my choice. But the words stuck in my throat like a day-old bagel. Because he wasn't wrong. I had nothing here except a dog, a hangover, and a positive pregnancy test from a man who gave me the wrong goddamn number.

"Fine," I muttered.

Dig threw his legs over mine. "I'll be able to stay for the first few days. That gives us enough time to get you settled and then ruin your new life."

Nancy whimpered.

And just like that, it was settled. One night with the wrong guy, one catastrophic voicemail, and I was trading my big-city burnout for Southern comfort.

God help Savannah.

CHAPTER TWO

Charlie

Morning light streamed through the tall windows of my River Street studio, catching the dust in the air and throwing gold streaks across the floorboards. I'd been up since before dawn, hands buried in the week's haul of discarded treasures—a teak porch swing with a busted slat, a box of tarnished brass drawer pulls, a stack of vintage postcards someone had tossed behind the antique shop on Bull Street.

Other people's junk. My livelihood. My comfort zone. The only religion that ever made sense to me.

Once the new finds were sorted into their usual pile of organized chaos, I spent the rest of the morning elbow-deep in salvaged wood and sweat. Which, in my opinion, beat dealing with whatever fresh hell Magnolia was spinning up. My sister had a way of turning everything into a melodrama, and I'd spent too many years trying to keep her from lighting it all on fire.

Figuratively. Mostly.

The rhythmic sanding of an old barstool helped drown out my thoughts, but not completely.

O'Malley's, our family's bar, was still standing, but barely. Magnolia had been doing everything she could to keep the place afloat since she'd inherited it after our uncle died, but it wasn't easy, not with the financial strain or the constant pressure of trying to make ends meet. And certainly not with that look she got sometimes—the one that said she was holding it together by force, afraid she couldn't do it on her own.

Her ex, Lee, returning to Savannah, had also stirred something in her. And if I were being honest, it had stirred something in me, too. He hadn't been back long—long enough to throw our routines off balance, but not long enough for anyone to admit how much it mattered that he was finally home again.

Leland Wilder. Magnolia's teenage heartbreak and my oldest friend. He was the reason I finally took that restless, half-formed part of myself that wanted to be an artist and turned it into whatever this career had become.

He was the first person who ever looked at my sketches and saw potential instead of pastime. Back when we were kids, digging through the junk piles his mom brought home from estate sales, he told me I had a rare eye. That turning trash into art wasn't just a way to cope—it was a calling. A way out.

He'd left Savannah over ten years ago, chasing music and Grammys and the shiny new life you can only find when you leave the town you grew up in. Now he was back, acting like no time had passed and the wreckage he'd left behind had just... vanished.

It hadn't. In fact, it had gotten a hell of a lot worse.

For the last decade, my life had been pretty damn simple: work hard, take care of the people I love, don't let anything fall apart. It wasn't glamorous, but it was steady. Predictable. I knew my role. I knew what was expected of me.

Since our Uncle Cole died, everything felt off—like a picture frame hanging crooked that I kept meaning to fix but never did. I kept thinking one day I'd wake up and things would feel right again. That day hadn't come.

Magnolia's name lit up my phone screen, cutting through the quiet.

Speaking of my crazy-ass sister.

I exhaled sharply and answered. "What's up, Mags?"

"Am I making the right choice?" she asked, skipping the pleasantries entirely.

I paused, sanding block hovering over the chair leg. "You're gonna have to be more specific."

Magnolia let out an exasperated breath, and I could picture her now—pacing behind the bar at O'Malley's, chewing on her thumbnail, pretending she wasn't unraveling at the seams. "Dane," she finally admitted. "All of it. The almost-engagement, the business, the way things are just... going."

Ah. So we were there now.

I didn't answer right away. I wasn't sure how to.

Her boyfriend, Dane, had nearly proposed a few weeks ago—even though neither of them was remotely ready for that kind of forever—and if that hadn't been enough to rattle her, Lee showing up out of nowhere certainly had. It got under her skin in a way I hadn't seen in years. The hesitation in her voice was new. I didn't like it.

"I don't know," I admitted, because I didn't. "Do you love him?"

She stayed quiet on the other line for a beat. And the hesitation, however small, was enough. Because she didn't know which "him" I was referring to—her boyfriend, or his brother who was back in town.

"You're a real shithead sometimes, Charles Abner Pruitt."

I smirked. "I try."

She heaved out a tired sigh. "Maybe I'll get some clarity today, and it will all click into place. I don't know."

"Let me know how that works out for you," I muttered.

She scoffed. "Go be crabby somewhere else. I'll see you later."

"Hey!" I snapped, pulling back the phone and staring at the screen like it had personally offended me. "You called me."

The call ended with Magnolia groaning as she hung up, but the restlessness didn't leave. It settled in my chest, low and heavy.

Magnolia got to spin out. That was her role. Chaos. Sparks. Big leaps and bigger crashes. And mine? I was the net. The extinguisher. The one who swept up the broken glass after.

I used to think it made me useful. Lately, it made me tired.

It could've been watching Magnolia start to question her own path. Maybe it was Lee, sauntering back into town like time hadn't laid a hand on him, stirring up every buried feeling in a ten-mile radius. Or maybe it was quieter than that. Deeper. The kind of shift you don't see coming until you're already standing somewhere different.

I'd spent my whole life making sure other people were okay. Making sure Magnolia didn't lose the bar. Making sure she didn't lose *herself.* Keeping the roof from caving in on what little we had left of our family.

I exhaled hard and rubbed the back of my neck.

No use thinking about it now. I had shit to do.

I grabbed the rag draped over my worktable and wiped down the chair leg I'd been sanding, sawdust clinging to my forearms, when the sound of footsteps echoed through the studio.

"Please tell me you have something cold to drink," Sutton groaned, stepping inside like she'd crossed the Mojave. She dropped a tote bag onto the nearest stool and started fanning herself with a takeout menu. "I am dying."

Sutton James had been around so long she felt like part of the furniture—loud, bossy furniture that constantly raided my fridge and never said thank you. She'd started as Magnolia's best friend and, somewhere along the way, became the unofficial mayor of our friend group.

Lee trailed in behind her, shaking his head with a grin. "You live in Savannah, Sutton. It's almost always hot."

She shot him a look as she kicked off her sandals. "That doesn't mean I have to *enjoy* it."

I sighed and tossed Sutton a cold bottle of water from the mini-fridge in the corner. "What do you two want?"

"Rude," she said, cracking it open. "Maybe we wanted to check in on our favorite neighborhood curmudgeon."

I gave her a flat look. She grinned like she knew she hit a nerve.

Lee perched on a stool and glanced around the studio. "Doyle and Jordan been by?"

I shook my head. "Haven't seen them since brunch the other day. What's up?"

"I had some things I needed to run by them. Bar stuff," he said with a shrug. "They're probably tied up."

Doyle and Jordan ran *Cheese, Please!*, the wine bar next door to my studio. They owned the building too, which made them my landlords, my neighbors, and my friends—though lately they were leaning heavier on the landlord side, since my rent was behind. Again.

Sutton arched a brow over her water bottle. "Or they're hiding from whatever fresh hell Magnolia's about to unleash now that she's got more money to play with."

"Probably," I muttered.

"Speaking of," Lee said, turning to me, "Is Magnolia really okay? With me buying into O'Malley's, I mean."

Lee had come back from Nashville and decided to embark on a clumsy, second-chance mission to win Magnolia back by putting his Grammy earnings into our family's bar. Part rescue mission, part steal his brother's girlfriend back for himself.

I scrubbed a hand down my face. "She says she is."

Sutton snorted. "So that's a no."

I exhaled hard. "She's got a lot going on. Keeping the bar afloat, figuring things out with Dane, trying to wrap her head around whatever business deal you're working out. She's thinking about the future for the first time in... ever."

Lee nodded slowly. "And you?"

"What about me?"

Sutton tilted her head, watching me too closely. "You know what's weird? I've known you for, what, eighteen years? And I have no idea what you actually want. Like, for yourself."

I tightened my grip on the sanding block. "I'm sanding these barstools for my baby sister and being the loyal, diligent big brother and best friend I always am. The rest doesn't matter."

Lee leaned back against the worktable, arms crossed, eyes steady. "It does, though."

I gave them both a look. "I don't need an intervention."

Sutton smirked. "That's exactly what people in need of interventions say."

I groaned, dragging a hand through my hair. "Both of you—out."

Lee grinned, holding up his hands in surrender. "Fine, fine. We're just worried about you, brother, that's all. Maybe it's time you tried expending all this energy on *yourself* for once."

Sutton hopped off the stool, stretching like a cat. "We're going to the wine tasting next door tonight. Don't be an old man. Come have a drink."

I sighed, but didn't argue. "Yeah, yeah."

The door shrieked as it opened, then slammed shut behind them. Through the window, they ducked into the alley, likely taking the shortcut toward Bull Street to dodge the herd of tourists clogging up the riverfront.

Thirty-three years old, and what did I have to show for it? A stack of half-finished projects, a sister still pretending she didn't need saving, and a front door that wailed like a beagle no matter how many times I fixed the damn thing.

Outside, clusters of ghost tour groups had already started to gather, their excited chatter floating in through my paint-streaked window. Savannah thrived on its haunted reputation—spirits in every historic home and moss-draped square.

But the real ghosts weren't the ones in the tour guides' scripts. They were the ones we carried inside. The might-have-beens and the what-ifs. The parents who never saw me graduate. The childhood that was cut short and rearranged.

And the whispers that had never quite left me: *Be responsible now. Look after your sister. Be the man of the family.*

I picked up a hammer, the weight of it familiar and grounding in my palm, and turned back to the barstool. Sometimes the only way to rebuild your life is to start with what was broken—what everyone else had tossed aside.

My friends were nosy. My sister was dramatic. My life was steady. Predictable. Routine.

So why couldn't I shake the feeling that something was about to break?

I shook my head and grabbed my tools.

Didn't matter. I had shit to do.

CHAPTER THREE

Tally

After two days of shoving my entire, pathetic life into two overstuffed suitcases, packing Nancy Reagan's extensive and frankly unnecessary wardrobe, and convincing Dig that no, he absolutely did not need to bring his tap shoes in case of a "dance-mergency," we crammed into Jordan's rental car and started the long, reluctant drive to Georgia.

As we crawled through bumper-to-bumper traffic out of Brooklyn, I watched my city disappear in the side mirror—the pizza shops, the bodega cats, the subway grates that used to feel like freedom. Now they just looked like bad decisions with good lighting.

I wouldn't be whole by the time I reached my brother. And still, all I wanted was for someone to be proud of me. To actually see into that part of me that had potential and help me dig it out from wherever I'd buried it.

My brother used to be the one to do that for me. But I knew what was waiting at the end of that car ride. Beneath the witty banter would be the same old reminder: Doyle was perfect without trying, and I wasn't.

We'd moved to New York together from Newnan, Georgia, shortly after Doyle graduated high school. We made promises. Big sibling dreams of being two kids taking on the city. We were supposed to grow together. Be there for each other.

Instead, he tucked himself into a wine shop job and found Jordan. They fell in love, realized their dreams didn't include me, and left for Savannah to open *Cheese, Please!*—a wine-and-cheese shop that probably smelled like a Napa Valley resort and smug perfection.

Meanwhile, I stayed. I failed. And I kept hoping he'd come back for me.

Leaving New York felt like losing the last shred of the life I thought I was supposed to have. It felt like quitting.

Arriving in Georgia felt like standing on the edge of the unknown. None of the worldly travel, the wild, artsy parties, or the hundreds of gigs I'd taken over the years could've prepared me for this—

Not just living under my brother's roof, but stepping into the biggest adventure of all: motherhood.

Dig, my best friend-slash-former roommate-slash-chaos twin, spent most of the ride buried in social media, planning his first trip to Savannah with the intensity of someone mapping out a three-week tour of Europe. By the time we hit Georgia soil, he had scheduled brunch reservations, ghost tours, a horse-and-buggy ride, and, by some miracle, had three dates lined up. He was more excited than I was to be back in my home state, though I'm pretty sure his enthusiasm had everything to do with skipping his dinner shifts at Errico's and escaping the city for a few days. I didn't mind the plotting or the scheming. I was glad he was there.

And then there was me. Unshowered, vaguely queasy, clutching an ancient poodle who smelled like a hot subway seat, rolling up to the front of my brother's luxury penthouse like I'd been personally evicted from the plot of my own coming-of-age story—despite the fact that I'd already face-planted into my thirties.

"God, I have never been happier to see a front door," Dig groaned, slumping against the wall.

Nancy Reagan, tucked under my arm like a sweaty handbag, let out a huff that sounded eerily like agreement.

"We're not even inside yet," I told them, nodding toward the wall of gleaming elevators. "This is just the fancy-pants lobby."

The entrance way smelled like expensive laundry detergent and new money and looked like the kind of place where you weren't allowed to speak above a whisper or sweat in public. The floors were marble, the lighting was flattering, and the concierge gave me a polite nod that screamed *You don't belong here, but I'm paid to be nice.*

This wasn't the dream Doyle and I had cooked up. That one had a shoebox apartment, burnt coffee, and a shared dream we chased from opposite ends of a borrowed couch. Not this.

"Hey y'all," the concierge sang out, jumping up to grab some of our bags. "Mr. Aden, how was your trip? Looks like you came home with a few more items than you did when you left."

Dig scoffed next to me and scanned his shiny name tag. "Hoyt, is it? Hi Hoyt. We're the Adens' emotional baggage, we'll be staying for a while."

A warm, friendly smile rose over his face, and he reached out to grab my hand. "You must be Tallulah, then. The Adens have told me so much about you."

"Ha, don't hold that against me, please."

Hoyt met my gaze, then his line of sight flicked to Jordan. "I never would, Ms. Aden. That's not my style."

The elevator dinged, and we all shuffled inside, Hoyt hitting the button for the penthouse, and we bypassed a few floors on the way. "On the first floor, we have an art studio and gallery run by a friend of Mr. and Mr. Aden. And, of course, *Cheese, Please!*. On floors two and three are offices. Four has some apartments, and the entirety of floor five is your destination, the penthouse."

The elevator doors slid open, and I was inside of Doyle's impeccably manicured world.

He appeared from the terrace holding a wine glass, wearing crisply ironed linen pants and a button-down so white it made my teeth ache.

"Tallulah," he said, sweeping in to kiss both of my cheeks.

At arm's length, he studied me. There wasn't judgment there, but a quiet ribbon of concern. My brother didn't know who, or what, would be walking into this apartment. I suspected, from his line of sight, that I was far less disheveled than he was expecting.

Nancy barked once, then twice, before launching herself into a tiny tornado of excitement. "Will you pick her up before she pees on your Restoration Hardware rug?" I asked.

"Right, yes." He scooped her up in time for her to lick his entire face. "Hi, Nance. You look... hydrated. Great."

Wine in one hand, dog in the other, he gestured around like he was presenting a prize on a game show. "Welcome home, sis. How are you feeling?"

"She hasn't thrown up in at least forty-five minutes," Jordan said dryly as he walked in behind us, carrying our luggage. Behind him, Dig staggered in under the combined weight of my second suitcase, the poodle's fashion trunk, and my giant salt lamp, which he cradled like a baby Jesus in a nativity scene full of poor decisions.

"Do not drop that," I hissed.

"I would sooner drop *you*," he said, breathless, struggling to get the door closed behind him with his elbow. "Why is it shaped like this? Is this lamp possessed? It feels possessed."

Nancy let out a strangled wheeze, wriggling out of Doyle's arms, and immediately began her usual reconnaissance mission, her claws clicking across the marble floor in search of anything edible or forbidden.

The penthouse was pristine. White walls. White furniture. Expensive lighting that made even my frizzy travel hair look editorial. It was like walking into a magazine spread about couples who start their own wine labels and name their children after yoga poses. And there we were—me, Dig, a forty-pound salt rock, and a dog that looked like a dust bunny with legs.

Doyle leaned in for another quick, unaffectionate hug. He pulled back enough to assess me once again, in disbelief that I'd landed in Georgia in one piece. His eyes flitted from the salt lamp wedged under Dig's arm, to Nancy, who had sneezed directly onto the leg of his couch, to the suspiciously duct-taped handle of my suitcase, covered in stickers from my travels.

Then his gaze landed back on me.

Something passed across his face, quick and flickering, before he caught himself and smiled, like he remembered that under my dry-shampooed hair and almost-put-together ensemble, I was still the sister he used to know. "Well, the good news is you made it."

"Barely," I said, shrugging off my bag. "Have you ever traveled a long distance with Dig? I had to suffer through eight hours of an a cappella version of *Hamilton* when Jordan refused to connect his Bluetooth to the car." I tossed my messenger bag onto the island. It split open, spilling receipts, ChapStick caps, and what might have been a half-eaten granola bar onto the counter. My camera tumbled out next.

Dig deposited the salt lamp onto the immaculate kitchen island with a thud that made all three of us flinch. "She insisted it come with us. For balance or witchcraft. It wasn't clear."

"It's grounding," I said, slipping out of my Birkenstocks, depositing them swiftly by the back door in a pile where there was no pile of shoes. "Besides, it gives off good light for indoor photos if the sun refuses to play along. Trick I picked up in Scotland. From, yeah… she was probably a witch." I lifted my camera from the table and scanned the penthouse through the lens. "We should plug it in over there, by the TV stand."

Jordan visibly winced.

Doyle's smile stretched too tight, his flawless life wrapped around him like armor. And there I was, dragging the ghosts of situationships past, impulse buys, and a dog who smelled like corn chips into his clean snow globe.

And suddenly, I hated how tired I was. Like I'd already overstayed a welcome I hadn't even used yet.

"Can we get you anything?" Doyle asked. "Food? Drink? Skincare?" He pointed vaguely toward the bathroom. "I picked up some essentials for you. Jordan said you didn't exactly have a routine."

I shrugged off the jab, snapping a quick photo of my brother leaning on the counter. "I need to take Nancy out. Do you want to come with me? Maybe we can catch up?"

Doyle's face flickered. "Can't. We've got a thing tonight, remember?"

"You said you'd be here tonight," I replied dryly.

"I left chicken and quinoa in the fridge," he said, ignoring me and patting my arm. "And ginger ale. But easy on the bubbles."

I blinked. "Should I come with you? To your thing? I can change."

Doyle and Jordan exchanged a married-people look. One that said, *You should handle this one*, and Jordan stepped in. "You should rest. We'll get you settled in Savannah soon enough."

Dig let out a low whistle. "Oof."

I didn't reply. I nodded and kept busy looking for the good light in the penthouse through my camera. The undeniable sting, however, was there. But I did what I'd always done and shrugged it off, keeping myself busy under the guise of a woman who desperately didn't want anyone to see how much she was hurting.

After they left, I changed into a sundress, dabbed on some unnecessarily expensive lipstick Doyle had set out for me, and tried—really tried—to feel like a person. Like someone worth bringing along. And, more importantly, like someone who had reset the timer on the last time she had gotten sick. *Ten minutes.*

I ran my fingers through my curls, stepped into my sandals, looked in the mirror, and told myself, *You're not the sad girl in the movie. You're the one who figures it out.*

Nancy wagged her tail like she bought it.

Dig and I took the elevator down to the lobby, and he jabbered on about his weekend plans. I nodded along, but my stomach was twisting. Once he left, I'd be solo with a poodle and my well-meaning, overly bearing brothers. Not exactly the dream scenario.

Hoyt waved us toward the back alley and nodded toward a nearby square for Nancy's walk. "Avoid the front of the shop," he said, grimacing. "Your brother's hosting a wine tasting tonight. You don't want to accidentally crash into his friends—you'll want a proper introduction."

I shot Dig a look that begged him not to open his big mouth—wide-eyed panic and silent pleading in full effect.

But, well… Dig did what he always does.

"So he wants to hide this insanely gorgeous woman from his stupid friends? Seems like maybe his friends are the ones who should have the honor of gracing my best friend's otherworldly presence." He gave a little shimmy, flicked imaginary hair from his shoulders, and I could do nothing but slap on a smile and herd him toward the back entrance.

We stepped into the sticky Savannah night, the air thick with gardenia and the heat of my own embarrassment, blinking against the sting of tears in my eyes.

Dig fell into step beside me, unusually quiet for someone who normally narrated everything from sidewalk cracks to passing clouds. I suspected his silence wasn't just a pause—it was calculated. Protective. Watching, waiting to see if anyone dared to jump out of the shadows and mess with me.

"Can we agree that this is really shitty?" I asked when we hit the edge of the alley and stepped onto the street.

Dig nodded. "We can agree on that, yes. But, aside from what I said back there, I do think you all need some time to adjust."

"Are you actually in agreement with my brother?" I scoffed.

He turned to me and took my hands in his, his face unreadable to the naked eye—but I knew that look. Even though he'd put someone through a wall for me, there was still a thread of pity there. "I found a hotel a few blocks away. I need to check in. You good?"

I let out a small, bitter laugh. "Peachy."

Because what else could I say? That I already felt like a smudged finger-print on my brother's immaculate life. That walking through his world made me feel like I'd never done anything right in my entire life.

He bumped his shoulder against mine. "Let's get one thing straight, love. You're not the discarded sister in this Southern soap opera."

I arched a brow. "No?"

He smirked. "No. You, my love, are the plot twist."

CHAPTER FOUR

Charlie

Most nights, the silence in the studio was a salve—soothing, earned. But tonight it pressed in, thick and damp and restless.

I should've been next door at the wine tasting, pretending to enjoy myself, pretending to sell art, pretending Magnolia wasn't circling the emotional drain like she did every time Lee Wilder showed up to any of our get-togethers. Instead, I cracked the side door open and hauled the half-sanded barstools out into the alley, hoping for a breeze while I worked. I lost myself in the rhythm of it—the scrape of wood grain, the burn of old varnish against my fingers, the scent of sawdust clinging to the thick, humid night.

It wasn't working.

Uncle Cole had been gone for a few months, but the loss still came in waves. Sharp. Relentless. Sometimes I'd be halfway through a text—usually a dumb question about plumbing in the bar or how to handle Magnolia's latest disaster—before I remembered he was gone. The ache had settled into background noise. I only noticed it when I stopped moving.

He wasn't just family. My uncle got me, no explanations needed. He was the guy who handed me my first toolbox and told me I could build something out of nothing. That there was a kind of beauty in giving discarded things a second chance.

Now, I wasn't sure what the hell I was building out of this life anymore.

And Magnolia—well. Between the on-again/off-again thing with Dane, the way she and Lee kept trading those ridiculous, hopeful looks every time they were in the same room, and the very real possibility that O'Malley's might not survive, I was one crisis away from losing my mind.

So, when I stepped into the alley to toss some scraps and found a woman crouched near the back door—muttering to herself as she fiddled with the lock to *Cheese, Please!*—I stopped cold.

I probably should've turned around and minded my own business. But I was already halfway to the dumpster, and it's not every day you catch someone staging a late-night cheese heist.

"You know I could call the cops, right?" I said, leaning against the studio's side door.

She startled so hard the poodle at her feet did a backflip. The dog, for its part, seemed rather proud of the party trick.

She spun around, dark curls sticking to her neck, eyes wide but defiant. "That seems excessive. Are *you* a cop?"

"Do I look like a cop?"

She gave me a once-over, then shrugged. "Everyone looks like the fuzz when they're standing in shadows."

"So what, exactly, is it that you're doing?" I asked, taking a half-step toward her.

"I could ask you the same thing. Creeping around like a Scooby-Doo villain in a dark alley."

I lifted the sander in my hand. "Pretty sure I'm not the suspicious one here."

She squinted. "Is that a weapon?"

"Sander."

"Yeah, okay. Still weird." She dusted herself off like she hadn't been caught red-handed, standing up straight, trying to look taller than she was. "I wasn't breaking in. I was… visiting a friend."

I glanced at the locked service door. "Through the back entrance?"

"I'm picking up groceries," she said, a little too fast.

I raised a brow. "Groceries. From a wine shop?"

She blinked. "Okay, fine. I left something in there during the last tasting. And hey, they sell cheese and stuff in there, too. I think…"

"They're having a tasting right now," I said, nodding toward the front. "You could try the actual door. Like a normal person."

Something crossed her face—shame, maybe. Or frustration. Hard to tell. But she straightened like she was bracing for a fight. "Guess I wasn't in the mood for a crowd."

She stepped forward, the building light catching the frizz haloed around her brunette ringlets. Savannah's humidity had claimed her as its latest victim, curls plastered to her cheeks, dress rumpled like it had given up on the night long before she had. Her shoes dangled from her fingers, the way a girl holds a weapon she's already surrendered, leaving her bare feet ready to crouch down and jimmy the lock.

She didn't belong here. Not in this alley. Not fiddling with a locked door under flickering bulbs and the scent of sour wine and rotting wood. She looked like she should be somewhere else. Anywhere else.

She had the kind of face you remembered long after you'd walked away. Big hazel eyes. A mouth with just enough curve to suggest mischief. She looked like trouble pretending to have its shit together.

Before I could say anything, before I could ask why someone so beautiful was hiding in a back alley, no shoes and no shame, she opened her mouth.

"Look, like I said, my friend owns this place. I was just—"

And then something slammed into my shins like a rocket-powered throw pillow.

I stumbled back in time to watch her scrappy little poodle launch itself into a frantic figure-eight around my legs, nails skittering on the pavement, ears flapping like it was gunning for takeoff.

I took a step back, tripped into a precarious stack of barstools, and barely had time to wince before they clattered down like a drunk game of Jenga.

Somewhere between the crash and my muttered, "Oh, for—" she made a sound.

Then she crumpled forward, hands on her knees, and let loose the unmistakable soundtrack of a body staging a full-scale revolt. Directly into the open sculpture frame at my feet. My yearlong masterpiece. Perfect.

Ah, fuck.

It wasn't the smell or the mess that got me. It was the sheer, unholy timing of it all.

It was a commissioned piece for one of Eunice Wilder's friends. Lee's momma had a whole network of them that loved to show off how well they could cut a check. And this one in particular had too much money and not enough taste, redecorating her alimony-funded penthouse after divorce number three. She'd seen one of my pieces at a gallery Magnolia had dragged me to, and next thing I knew, her assistant was sending me Pinterest boards labeled *"Mixed Media Madness"* and *"Moody Metal That Says Healing."*

She wanted a bespoke piece. "Raw but elegant," she'd said on the phone. "Something that whispers reinvention." It was meant to sit between her champagne fridge and the antique mirror she swore came from a Tuscan palace. A showpiece for the entryway. A conversation starter. The kind of installation that would impress whoever she invited over next.

The *fuck you* piece she hoped he'd stumble across on Instagram and immediately regret losing all of his money in exchange for a younger woman. Her words. Not mine.

But for me, it had turned into an escape hatch. I kept working on it long after the check had cleared, and I wasn't done yet. I kept adjusting the angles, smoothing the welds, staring at the shape until I didn't know exactly what it was I was trying to fix.

It wasn't just a job. It was the gateway to countless opportunities. If this went right, who knew how many other multi-divorced women would seek me out to decorate their new homes with metal and ungodly amounts of money. Now it was covered in whatever this stranger had eaten for dinner.

I stared, mute. Powerless. Like the universe had kicked me in the shins, too.

The back door of *Cheese, Please!* banged open and Lee stumbled out, beer in hand, laughter already bubbling from his throat.

"Oh my God," he called out. "Someone's hurling into your latest masterpiece."

He sloshed beer onto his shoes like it was part of the bit. My stomach twisted.

It wasn't the mess itself; it was the way she sank into it, like everything had finally caught up with her.

"Jesus," I muttered, stepping forward. "What the hell?"

She lifted her gaze, her skin pale beneath the flush, her eyes glassy but clear enough to know something had gone wrong. Sweat-damp curls clung to her face, and for a second, I thought she might apologize again—but she blinked, unsteady, as if the world had tilted.

"I'm sorry," she said, voice barely audible. Then she bent again, her shoulders rounding as she fought to steady herself.

Lee was already moving. He came back with a stack of napkins and crouched beside her, his voice soft and steady. "Are you all right?"

She nodded, dabbing at her mouth with a cocktail napkin like it might erase the last thirty seconds.

"This is my poodle, Nancy Reagan," she said, and that was truly the last thing I expected to come tumbling out of her mouth.

I looked at her. Then the dog. Then back to the sculpture that now had a new layer of residue I hadn't planned for.

Sensing my ever-rising blood pressure, Lee shot me a look. "Calm down," he whispered. "Don't make it worse."

Easy for him to say. He hadn't spent the last few months building that piece one weld at a time. He hadn't been the one left holding the wreckage when someone else unraveled in front of him.

"Very nice to meet you, Nancy, but is your mother okay?" Lee quipped, trying to tamp down his building laughter as he kneeled beside her to pet the dog.

"I'm fine," she insisted. "Totally fine. Happens all the time."

"It happens all the time?" I repeated.

"Low blood sugar," she said confidently. "And stress. And heat. And, probably, Mercury in retrograde? I don't know. I'm not a scientist."

Nancy Reagan sneezed and curled up next to her like she'd seen worse.

I scrubbed a hand through my hair and stared down at the carnage beside her. "You know you just ruined a commissioned sculpture, right?"

Her eyes darted toward it. "Oh. Shit. That's art?"

"Yes."

She winced. "I thought it was a bike rack."

My jaw worked, but nothing came out.

Fused from an old, weathered steel drum with salvaged metal rods, twisted rebar, and chains, from a distance it *could* be mistaken for a modern, industrial bike rack or abstract furniture. But it was meant to evoke the idea of a heart, hollowed and guarded. The rods were bent outward in curves that loosely mimicked rib bones or a cage, and at the center of the drum was a flickering battery-powered light meant to resemble a low-burning flame. I'd been building it for months, unsure why I kept returning to it over everything else I'd been working on.

For my client, the piece was a status symbol—a way to show her friends how quickly she could burn through her ex's money. But for me, it was about containment and protection—of grief, of hope, of memory. The steel drum, once meant for oil or waste, had been reborn as a vessel for light. A quiet tribute to Uncle Cole, to loss, and to the belief that even the ruined can still reflect beauty.

And that light had sputtered out.

"Art is subjective?" she tried.

Lee took a sip of his beer at the exact wrong second, choking and hacking as he fought to keep it from spraying everywhere.

"I'll pay for the damage," she added.

"You got six grand on you?"

"Six grand for a bike rack? Maybe in Monopoly money."

She looked like someone who lived on freelance checks and espresso shots—equal parts shaky confidence and sheer determination, like she'd been running on fumes long before tonight. Something about her reminded me of Magnolia before she'd settled down. That same restless energy.

I let out a slow breath. "Forget it. It's going to be okay. Just... sit. Breathe. Don't touch anything."

She nodded, folding down onto one of the half-sanded barstools with the kind of compliance that only comes from narrowly dodging a full-on disaster. Nancy Reagan immediately sprawled across her feet like a soggy welcome mat.

Lee, ever the host in a crisis, appeared at her side with a half-full water bottle and a slightly baffled smile. "You're officially our weirdest visitor this week. And that's saying a lot. This place has quite the reputation."

She accepted the bottle, tipped it toward him in thanks, then flicked her eyes back to me—less panicked now, but still dazed around the edges. "Bathroom?"

I jerked my chin toward the open studio door. "Down the hall. Second door. Do you need help?"

"No." She stood, gathered the dog in her arms, and slipped inside without another word.

Lee and I followed her quietly, the door clicking shut behind us. I stayed near the exit for a beat, listening for any ungodly noises coming from the back of the studio, one hand braced and ready to bolt if necessary.

Lee leaned against the worktable, watching me with that knowing look I hated. "She's something," he said, voice low.

I wanted to skulk down the hall to make sure she was okay. Which was ridiculous, because I didn't know this girl. Didn't owe her anything. And she'd destroyed months of work. But for some reason, it felt less noble and more creepy, so I stayed put by the door, standing guard.

There was something about the way she'd held it together—even while falling apart—that stuck with me. The stubborn tilt of her chin. How she'd offered to pay six grand she clearly didn't have, even if it was in Monopoly money. The way her hands shook when she took the water bottle.

What kind of night ends barefoot in an alley, trying to break into a wine shop?

"She's cute, though," Lee said, grinning like he could read my mind.

I shot him a look. "Don't."

"Too late," he winked. "You're already thinking about it."

He wasn't wrong. And I hated that.

Suddenly needing air, I turned the handle and stepped back outside. The heat pressed in again, thick and still. That same mix of scorched metal, sour wine, and rot clung to the air. From around the corner came the muffled sounds of music and laughter—easy, familiar noise from people whose lives hadn't been cracked open on the concrete.

Lee stepped outside and squeezed my shoulder as he passed. "Try not to fall in love while I head next door for a refill."

He walked off toward the front of the shop. I stayed, though every instinct I had was screaming at me to run in the opposite direction of whatever was happening in my studio.

I leaned over to assess the damage. The sculpture was still standing. It wasn't ruined, just interrupted. I'd clean it, fix what needed fixing, and bring it back to what it was supposed to be, even though I still had no idea what that was.

I kept thinking about the look on her face. That first second when she realized what she'd done. Not only the mess, but the meaning of it. She didn't just wreck my work, she landed in the middle of it and managed to take what was mine and make it hers, just by showing up and falling apart.

I didn't know what to do with that yet. But a part of me knew she wasn't done causing trouble, and I wasn't done cleaning up the mess.

CHAPTER FIVE

Tally

The streaky, paint-splattered bathroom mirror wasn't doing me any favors. I braced my hands against the edge of the sink and took a half-hearted look at myself. Not my full reflection, not yet. My eyes stayed half-lidded, like I could soften the blow by only taking in small pieces of myself at a time.

My dress was a mess. *I* was a mess. The neckline had slipped to one side, the hem looked like it had been through a wind tunnel, and the whole thing clung in places it shouldn't, while sagging in places that only made me feel worse. So much for fun and flirty. The fabric, once smooth and light, was now wrinkled and damp. My curls had surrendered to the humidity, ballooning into an unpredictable nest of knots and plastering themselves to my forehead. My skin was flushed, my eyes glassy, and there was a smear of goo near my collarbone I wasn't brave enough to identify.

I reached for a paper towel, tore off too many, and dabbed under my eyes. It didn't help. Nothing really would at this point.

This was the part where I would usually come up with a joke or a distraction. A shiny personality quip to wave around so no one would notice the parts of me falling apart before I did what I always did.

Run away. Start over. From experience, Iceland was very nice this time of year.

But there was no one to run from, except for myself, and even if there had been, I didn't have it in me. Not tonight.

I looked back at the mirror, this time a little more directly. My face stared back, worn and tired. I hardly recognized myself.

I ran cold water over my wrists and tried not to think about getting sick in an alley, onto what was apparently actual art. In front of a man who asked if he looked like a cop, and somehow managed to make it sound like a threat and a pickup line at the same time.

My cheeks burned. I couldn't tell if it was from embarrassment or the heat closing in from all sides.

Nancy Reagan gave a soft boof from her spot near the door. She didn't bother lifting her head. Her entire body had melted into the tile, and I didn't blame her. I was half a second away from joining her myself. Every part of me felt wrong—my hair, my skin, the way my dress stuck to my body like cling-wrap. The bathroom air was stifling and stale, and my legs still felt shaky from standing too fast.

I splashed water on my face again, pressed the towel to my cheeks, and waited for my pulse to settle. It didn't. Not really.

From the other side of the door, voices carried in. One was deep and quiet, rough around the edges. That had to be Mr. Not-a-Cop. Another was warmer, almost teasing. A third voice joined in—female, polished, and Southern in that way that made everything sound both friendly and like a warning.

I cracked the door open.

The hallway was dim, the light from the studio barely reaching this far back. The floor was solid concrete, uneven in places, and covered with a faded rug that looked like it had been walked over a thousand times without anyone bothering to straighten it. To my right, a curtain hung slightly out of place. Behind it, I could make out a bed pushed against the wall and an armchair with a sketchpad tossed onto the seat. No door. Only fabric and shadows. It wasn't much, but it was lived-in, pulled together with care, even if nothing matched.

Nancy trotted ahead of me like she'd been there a hundred times before, her nails ticking quietly across the floor. I followed behind, slower, each step making the tight feeling in my chest worse. My brother's voice was already forming in my head, barbed and disbelieving. *You did what?*

The studio opened up around me in a way that made it hard to tell where one thing ended and the next began. Ceilings stretched high, wooden beams exposed, while streetlights spilled through the wide front windows, washing everything in a pale, borrowed glow. The air carried sawdust and metal, cutting and earthy, with a faint trace of whatever chemical someone had used to mop up after a bad date with a power tool.

Sculptures stood frozen mid-process, flanked by bins of parts and scraps. Table legs leaned like they were gossiping with rusted chains and shards of glass waited in neat little piles. It was messy, sure—but the kind of messy that made sense if you lived there. Nails sorted into coffee tins, chains coiled like snakes on the floor, canvases leaning in a row as if waiting their turn. Nothing about it felt abandoned; it all carried the weight of someone's hands, someone who didn't mind leaving fingerprints on their work.

Compared to the penthouse above, it was almost laughably unrefined. Nothing matched, nothing gleamed, and yet, in its quiet chaos, it felt more like home than all the coordinated perfection upstairs.

Three people surrounded the long central worktable. The artist hunched over a half-sanded slab, sleeves shoved up, muscles flexing tight as he worked the edge smooth. His friend had claimed a stool as if this were his living room, lounging easily with a grin tucked in the corner of his mouth. Beside him, a woman in a tank dress—plain in theory, unfair in execution—balanced a mason jar of beer so hazy it could've passed for juice.

Nancy darted straight toward them like she was meeting up with old friends.

I followed, determined to reenter the room like a normal person and not someone who had recently expelled the contents of her stomach into a piece of commissioned art.

"Hey," I croaked.

Three heads turned at once.

The artist kept his face locked between focus and a scowl. His friend, though, wore the opposite—open, easy, a teasing grin with a trace of kindness tucked in behind it. And the woman? Her gaze swept over me like a scanner at checkout, one brow quirking. Not judgment, exactly, more so cataloging everything for future reference. Blonde curls tumbled over sun-warmed shoulders, and she looked effortlessly put-together in that maddening, Savannah-cool kind of way.

"I'm… better," I lied, though no one bothered to ask. My voice cracked at the end, which didn't help the illusion. "Sorry about the mess."

"You sure?" Not-A-Cop's friend asked, already pulling a stool out with his foot and nudging it toward me. "You kind of went full exorcist out there."

The woman passed me a clean glass of water without a word, her eyes softening—slightly—when our fingers brushed. The artist still hadn't spoken—he stood there with his arms crossed, watching me like he wasn't entirely convinced I wouldn't unravel in front of them. Beside him, the blonde gave me a deliberate once-over, trying to look unimpressed, and almost succeeding, but there was warmth there.

"I'm Sutton," she said finally. "And you are—"

I opened my mouth, but Nancy cut me off with a sharp, accusing bark that ricocheted through the room.

And that's when it hit me.

My stomach knotted, and a cold sweat prickled across the back of my neck. The air got thick, and every breath felt like work.

"Oh no," I whispered.

The floor lurched. My vision smeared at the edges. I turned toward Not-a-Cop, scrambling for words—an apology, a warning—but nothing came out.

Then the room tilted, and everything went dark.

***

I came to slowly, my head pounding with a heavy, dull rhythm that felt like someone had set up a bass drum behind my eyes. My mouth was desert-dry, my tongue thick, and I was sprawled out on an object that was very much not a bed. The surface beneath me was cool, a little sticky, and almost certainly never advertised as a place for human recovery.

Voices bled in and out. Blurry shapes hovered above me—three of them, close enough that their expressions came into focus. One looked genuinely concerned, another hovered in that awkward limbo between *should I help and please let this not be my problem*, and the third—arms crossed, mouth pressed tight—looked about five seconds away from dragging me to the curb.

"Is she breathing?" Sutton asked finally, tone flat, eyes locked on me with the kind of bored precision that made it clear she was not thrilled about her role in tonight's drama.

Then, apparently deciding I wasn't dead enough to warrant panic, she uncrossed her arms and plucked my wallet from the mess on the table. With a sigh, like this was the last thing she had time for tonight, she started flipping through it—slow, deliberate, every movement laced with judgment. ID, punch cards, a receipt for what I was *hoping* was pizza and not a cry for help—all of it examined like clues at a crime scene.

Not-a-Cop—the only name I had for the artist pacing like a lunatic nearby—ran both hands through his hair again, making it stand on end like he'd stuck his head in a dryer vent. He looked equal parts furious and deeply inconvenienced.

His friend hovered off to the side, holding his phone in both hands as if he expected someone else to take over and tell him what to do. His thumb hovered above the screen, but he didn't move.

"She's Doyle's cousin, or maybe sister," Sutton said excitedly, holding up my ID like she was announcing the winning raffle ticket. "Tallulah River Aden. Does that ring any bells to either of you?" She glanced at the guy looming over me. "Dude, why are you glaring at her like that?"

The artist squinted, like the name had lodged somewhere in his memory but hadn't fully surfaced. He leaned back on his heels, finally out of my face.

"Aden. Wait—Doyle Aden?"

The friend was already dialing. "Doyle's not picking up. Let me try Jordan."

I blinked up at the exposed beams overhead, willing the room to quit its carnival spin. My limbs were useless jelly, my stomach staging a full-blown mutiny, and the best I could manage was staying flat and not making things worse.

"Magnolia's on her way," Sutton said, dropping her phone beside me.

The studio door squealed open a moment later, like it was bracing for impact.

A woman strode in—tall, striking, with a sharp red bob that looked like it hadn't seen a brush in days but still managed to fall into place like it had a stylist on retainer. Jeans, scuffed boots, a faded tee with some band logo I was definitely not cool enough to recognize. No heels, no frills—the kind of quiet confidence that says *I've seen worse and dealt with it before breakfast.*

She hadn't finished shutting the door before her eyes locked on the artist's buddy.

"You've got to be kidding me, Lee," she said. "I thought you went home."

Lee straightened from his stool, lifting a hand in mock salute. "Nice to see you too, Magnolia. You're glowing."

"I'm sweating," she deadpanned. "And if I'd known *you* were part of whatever this is, I'd have taken a longer route."

"Don't lie. You missed me," he said, grinning.

Magnolia crossed her arms. "I missed having peace and quiet in my city. That's what I missed."

"Still feisty as ever," he said under his breath, then turned to the blonde next to him. "Did *you* miss me?"

Sutton didn't look up from my wallet she had resumed rifling through. "I didn't miss watching this exact conversation play out every single day of my life."

Magnolia took one look at the room—at me sprawled on the worktable, at Nancy sniffing what I hoped was a rag pile, at the artist whose table I had apparently commandeered with my entire body, now pacing like he wanted to burn the whole building down—and sighed like someone who'd walked into a party she had very much not RSVP'd for.

"Jesus," she muttered, folding her arms across her chest. "We were trying to have one normal wine tasting, and now we're one poodle and a public crisis deep. Another Tuesday in the ongoing saga of our deeply cursed family group chat."

"She's Doyle's sister. Or, cousin. Or! Could be his mom? Doyle has great genes, I can tell," Sutton said again. "Also, she yakked all over the sculpture the Black Widow commissioned."

Magnolia tilted her head, staring at me with open curiosity. "Well. She doesn't look dead. That's promising."

"You can only be a Black Widow if you kill your husband," Lee muttered, eyes cutting toward Magnolia. "Black Widows don't rack up failed marriages to men they shouldn't have dated in the first place, even if they *are* loaded."

She ignored him completely, aside from a resigned sigh, and glanced over her shoulder. "Charlie, you want to explain why there's a half-conscious woman on your worktable? Or are we collecting strays now?"

Charlie. So that was Not-a-Cop's name. He didn't say much, but his posture eased once he was close.

"She passed out," he said, rubbing a hand across the back of his neck. "She... folded. I didn't know what else to do."

Magnolia raised a brow. "Well, dragging her onto your work table like some kind of DIY Florence Nightingale situation isn't exactly the standard protocol."

"Didn't see anyone else volunteering to do anything different," Charlie muttered. The bite was there, but only on the surface.

"I didn't mean to—I wasn't trying to cause trouble," I croaked, pushing myself upright. It clicked then, and the revelation did nothing to slow down my pounding pulse. These were my brother's friends, weren't they? "I didn't know who you were. Any of you. Except Lee. I mean—" I looked over at him, blinking a few times as my brain caught up with everything else. "I recognize you. From your music. I loved *Walk Away Slow.*"

The tension in the room bubbled, and no one looked directly at anyone else.

Lee, to his credit, grinned like I'd handed him a piece of birthday cake. "Well, thanks, darlin'. That one's a favorite of mine, too."

Magnolia muttered under her breath, too low for me to catch. Charlie stared down at the floorboards like they'd suddenly become fascinating. And Sutton? She tipped back against the worktable, arms crossed, her expression parked somewhere between unimpressed and mildly entertained—like she'd seen this show before and was curious how bad the ending would get.

"Okay, real question," she said, her voice clipped. "Are you drunk? Are you high on drugs?"

"Sutton," Lee said, shooting her a warning glance. "Jesus."

She blinked, all wide-eyed innocence. "What? We were all thinking it. She was breaking into the shop, and now she can barely lift her head. I'm the one rude enough to say it out loud. Also, where are her shoes?"

Charlie sighed and tightened his jaw, fingers drumming against the edge of the table, the picture of someone trying to talk himself down.

"I'm not drunk. Or high," I said, quieter than I meant to. My pride bristled, even if she was entirely wrong about me. "It's just heat exhaustion. Or dehydration. Or pregnancy. Take your pick."

Sutton's eyebrows shot up. "Oh, good. An overachiever."

"So why were you breaking into the shop?" Charlie asked, hovering over me.

"I just… I wanted to see what was so special about my brother's friends that he wouldn't let me meet them."

Lee gave a low whistle, dragging a hand down his face. "Well. Tonight's really going for gold."

Magnolia snorted. "Y'all leave for ten minutes and come and adopt a human disaster. Impressive, even for you."

"You want to get off the table?" she asked, nodding toward a nearby stool. "Or lie down again, if your dramatic flair hasn't quite run its course."

I managed a faint smile, grateful for the hint of kindness tucked beneath the sarcasm. "I think I'll stay put, if that's okay. Kind of afraid to test gravity again."

As if summoned by sheer awkward energy, the studio door creaked open again—and this time, Doyle and Jordan came rushing in, talking over each other.

"Oh my god, Tally—"

"Sorry, we came as soon as—"

"—we thought you were just being—"

"—melodramatic," Jordan finished helpfully, then winced. "But obviously this is… more than that."

Doyle dropped to a crouch beside me, worry etched across his annoyingly symmetrical face. "Jesus, Tals. You good?"

"Not exactly the quiet entrance you had in mind for me," I muttered, pressing my fingers to my temple. "Really killing it on the new-girl-in-town front."

I looked up at Doyle, guilt threading through the nausea still curling in my stomach. He was here. He'd shown up. He was saying all the right things, doing the concerned brother routine like a pro. But I could see it. That look that said *you promised you wouldn't screw this up.*

Charlie stood stiffly to the side, arms crossed. "She also passed out in the middle of the studio. Kind of a whole… production."

"Thank you, Not-a-Cop," I muttered under my breath.

Jordan straightened and scanned the room. "Wait—where's Dane?"

A collective groan went around the room like a wave at a particularly tragic sporting event. Magnolia didn't turn around as she muttered, "He sniffed the drama and decided it was bad for his image."

Sutton gave an exaggerated eye roll. "Big surprise."

But I caught the way Magnolia's gaze cut to Lee, who didn't say a word. He met her eyes like they'd said it all a long time ago. The smirk faded, replaced by an intimate softness I don't think I was supposed to witness.

"Dane's not really the 'ride or die' type," Lee said eventually, voice casual but not unkind, eyes still locked on the redhead standing before him. "He's Magnolia's boyfriend, by the way. He's also my golden-child older brother. Which basically makes him an expert at being in two places at once—everywhere but here, with his girl, like he should be."

Magnolia's lips twitched, but she didn't say anything. Charlie shifted his weight, restless beside her, clearly itching to step in but not sure if it was his place. The mood in the room curdled, thick enough that even my brother flinched.

Doyle patted my leg twice, a little too forcefully. "Anyway! You're awake, and that's what matters. Let's head upstairs, get you settled, and let the rest of these people salvage their evening. What do you say?"

There was a tightness in his tone I recognized immediately, the sound of him trying to be the responsible one, the one in control. But it felt different. Not like when we were younger, when the world felt like it might fall apart unless we held it together ourselves. This felt more practiced, like someone performing concern at the exact pitch they thought people needed to hear.

He sounded like our mother. Controlled and measured with enough warmth to disguise the edge beneath it. A shiver crawled down my spine, thorny and unwelcome.

I glanced at Jordan, who gave me a warm, apologetic smile and set a bottle of water on the table beside me. "Sorry again. We thought you were being dramatic."

"I mean," I said, wryly, "you weren't entirely wrong."

Jordan grinned and offered Nancy Reagan a pat. "Well, if she's okay, that's what really matters."

Nancy promptly licked his fingers like he was the one who'd personally delivered her from darkness.

Doyle turned to Jordan, already reaching for my bag, ready to get me out of there and sweep all of this under the rug. "Can you take her upstairs? I'll stay and help Charlie clean this up."

His voice was soft—polite, even. The version of Doyle that people trusted. The version that sounded calm and dependable. But I caught the edge in it. The urgency. The quiet strain. But it wasn't care. It was containment.

"I'm fine," I murmured, but no one heard me.

Charlie's voice cut through the space, low but firm. "Shouldn't she go to the hospital?"

I glanced up. He was watching Doyle—not me—with a subtle frown, trying to make sense of what was happening, almost like he'd seen this kind of deflection before.

Doyle's head snapped up, a too-bright smile already in place. "That's a great idea," he said quickly, throwing an arm around Jordan's shoulders. "Jordan can take her. Just to be safe."

And that was that. I was being passed off like a hot potato nobody wanted to hold too long.

"I'll go, too," Lee chimed in, casual but already moving toward the door. "It never hurts to have backup. Or snacks. I'm great with a vending machine."

Doyle didn't acknowledge him. He was too busy grabbing a handful of napkins and making a show of helping Charlie wipe up a puddle of water I'd knocked over near the worktable. Crisis diverted—damage managed.

No one would ever suspect that Doyle had been cleaning up messes of mine, just like this, our whole lives.

I opened my mouth to protest, then shut it again. My head throbbed, my stomach rolled, and every cell in my body begged for a shower and some kind of dignity reboot. Maybe it wouldn't hurt to have a medical professional, and not a group of half-wine drunk millennials, give me a once-over.

Charlie met my eyes briefly, and for the first time all night, there wasn't irritation behind his expression. A quiet concern lingered there instead. But he didn't say anything more.

And Doyle? Doyle wouldn't look at me.

CHAPTER SIX

Tally

I could barely feel my legs by the time we left the hospital. My body hummed with that hollow ache that comes after you've hit a wall so hard, it knocks the breath clean out of you. My hands still smelled faintly of antiseptic. My mouth was dry. I'd nodded along while the doctor listed off everything I'd been neglecting—hydration, rest, food that didn't come in a wrapper—and each word landed like a stone. She hadn't scolded. She didn't have to.

Because I already knew.

This wasn't exhaustion. It was consequence. Every skipped meal, every "I'm fine," every tomorrow I'd promised myself had stacked up until the weight finally toppled.

By the time we reached the penthouse, the pressure in my chest had turned sharp, wrapping tight around my ribs. Not nausea. Not heat. Guilt. Shame. Fear. All of it pressing in at once.

The elevator doors slid open, and there they were—Doyle and Dig, parked at the kitchen table like they'd been waiting all night. Empty plates. Half-drained cocktails. Doyle's head snapped up, his chair scraping back before I even crossed the threshold. He didn't come to me. His focus locked on Jordan, who hovered behind me, shoulders heavy with whatever truth had followed us home.

Dig, on the other hand, sprang from his seat like it was a trampoline. "Oh my God, you look like warmed-over hell," he whispered, arms wrapping tightly around me as he squeezed. "I mean that with love. You're still prettier than ninety percent of this city."

I clung to him like a lifeline, grateful for the warmth, for the familiarity. For someone who didn't make me feel like a burden.

Behind me, I caught snippets of Doyle and Jordan's low, tense conversation. Words like "rest," "plan," and "tomorrow" floated into the air, clipped and quiet. They were always like this—two halves of one unit, locked in their own orbit. It hit me all over again, like it always did. When it came down to it, Doyle had chosen his future, and I hadn't been part of it.

Not really.

"You wanna go for a walk?" Dig asked, his voice soft as he tucked a piece of hair behind my ear. "The two of us? After you clean your raggedy-ass self up first, of course."

"Off a short pier? Yes." I sighed, twisting a damp curl around my finger until it tugged. "I wish he'd let me explain. I almost get the sense he's more angry with me than worried."

Through the glass doors, Doyle and Jordan had migrated to the lanai, whisper-shouting like it was an Olympic sport. I caught a flurry of Doyle's hand gestures—sharp, frantic, blaming. Jordan answered with slower movements, deliberate and tired from hours spent bedside at the hospital.

No wonder I always wanted to bolt. The drama didn't start with me—it stuck to me better than it stuck to anyone else.

"This is usually the part where we'd get drunk," Dig said lightly, nudging me. "But you're, like, aggressively not fun anymore. Something about creating life?"

There he was—my favorite person.

I stood, reaching for his arm and pulling him to his feet. "I can't sit here and watch him spiral. I already feel like shit. And he's really out there flailing, looking like a better Botoxed version of Momma."

Dig raised his brows. "Tell me how you really feel."

I let out a long breath. "Sorry. I'm just… tired. And I need to get my shit together. For me. For the baby. Not only because Doyle's cleaning up after me again. And this time I can't book some European photoshoot and forget that my family even exists."

Dig looped his arm through mine as we headed toward the guestroom and the long, scorching shower I had been dreaming of for hours. "He's still a control freak in linen pants. Some things never change. Try to remember that."

"Fucker," I muttered.

"Now *that's* the girl I dragged out of Brooklyn."

Arm in arm, Dig and I wandered aimlessly through Savannah's crooked cobblestone streets, the kind that made it impossible to walk in a straight line, like the city was gently nudging you to slow down and take notice. Gas lamps flickered to life above us as dusk stretched long over the moss-draped oaks, and everything—the light, the air, the way the magnolias clung sweetly to the breeze— felt a little too beautiful for how deeply unsettled I was.

We passed weathered brick buildings that leaned into each other like old friends, patios strung with fairy lights spilling warmth onto the sidewalks. Bars hummed with laughter and clinking glasses. Somewhere above, a woman's voice carried on a balcony; somewhere else, a saxophone moaned down a side street, as if it had a story it couldn't keep to itself.

Dig and I had an unofficial bar taxonomy. In New York, when we scraped together enough money from our dead-end jobs to feel flush, we wanted noise and neon—places where you could dance on sticky tables and drink an electric-blue cocktail without anyone judging you for it. On our rare confident days—when we remembered we were funny and smart and maybe even a little magnetic— we went for velvet booths and dirty martinis in sleek downtown places with real menus and tiny, expensive appetizers.

But tonight wasn't for swagger or celebration. It wasn't for glossy surfaces or dancing on tables.

Tonight was for four walls, low lights, and maybe a bartender old enough not to ask questions.

"I want something haunted," I muttered. "Like… emotionally. Spiritually. Maybe even literally."

Dig squeezed my arm. "This is Savannah, baby. Everything's haunted."

We turned a corner into one of the quieter squares, where ivy curled around cast-iron fences and Spanish moss dangled like the city's own lazy sigh. The hush of it all pressed into me, gentle but insistent.

The more we walked, the more I didn't hate the feeling.

"This place looks promising," Dig said, eyeing the weathered sign swinging gently above us. "I can already feel the kind of charm that guarantees we'll be the hottest bitches in the room. Mostly because the average age of the competition is… retirement-adjacent."

I smirked. "Sixty is the new forty. Grey is the new bombshell."

He gasped, clutching his imaginary pearls. "And I am the new Ethel Merman."

I snorted, grabbing the warped mahogany handle. "You *wish*, babe."

The door stuck like it was clinging to its final shred of dignity. I gave it a tug, then another, before it finally gave in with a sticky groan and a sad, warped jingle of the overhead bell.

We stepped inside, blinking against the dimness and taking in the smell of lemon oil, old stories, and a little bit of beer that never fully left the floorboards. The bar stretched long along the right wall, polished to a low shine under golden sconces that looked like they'd been installed before electricity was a given. A scattering of small square tables filled the rest of the space, their mismatched chairs huddled close like old friends sharing secrets. Toward the front, a short, squat stage waited beneath a dusty spotlight—currently dark, but clearly well-loved.

Dig leaned in. "Okay… she's giving haunted dive bar realness. I like her."

And to my own surprise, I did too.

A television angled awkwardly toward the bar played a grainy episode of some kind of dating competition. Lots of tanned people shouting over champagne flutes and forced intimacy. Beneath it, rows of half-drained liquor bottles gleamed under a dusty strip of LED lighting, casting a low amber glow across the worn mahogany.

No bartender in sight.

"Maybe they're closed," Dig whispered, inching closer to me like the air had suddenly turned hostile and a ghost was going to come hurtling toward us with a drink menu in one hand and a machete in the other.

The silence closed in around us, thick and expectant. The air buzzed with that same itchy unease that came from stepping into a place that didn't quite expect you. Like maybe we were intruding. Or worse, like the place was holding its breath, waiting to decide what kind of people we were.

"Can I help y'all?"

The voice cut through the quiet as a tall redhead stepped out from the back, letting the door swing shut behind her. She looked tired—like someone who'd been holding up too many things for too many people for too long— but when she spotted us hovering near the bar, her posture straightened, eyes brightening enough to pass for enthusiasm.

Then her gaze landed on me.

"Well, hell," she drawled, blinking like she wasn't sure I was real. "You're the girl who passed out in my brother's studio last night."

Dig nudged me with his elbow. "Wow. You really know how to make an entrance."

Magnolia's brows lifted as she moved behind the bar, slipping into motion with the ease of someone who'd done this dance a thousand times. She grabbed a rag and started polishing a glass that didn't need polishing, but clearly gave her something to do with her hands.

"We're not technically open yet," she said, "but if y'all promise not to faint, or worse, I'll happily make you a drink."

There was a bright smile on her face, but a thread of wariness behind it mixed with a kind of hopeful desperation I recognized all too well. Maybe she needed us to sit down more than we needed the drink.

"I'll have… actually, I don't know. I've never been so stumped before," Dig said, eyes darting between the menu and the rows of liquor behind the bar like he was selecting a wedding cake.

"You like bourbon?" Magnolia asked, southern twang twinkling through the room, already reaching for a bottle. "I make a pretty decent drink with peach liqueur. It's like sippin' on Savannah."

Dig lit up, practically bouncing on his stool. "Sold."

Magnolia turned to me next, one brow lifting. "And for the lady? I'm guessing something less boozy, on account of your… situation?"

She cut a quick glance toward Dig, like she wasn't sure if he was in on the secret.

Dig raised both hands. "Don't look at me. I didn't get her into this mess, I'm just the support staff."

I gave him a shove with my elbow and looked back at Magnolia. "I'll take an iced tea, if you've got it."

She grinned and turned toward the fridge. "This is the South, hunny. They'd shut me down if I didn't."

As it always happens when a screen is within reach of a human attention span, Dig and I turned toward the TV while Magnolia fixed our drinks. He started talking, mostly to himself, about the show's dynamics and which contestant had won him over. I hadn't seen a single episode, so I wandered off to check out the photos lining the wall.

Black and white frames stretched along the length of the bar, running from the edge of the stage to what I assumed were the bathrooms and office. I paused at each one, following the quiet story they told. The outfits and haircuts changed with the decades, but the bar itself looked mostly untouched.

At the last frame, I stopped. A man in a scally cap stood behind the bar, smiling, with two kids propped on either side of him. Their small hands rested near pint glasses that were hopefully filled with root beer. The girl had to be Magnolia. She looked about twelve, freckles clear even in black and white, smiling like she already owned the place.

I hadn't heard her come up behind me and nearly jumped when she slid a glass of iced tea onto the table in front of me.

"That's my Uncle Cole and my brother, Charlie," she said quietly, eyes still on the photo. There was a weight to her voice, the kind that settles somewhere deep in your bones. She let out a slow breath, scanning the wall of photos like they were old friends. "This bar's been in my family a long time. I'm Magnolia Pruitt, by the way. We weren't properly introduced last night."

She offered her hand, and I took it for a slow shake. "Tally Aden. Doyle's older sister, as you know. I'm sure he's already given you the highlight reel."

Magnolia's mouth curved, her laugh low and easy. "I've heard a few things here and there." She gave me a quick wink. "Nothing you need to worry about. Your brother loves you."

That was hard to believe.

From his stool, Dig perked up, cocktail in hand, and sauntered over. "And I'm the comedic relief—Diego Salvador. But you can call me Dig." He leaned in to get a closer look at the photos, stopping every few steps. "Wait, this place is yours?"

"This place is mine," she said, falling into step with us as we made our way along the wall. "O'Malley's is legendary in Savannah. Or at least it used to be."

Dig lit up, shimmying like he'd been handed a backstage pass. He started firing off questions, one after another, and Magnolia answered each in that easy Southern rhythm, telling us how her family came over from Ireland and how the bar had survived wars, hurricanes, and more than a few city ordinances.

My chest ached when she mentioned losing her parents. And when she said her uncle had passed recently and left the bar to her, I blinked back the tears. Damn hormones.

Still, she rallied, her voice steady as she moved into lighter memories. She told us about the time she and her friends snuck in and threw a party that lasted until sunrise while her uncle was out of town. She pointed to a framed photo near the door and explained how, according to local legend, the first St. Patrick's Day parade in Savannah had started right outside the front door.

There was an ease to the way she spoke, as if the bar had shaped her just as much as her family had. And maybe it was the lighting, or the comfort of hearing someone talk about a place they loved, but one of the tight spools of anxiety I'd been carrying around started to unfurl a bit. Not all the way. But enough for me to take notice.

If you lifted this building, you'd find Magnolia's roots. And I'd wondered, briefly, where mine would ever be planted.

"I love this place," Dig said, raising his glass in a toast to the ceiling fan. He settled back onto his barstool, eyes already scanning the cocktail menu like he was preparing for another round—or five. "Can we stay forever? Magnolia, is the storage closet available for rent?"

Before she could answer, the door at the back of the bar creaked open. A tall, broad silhouette filled the frame. There was a pause, then the scrape of a box being shoved aside, the clink of bottles, and a string of low, muttered profanity that grew louder with each step.

Magnolia didn't look up. She poured another glass of sweet tea into a mason jar with steady hands, her voice flat. "That'll be Charlie."

Another thump. A grunt. A string of curse words that would make a nun blush. "Magnolia, I swear to God, you need to have someone clear out all these boxes. I can't get the wine in if I've got to hurdle over every single piece of yours and Lee's crap."

He stepped into view, stopped short when he saw me, and went perfectly still, eyes locked on mine. Recognition flickered, then confusion. Or annoyance. Possibly abject horror. Hard to tell.

I gave him the kind of careful smile reserved for someone who's seen you at your worst but hasn't figured out where they know you from yet.

He didn't smile back. He stood there, completely still, like someone had hit pause on the movie of his life.

"What are you doing here?" he finally asked, voice low and flat, directed squarely at me.

Dig, still nursing his drink, glanced between us with a spark of curiosity. "Well. This just got interesting." Then, behind the rim of his glass, he added in a low whisper, "You neglected to mention he's hot."

Magnolia tossed a rag over her shoulder and gave me a look. "Ignore my brother," she said, nodding toward Charlie, who was still planted by the door like he was debating whether or not to bolt. "He barks louder than he bites. How long are you in town?"

Charlie muttered a string of words under his breath that sounded suspiciously like "*not wrong.*"

"I'm staying with Doyle and Jordan for a little while," I said, tucking a strand of hair behind my ear. "Just until I… figure some things out."

Dig, perched on the stool beside me, took a long sip of his cocktail and, without missing a beat, said, "I'm in town for the weekend, hanging with my baby mama while she gets settled. And it appears she's doing *great* at making friends already, aren't you, sweetie?"

He shot me a grin so dazzling it probably should've come with a lens flare, then patted my knee like we were starring in some twisted version of domestic bliss.

I jabbed an elbow into his side, hard enough to earn a satisfying yelp.

Magnolia blinked at us. "Oh. Wow. That's—"

"A lie," I said quickly, offering a smile that barely passed for polite. "All of it. Except for the part where he's only here for the weekend. Unfortunately, that one's true."

"Rude," Dig muttered, rubbing his side. "I was going to take you to brunch tomorrow. Now I might fake my own death."

"You already did that," I said. "In 2017. After that guy ghosted you and you couldn't face your co-op shift."

"That was a spiritual death, Tally. Totally different."

Charlie looked like he was trying to decide whether to ask more questions or walk straight into the ocean.

He stepped up beside Magnolia, resting one forearm on the bar in practiced comfort, but there was a chip in his armor, in the set of his shoulders, like he couldn't tell if he was joining a conversation or crashing it.

Magnolia shot him a blink-and-you'll-miss-it side glance—a quiet little *well, look who's participating in group dynamics* moment.

"So," Charlie said, voice low and a shade too careful. "You two aren't… together?"

Dig and I both barked out a laugh at the same time.

"No," we said in perfect unison.

"But she is my soul mate," Dig added, clutching his chest with all the theatrical flair he was born with. "We've just transcended the need for physical intimacy."

"Or basic communication skills," I muttered, elbowing him again.

Magnolia's brows lifted ever so slightly as she turned to look at her brother. Not with surprise exactly—more like she was trying to clock whatever new social calculus he was running. She passed him a beer from the tap, and he took it without taking his eyes off me.

Charlie didn't say anything. He watched me over the rim of his glass, his expression unreadable. Almost as if he hadn't decided yet if I was trouble, or if he already knew I was.

"Doyle mentioned he had a sister," Charlie said, his tone low and grouchy. "Didn't realize she was the type to lurk in the shadows, breaking into places after hours."

I straightened, lips parting, ready to fire back—but he kept going. "So. You're crashing here for a while, figuring things out?"

It wasn't hostile. Not really. But there was an obvious edge underneath it. A warning. Like, *don't come in here and blow up their lives.*

Dig set his drink down with a little more force than necessary. "You make it sound like she crawled in through a window. Doyle invited her. She belongs here."

Charlie's brow ticked up. "Didn't say she didn't belong here. It's just funny that Doyle left out the part about her proclivity for breaking and entering. Especially with a baby on the way."

My pulse jumped. The sting hit quick—like someone squeezed lemon juice over an open cut.

I let out a dry laugh. "Well, sorry I didn't introduce myself with a PowerPoint. Would you like a printed itinerary of all my failures, or should we go with bullet points?"

"Well, a PowerPoint would have been a hell of a lot neater than you attempting to break into your brother's shop and then… well, you know the rest."

Magnolia shot Charlie a pointed look but didn't comment. Instead, she turned to me. "What do you do, Tally? If you're looking for some temp work while you're in town, I have a few connections."

I hesitated. "I'm sort of… in between things right now."

Dig rolled his eyes. "Don't let her blasé tone fool you. She's talented in that New York kind of way where she could do ten things brilliantly but chooses to do one incredibly well and pretend it's no big deal."

He turned to Magnolia. "She's a photographer—one of the good ones. The kind who sees people—like, really sees them. Even when they wish she wouldn't."

My throat tightened again, this time for a different reason.

Magnolia leaned back against the bar, tapping a finger to her chin like she was chewing on a thought. After a few beats, her eyes lit up.

"Lee's playing at this charity gig his mom, Eunice, is putting on for the Daughters of Savannah Civic Society. I'm bartending, Charlie's showing a piece, Doyle and Jordan are handling refreshments, and Sutton's catering. A photographer is the missing piece."

Beside her, Charlie groaned and dragged a hand down his face.

She shot him a look. "Not a word from you. Eunice owes me a favor anyway." Then she turned back to me, eyes glinting. "You brought your camera to Savannah, I hope?"

I opened my mouth to answer, but Charlie beat me to it.

"Shouldn't you run this by Doyle and Jordan first?" he asked, not unkind but cautious, like I needed permission to be alive.

My stomach twisted, and heat rose in my cheeks before I could stop it.

"Well," I said, plastering on a brittle smile. "When you get in touch with my handlers, let me know. In the meantime, I have my camera. I always do."

I turned on my heel, scooping up my bag. "Come on, Dig."

He scrambled after me, clutching his drink like a talisman. "Wait up. You forgot your emotional support person." He turned back to the bar, waving dramatically at Magnolia. "Can I get this in a to-go cup? Savannah's open-container laws are the only thing keeping me upright right now."

The door swung shut behind us with a bang that echoed louder than I meant it to.

CHAPTER SEVEN

Charlie

The bar door slammed, rattling the frame and the bell that was barely clinging to life above it.

Through the warped glass, I caught Dig—Tally's pint-sized sidekick—planting himself in the window like a Broadway villain, both middle fingers raised in a curtain-call flourish. His grin was wide and feral, the kind that comes from equal parts drama club training and a lifelong commitment to petty vengeance.

Tally appeared behind him, catching his arm and hauling him back with a sharp tug. She lingered for a beat, long enough for our eyes to catch through the glass.

Her face wasn't furious anymore. The anger had drained out, leaving only a hint of sadness in its place. Or disappointment—like I'd confirmed something she'd already suspected.

I looked away first. I didn't know who she'd been hoping for, but last night I'd shown her exactly who I was, even if that wasn't the man I wanted to be.

I wiped the same stretch of bar three times, even though there wasn't so much as a ring on it. My shoulders itched with the weight of Magnolia's silence.

She didn't say anything right away, which was worse than yelling. That meant she was working it up, letting it marinate. And sure enough, after a beat, she settled onto the stool behind me, that pointed quiet of hers like the cocking of a gun.

I heard the subtle clink of ice against glass—her cocktail, untouched since she'd mixed it. She exhaled, long and theatrical, like she was centering herself before she took aim.

"You wanna tell me what that was?" Magnolia's twang was syrupy sweet, but there was enough bite in it to draw blood.

I didn't turn around. "Not sure what you mean."

"Charlie," she said, drawing my name out like a warning. "You ran her off."

"She didn't exactly tiptoe in here with a warm plate of cookies," I muttered. "Last night she's jimmying the lock at *Cheese, Please!*, then she keels over and has to be hauled off to the ER. Now she's showing up like she's been part of this circle all along. I'm just—" I finally faced Magnolia, hands spread. "I'm trying to figure her out. That's all."

Magnolia scoffed behind me. "So your instinct was to humiliate her? Classy."

I finally turned around. She was already watching me like she knew every excuse I was about to offer and already didn't buy a single one.

"Am I supposed to braid friendship bracelets with her?" I was getting worked up, but I didn't back off. "You saw her. Did you see the way she looked at me? And clearly something's up, or else Doyle, who I've known for ten years, would have introduced us to her right off the bat."

Magnolia's brow arched. "And that gives you permission to act like a jackass?"

"It gives me a reason to be cautious," I said, my voice dropping. "You didn't see her last night. She was out of it. Shaking. Barely conscious. And now she's suddenly showing up here with some loud theater kid who keeps calling her his baby momma?"

"You mean Dig? The sweet one with the nice shoes and an alarming obsession with reality TV?" She shot me a look. "Yeah, really dangerous."

I opened my mouth. Closed it again. She had a point, but I wasn't ready to admit it.

She stood and walked past me, fingers trailing along the bartop. "Doyle's the one who should be explaining things," she said, her voice lower now, more tired than angry. "But until he does, maybe try not being the worst version of yourself just because someone walks through the door and doesn't fit your idea of how things should go."

She moved with an easy sway, the click of her boots echoing across the floorboards. The air still carried that familiar mix of citrus cleaner and old wood—stinging, grounding, unmistakably O'Malley's.

Unmistakably Magnolia.

She was my anchor. The reason I showed up, stayed steady, kept my head down, and handled what needed handling. I was her keeper. Always had been. And getting pulled into someone else's chaos, especially Tally's, couldn't happen.

Magnolia let the silence stretch, then added, "She's a mess, Charlie. But so are the rest of us."

"Heyo!" Lee's voice landed loud and unapologetic as he swung through the back entrance, boots thudding across the floor. His guitar was strapped across his back, same as always, and he looked freshly showered, annoyingly energized, and like he hadn't walked into the middle of a situation he was bound to make worse.

Magnolia didn't respond; she gave me a pointed glance before turning her back to him and grabbing a rag off the counter.

Lee slowed, taking in the tension in the room. "Okay. What did I walk into?"

Sutton followed behind him, arms full of cooking magazines and a sweating iced coffee that was threatening to slip right out of her hand. She didn't speak either; she looked at the three of us like she'd walked into the wrong room at a family reunion.

I didn't offer an answer. I let everyone shuffle around and quietly hoped one of them would change the subject. Sutton usually had an unhinged tale to share from whatever event she'd catered that day. And Lee always had some story that spun way off course and took the attention with it. Or, if the universe felt like cutting me a break, he'd finally blurt out how he really felt about Magnolia, and they could spend the next hour arguing about whether she should marry him or his brother. Literally anything else. Anything but sitting there, feeling like the world's biggest asshole.

Because the truth was, I'd been a dick. And worse, I didn't even know what I was trying to prove. I saw her last night—barely upright, clearly terrified, holding it together by a thread. Then today, I treated her like she didn't belong. Like I had some authority over who was allowed into this circle. I hated that. It didn't feel like me. At least, I hoped it wasn't.

Still, there was a pull to her I couldn't shake. The way she looked at me was like she was bracing for impact, already convinced I wasn't worth trusting, and I'd proven her right. Those eyes saw too much and gave nothing back. It bothered me. I didn't know what she was searching for, but I knew I'd only made it harder for her to find it.

"Uh, hello?" Sutton waved a hand in front of my face. I blinked, realizing I'd been staring at the wall. "Are you brooding? Lee—he's brooding."

Magnolia didn't even look up from the cooler she was restocking, but I caught the rise and fall of her shoulders in a quiet chuckle. "Oh, he's broody and moody, all right. Scared off Doyle's sister like she'd wandered into a damn ambush. She barely set foot in Savannah before he made her feel like a dog begging for scraps."

Lee let out a low whistle. "Damn, man. That's twice now. Are you planning on running off every woman who accidentally makes eye contact with you, or just the really cute ones?"

I muttered, dragging a hand down my face, "I didn't run her off."

"You think she's cute?" Magnolia asked, popping up from behind the beer chest.

Lee laughed. "She's adorable, Maggie. Does that make you mad?"

Magnolia didn't say a word. She threw her hands toward the ceiling like she was hoping the universe might beam her out of the conversation entirely. I was genuinely hoping for the same to happen to me.

Sutton squirmed in her seat, her iced coffee puddle stretching across the bar. At least it gave me something to wipe up. "Okay, but like… did we get any good gossip out of her? What's she really doing here? And are Jordan and Doyle actually that perfect, or do they lock themselves in the penthouse at night and bathe in salmon sperm to keep that youthful glow?"

Everyone turned slowly to look at her.

"What?" Sutton blinked, all innocence. "It's all over the internet. It's the new fountain of youth."

Lee choked on his beer. Magnolia blinked like she was reconsidering every life choice that had led her here. I stared at Sutton, completely unamused.

"You scare me," I said.

"Rightfully so," she replied, taking a slow sip of her coffee.

Lee lifted his hand like he was about to make a toast. "Well, this isn't exactly gossip, but I heard Doyle and Jordan mention it at brunch a few weeks ago—and it was confirmed when I ended up at the hospital with her last night."

Sutton's eyebrows shot up. Magnolia paused mid-wipe on the bar.

"The baby's father kind of ghosted her after a… situationship." He cringed. "I can't believe I just used those two words in a sentence."

I winced. That was… brutal.

Sutton let out a soft, "Yikes."

Magnolia muttered under her breath, and I caught enough to know it wouldn't make the Sunday bulletin.

Lee ran a hand over the back of his neck. "Anyway, I don't know the whole story. But it sounded like she's been through it. And now she's here, alone, trying to figure things out."

"She's a photographer, you know," Magnolia said, reaching for a wine glass. "I was thinking about asking your momma if she could shoot that pre-holiday charity event we'll all be at. It'll give her a chance to meet people and maybe soften Doyle up a little."

Lee perked up. "Jordan said the same thing last night. Said she's the real deal. Apparently, she's done work in like a dozen countries—photojournalism, weddings, travel stuff. He said there's this one shot she took in a monsoon, of a bride laughing barefoot in the rain, and it went viral. Got picked up by a few magazines. He showed me her site—her photos don't just look good, they make you *feel*. Like she sees things most people miss."

Magnolia's brows lifted. "So why isn't she doing that now?"

Lee shook his head. "Jordan's not sure. Said she was bouncing from country to country, gig to gig, and then… she just stopped. Went back to New York, picked up some odd jobs. Started doing local stuff again. He said it seemed like something happened, but she never really talked about it."

Magnolia let out a low whistle. "That's a hell of a pivot. Bet we can guess what that something was that happened."

It was one thing to be new in town—jobless, pregnant, clearly hanging on by a thread. But to hear she'd been all over the world, then went back to New York and somehow landed here in Savannah, alone, after some guy bailed on her completely? That kind of hurt didn't bruise. It left a mark you couldn't scrub out.

The guilt hit fast and searing, gnawing at the edges of my conscience. I stepped out from behind the bar and started pacing, dragging a hand through my hair like that might help untangle whatever was clawing at my chest.

"I should apologize," I muttered, mostly to myself. "How do I always end up looking like the asshole?"

Sutton tilted her head, eyes narrowing like she was clocking a new development. "Oh my God. Is Charlie Pruitt actually making this about himself for once?"

Lee let out a low, slow laugh. "Maybe," he said, careful now, like he knew he was edging into dangerous territory, "You're not the asshole. Maybe you're mad because she got under your skin, and you're not used to people doing that."

I stopped at the front of the bar, leaning on the edge of a worn barstool. "You realize you're trying to give me advice in my own sister's bar, standing exactly two feet from the spot where you shattered her heart and ran off to Nashville, right?"

He lifted his beer and grinned, shooting an unbothered wink at my sister. "And yet here we are."

I didn't say anything after that, mostly because I didn't have a comeback that didn't sound like a tantrum.

My whole life, I've been the loyal one. The dependable one. The guy who picks up the phone at midnight, who shows up with tools when your sink breaks or bourbon when your heart does. Charlie Pruitt. The solid one. The one who holds it all together.

I've been the foundation. For Magnolia. For Sutton. For Lee. For everyone else in our circle. Even when it felt like I was barely hanging on myself.

And somehow, within one night, Tally had turned me from the golden retriever best friend everyone could count on into the guy in the corner, snarling and snapping, unsure how to clean up a mess for the first time in my life. She didn't just rattle me. She'd looked straight through me and saw something I didn't want seen.

She saw the asshole underneath.

And I hated that. Hated how it made me feel like I wasn't as unreadable as I thought. Like perhaps the armor I'd spent a decade welding around myself wasn't as bulletproof as I needed it to be.

Because if she could see the mess behind the curtain after knowing me for all of two minutes… how long until everyone else did, too?

I was the guy who held everything together.

But standing there, elbow-deep in dish soap, thinking about the flash of her eyes and that defiant curl of her mouth…

I couldn't shake the feeling that maybe *I* was the one coming apart.

***

Back in the studio, I tried to work. Opened my sketchpad. Stared at a blank page.

I kept thinking about last night—her lying on that table, barely conscious, and the worry that shot through me even though I didn't know her. And then today, when I actually got the chance to talk to her, I'd been a complete ass.

I glanced down at my forearm—the linework I'd finished last month, tributes to mentors I'd lost and the people I loved. I wondered if she'd noticed the ink last night. The way her eyes had flickered over my arms before she went down.

The sketchpad dropped to the coffee table. I grabbed my beer and took a long pull.

I'd spent my whole life being the foundation—for Magnolia, for everyone. Solid. Steady. Dependable.

So why did one night with a stranger make me feel like I was the one coming apart?

CHAPTER EIGHT

Tally

I was halfway through a list of things I needed. So far, it included exactly one item: "The will to live." Not super helpful, but at least I was setting the bar low.

My camera bag sat open beside me, holding the essentials. A couple of flashes, two charged batteries, a wide-angle lens, and my 50mm prime—which, despite everything, I still called my favorite like it was a person. But the rest of my gear? Light stands, tripod, reflectors, editing setup—all of that was still in Brooklyn. Along with any real intention of making this a job again. Even if, once upon a time, it had been the dream.

I leaned back on the ridiculously plush couch. One of those expensive, designer monstrosities that felt more like a cloud than furniture and definitely did not need a crusty poodle turning circles on it. I let out a breath so long and shaky it felt like my bones deflated right along with it.

I'd been taking pictures for as long as I could remember. My camera hung around my neck like armor, steadying me when nothing else did. It made me feel real. Seen. Like I had purpose, even if I wasn't the one being captured.

In high school, I was president of the photography club and worked on the yearbook. Entered every contest I could find, from the ones printed in the back of glossy magazines to the dusty state fairgrounds where judges smelled like menthols and funnel cake. I built a portfolio full of ribbon-winners, the kind of work teachers said would take me far.

And they were right. I got into some of the best photography programs in New York. Full scholarship. A golden ticket.

But I didn't go.

I'd been waiting for Doyle to graduate so we could move together, the two of us taking on the city we'd imagined in endless conversations and late-night dreams. When the time came, my admissions had expired, but I didn't bother to reapply. My brother and I had finally made it to New York together, and we could conjure up a new dream—a different one we could hold onto together.

And when that didn't work, and Doyle eventually found his own path lit by the embers of a love I'd never known, I set off on my own, chasing a meaningful life the way other people chased love. Weddings in Tuscany, street food in Bangkok, fireworks over Tokyo—proof I could build a life through my lens.

And then, in Australia, I met a boy with salt in his hair and a laugh that made me forget what I was running from. We fell fast, burned bright, and when he eventually left, because they always do, I told myself it was just another picture that didn't develop. That's how it always went—catching love, never keeping it.

It had been a little over two weeks since I'd landed in Savannah, and I was already unraveling. Unsettled. Embarrassed. Exhausted—not only from the pregnancy, but from that deeper level of tired that settles in your chest and makes everything feel too loud, too bright, too much. The what-have-I-done sort of tired.

The kind that comes from trusting the wrong person. Again. From mistaking chemistry for connection and ending up with a nine-month reminder. The fallout? All mine to bear alone.

The world may have chewed me up and spit me out, but at least it usually had the decency to let me disappear. Wherever I landed, I could blend in—no reputations to manage. No family watching.

But here in Savannah, everything felt exposed. Like a magnifying glass hovered over me, every choice examined, every step too loud. I knew it was only a matter of time before I screwed it all up again.

Magnolia had been texting nonstop, practically buzzing about me meeting Eunice Wilder. Apparently, the Daughters of Savannah Civic Society needed someone to take photos for their social media and newsletter, and Eunice had started looking right before I got into town. Total coincidence. Obviously.

It sounded great in theory. But I had no editing supplies. No workspace. And at that exact moment, not even the will to live, according to the checklist in front of me. I was mentally drained, anxious, and already spiraling about the idea of disappointing a woman I'd never even met.

Nancy twitched in her sleep beside me, a soft little snore escaping her as the sunlight caught the wiry curls on her head. Her body curled toward mine, trusting, unbothered. She didn't seem to care that I had no idea what I was doing. She didn't question whether I deserved her. She was here, warm and real and mine.

And God, I envied her for it.

I looked down at the pen in my hand, still hovering above the notebook, my fingers twitching with the familiar ache of wanting to get it right and knowing I probably wouldn't.

What did it mean to belong somewhere? To wake up and actually recognize your own life. To feel anchored instead of adrift. Maybe it wasn't about the place at all, but about finding someone who made the chaos quieter by existing.

I had always been a girl in motion. A girl with a suitcase half-packed. A girl who didn't hang art on the walls because it felt like a lie to pretend she was staying. I moved through cities and apartments and people like wind through trees. Felt for a second, then gone. There was never any time to grow roots when you were already halfway to the next exit.

And now? Now there was a tiny, flickering life inside me. One that didn't get a choice about whether I stayed or ran. One that was already counting on me to be someone I'd never been before. Anchored, stable, enough.

I wasn't failing myself anymore. I had the very real possibility of failing someone who hadn't even arrived yet. Because deep down, in that raw place I didn't let anyone touch, I didn't want to run this time, I wanted to try. But I didn't know how.

Some people had families. They had mothers to guide them when they were bringing new life into the world. Mothers who mailed parenting books and knitted tiny sweaters and called three times a day to say, *You've got this.*

Mine didn't even know where on this planet I was. She didn't even know I was pregnant. And if she did… I didn't want to think about it.

The truth was, my mother had a way of turning everything into a reflection of herself. My choices weren't mine. They were statements about her. Embarrassments. Proof that she had sacrificed everything and still ended up with a daughter who couldn't hold it together for longer than a calendar month.

She would have called this moment—me, alone on someone else's couch with a crusty dog and an even crustier reputation—a cry for attention. Or worse, a pattern. As if I enjoyed the constant feeling of barely staying afloat. As if chaos made me feel alive instead of exhausted.

I folded my arms across my middle and sat with the weight of it. The silence. The pressure. The absence of someone who should have cared enough to check in. To ask if I was okay.

But she didn't. And I knew she wouldn't.

I pushed myself deeper into the couch cushions, staring at the ceiling, hoping it might hold answers I hadn't thought to ask yet.

Nancy stirred beside me, lifting her head with a quiet huff, confused by my antics. I didn't move. I sat there for a moment, eyes fixed on the one-lined list I'd written, wishing the rest would somehow appear on paper. Then I folded it in half, slid it under the throw pillow, and tried to pretend it wasn't there.

Maybe I wouldn't go to this meeting with Eunice.

Magnolia would get over it. Eunice didn't know me, not really. I could say I wasn't feeling well, which everyone would believe at this point, given the history. Or I could say I'd double-booked. I could say anything, really, because if I didn't show up, there'd be no photos. And if there were no photos, there'd be nothing for me to ruin.

That was the part no one ever said out loud—the way not trying sometimes felt safer than trying and failing. If I backed out before anyone got their hopes up, I couldn't disappoint them. Couldn't confirm whatever quiet suspicions they might already have about me being a mess, or a flake, or someone who wasn't quite cut out for the life she claimed she wanted.

Being invisible was safer. It was also lonelier.

The front door creaked open, and Jordan stepped inside, holding two iced coffees. His eyes found mine with a quiet steadiness. It wasn't pity. He knew better than that. It was a softness, like he could sense I was coming apart and didn't want to press on the bruise.

"I come bearing gifts," he said, crossing the room and offering one of the cups. "One sad, soulless decaf for you. One proper caffeine bomb for me."

I took it, half touched, half offended. "Decaf? Are you trying to make me suffer more than I already am?"

Jordan settled into the armchair across from me. "It's called protecting the baby. Or, more specifically, protecting Doyle from having to deal with both you and a caffeine crash at the same time."

I groaned but sipped. "Fair."

He leaned forward, elbows on his knees. "I also come with a mission."

"A mission?"

"A *Cheese, Please!* emergency," Jordan announced, already sounding exasperated. "The walk-in needs restocking, the wine display looks like a raccoon blew through it, and your brother has buried himself in spreadsheets and quarterly projections like he's running a Fortune 500 company instead of a glorified snack boutique. So that leaves me. And—lucky you—*you.*"

I blinked. "You want *my* help?"

He gave me a look. "You've got a few hours until you meet with Mrs. Wilder. Unless you'd rather keep letting your dog psychoanalyze your existential spiral from the couch."

Before I could argue, he added, "Also, if you're up for it, I was hoping you might take a few pictures. Some product shots for the website, maybe a few behind-the-scenes things for socials. We're way overdue for an update, and everything you've posted online has looked... I don't know, cool. Like, actually cool."

My mouth opened, but nothing came out.

"I mean, only if you want to," he added quickly. "It's not a job-job. I mean, of course, we will pay you. I thought you might want something to do that didn't involve... whatever this is that you're doing now. Which is what, exactly?"

I shrugged and glanced down at myself—an old t-shirt and linen pants that hadn't seen daylight since I arrived. No stains, no leftover breakfast crust. Functional. Maybe even employable.

I took another long sip of the decaf. "Okay. I'll help."

Jordan smiled. "Thank you."

I paused. "But only because I'm wearing real pants."

His grin widened. "Hey, we take progress where we can get it."

And for the first time in a while, a flicker of purpose stirred. Small, fragile, but real.

It was a start.

***

Cheese, Please! was bright and welcoming, filled with the warm scent of fresh bread, aged cheddar, and an herby note I couldn't quite place. It was annoyingly charming, like a Pinterest board had come to life and decided to run a cheese and wine empire.

Muted golds and soft greens wrapped around the space like a hug, and hand-lettered chalkboard signs pointed the way toward truffle brie and house-made jam. A floor-to-ceiling cooler hummed quietly along the wall, stocked with crisp white wine and those little jars of pickled things I could never afford but always craved.

I'd seen a few of their posts floating around on social media. Jordan had a solid eye for branding, but he wasn't wrong. The photos didn't quite match the vibe. The space itself was effortlessly cool, but the images fell short.

Still, stepping through the door now hit me in a way I didn't expect. It wasn't jealousy, and it wasn't regret. It was pride. Real, breath-catching pride.

My brother used to eat peanut butter straight from the jar and swear he was destined to be the next Anthony Bourdain. Now he was part-owner of a place that looked like it belonged in a glossy spread about hidden Southern gems. And Jordan, with his soft-sweater warmth and love of the perfect blend of tannins and age of grapes, had helped turn the vision into this beautiful, tangible reality.

A smile crept in before I could stop it. My eyes probably said more than I meant them to, but I didn't bother hiding it. For once, it felt good to be proud, even if it wasn't mine. Even if I was standing on the edge of it all, looking in.

I held onto that feeling for as long as I could. Long enough to forget that Doyle had left me behind in New York without a second thought. Enough to quiet the part of me that still felt a little abandoned. For a few minutes, awe was louder than bitterness. And that felt akin to progress.

Jordan handed me an apron—hunter green with a tiny wedge of gold, metallic cheese, and the words *Cheese, Please!* stitched across the front. I tied it around my waist and tried not to let my hormones tackle me to the ground. It was just an apron. But it felt like more. A tiny signal that I wasn't just floating. That maybe I had a place here.

I followed him behind the counter, rolling up my sleeves with the confidence of someone who *might* know what she was doing. And somehow, I did. I stocked the fridge, sorted crackers by expiration date, and lined up glass jars of imported olives with labels I couldn't pronounce but instinctively respected.

Jordan didn't hover. He let me work and trusted me to get it done.

It was simple, repetitive, a quiet rhythm that let my brain go soft around the edges. I hadn't realized how much I'd missed using my hands and my brain, moving around without the weight of judgment pressing on my shoulders.

I'd held so many odd jobs over the last few years that none of this felt particularly intimidating. I'd been a yoga instructor, a cashier, a wedding planning assistant, a hairdresser—sort of, but that's a long story—a mortician, and a beekeeper. Also, a waitress. A really bad one. And in between all of that, I kept trying to make photography stick. I'd book a few weddings, snap some engagement shoots, and once even did a full-day elopement marathon in Central Park with twenty-nine couples and one extremely aggressive squirrel.

No matter how chaotic things got, holding a camera gave me a sense of purpose. It was the one thing that made me feel capable, useful. But the feeling never lasted. The money was inconsistent, the pressure crept in, and eventually I'd fold. I'd take the next job that came along and convince myself it was only for now, a placeholder until I figured it all out.

The problem was that I never gave myself the grace of loving the craft of photography enough to try and make it a career. I took it too seriously and would quit before I could fail.

"You're good at this," Jordan said, tossing me a bar towel to wipe down the counter. "Are you sure your résumé doesn't say *cheesemonger in a past life*?"

I snorted, catching the towel one-handed. "I'm adding it now. Right between 'beekeeper' and 'bridesmaid wrangler.'"

My résumé flashed through my mind—a dozen half-finished jobs, none lasting longer than a year. I'd need to find a real, consistent job in Savannah. But who was going to hire someone whose longest stint at anything barely lasted longer than a podcast episode? And then to show up visibly pregnant on top of that? Lord, I was about to spiral.

I grabbed my camera and slung it around my neck, trying to settle my nerves by focusing on the one thing I still, somewhat, trusted myself to do.

The light in the shop was shockingly good. Warm, directional, and soft enough to work with. I started circling, testing a few angles, checking how the shadows fell across the shelves and counter. I adjusted the light sensitivity, bumped my aperture enough to blur the background, and zeroed in on a cluster of jars that looked more artisanal than anything I could afford.

Near the front, a round display table made from a reclaimed wine barrel caught the afternoon light just right—practically begging for a shot. I moved a wedge of cheese an inch, angled the wine glass, dropped a tiny bowl of pickles in for balance. Then I crouched, framing the shot so the curve of wood and glass did all the work.

Click.

I adjusted a smidge to the left and took another.

Click.

I was so focused, I didn't hear Jordan approach until he spoke. "I have absolutely no idea what you're doing, but it looks cool as hell."

I glanced up at him, half-laughing. "Oh, you know, trying to make fermented grapes look sexy."

He looked at the setup, then nudged the barrel with the toe of his shoe. "Charlie actually made this table. It was the first commissioned piece we bought from him when we opened."

I looked at it again, noticing the clean weld lines and the slight asymmetry in the woodgrain. The intricate detail in the smooth edges reminded me of him lurking in the shadows the night we met, a sander in hand and a crooked smile on his lips. Was he really that annoyed with me that night, or did I miss the part where maybe he was kind of charming in a grouchy sort of way?

"Of course he did," I murmured.

Jordan didn't press, only handed me a folded dish towel. "You've got pickle juice on your elbow, Ansel Adams."

The bell over the front door jingled, and Jordan's posture stiffened slightly, enough to make me pause.

My brother strode in, sunglasses still perched on his nose like he hadn't fully committed to being indoors. His gaze swept the room, already carrying that air of *what did I walk into.* Then he saw me, and his eyes narrowed like Jordan had asked a possum to restock the shelves.

"What are you doing down here?" he asked, voice laced with that signature cocktail of judgment and disbelief.

"Helping," I said, holding up a wheel of Gouda as if it proved my point.

His mouth curved—not quite a smile, not quite approval. "Oh, photography again? Adorable."

Jordan made a noise low in his throat and stepped between us before I could come up with a response that wasn't laced with profanity.

"She's taking shots for the website," he said calmly. "And actually doing a damn good job, if you're curious."

Doyle's sunglasses slid down enough to reveal the quick flick of his eyes over me. "Sure. Great. Just… don't knock over the display." He moved behind the counter, gruff but not entirely dismissive.

I swallowed whatever comeback was building in my throat and quietly set the Gouda back on the counter, trying not to let my hands shake. I grabbed a damp rag and started wiping down the tasting table, focusing on the sticky wine rings like they were the most important thing in the world. I could pretend his words didn't sting, but they did because he wasn't wrong. I had picked up photography again. Just like I'd picked it up the last time. And the time before that. I just never managed to hold on.

I was rearranging the sample cups when Doyle pushed his sunglasses up onto his head and gave me a once-over, his brows lifting at the apron. "Since when do you 'help,' Tallulah?" His tone wasn't cruel, just skeptical—like he was trying to figure out if this was a bit or a breakthrough.

Jordan coughed in the background, clearly not eager to referee the Aden sibling apocalypse this was on the verge of becoming. He scurried to the back of the shop, refusing to make eye contact with either of us.

My brother's expression caught my eye as I lowered my camera and adjusted the strap around my neck. The dynamic between us had changed since I'd been in Savannah. His usual cadence and banter with me—typically a little judgmental but mostly playful—had curdled into a shade shy of animosity. Almost like he saw me as a burden.

"Remember, my darling brother," I touted, leaning against the repurposed wine barrel. "You're the one who invited me into your lair. Or was this all an elaborate plan to make me feel more like shit than I already do?"

My brother shrugged, but something flickered in his expression. A smug look flashed across his face, and he leaned a hip on the counter, folding his arms across his chest.

"Heard you're meeting with Eunice Wilder."

"I am," the words came out steadier than I was.

His mouth tugged sideways. "Good luck with that. Eunice will probably send you home with cookies and a five-year plan. Don't say I didn't warn you."

We stared each other down for a minute before he turned and made his way to the office in the back.

I pivoted back to the window where my shot waited. The light had drifted, catching the curve of the wine glass and scattering across the brass inlay of the sculpture beneath it—the old wine barrel I'd used as a stand. The carvings were there all along; I was seeing them now.

I stepped closer.

"Who wants Manchego and a better attitude?" Jordan called, emerging from the walk-in fridge with a plate of cheese samples.

I laughed, then I adjusted the frame, leaned in, pressed the shutter.

Click.

This time, I didn't second-guess it.

***

As the afternoon wore on, my confidence climbed. *I could do this,* I thought, falling back into the familiar rhythm of photographing still life—the quiet, predictable kind that didn't blink or move or ask to see the back of the camera. It felt good to have purpose, even if it was only for Jordan's social media feed. And now, with the golden light flooding in through the front windows, it was time to graduate to the hard stuff. People.

"Jordy," I called, dragging a pair of rustic barstools into position around one of the high-tops by the window. I'd already staged the shot—two crisp wine glasses, a tiny but adorable charcuterie board, folded napkins that looked impossibly casual in a curated kind of way. "You and Doyle get out here. This light is unreal."

Jordan poked his head out from behind the bar, arms full of packages, and made a face. "Your brother's knee-deep in invoices. I don't think he's leaving that cave anytime soon."

"Just try," I pleaded as I crouched low, testing shadows and shifting the angles. I had maybe two minutes of that perfect, glowy light. If I could get them in position, the whole scene would come to life.

Jordan sighed and ducked into the back, murmuring a few words that were met with a familiar, stubborn grumble. No surprise there—Doyle couldn't take a break if it came with a bow and a paid invoice attached.

Footsteps echoed behind me as I angled the wine glasses again, chasing the way the light curved across the glass. "Let's go, people. The sun waits for no one."

"Wow," came a voice that slid into my spine, warm and amused. "Those invisible people you're shooting look like they're having a great time."

I turned on my heel, already smiling, and spotted Charlie walking in, two crates of empty bottles balanced in one arm. The late afternoon sun angled low between the buildings, spilling through the front window and catching his tousled auburn hair, gilding the curls that had slipped free from beneath his backward cap. His green eyes met mine, calm and steady, holding a hint of curiosity that made me forget, for a second, to keep my distance.

"Very funny," I muttered, gesturing toward the crates. "What are you doing? Building a wine spaceship? Should I be concerned about your hobbies?"

That smirk bloomed—slow and crooked and a little bit dangerous. "Maybe you've got more of the artist's streak than you think, darlin'." He nodded toward the table, where the light had pooled in a perfect golden spotlight. "You're not wrong about this, the angle's perfect. This shot would look great online."

"I'm going to miss it," I groaned, sinking onto one of the barstools. "The good light's fading and my models are a no-show."

Charlie set the crates on a lower table, then surveyed the setup. "I assume you don't have a tripod?"

"I have a timer."

He held out a hand. "Then hand it over and sit."

Our fingers brushed for a second, and a jolt went straight through me. I ignored it and slid the camera into his hand. Charlie adjusted the lens, balanced it on the crates, then sat across from me.

I blinked, trying to figure out what to do with my hands—or my face—or the walking contradiction sitting across from me, suddenly acting all cooperative.

He leaned forward and gently turned my chin toward him with two fingers. "Look at me. Pretend I just said something funny."

But I couldn't—not because he hadn't, but because everything in me had suddenly gone still, and all I could do was stare.

He chuckled low in his throat, reset the timer, and dropped back into his seat, this time arranging my hand beneath my chin. "Alright, then. Don't fake a laugh, I'm not that funny, anyway—lots of dad jokes and bad innuendos. Maybe pretend you don't hate me. You can manage that for ten seconds."

I snorted out a laugh despite myself. "I don't hate you, I barely know you."

He reached over again, adjusting the placement of my other hand so it rested lightly against the base of the wine glass. His own hands landed on the table, broad and steady, curling around his glass in a way that made the whole image feel—real.

The timer began to click, slow at first, then faster.

His gaze locked on mine.

"You have the most beautiful eyes," he whispered as the shutter clicked.

If I had to guess, the photo probably captured me mid-blink, mid-heartbeat, caught somewhere between stunned and unsure whether to breathe.

There wasn't time to check. The back door creaked open, and Doyle came striding out with Jordan close behind.

"Hey, Charlie," Doyle called, his tone clipped. "I left those empties in the hallway. You didn't need to come all the way in."

I turned toward Charlie, wondering if he'd noticed the slight edge in my brother's voice. But when I looked at him, he wasn't watching Doyle at all.

His eyes were still on me.

"Just helping Savannah's newest photographer catch the light," he said casually, tipping his chin toward the camera. "Didn't want her missing the shot."

Jordan coughed, poorly masking a laugh.

"Having fun playing photographer, or are you actually planning on doing anything useful today?" Doyle asked. His grin tugged sideways, enough to show he meant it as a joke, though his delivery still landed rougher than he probably intended.

Charlie rose from the stool, slow and deliberate, and took a few steps toward us, positioning himself slightly in front of me. Not confrontational, not overt—but enough. "We were having a lot of fun, actually," he said, eyes steady on Doyle before flicking to Jordan. "Grab a seat so she can catch the rest of the light."

The shift in the room was instant. Jordan and Doyle exchanged a glance, both of them blinking like they weren't used to hearing Charlie speak with that kind of edge. Still, they moved, settling into the seats across from each other without another word.

Charlie handed me my camera without making a show of it, and I gave him the smallest thank you, a breath of it, so soft only he would hear.

I snapped into motion, directing them into place as the light dipped lower. Once we found our groove, I moved Jordan and Doyle around the shop, catching detail shots and even getting my brother to pose for a few headshots in front of the fully stocked wine shelf.

Charlie stayed close, watching as I shifted angles and fiddled with settings, tossing in the occasional quiet suggestion but never hovering. He gave me space to lead, to work, to actually be good at what I knew I was capable of doing—and he didn't make a big deal out of it.

By the time the sun slipped away completely, we were the only people left in the shop. I cleaned up the space and wiped down the counter, slipped off my apron, and smoothed a hand over the subtle curve of my stomach. It wasn't obvious yet, not unless you knew to look, but the gesture had become second nature. A reminder. A promise to do better this time.

When I looked up, Charlie was watching me. The amusement from earlier was gone, replaced by a quiet reverence.

"Tally," he started, voice low and careful. "About the night we met… I feel like we got off on the wrong foot. I've been thinking about it. About you. I'm usually the one people can count on—the steady one. But with you, the last couple of times, I wasn't myself. And you saw right through it."

I didn't want to meet his eyes. Didn't want to open that door. But I looked anyway. And there it was—that softness, that quiet pull that made it impossible to breathe properly.

His fingers flexed at his sides. "You don't need a camera to see people for who they are. That's what rattled me. So maybe… maybe give me another chance. To show you the version of me that isn't all built-up walls and bad timing."

He didn't move after that, but held my gaze, steady and unblinking, ready to tackle every excuse I might throw at him.

"Don't," I whispered. "Don't look at me like that."

"Like what?"

"Like I'm broken. Like I'm something that needs fixing."

He stepped closer, slow and deliberate, his eyes never leaving mine. He reached out and brushed his thumb across my cheek, catching a tear I hadn't realized had fallen.

"You don't seem broken to me," he rasped, his voice rough but steady. "And I'm not trying to fix anything."

I wanted to believe him. But the way Doyle had looked at me had pulled me straight back to being seventeen with a secondhand camera and not a soul alive who believed I'd do anything real with it.

Charlie tipped his head, letting a lock of hair fall across his brow. "Give yourself a little credit. Every time I've seen you since that first night—hell, maybe even then—I haven't seen someone falling apart. I've seen someone trying. Someone who keeps showing up, even when it's hard. And you're good, Tally. If you wanted it, you could make a career out of this."

I couldn't speak. I stood there, letting it all hit me—the sawdust, the warmth rolling off him.

"You don't have to have it all figured out to matter," he said. "You're allowed to be here, even if you're still piecing things together. You don't need anyone's permission. Not your brother's. Not mine. No one's."

I wasn't sure what to say, so I busied myself with closing up for the day—wiping down the last counter, gathering empty glasses, flicking off lights until the shop dimmed into soft shadows and quiet.

Charlie rocked back on his heels, watching me without pressing. Then, with a half-smile and a shrug, he said, "Come on, darlin'. Let me walk you home so you can get ready for this meeting with Eunice. It's on the way anyway."

I set the last clean glasses on the shelf beside him and looked up. "You live downstairs from me," I said, the charm of him wrapping around me like an old quilt.

"Well," he mused, "Isn't that convenient?"

I grabbed my camera bag, turned off the last light, and let him walk me home.

CHAPTER NINE

Tally

I yanked what used to be a form-fitting black cocktail dress over my body, which was now—unceremoniously—more full than it had been a few weeks ago. But if I had to guess, my secret wasn't much of a secret anymore. And if there was one thing I knew about these Savannah natives, it was that they didn't just gossip. They curated it.

If Eunice Wilder didn't already know I was pregnant, it'd be a miracle.

I took the elevator down to the lobby and found Charlie leaning casually against the front desk, deep in conversation with Hoyt. As I approached, Charlie straightened, one arm still resting on the counter, and gave me a look—half grin, half smirk—that tugged at what was left of my composure

"Ms. Aden," Hoyt said, springing to his feet. He looked one breath away from a panic attack. "Can I call you a cab?"

I shook my head. "That won't be necessary. Are you okay?"

Charlie came to stand beside me. His eyes traveled down my dress and landed, with entirely too much focus, on my lips.

"I'll walk her to Eunice's," he said, casual as ever. "Fill her in on the way."

He held out his arm, and I slid mine through his, ignoring the warm press of muscle and that fresh, woodsy scent—like a man who'd recently showered or singlehandedly rebuilt a cabin. I tried very hard *not* to picture him stripped down, hammering nails into chopped pine, sweat dripping down his—

"I bet she can come up with a solution for your little problem," he said, voice low, yanking me out of my spiral.

"I don't want to be a burden, Mr. Pruitt," Hoyt mumbled, deflating back into his seat. Whatever was gnawing at him had taken up permanent residence in his spine. "Tell Mrs. Wilder hello for me."

Charlie pushed the door open with his back, guiding us onto the sidewalk, eyes locked on mine. "Will do, Hoyt," he called.

"What was that about?" I finally asked as we reached the crosswalk on Broughton. I hadn't wanted to break the spell—the two of us, arm in arm, moving leisurely through Savannah like we had nowhere else to be.

Charlie hit the button for the light and turned toward me. "Hoyt and his fiancée, Charlotte, were supposed to get married next summer. Some destination wedding in the South of France."

The light changed, and we crossed the street, still linked, close enough to feel his steadiness as if it were my own.

"Oh," I said, still failing to see why Hoyt had looked like someone had kicked his puppy.

Charlie paused in front of a bakery, studying the window for a moment before continuing. "Turns out Charlotte's mom is sick and they need to move the wedding up."

He stopped again, this time outside a florist, squinting at the storefront. "No, this isn't the one Eunice usually uses. I'll have to ask her when we get there."

"What's going on, Charlie?"

He stopped walking and gently unhooked our arms, taking my hand in his. His palm was rough and warm, calloused and sure. The type of hand that could steady you. The type of touch that could undo you.

"They can't find vendors on short notice. Hoyt's been calling around to bakeries and officiants. Trying to line up a florist. Photographer, too. He's having a hard time."

I slipped my hand back, not entirely trusting myself to hold it together. "Oh, is he now?"

Charlie laughed, low and unbothered, then took my arm and tucked it back through his again. We picked up the pace, heading toward the stately homes lining Jones Street.

"He is. And wouldn't you know it, a photographer—who's won state fair blue ribbons, gone viral, and is single-handedly revamping the social media profile of *Cheese, Please!*—so happens to live in the building he works in."

I rolled my eyes. "Yeah. What luck, indeed."

We stopped on the old brick sidewalk in front of the Wilder House. A wide, wraparound porch ran the length of the front and curved away to a shadowed courtyard tucked behind a large arched gate. Navy shutters sat neatly against the white clapboard, and the deep front door caught the evening light like it belonged to a postcard. Two white rocking chairs waited on the porch, a riot of hot-pink azaleas bursting between them, their perfume drifting down the steps.

I stared at those rocking chairs a little too long.

Of course it was the nicest house on the block. It had to be the Wilder House.

"You'll do it," Charlie said as we climbed the stairs. He turned toward me, gaze locked on mine as he knocked. "You're not the kind of girl who lets people down. Or did I read you all wrong?"

I stared at him, heart thudding in my throat.

Yeah. He read me all wrong.

But I didn't have time to argue, because the door swung open, and a woman who looked like she'd floated off the pages of *Savannah Living* greeted us with a warm, practiced smile.

"Tallulah Aden, what a pleasure," she said, pulling me into a hug that was somehow both graceful and commanding. Then she glanced at Charlie, offering a tilt of her head and a soft, quizzical smile. "My Charlie. What a surprise. Will you be joining us for dinner?"

Charlie rocked back on his heels. "Well, you know what, Eunice? That sounds perfect."

The Wilder home was everything the penthouse tried to be, but couldn't quite touch. Word was, Eunice Wilder had designed every inch herself—with help, of course—but the vision was all hers. Southern charm met modern elegance: wide plank wood floors warmed the rooms, rugs layered like soft punctuation, and soft lighting made everyone look like they'd been airbrushed. Antiques lived alongside clean-lined sofas; a brass tray of well-loved cocktail glasses balanced a stack of travel books; framed family photos marched up the staircase like a well-curated biography. There were little, undeniable Eunice touches everywhere—a bowl of fresh lemons on the sideboard, monogrammed linen napkins folded with meticulous care, a faint whisper of polishing oil and old wood in the air—so that nothing felt stuffy and everything felt deliberately hospitable. Beautiful in that effortless, expensive way.

She led us through the foyer and into a formal sitting room, where Lee was nursing a drink—and what looked like a bruised ego. An older man sat across from him, his frown lifting slightly when he saw Charlie walk in.

"Charlie, my boy," the man said, easing out of his chair and clasping Charlie's hand—not stiff or performative, but familiar.

"Tally," Charlie said, nodding toward him, "this is Vance Wilder, Esquire. Lee's father."

Vance gave me a polite nod, but his attention flicked quickly back to the others. Lee crossed the room, gave me a quick hug, and then clapped Charlie on the back with the enthusiasm of someone performing for his parents.

The energy in the room felt more rehearsed than real—a different version of the two of them than what I'd seen at the studio.

"It's nice to meet you," I said, settling into a seat as Eunice gestured for us to sit. This was second nature to me. I crossed my ankles, took the drink in my right hand, napkin in my left, and nodded at the neck when saying thank you. I could play a polite debutante in my sleep.

Some days, I really was Momma's dutiful daughter.

"So," Eunice said, once the obligatory small talk had passed, "Magnolia tells me you have a photography business?"

I laughed lightly. "Oh no, not a business. I just… have a camera."

Beside me, Charlie coughed pointedly, lifting his glass again. "She's being coy, Eunice. She's incredibly talented. I watched her shoot for the Adens' shop today. She's got an eye."

"That's wonderful," Eunice said. "I thought perhaps you could photograph our upcoming charity event. If that goes well, we could talk about some ongoing projects—maybe boosting our social presence a bit."

Across from us, Lee perked up. "Jordan told me she's traveled the world, shot weddings, festivals, and portraits that landed her in magazines. And she went viral."

Vance arched an eyebrow. "What's viral?"

Eunice chuckled softly. "We don't need a resume, boys. I only need to know if she wants the job."

Sutton popped her head in, wearing full chef regalia, her expression sheepish in a way that surprised me. She looked nothing like the bossy girl I'd first met in the studio.

"Dinner's ready, Mr. and Mrs. Wilder," she said, stepping back as everyone began to rise. She caught Eunice's attention and leaned in to whisper, "I heard she once saved a dozen babies from a landslide with her camera alone."

Eunice placed a hand on Sutton's shoulder. "She has the job, my dear. She only needs to say yes."

"Oh. Okay," Sutton said, trying not to laugh as she ducked away.

Eunice led me toward the dining room, her voice softer, for me. "In case you haven't noticed, my son's friends are fiercely loyal. When they pull someone into their circle, they tend to hold on."

I thought of my brother, and how I still wasn't sure if I was in with *him*— or hovering somewhere on the edge.

I took my seat at the long dining table, trying not to slouch, pretending it didn't mean the world that these people—Charlie, Lee, Sutton, even Eunice— were putting in this level of effort for someone who felt like she barely belonged.

Eunice, who had known me all of five minutes, looked like she had more faith in me than my own mother ever had.

"I'll do it," I said, my voice carrying loud enough to cut through the hum of conversation.

Charlie leaned back in his seat, eyes landing on mine, a wide grin spreading across his face. "Of course you will, darlin'."

CHAPTER TEN

Charlie

Every year, the Daughters of Savannah Civic Society put on a pre-holiday charity event that, once upon a time, took place in the grand ballrooms of the city's finest homes. But Savannah was changing, as cities tend to do. Most of those old buildings had been snatched up by Savannah College of Art and Design or turned into bed-and-breakfasts.

The old families—once the epicenter of Southern society—had mostly moved on from the city center. But the money they left behind? That stuck around. And the people still holding onto it liked to toss it around like confetti.

This year's event was being held at Trustees' Garden, one of Oglethorpe's old experiments, where he once tested which crops could survive Georgia's soil. Now, it was a sprawling event venue crawling with Savannah's elite—ready to outbid their friends at the silent auction and spend top dollar on the art we'd all graciously "donated." I use that word loosely. Eunice was giving most of the artists a cut, seeing as we were all, well, broke.

I parked in an empty spot and looked to the woman beside me—who, judging by her expression, was about three seconds away from recreating the night we met and losing it all over my dashboard.

"You got this, Tally," I said gently.

She nodded but didn't speak. Hadn't said a word since I picked her up—well, since I took the elevator up to get her. Silent in the garage. Silent the whole drive. Her hands were folded in her lap, knuckles white.

Every day, her belly grew a little more noticeable. Instead of dressing in head-to-toe-black, like a photographer who could blend into the wallpaper, Eunice had sent for a custom ballgown, claiming Tally needed a showstopper to help her *"mingle with the donors and look divine doing it."*

She already looked uncomfortable as hell before we even left, but now, watching her try to climb out of the truck with her camera bag in one hand and her dress hiked up to her thighs in the other, she looked like she was about to crawl out of her skin.

I rushed around to the passenger side, grabbed her gear, and took her hand to help ease her down. She looked pale, shaky—nothing like the woman who, in a few minutes, would walk into a room looking drop-dead gorgeous and possibly land the biggest opportunity she'd had since showing up in Savannah.

"Are you feeling okay?" I asked, brushing a loose curl from her cheek. Her hair was pinned up in some fancy, low bun, little ringlets springing loose to frame her face. "I can take you home right now if you're feeling sick."

She shook her head. "No, it's not that."

Her voice was quiet. She chewed her bottom lip, eyes soft and scared in a way that made my gut tighten.

"I'm just nervous," she whispered.

I cupped the back of her neck and made sure she met my eyes. "Hey, darlin'. You're gonna do great. I'll be there. Lee, Sutton, Magnolia—hell, even your brother's inside, spending his money like the rest of 'em."

"Ugh. That's what I'm afraid of," she mumbled, eyes flicking toward the sound of Lee and Ryan, Lee's songwriting partner, warming up on stage. "I don't need Doyle judging me. Or worse—thinking I'm gonna screw it all up."

I shut the truck door behind her and slid my fingers between hers. She looked up at me with those wide, nervous eyes that nearly undid me. The way she was dressed, the way her hair was done, the light makeup—it wrecked me.

And for a second, I let myself pretend we were two regular people walking into a gala together. Not the hired help.

Because tonight? This girl deserved to feel like a damn queen.

We entered the main room where the band was set up, and Lee waved us over from the stage. Sutton and Magnolia were leaning against the rail, shouting at Lee and Ryan, who were both fiddling with the amps. As we got closer, I caught the tail end of Sutton yelling, "It sounds like shit," before both guys threw their hands up and rolled their eyes in perfect unison.

My sister turned around, and the second she clocked our joined hands, her eyes went wide as saucers. She smacked Sutton in the arm.

Magnolia was dressed in full bartender attire, Sutton in her more formal, all-black chef's gear, but they'd clearly done their hair and makeup. As always, they looked stunning. I leaned in and kissed my sister on the cheek, then did the same to Sutton.

"Hi, Tally," Sutton giggled, shooting a look at Magnolia. "Charlie Pruitt, my my my. Haven't seen you hold hands with a girl since we were in middle school."

Suddenly aware of our touching, Tally snatched her hand back and wiped her palm down the front of her dress. "Sorry, Charlie," she mumbled, leaning in to give the girls half-hearted hugs as they all exchanged overly polite compliments like a gaggle of geese seeing each other for the first time in years.

Lee hopped off stage and made his way to Tally. "I'll take you to Momma," he said, kissing her on the cheek. Color bloomed up her neck and a wave of unnecessary jealousy slammed into me. My brain went dark. If he couldn't have my sister, would he go for her?

Tally offered us a little wave as Lee led her off, and Magnolia stepped beside me.

"Get that look off your face right now, Charlie Pruitt," she hissed under her breath.

I curled my lip at her. "I have no look, Magnolia."

"You do. It's that Viking staredown you pull when you're two seconds away from pummeling someone. You look like you might knock Lee on his ass for touching your girl."

Sutton, nosy as ever, inched closer to eavesdrop, eyes lit with gossip-induced glee.

"She's not my girl," I said flatly. "She's my friend. And she's scared to death. Especially of her brother. Who, by the way, I'd like to have a conversation with if you've seen him."

Magnolia laid a gentle hand on my shoulder, grounding me. "Charlie," she said, voice soft but firm, "You do *not* want to get in the middle of whatever those two have going on. Same way you wouldn't want anyone interfering in our shenanigans."

I exhaled hard, trying not to rip off my tux or rake my hands through my hair like a man on the verge. Instead, I paced a few steps around her. She had a point—a good one. And one of those 'don't-intervene' moments was walking toward us right now.

"Hey, babe," Dane Wilder said, leaning in to kiss my sister's cheek. Sutton vanished like smoke, Ryan right behind her. Dane turned to me with a slick grin. "My future brother-in-law," he said, going in for a hug. "So, who was that I saw you strolling in here with?"

"Shit, I gotta run," Magnolia muttered, fleeing toward the bar where guests were beginning to line up.

I turned to Dane. "How've you been? We haven't seen much of you around lately."

Dane laughed, chewing the end of his martini olive. "Busy. Trials. You know—*real* work."

His gaze swept the room, then he started toward the far corner where Tally was standing with his mother, the two of them deep in quiet conversation.

"I should probably go introduce myself," he called over his shoulder. "Make the new girl feel welcome."

I made my way to the silent auction table across the room as Dane introduced himself to Tally in that smooth, slick way only Dane Wilder could pull off. She looked absolutely *thrilled* to meet him—until he moved on to the next group and she stuck her tongue out at his back.

Her eyes scanned the crowd and landed on mine, sitting behind a table in front of the pieces I'd donated. She lifted her camera and snapped a photo, and I'd have bet good money that when she developed it, I looked absolutely smitten.

As the night went on, her confidence bloomed. She floated around the room taking candids, gently directing folks where to stand, who to gather with. She plucked wine glasses from tipsy hands, corralled overzealous men away from unsure women, and always—*always*—kept herself out of her brother's line of sight.

Good girl, I thought, half-laughing at myself and watching her like she belonged to me. She didn't, of course. But as she made her rounds—stopping to chat with Magnolia and Sutton, catching Jordan alone, joking with Lee and Ryan during their break, even humoring Dane *again* when he cornered her—I realized something.

She didn't belong to *me*. But she was starting to belong to *us*.

"Hey, you," she beamed, saddling up next to my table. "Eunice says I'm free to mingle—maybe even dance a little. Think you can abandon ship for a boogie or two?"

I laughed, coming around the table and linking our arms. "A boogie?"

"Or two, like I said." She grinned, and we headed toward the dance floor, where Sutton had shed her chef's coat to reveal a cocktail-length black dress.

Magnolia flitted by with a tray of drinks and dropped them off. "You looked great out there, Tally!" she shouted over the music—an upbeat and poppy tune that Lee and Ryan were sweating through.

Eunice and Vance joined us, Dane trailing behind. For a minute, things felt... normal. The kind of normal a gala was supposed to feel.

But nothing good lasts forever.

"Tally, what are you doing?" Doyle's voice sliced through the music as he appeared at her side, grabbing her by the arm and pulling her out of the circle.

The look on her face made everyone stop. I could even hear Lee trip over a riff on stage. Doyle yanked her off to the side, and I lunged forward, but Magnolia caught my arm.

"No," she said sharply. "Don't."

"It's not fair," I growled, yanking my arm back.

"It's also not our business," she snapped, eyes locked on mine.

Eunice, calm as ever, leaned in. "Is everything all right with Tally?"

Jordan appeared at her side, all polish and charm. "Everything's fine, Mrs. Wilder. Doyle's worried she's getting dehydrated. He thought she should rest a minute." He turned to me. "Charlie, can I talk to you for a second?"

I deadpanned. "Can I talk to *you* for a second?"

He smirked. "Fair enough."

He led me off the dance floor, away from Doyle and Tally. Outside, the air was cooler, and my nerves start to fray. But still, I met his eyes across the cocktail table.

"What the hell was that?" I asked.

Jordan sighed. "He didn't know Eunice told her she could let loose. He thought she was slacking off."

"She was *dancing* with Eunice. And even if she wasn't, who *fucking cares*?" I started pacing the edge of the pavilion, raking my hands through my hair, gel sticking to my fingers in tacky strands. I probably looked half-feral.

"Charlie," Jordan said calmly. "Whatever's going on between Doyle and Tally is theirs to work out. He asked us not to interfere—and you should respect that."

"Oh, so *now* we're just supposed to stand around while another woman in this group gets talked down to? And what? Let it go? Smile and nod and call it Southern hospitality?"

Jordan's eyes dimmed. His shoulders tightened. "Isn't that what you asked us to do with your sister?"

He had me there.

I'd asked my friends to back off Dane. Not to interfere. Not to make waves. And they had—reluctantly.

But this felt different. This was *family.* Her own brother had dragged her off the dance floor. I'd never seen Doyle act that way before.

Was he changing? Or was I forgetting who I was?

"Jordan," I said, quieter now, "Tell Doyle she's trying. She did a great job tonight. Eunice is thrilled. Let her have this win. Give her a damn chance."

"I'll do my best," he said, eyes sincere. "But you don't know how many years Doyle spent cleaning up after her—bad choices, wild ideas, boyfriends who disappeared with her rent money. We used to get postcards from Australia and eviction notices from apartments we didn't even know we'd cosigned on. He's scared, Charlie. He's scared she's gonna tank this and take us all down with her."

I swallowed hard. "Maybe. But we'll never know unless we give her the chance to stand or fall. We don't get to decide for her. We don't get to protect her from becoming who she wants to be... just because we're afraid she might."

Dane sauntered onto the patio, cigar between his lips. "What's up, boys?" He grinned, smoke curling behind him. "Charlie, your new girlfriend said to tell you goodnight. She left."

I nodded tightly and pushed past him without a word.

"Fix your hair, Pruitt," he called after me. "You look like you just got out of a damned straitjacket!"

That night, lying in bed, I kept replaying the look on Tally's face. The pure humiliation as Doyle dragged her off the dance floor like a child who didn't know better.

I tried, with everything in me, to see it through his eyes—a brother who'd watched his sister come apart more than once. Who'd spent years piecing her back together. Who believed he was the only one who could keep her safe from herself.

And then it hit me—what haunted me wasn't what Doyle did. It was what I hadn't done.

I never stepped in Magnolia's way. Never stopped her from making choices I knew might break her. I stood back, let her do it, and swept up the pieces afterward.

And maybe that made me a better brother.

Or maybe it made me worse.

CHAPTER ELEVEN

Tally

The light in the penthouse was too pretty for editing photos, but there I was, doing exactly that. Every click of my trackpad sounded accusatory, the light dancing across the tops of my hands as I moved the specs around, taunting me to stop what I was doing and lift the camera, for God's sake. Nancy Reagan snored beside me on the couch—dead center on one of Doyle's poached cashmere sweaters, probably getting the stench of corn chips embedded in the deep, woven fabric.

"Oh well," I shrugged, moving on to the next round of edits.

The fundraiser photos came out better than I could have imagined—Magnolia mid-laugh, Eunice glowing beside her husband, Jordan and Doyle in their usual, unbothered bliss. And Charlie—no. I'd cropped him out of most of them. Not out of spite. Just self-preservation disguised as composition.

My phone buzzed, and Dig's face filled the screen, too close and upside down. He was wearing a sheet mask and what I think was a towel turban. The man commits to skincare like it's a religion.

"Tell me you're alive and hydrated," he said through bites of what looked like cereal in a coffee mug. "And please say you're not editing in 200% zoom again because that way lies madness."

"Hi to you, too," I said, propping the phone against a candle. "And these pores aren't going to edit themselves."

Dig blinked slowly. "Those are pixels, babe."

"Semantics."

He shifted, which in Dig language meant he was settling in for A Talk. "Okay. Give me the status report. You are currently in Savannah, the city of historic architecture and unresolved feelings. Have you kissed the carpenter yet?"

"Absolutely not. Also he's an artist, he's not a carpenter."

"Tomato, tomahto, he looks like he can lift a house. What happened after the fundraiser? I heard you two were giving smolder and a half."

"I haven't seen him," I shrugged. "Not since that night. Also, where are you getting this information from?" I scanned the room looking for cameras Dig might have planted on his last trip. I truly would not put it past him.

Dig paused, the cereal spoon hovering midair. "Excuse me? And Tally, what do I always tell you?"

I sighed as we both announced, in unison, "Don't question my methods."

"Good girl. So where has the carpenter been? Girl, if you're going for slow burn, we are fried as hell over here."

"He's been… busy?" I tried, not correcting him again. "And I've been working. And then every time we're in the same room, it's like—" I made a gesture that could have been fireworks or indigestion. "Moments. Plural. Then nothing."

"Moments," Dig repeated flatly. "Did we make eye contact for longer than three seconds? Did a hand graze occur? Was there a meaningful silence longer than a Vine?"

"First of all, you're ancient. Second, yes to all of the above."

"And he hasn't called?"

"I mean he texted. Once. 'Great job at the fundraiser' with two clapping emojis, which is either wholesome or deranged, I can't decide." I pulled my cardigan tight around me. "I feel like I'm fourteen again and refreshing AOL for away messages."

"Sweetheart, if his emotional availability were a beverage, it would be room-temperature seltzer," Dig said. "Flat, vaguely apologetic, and somehow still disappointing."

I laughed, which came out more like a hiccup. "I keep thinking I made it up. The… whatever it was."

"You didn't make it up," Dig said, voice gentler. "You are many things— dramatic, talented, chronically dressed like a tragic bohemian witch—but delusional is not one of them. From what I heard, the man stared at you like you'd invented light."

I pressed my fingertips to my temple. "Then why do they always disappear?"

"Because men are obsessed with the conquest. The second you're actually available? Crickets. It's like their dick and their feelings can't be in the same room."

"I'm guessing this is coming less from a place of love and more from your newest situationship ghosting *you*." I quipped.

"Obviously," he said. "But also—look at me." He leaned so close I could count every one of his eyelashes peeking through his face mask. "Sometimes people back away because they care more than they know how to. Sometimes they back away because they don't. You'll figure out which one he is. Either way, you're fine."

I swallowed. "I hate that you're right."

"I know. It's my curse."

We sat in the shared quiet you only get with the person who's seen you ugly-cry into a martini. Savannah's afternoon light slanted across the floor, turning Nancy Reagan's fur into a halo.

"Oh—before I forget," Dig said, digging around off-camera. "I've been meaning to tell you. I ran into that human khaki pant at McGreevy's."

A cold pinprick walked down my spine. "What?"

"Nick," he clarified, then winced. "Sorry. I should've opened softer. He was having drinks with a bunch of his bros. I may have… gently introduced my fist to his face."

"You punched him?" I sat up so fast the phone dipped, giving Dig an accidental tour of the guestroom ceiling and probably whatever was up my nostrils. "Diego!"

"Lightly!" He held up his hand. "As someone who has had several plastic surgery visits, you never know whose nose cost more than a Ferrari." He shrugged. "Anyway, he was asking about you. He'd heard a rumor—don't ask me from where because I protect your secrets like the Holy Grail—and wanted to know if you were in Savannah and if you were, quote, 'okay'. Which is rich."

My skin went too hot and then too cold. "And you didn't think to tell me when it happened?"

Dig's mouth softened. "I didn't want to put him in your head if he wasn't going to be in your life. He doesn't deserve rent-free space. But. If he shows up— call me. Or text the avocado emoji, we'll make it a code."

I exhaled, long and uneven. "Okay."

"You okay?"

"No," I said honestly. "But also… maybe."

He smiled. "There she is."

We stayed a little longer, talking about nothing and everything: Sutton's drama at the catering company, Magnolia's latest verbal takedown of a board member who thought "content creator" meant "girl with ring light," the way my mother's voice still lived in the corners of my brain like black mold. I was telling their stories like they belonged to me. Like I belonged to them. Finally Dig checked his watch and made a face.

"Go take pictures," he said. "You're hotter when you're looking at beautiful things."

"Bossy."

"Gorgeous," he winked.

We hung up and the apartment fell back into its expensive hush. On the black screen, my reflection looked like a woman I almost recognized—tired, sure. But still standing.

I closed the laptop and sat there for a minute, palms heavy on my knees. Charlie's face tried to walk into my head and I pushed it away. I thought about patterns. About running and holding and letting go. About how many times I'd mistaken momentum for meaning. About how a man could look at you like a promise and then forget your name when the lights came back on.

I also thought about the night of the fundraiser—the way Charlie had hovered a breath behind me without touching me, the way my body had known he was there before my brain caught up. How safe I'd felt with him nearby.

But safe is different than saved. And I was very tired of waiting to be rescued from a life I had built myself.

"Okay," I told the room, and possibly the hidden cameras I still wasn't convinced weren't planted. "New plan."

Nancy Reagan blinked one eye, unimpressed.

I slung my camera over my shoulder, jammed my feet into sneakers without untying them like a complete menace to society, and grabbed a granola bar that tasted like sugared cardboard. In the lobby, Hoyt asked if I was "headed out to make some magic," which feels like a thing men say when they want to be supportive but also have no idea what you do for a living. I smiled anyway.

Outside, the air had that clean-edged chill Savannah gets right before sunset—cool enough to pretend it's winter, warm enough to call yourself dramatic for pretending. The river breathed. Tourists argued with map apps. Somewhere a street musician was in a committed relationship with "Stand by Me."

I started toward the water and let my camera find its way into my hands. The first few shots are always bad on purpose, like stretches before a run. A lamppost with a halo of gnats. The curve of a cast-iron balcony. A forgotten ribbon caught in a live oak.

The city gave me back my eye in increments. A woman fixing her lipstick in a storefront reflection, not looking at herself so much as gathering. A boy teaching his little sister how to skip stones and almost hurling his whole body into the river, causing a complete chaotic tumble with the supervising adults. Two men sharing a carton of fries on a bench, the comfortable quiet of people who have known each other for a lifetime.

I found a sliver of light leaning across the cobblestones and stood in it until I warmed. I took a photo of my shoes and laughed at myself. I let my shoulders drop. The noise in my head dialed down from football stadium to coffee shop.

At the railing, the river shrugged by, heavy and full of life. I focused on the shimmer where the current folded over itself and clicked three times, then checked the screen. The exposures were a hair dark. I adjusted, tried again. Better.

A couple wandered into frame and didn't notice me, which is how I like it—her elbow hooked through his like it was a promise they knew how to keep. I caught them in the corner of the shot and didn't hate the ache that rose in my throat. It meant I was still here. It meant I still wanted what I'd always wanted.

My phone buzzed in my pocket. For a second my whole stupid body hoped. I glanced down.

Dig: **Remember: avocado emoji if the gremlin appears.**

I sent back a middle finger emoji. He replied with a bicep and a tiny boxing glove.

"Okay," I told the river. "I've got me."

The wind flipped my scarf into my face. I tightened it and lifted the camera again. The water. The lights. The long bruise of sky. Somewhere behind it all, men were making choices that would ripple through my life without ever asking first.

I could choose this. I pressed the shutter and felt, for the first time all day, like I hadn't been left behind. The camera clicked again. And again. And again.

CHAPTER TWELVE

Charlie

The studio smelled like sawdust and peppermint. Not because I'd suddenly caught the Christmas spirit, but because someone had commissioned a piece made out of candy canes and vintage tinsel, and now the smell had settled in like a tenant who'd moved in for the season.

It did add a little festive flair, I suppose. And, the good news was, *I* was paying rent thanks to the uptick in custom holiday orders.

A crooked little Christmas tree slouched in the corner, half-lit and lop-sided, as if it had run out of ambition sometime around December 1st. Sutton had decorated it with string lights and what looked suspiciously like paperclip ornaments—leftovers from a staff meeting at LaMonte's, the catering company where she worked.

"You know," Sutton said, flopping onto the stool by the worktable, "when Magnolia sent that group text about picking a maid of honor dress in 'a shade that evokes oyster shells at dawn,' I almost threw my phone into the river."

Lee didn't look up from the box of old photographs he was sifting through. "At this point, I'm convinced she's marrying him to spite us all."

I carefully positioned a photo of Magnolia, Lee, and Dane—fitting, given the conversation—right above the curve of her ear.

The piece had been Lee's idea. A large-scale portrait of Magnolia, based on a candid I'd taken on my phone one lazy afternoon in Forsyth Park. From a distance, it looked simple—her, laughing, mid-reach for her cocktail. But up close, it told a different story. The entire thing was built from tiny, mosaic-like snapshots: family photos, Savannah landmarks, old memories from O'Malley's. And threaded through it all were handwritten lyrics pulled from Lee's albums. Every word he'd ever written about her, stitched together with glue and grief.

I huffed out a laugh. "Well, you gave it your best shot, buddy. Valiant effort."

It had been a few months since Lee came back to Savannah from Nashville. He'd tried, really tried, to win my sister back in one of those grand, let-me-prove-everyone-wrong moments. But Magnolia had decided to accept Dane Wilder's proposal instead—asshole, esquire.

Lee held up a small photo. Magnolia and Uncle Cole stood in front of O'Malley's, smiling like the worst of the world hadn't touched them yet. His own smile flickered, then disappeared before it had the chance to settle. He handed me the picture without saying a word.

He sifted through the box again and pulled out another. This one showed him and Magnolia, eyes locked, that unmistakable closeness between them. It was the kind of look people only ever gave each other when they thought they had forever. Back when they were best friends who fell hard, when we all believed nothing could come between them.

"It's not over till it's over, *buddy,*" Lee snapped as he passed me the next one.

I chuckled under my breath and turned toward the floor-to-ceiling windows. Outside, Savannah was dressed for the season, strung with lights that wound through the trees and wreaths clipped to every lamppost in tidy, ornamental rows. Tourists meandered along River Street in a slow-moving tide, wide-eyed and uncertain, as if trying to make sense of all the holiday sparkle. The river behind them stirred restlessly, slate gray and rippling beneath the surface, as if it were one strong gust away from breaking loose.

It matched the energy in the room.

I hadn't seen Tally in weeks. Not since Doyle dragged her out of the gala like a child who'd misbehaved. The shame on her face was burned into my brain—permanent. I'd made myself available in all the usual places, hoping we might happen to cross paths. But either she was avoiding all of us... or avoiding me.

"We should go do something fun," I said, and two sets of eyes snapped to me like I'd suggested robbing a bank.

Sutton crossed her arms. "Hate to break it to you, Charlie, but this *is* your idea of fun."

Sutton's tinsel crown was starting to shed.

Which would've been fine if she wasn't actively trying to reattach it using nail glue she found at the bottom of her purse and the condensation from her cocktail glass to "thin it out".

"You're going to permanently glue that to your forehead," I said flatly, brushing glitter off my sweater for the third time.

"It's called commitment, Charles," she replied, tipping her drink back with all the confidence of a woman dressed like a Christmas Tree who had clearly never known shame. "I am so glad I kept this sweater dress," she said, marveling at the oversized green garb decorated like a balsam fir.

Lee, wearing a velvet green blazer and a Santa hat that said *Let's Get Elfed Up*, slid another round onto the high-top table with a flourish. "One more for the road?"

"I swear to God," I muttered, but I took the drink anyway.

This place, Jingle Hell, the self-proclaimed "Grittiest Christmas pop-up in Savannah," was a fever dream. Fake snow machines, a wall of broken nutcrackers, a bartender in a full Grinch costume who wouldn't make eye contact.

And we'd been there *way* too long.

I was wearing a sweatshirt with a giant, buff elf torso on it. An elf. Torso. Sutton already had her outfit from the Historical Holiday Tour we helped Magnolia with, but Lee and I still needed festive attire, so Sutton dragged us to the Christmas section of the Salvation Army. Lee handed me the sweatshirt like it was a peace offering. And me, being the idiot I am, I put it on.

"I can't believe I let y'all talk me into this," I said, dragging a hand over my face as the "Wham!" Christmas album blared overhead.

Sutton clinked her glass against mine. "Excuse me, but you're the one who wanted to go do something fun." She spun on her stool and took in the sad, slapped-together plastic holiday decor covering the walls of the old tux shop. "You love it. Admit it."

"I love seasonal depression and bourbon," I muttered. "This is just… tinsel and regret."

Sutton let out a gasp so dramatic I thought someone had died. "Oh my god, there's a pop-up holiday market on River Street!" she screeched, shoving her phone in my face. "Let's take these drinks to go and *shoooopppp*."

She dragged the word out like it had its own sleigh bells.

Before I could protest, she slid off her barstool in a glittery wobble, slunk behind the bar like she was on their payroll, and snatched a few to-go cups while expertly dodging the Grinch bartender, who was mid-existential crisis in front of the beer taps.

"I don't *shoooopppp*," I grumbled as she sloshed our cocktails into plastic cups with the concentration of someone defusing a bomb.

"You do now," she chirped, handing me my drink.

Lee leaned over to inspect the operation. "I should get a gift for my mom."

Sutton let out a bark of laughter. "Your mom? Good luck. That woman has everything—*including* a full-blown fine-art collection and zero tolerance for handmade crap."

Lee shrugged. "Yeah, but she likes Christmas ornaments and local soap. I'll find something."

Sutton wedged herself between us, looping her arms through ours, her head bobbing between our shoulders as we shuffled toward the door. Her tinsel crown was now a sideways tiara, glitter and glue smudged across her cheek.

"I just *love* you guys," she hiccupped, swaying as we stepped out into the crisp air. "Even when you're grumpy and judgmental and dressed like a half-naked elf."

The crowd thickened as we made our way off Bay Street, winding down the old stone steps toward River Street. Lights twinkled along the railing, strung from lamppost to lamppost as if someone had tried to tie the whole city up in a bow. Holiday music floated through the air, faint and slightly warped by the wind and overlapping speaker systems. The scent of roasted nuts and kettle corn drifted around us, curling through the crowd with the kind of festive pull that was impossible to ignore.

Sutton had already tripped twice—once over her own foot and once because she stopped walking entirely to scream over a dog in a Christmas sweater, which caused Lee to bump right into her and knock her over.

"I want that dog," she declared, pointing dramatically as it waddled away.

Lee snorted into his to-go cup of mulled wine. "You've already permanently glued your crown to your forehead and scraped both knee caps. Maybe pace yourself."

Sutton squealed at the sight of a booth covered in homemade soaps and disappeared into the crowd with a dramatic flounce of her velvet skirt.

I lost her instantly.

Turning in a slow circle, I scanned the crowd, squinting through the horde of shoppers. "I swear to God, if she joined another caroling group…"

"She's having fun," Lee said, voice wry, sipping from his to-go cup like we weren't chasing a human ornament through one of the busiest Christmas pop-ups in the city. "You gotta let her live."

I grumbled under my breath about adult supervision and tried to keep my eyes on anything sparkly and human-sized, weaving past families in matching pajamas and parents dragging wide-eyed toddlers hopped up on peppermint bark. Right as I passed a booth covered in handknit dog sweaters and bourbon-scented candles, I spotted her.

The *Cheese, Please!* booth, glowing under strings of Edison bulbs, was bustling. Little sample trays lined the edge of the booth, and in the middle of it, perched behind a table covered in gingham and wedged between waxed cheese wheels and a sign that said *Savor the Season*, was Tally.

She looked different.

Her hair was down in loose waves, her skin warm and flushed from the snap of cold or maybe from laughing at whatever Sutton had whispered in her ear. She wore a bright red cardigan that hugged her shoulders and a long scarf she was fidgeting with, as if she wasn't sure what to do with her hands. And yeah— she was definitely showing now. A little more than a few weeks ago. Enough that my brain stalled.

Not seeing her these last few weeks only made the pull toward her stronger. I'd seen the photos from the winter gala, and what she'd done to the *Cheese, Please!* website—both were getting attention. Two big wins, and word around town was that she'd landed a permanent gig as the official photographer for the Daughters of Savannah Civic Society. Part-time, of course.

Not that I was asking around about her or anything.

I'd thought about inviting her to dinner. Or lunch. Or to sit across from her and hear her talk. But the way Doyle had looked at us that night—the way his jaw tightened when he saw her laughing with us—and what Jordan had asked of me, made me think twice.

But standing here now, watching her move through the space like she finally belonged, the grip in my chest eased. Then tightened.

She lifted her camera and snapped it in Sutton's direction, catching her mid-bite with a cube of cheese halfway to her mouth. My own lips pulled into a half smile at the way her eyes lit up as she lowered the lens, tucking it against her chest.

"I don't like that look on your face," Lee said, appearing at my side.

"I don't have a look."

"You absolutely have a look. It's the same one you had when Magnolia brought Pickle home as a kitten and you claimed she hated you, then let her sleep on your pillow for three weeks straight."

"She bit me," I muttered. "And Pickle still hates me."

"Exactly," he said, sipping his drink. "You're doomed."

We reached the booth, and I stepped up beside Sutton, nudging her shoulder with mine to let her know we'd caught up. Tally hadn't noticed us yet. She was busy snapping photos and handing out samples, wrapping up little gift boxes, laughing softly as she chatted with strangers like she did this every day.

"This is life-changing," Sutton whispered, reaching for another toothpick.

Tally looked up then, her laugh still caught in her throat. Her smile faltered when she saw me, but she straightened her shoulders and gave a polite nod.

"Evening, gentlemen," she said, voice bright and composed. "Here to sample the seasonal Gouda or just babysitting our friend before she ends up going viral on Instagram?"

Sutton waved a toothpick in the air like it was a victory flag. "I'm supporting local business."

"You're eating all the samples," I said, folding my arms.

"I'm eating with purpose," Sutton replied, entirely unbothered. "And sopping up all the festive booze."

Lee leaned against the counter, relaxed and grinning as he flashed Tally one of his signature smiles. "This setup looks amazing."

"Thanks," she said, her eyes dipping for a second like the compliment had snuck in and caught her off guard. "Jordan asked if I wanted to help and snap some photos for social media. I've still been trying to earn my keep."

Her voice carried a brightness that didn't quite hold, a thin crack running through the middle of it that stopped me cold. I thought back to the conversation we'd had a little over a month ago in the darkened shop, where she told me that she wasn't someone who needed to be fixed. I knew she wasn't, and it almost looked like she was on the road to believing it now, but something was still standing in her way.

Sutton popped another cheese cube into her mouth and stage-whispered, "So glowy," like Tally wasn't standing directly in front of her.

Tally laughed, an unfiltered, head-tipped-back kind of laugh. And for some reason, that sound got to me more than anything else she'd done since showing up in Savannah.

"You good?" Lee asked quietly, angling toward me without drawing attention.

I nodded but didn't say a word.

Tally glanced up from behind the booth, eyes narrowing slightly when they landed on me. "Well, if it isn't Savannah's most reluctant customer," she said, her tone light but edged with a thread of ice.

Sutton snorted into her cider. Lee suddenly found the string lights very interesting.

"I'm here for the cheese," I said, more rigid than necessary for a Christmas market.

Tally tilted her head, appraising me like I was part of the inventory. "We've got cranberry cheddar, honey goat, and a limited supply of men who don't ghost after a good time."

That earned me an elbow from Sutton and a snort from Lee.

She didn't smile when she said it. But I did.

And of course, she noticed.

"I didn't ghost you," I said, voice quieter than I meant. "I was giving you space."

I couldn't tell her that Jordan had asked me not to intervene. Not to get involved. But did he mean with their sibling drama—or with her?

She tilted her head, arms still crossed. "Huh. Funny. I thought we were getting along just fine that night."

Sutton and Lee both froze, turning to stare at me like I'd pulled a fire alarm in a library.

I opened my mouth. Closed it. "It wasn't—We didn't—I just…"

Nothing. Not a single decent sentence came to the rescue.

Sutton clapped her hands once, sharp and decisive. "And on that note, I'll take a water if you've got it."

Tally raised one perfect eyebrow, spun on her heel, and disappeared behind the counter.

"Smooth," Lee muttered under his breath as she walked away.

***

As the night wore on and the crowd thinned into loose clusters of couples and last-minute shoppers gripping half-eaten gingerbread and lukewarm cider, someone killed the string lights overhead. The booths fell quiet, shadows stretching across the cobblestones, the river throwing back soft reflections.

For a moment, it felt like Savannah had been paused mid-breath.

Lee had taken Sutton home after she tried to serenade a basket of pretzel rolls and declared one of the vendors looked like "If Bradley Cooper and Santa had a baby." I gave him a look that said *good luck* and ducked out before he could rope me into Uber duty.

Now I was alone, heading toward the water, hands shoved deep in my pockets. Grateful for the quiet. Thankful for the break from the glitter-fueled chaos.

Honestly, the night hadn't been half bad.

It got me out of the studio, away from Magnolia's relentless wedding group chats. I didn't have to answer texts from Dane asking what my sister was doing and why. And for a while there, I almost convinced myself I was just a guy having a drink with his friends. Not a walking collection of pressure points barely held together by bourbon.

But then we ran into her. And suddenly, I wasn't laid-back, half-loose Charlie Pruitt anymore. I was the Grump Who Stole Christmas.

Speaking of the glowing, gorgeous new resident of Savannah.

Tally was sitting on a bench near the Waving Girl statue, her scarf draped around her shoulders, curls spilling down her back in soft waves. Nancy Reagan, fully committed to her role in a tiny reindeer suit, sat tucked beside her, ears twitching at the sound of my footsteps on the cobblestone.

Tally turned her head before I could even think about pretending I hadn't been looking.

"You again," she said, voice low, carrying the faintest note of surprise.

I glanced down at the bench beside her. "This seat taken? Or are you saving it for someone who won't make things weird?"

She turned toward me, eyes scanning my face, then the quiet stretch of the river beyond us. "You can sit," she said, patting the empty spot. "I promise not to throw up or pass out this time."

"That's a relief," I said, lowering myself onto the bench. "I didn't bring a poncho."

The breeze off the river lifted the ends of her scarf and tangled a curl behind her ear. She looked tired but steadier now, more grounded. She lifted her camera, altered the settings, and captured a shimmer on the water I hadn't noticed before—or maybe hadn't known how to see.

She glanced over and caught me staring.

"Everything all right?" she asked, brow raised.

I shrugged, dragging the toe of my boot along the edge of the cobblestone. "Been a long night."

She gave a quiet nod, hands folding neatly in her lap. "Yeah. Same."

The silence that followed wasn't uncomfortable. But it wasn't empty either.

I leaned back, noticing how still she was. The breeze carried a strand of hair across her cheek, and she didn't bother to move it, only sat there watching the river slide past the bank.

"You look…" The words caught in my throat before I could finish. I bit them back, unsure if saying them would cross some invisible line. Still, the thought burned in my chest.

She turned to me, a faint smile playing at the corner of her mouth. "I look what?" she asked, tone light but eyes sharp. "Don't say glowy. I already got that one tonight."

I looked at her for a long second, not smirking, not teasing but really seeing her. The curve of her jaw. The quiet exhaustion around her eyes. The way I wanted to lean into her.

"I was gonna say beautiful," I said finally. Honest. Steady. No way out of it now.

Her breath hitched—not much, but enough for me to notice—and she looked away like the river might rescue her.

It didn't.

She recovered quickly, eyes narrowing in suspicion. "Are you drunk?"

"No."

"Then why are you being... nice?"

I let out a breath. "I feel like I was nice the last time I saw you. You said it yourself, we had a good time that night."

She stood then, arms folding across her chest. "And then you've been ignoring me ever since."

"I haven't—"

"You have." Her gaze flicked to mine. "We live in the same building, and I haven't run into you once."

I stood, and she looked up at me, chin tilted with quiet confidence. Her eyes lingered, tracing a path from one of mine to the other, then down to my mouth before finding their way back again.

Without thinking, I stepped closer. The river moved behind her, catching the glow of the lights and breaking it into a shimmer. One stubborn curl had fallen loose, brushing her cheek. I reached out and tucked it back, my fingers grazing warm skin.

I didn't go around touching people. That wasn't me. But something about her made it hard to stay still.

"I'm not trying to ignore you," I said, voice lower than before. "I think I'm just..." I huffed out a breath and shook my head. "Shit, maybe I am drunk."

That made her smile.

"Every time we cross paths, I feel drawn to you. Even when I know I probably shouldn't be. I catch myself walking the long way behind the studio, hoping you'll be out there. Even if we don't talk. Even if you're just standing in the sun or scolding that dog of yours."

She didn't say anything, but the softness in her expression said enough.

"I might be guilty of ghosting you. But it's not like you came knocking on my door, either."

She stared at me, an unreadable expression passing over her face.

"The only thing I'm guilty of," she said, almost to herself, "is trying to figure out where I fit in here. And it's getting easier, but I still feel... unmoored sometimes. Everyone has their thing. Their people. And I'm starting over again."

She looked down, fiddling with the edge of her scarf.

"I'm about to be a mom," she added, softer now. "And I don't really have anyone here other than my brother, who's doing his best to keep me at arm's length. I have no real tribe. Some days it feels like I'm doing it with duct tape and blind optimism."

I took another step closer.

Close enough to see her scarf sliding off one shoulder. Close enough to notice the faint freckles across the bridge of her nose, the tiny tremor in her bottom lip. The wind tugged another curl loose, brushing against her neck.

She turned slightly, her gaze landing on the bronze statue beside us—a woman frozen mid-wave, a dog at her feet, both of them looking out at the horizon.

"You know about her?" she asked quietly.

I glanced at the statue. "The Waving Girl. Florence something."

"Martus," she said, her voice steadying with the kind of rhythm that came when she was telling a story she'd told before. "Her dad was the lighthouse keeper on Elba Island. When he passed, her brother took over. They lived out there in isolation for years. No electricity. No running water. Just the sea, the sky, and each other."

She stood, pulling her camera from her bag and snapping a few photos—of the statue, the low-hanging clouds, the way the moon caught the river.

"People say she waved to every ship that came through the Savannah River. Every single one, for over forty years. Morning and night. Rain or shine." She turned back to me, lowering the camera. "Can you imagine that kind of devotion? Standing in the same spot, every day, hoping someone sees you?"

I didn't answer. But I couldn't tear my eyes away from her.

"Some say she was waiting for a sailor she fell in love with when she was young. That he promised to come back for her, and she waved until the day she died, hoping to see his ship." She turned toward the bronze figure again. "But Florence always insisted it wasn't about love. She said she did it because she didn't want to feel alone. That waving made her feel connected. That if she could make someone smile on their way in or out of the port, maybe it would mean she mattered to someone, even for a second."

She crossed the short distance to the base of the statue and gently rested her hand on the bronze dog's head.

"Loneliness," she whispered, "makes people do the most unbelievable things."

I crossed the space between us and slid my arms around her, steady and warm. Not possessive. Not demanding. I held her still while everything else seemed to move. I pressed my lips to the top of her head, slow and sure, and she tilted her chin to meet my eyes.

The world quieted.

"I think," I said, voice low, "you're a lot closer to finding where you belong than you realize."

Her eyes glossed with unshed tears, but she didn't look away. For a second, she leaned into me—just barely, enough that I thought maybe this was it. Then something shifted behind her eyes. A wall went up, quiet but unmistakable.

She stepped back, out of my arms, and wrapped her scarf tighter around her shoulders like she was gathering herself back together.

"Goodnight, Charlie," she said softly.

Not angry. Not bitter. Just... careful.

And before I could find the right words to stop her, she was already walking away, Nancy Reagan trotting at her heels.

I stood there by the statue, watching her go. Florence Martus kept waving at ships that might never return.

And I wondered if I'd just become one of them.

CHAPTER THIRTEEN

Tally

I was officially lumbering through the awkward, swollen stretch of my second trimester, with Christmas crashing toward us and the slow-building, mutually assured emotional implosion between my brother and me ticking closer by the day. Most of the time, we held it together—if we weren't home at the same time, or speaking, or occupying the same general airspace. Some days, even the knowledge that the other existed felt like a personal affront.

I kept trying to pinpoint the moment it all shifted, when the thread between us frayed and the space grew quiet in a way that wasn't peaceful anymore. We used to be close. Even when I was still across the globe, we checked in. We'd send stupid memes. Called when the world felt heavy or stupid or too much. And now, I was sleeping two doors down in his meticulously polished penthouse, and somehow I had never felt more like a guest in my own family.

I missed him. Not only in the nostalgic, wish-it-were-different way. I missed him with the deep ache of someone who remembers what it felt like to be understood without having to explain anything. We used to move through the world like a two-person team, taking turns as the mess and the fixer, always knowing the other would show up when it mattered. And somewhere along the way, without meaning to, Doyle became the one who kept everything running—who paid his bills on time, who held the line, who became the steady one I pretended to be. I missed being the big sister who could take care of things. I missed being his soft place to land. And lately, it felt like I had become a problem he didn't quite know how to solve, a presence he tolerated out of obligation.

But aside from all that, Savannah was settling into my bones, the way a blanket does when it's been washed a hundred times and always smells faintly like home. I'd started carrying my camera everywhere, picking up odd gigs when I wasn't at *Cheese, Please!* or managing the Daughters of Savannah Civic Society's social media feed.

I'd just about finished planning Hoyt and Charlotte's elopement—we nailed down a cake, a florist, and, by some miracle, Pastor Dave Donnelly, a newcomer trying to establish himself as Savannah's latest pop-up minister. I'd met him at one of Eunice's business mix and mingles, courtesy of Magnolia's not-so-subtle matchmaking shove.

But with no actual, steady job in range, I'd been happy getting what work I could and putting away some money for my own space.

Avoiding the penthouse had become somewhat of a full-time job in and of itself. But eventually, I had to go home. And, when I did, the fireworks were inevitable. Not the fun kind. No, these were full-blown, nuclear-grade blowups—the kind only the Aden siblings could truly ignite.

"I just don't understand what you have against kale," Doyle huffed, stabbing at his own quinoa-and-sadness bowl. "It's full of micronutrients. It's good for your skin, which—frankly—doesn't look like you're taking care of no matter how many serums and creams I throw your way. But why am I even talking? You're not listening."

Across from us, Jordan didn't say a word, but I saw the way he sat up straighter. His spine stiffened in that barely-there way it always did when Doyle started to spiral. He didn't interfere—he never did—but his silence carried its own kind of tension.

"I just don't like it," I said, my voice low and flat. I rubbed a hand over my stomach. "I don't have to justify anything to you, Doyle. It's rabbit food. I'd rather have a burger."

"Technically," Jordan said under his breath, "That's a salmon burger."

Doyle gave him a pointed look, then turned back to me with a little exhale, trying to stay calm. Pretending, as always, that he was the reasonable one. "Tally, you said you wanted to eat better for the baby. So yeah, when I make you a healthy dinner, I expect you to—"

"Expect me to what?" I cut in, setting my fork down with a quiet clink. "Eat it and say thank you even though it tastes like compost and makes me nauseous?"

Doyle blinked at me, clearly surprised I was pushing back. "No, I expect you to take some basic care of yourself. And your baby. Jesus, Tally, it's not like I'm asking you to run a marathon."

"I didn't ask you to make me lunch."

"You didn't have to. You're staying here for free, taking up space like you always do and expecting the world to bend around your preferences."

My whole body went still.

"You asked me to come," I said, quiet but unwavering. "You told me to come stay with you. And I thought it would be like it always was. We'd hang out and talk and laugh, and you'd still be my best friend even if everything else felt like it was falling apart."

Doyle's mouth pressed into a hard line.

"But instead," I went on, pushing the words out even though my throat was burning, "You've been keeping me at arm's length since the minute I got here. Avoiding me unless it's to criticize whatever I'm doing or not doing. I don't even know what I did wrong."

His jaw worked like he wanted to argue, but couldn't quite find the right words.

"You've been walking around like I'm an inconvenience, like I'm embarrassing you, and I don't get it, Doyle, I don't." My voice cracked, and I hated that it did, but I didn't stop. "You hated Mom. You hated how she judged us. How nothing we did was ever good enough. And now you're just like her."

His eyes snapped to mine.

"You stand in front of me, preaching about vitamins and discipline, acting like you're so much better than me, and for what? You're exactly what she was—cold and righteous and impossible to please."

Doyle slammed his fork down. "You don't get to say that."

"Why not? It's true. You can't even look at me without that face. That face that says I've already disappointed you and I haven't even opened my mouth yet."

"Well, maybe being like Mom isn't perfect," he said, voice sharp with frustration, "But at least I'm not repeating the same mistakes on a loop."

I scoffed. "I mean, to be fair, getting knocked up is kind of a new thing for me."

Jordan let out a quick huff, but my brother didn't so much as blink.

There was a long, awful beat of silence. Then Doyle dragged both hands down his face. Some of the fire had already drained out of him.

"You want to know why I'm distant?" he said, his voice lower now, the edge cracking. "Because I'm tired. I'm tired of being the one who keeps it all together. I'm tired of watching you make the same choices and then act like you're shocked when it falls apart. You want support? Great. But support doesn't mean coddling. It doesn't mean pretending you're not the one holding the matches."

I stood too. I didn't even realize I'd shoved the chair back until it bumped the ledge behind me.

"I'm not asking you to coddle me," I said. "I'm asking you to see me. Not as a problem. Not as a failure. Just… me. Your sister."

He shook his head. "I don't even know who that is anymore."

"Well, maybe if you stopped judging me long enough to actually talk to me, you'd find out."

Doyle didn't say another word. He stepped back from the table too quickly and stormed off the veranda without bothering to clean up his half-finished bowl of quinoa or the trail of judgment he'd left in his wake. The penthouse swallowed him up a second later, the sound of a door closing somewhere inside cutting off the last of his exit.

Jordan stayed behind long enough to glance in my direction, the slightest flicker of apology in his eyes, although whether it was for Doyle's behavior or for not saying more, I couldn't quite tell. He didn't speak as he reached across the table and gently stacked our bowls, as if cleaning up could somehow sweep away the damage left behind. Then he followed after my brother, quiet as ever, and I was alone again.

I stepped to the edge of the railing and looked out at the river. The late afternoon sun was slipping low over the rooftops, painting the sky in soft, washed-out colors that didn't quite manage to feel comforting. The breeze rolled in from the water, cool and clean, carrying the distant murmur of traffic and tourists below.

I sank back into one of the chairs, every part of me heavier than it had been earlier. No tears, just that stubborn lump in my throat and the tightness in my chest from all the words I kept swallowing to keep the peace.

And then, beneath the weight of my hand, a tiny shift. A flutter. A soft, sure movement from inside me, like the baby was reminding me they were still there. Another nudge, firmer this time, and I stilled completely, both hands now resting over the small swell of my stomach.

I wasn't alone, not really.

But God, it sure felt that way.

***

Unable to shake the pressure of the conversation with my brother, I slipped out the front door and wandered away from the penthouse, hoping the fresh air would do what deep breaths and counting to ten hadn't managed to pull off. I didn't have a plan, only a vague urge to keep moving, to feel the ground under my feet and put a little distance between myself and the words still echoing in my head.

And while I was at it, I decided to treat myself to something hot, greasy, and about as prenatal-approved as a margarita. The walk-up window at McDonald's called to me like a beacon of poor choices, and I stood under the yellow glow of the menu board ordering a large fry and a large orange soda—the kind that probably glows in the dark—glancing over my shoulder every few seconds like Doyle might pop out of the hedges and tackle the bag out of my hands.

I strolled from square to square, the bag growing greasier the longer I went without opening it. I'd been hoping for a quiet bench, but eating alone felt too pathetic.

I needed a friend. Someone who wouldn't judge me for stress-eating fast food or falling apart over a kale salad. Someone who might actually understand.

My feet carried me toward O'Malley's.

The bar sat tucked on a corner just off the main drag, weathered brick and a hand-painted sign that looked like it had survived a few hurricanes. A single light glowed in the window. Through the glass, I could make out the long mahogany bar, the rows of bottles catching the dim light, and a familiar figure moving behind the counter.

Charlie.

I hesitated at the door, suddenly second-guessing myself. But before I could back out, he looked up and caught my eye through the window.

Too late now.

I pushed the door open, and the smell hit me immediately—old wood, lemon oil, and something faintly hoppy that had probably seeped into the floorboards decades ago.

Charlie straightened from where he'd been wiping down the bar, a dish towel slung over his shoulder. He wore a faded O'Malley's t-shirt and jeans, sleeves pushed up to his elbows, forearms dusted in what looked like sawdust and paint spackle.

"We're closed. Don't open for another hour," he said, but there was no bite to it. His eyes scanned my face, then dropped to the McDonald's bag in my hand. "Though I'm guessing you're not here for a drink."

"I was looking for Magnolia," I admitted, hovering near the door like I might bolt at any second. "Is she around?"

"Dress fitting," he said, tossing the towel onto the bar. "I'm covering. Lucky me."

I shifted my weight, suddenly feeling ridiculous. "I can go—"

"Don't." He gestured to one of the barstools. "Sit. You look like you need it."

I hesitated, then crossed to the bar and climbed onto a stool, setting my contraband on the polished wood. The bag crinkled obscenely loud in the quiet.

Charlie eyed the McDonald's logo, one brow lifting. "That from the walk-up on Broughton?"

"Maybe."

"And you're eating it alone in a closed bar because...?"

"Because my brother is a judgmental ass who thinks kale will solve all my problems," I said, pulling out a fry and biting into it with more aggression than necessary. "And I needed to eat something that wouldn't make me want to cry."

Charlie's mouth twitched. Not quite a smile, but close. He pulled out his phone, tapped at it a few times, then set it down.

"What are you doing?" I asked.

"Ordering reinforcements," he said. "Those fries aren't gonna cut it."

"I didn't come here for you to feed me."

"Yeah, well." He shrugged. "I was gonna eat anyway. Might as well have company."

I took another fry, slower this time, and let the silence stretch. The bar felt different now—quiet, but with that pre-show buzz, the sense that any minute it'd all come back to life.

Charlie grabbed a glass and went to work, pouring grenadine and soda, stacking in extra cherries and orange slices before sliding the drink my way. "It's the only mocktail I know how to make," he said with a shrug.

I took the skewer of cherries and wrapped my lips around them, popping each one off in slow succession. Sweet syrup clung to my fingers, the taste bright and sticky as I caught the last trace with my tongue.

Charlie leaned against the counter, arms crossed, watching me with a look I couldn't read.

"So," he said finally. "Kale?"

I let out a bitter laugh. "Kale. Quinoa. Micronutrients. Apparently, I'm not taking care of myself or my baby, according to Doyle's expert opinion."

"Ah."

"And when I said I didn't want to eat it, he told me I was taking up space and expecting the world to bend around my preferences." I stabbed another fry into the corner of the bag, hunting for rogue salt. "He invited me here, Charlie. He told me to come. And now I'm some kind of burden he's stuck with."

Charlie didn't say anything right away. He only listened intently, letting me get it all out.

"I told him he's just like our mom," I admitted, quieter now. "Cold and righteous and impossible to please. And he didn't even deny it."

"That probably hit him hard," Charlie said carefully.

"Good." I popped another fry into my mouth. The mix of salt and grenadine was sinful enough to pull a quiet moan from my throat. "Maybe he needs to hear it."

A knock came at the door, and Charlie pushed off the counter to grab the takeout. He came back with a Treylor Park bag, setting it between us and pulling out fried chicken sliders, extra pickles, and a side of mac and cheese that looked obscene in the best way.

"Here," he said, sliding the sliders toward me. "Real food."

I stared at the bag. "You didn't have to do that."

"I know."

The first bite hit me square in the soul. I closed my eyes, savoring the warm, vinegary crunch, and when I opened them again, Charlie was watching me with something that looked almost like amusement.

"This doesn't mean we're friends," I said, mouth full.

"God, no," he deadpanned.

I snorted despite myself, licking hot sauce off my thumb. "Why are you always so nice to me? Even when I'm a mess?"

Charlie leaned forward, forearms bracing against the bar. "Maybe because I get it."

"Get what?"

"What it's like to love someone who doesn't know how to let you in." He paused, gaze dropping to the sliders. "My sister's getting married to Dane Wilder. Lee's brother."

I blinked. "Yeah, I'd heard rumors. That's... complicated."

"She thinks it's the only way to save this place," he said, gesturing around the bar. "That if she marries him, he'll sign over his part of the family trust and O'Malley's stays in our family. She really believes it's her only option."

"And you're just... letting her?"

His jaw tightened. "I'm not *letting* her do anything. She's a grown woman. She makes her own calls." He looked at me then, eyes steady. "But I'm standing by, ready for whatever she needs, whenever she needs it. That doesn't mean I don't tell her how I feel. And sometimes she hates hearing it."

"Why are you telling me this?"

He inched closer, gaze sweeping my face. "Because when you're stuck in the middle of one of life's messes, it's hard to see straight. And sometimes the people who sound the most critical are the ones trying hardest to look out for you. Even if they don't always get it right."

I set down the slider, suddenly not hungry anymore. "So you're saying Doyle's being an ass because he cares?"

"I'm saying he's scared," Charlie said. "And fear makes people do shitty things. Doesn't make it okay. But it might explain why he's holding on so tight."

I wrapped my fingers around the edge of the bar, grease still slick on my skin. "I came here thinking we'd fall back into a rhythm. That we'd be siblings again. But he's keeping me at arm's length, like he's embarrassed to be seen with me."

"I've known Doyle a long time," Charlie said. "He's not always great at handling things he doesn't understand. He's used to being the responsible one, and sometimes that makes him hold on too tight or push harder than he should." He paused. "He reminds me a lot of myself sometimes. Especially the way I am with Magnolia."

"From what I've seen," I said, trying not to laugh, "you and Magnolia are nothing like Doyle and me."

"We can be," he admitted. "Right now, she's making a decision I don't understand, and I don't know how to support it. I slip up. I let my fear show. I go about it the wrong way."

He looked at me then, really looked at me, and something in his expression made my chest ache.

"But I'm trying," he said. "And maybe that's what Doyle's doing too. Trying. Failing. But trying."

I let out a shaky breath. "I don't know if I can keep doing this. Living there. Pretending it's fine when it's not."

"Then don't," Charlie said simply. "You don't owe him perfect. You don't owe him easy. You just owe him the truth."

A breeze swept in from somewhere—maybe the back door was cracked— and I wrapped my arms around myself, suddenly cold.

"I'm sorry," I said quietly. "Not just for tonight. For all of it. For blowing into town like a hurricane. For ruining your artwork. For not knowing how to take a compliment."

Charlie shook his head. "You don't need to apologize for trying to start over or being afraid. We're all scared of something."

"Even you?"

"Especially me," he said, voice low. "I'm terrified of watching my sister marry the wrong guy. Of standing by while she makes a choice I can't undo. Of not saying enough or saying too much." He dragged a hand through his hair. "But I show up anyway. Because that's what you do for the people you love."

I stared at him, this man who kept showing up when I least expected it and most needed it, and felt something shift in my chest.

"Thank you," I whispered. "For the food. For listening. For not making me feel like an idiot."

"You're not an idiot," he said. "You're just human. And that's allowed."

We sat there in the quiet of O'Malley's, the weight of the day finally starting to lift, and for the first time since the fight with Doyle, I didn't feel quite so alone.

CHAPTER FOURTEEN

Charlie

"Oooh, chicken and waffles," Magnolia said, her eyes lighting up as she peeked into the takeout bag on the counter. She dropped a dog-eared bridal magazine on the bar and curled one leg beneath her on the stool she kept parked by the to-go window.

"Yep. Fried chicken," I muttered, wiping my hands on a dish rag. "Even though your best friend makes it way better than anyone else in this city. And waffles to bat down what you described over the phone as I quote, 'seasonal sads.'"

She hopped off the stool. "I don't know if you can technically get seasonal depression in the South," she said, pulling open the bag and inhaling dramatically, "but if you can, I definitely have it. So I want to eat like I'm gearing up for hibernation."

I leaned against the bar and rubbed the back of my neck, eyeing her with suspicion. "You sure you're not like… regular depressed? Because last I checked, you're engaged to a guy who gets hammered and sends you Shakespearean-level passive-aggressive texts at midnight because he can't handle your sass."

Magnolia rustled around inside the takeout bag. "Where's yours?" she asked, frowning over her shoulder. "I thought we were eating together."

I gripped the edge of the bar, eyes on my boots. "Wasn't all that hungry."

Through a mouthful of waffle, she let out a muffled snort. "Don't be judgy, Charlie. You might not have the seasonal sads like I do, but you've definitely had a scowl on your face since I walked in here."

I shrugged and made my way behind the bar, reaching for a highball glass and the good bourbon I kept tucked away from the regular shelves. There was a comfort in moving behind the bar again and stepping into the familiar rhythm of it, even if only to fix a drink, that settled into my chest like muscle memory. The lights strung across the ceiling, the garland half-heartedly taped to the taps, and the handmade snowflake ornaments leftover from the Historical Holiday Tour added a layer of nostalgia that hit harder than I expected.

In a breath, the comfort unraveled, exposing what had always been waiting beneath it.

Grief.

Maybe it was the holidays and how much our momma used to love Christmas, the way she'd string lights across every square inch of our porch on Tybee Island as if she were trying to signal low-flying aircraft. Or maybe it was the drink in my hand, mixed exactly the way Uncle Cole taught me—muddled maraschino cherry, one oversized cube, stirred slow, never shaken. A ritual I hadn't even realized I still followed, like tradition passed down in the blood.

Either way, grief was tugging at me, wrapping itself around the soft parts of my heart I usually kept locked away.

Maybe it was the cold front moving in. Maybe it was the sadness that always showed up when the lights dimmed and the music got merry and the quiet crept in, no matter how crowded the room was.

Or maybe it was the conversation I'd had earlier tonight with a very pregnant woman who'd shown up at this bar looking like she was barely holding it together. The more I talked to her, the more I realized she wasn't just beautiful—she was raw, honest in ways most people weren't, and trying her damn best.

And I couldn't stop thinking about her.

Testing the waters, I took a slow sip, let the silence stretch, then asked, "Have you talked to Tally lately?"

Magnolia didn't answer right away. She took another bite of waffle, chewing slowly, one eyebrow raised, like she knew damn well I wasn't asking just to make conversation. After a long pause, she swallowed and leveled a look at me.

"Why are you asking me this?"

I shook my head. "She stopped by earlier," I said, too carefully. "Seemed like she was having a rough night."

Magnolia narrowed her eyes. "Yeah, she texted me. Said you fed her and let her vent about Doyle. That was rather nice of you."

I didn't answer. I kept busy behind the bar, stirring the cocktail I'd already finished and wiping the countertop—anything to avoid eye contact.

"So," I tried again, casually—too casually, probably—"do you think she's planning on staying in Savannah? Or does she have… I don't know. Another plan?"

Magnolia froze mid-bite.

Then, in one fluid, furious motion, she hopped off the barstool, which scraped back so hard it smacked the counter with a clang that echoed through the room.

"Charlie, no. Absolutely not. You cannot start developing a freaking crush on Doyle's extremely pregnant, highly emotional, very much-in-transition sister. I forbid it."

I scoffed. "You're marrying Dane for a business deal, basically. And *you're* worried about *me*?" I carefully handed her the drink I'd just made, in case she decided to start swinging. "But to answer your extremely dramatic question—no. I am not *developing* a crush on Doyle's sister."

She wasn't Doyle's sister, not to me. Her name was Tallulah River Aden. And I'd long since blown past the developmental phase of anything. I was already in freefall. No guardrails. No plan. Falling, and too far gone to stop.

The moments we carved out together—the quiet stretches, the easy back-and-forth that belonged only to us—got under my skin. Even if she thought I'd ghosted her. Even if I told myself I was doing the right thing by keeping my distance.

What sat between us now wasn't loud or obvious. It felt like finally being where I was supposed to be.

And this was wildly, ridiculously out of character for me.

Because I was the dependable one. The golden retriever of a brother and a friend, the guy everyone counted on when the wheels came off. I picked up the late-night phone calls, drove across town without asking why, showed up with a toolbox or a shoulder when somebody needed it. The one people leaned on—not because I begged for the job, but because I'd proven, over and over, that I wouldn't let them fall.

I'd built my whole identity around being solid. Predictable. The one who held it together.

And then she blew in, Hurricane Tally with her wild curls and sharp comebacks. Those sundresses she kept wearing, no matter the weather, that clung to every new curve. Eyes that caught too much and offered back almost nothing.

She didn't even have to speak for me to lose my senses. She was a contradiction in every direction. And it was no wonder she somehow got under my skin.

"Hey. Earth to my big brother. Can we shift focus to the wedding, please? That is, if you're done spacing out and definitely not thinking about the woman you, of course, don't have a crush on."

Magnolia was watching me now, eyebrows lifted in that way she did when she was trying to be playful but also keeping score, waiting for me to say something. To be useful. To be steady. To be the version of me she depended on without ever having to ask.

But she didn't really see me. None of them did. Not the part of me unraveling in the quiet moments. Not the version that lay awake most nights, wondering what it would take to feel whole instead of held together by expectation and obligation.

They saw the guy with the checklist. The fixer. The anchor. But never the weight I was dragging to stay upright.

"Of course we can, Mags."

She lit up at that, her shoulders relaxing as she pulled out a notebook from under the bar, already in motion, already onto the next thing.

"I was thinking of a bourbon-based cocktail for the signature drink," she said, tapping her pen against the page. "And maybe passed appetizers—festive, but not… I don't know, heart-shaped meatballs or anything."

I nodded along. Let her fill the space with plans and details that made her feel in control.

And I slipped back into the role I knew best. The steady one. The strong one. The one who could pretend, for a bit longer, that everything was fine.

CHAPTER FIFTEEN

Tally

I'd been running myself ragged all morning—half event planner, half cheese monger, full-time emotional disaster. With Sylvie off in Cabo living her best life, I was holding down the fort at *Cheese, Please!* while prepping Hoyt and Charlotte's elopement later that afternoon.

On paper, everything was handled. Eunice's florist had delivered the flowers. Sutton's cake was chilling in the back. My camera battery was fully charged. Pastor Donnelly was likely somewhere vibrating with excitement about his first Savannah elopement.

But my chest carried that restless hum—the one that made every sound too loud, every light too bright.

The bell over the door jingled.

"Be right with you!" I called, ducking behind the counter to grab champagne bottles from the cooler. My reflection in the glass looked unhinged: hair frizz halo, apron streaked with honey, the faint glow of someone pretending her life wasn't unraveling inside an artisanal cheese shop.

I straightened, balancing three bottles on my swollen belly. "If you like Gouda, there's a great potato chip variety that—"

"Hey, Tal."

The bottles nearly slipped from my hands.

That voice.

I knew that voice.

My body knew before my brain caught up—stomach dropping, skin going cold, breath catching somewhere between my lungs and my throat.

Nick.

He stood by the cooler in a worn leather jacket I used to borrow when I got cold at the bar, hands shoved in his pockets as if he'd just wandered in for brie like any regular customer. His hair was still gel-slick, that lazy smirk tugging at his mouth—only now it looked smaller. Uncertain.

A faint bruise shadowed his temple. Dig's handiwork. I fought down the smirk.

"What are you doing here?" My voice came out flat and distant. Like it belonged to someone else.

His gaze dropped to my belly right as the baby kicked.

Perfect timing.

His face changed—shock, then recognition, then something that might've been fear. "Shit," he breathed. "So Dig wasn't exaggerating."

"You need to leave." I set the champagne bottles down before I dropped them. My hands were shaking.

"Tally—"

"Now."

He didn't move, only stood there, staring at me like I was a problem he hadn't planned for. "We need to talk."

I bit out a sarcastic laugh. "No, we really don't."

"I came all the way to Savannah—"

"I didn't ask you to." My voice cracked despite my best efforts. "How did you even find me?"

"Your Instagram's public," he shrugged, like it was obvious. "And you're tagged in every *Cheese, Please!* post. Wasn't exactly hard."

Of course. The one time social media actually worked, it led my ex straight to my door.

"The rumor mill went wild with this one. And Dig all but confirmed it when he tried to knock me out," Nick continued, taking a step closer. "I needed to know for myself if it was true."

"Well, now you know." I crossed my arms over my chest—or tried to. My belly got in the way. "You can go."

"Is it mine?"

The question hung in the air like smoke.

I stared at him. "Are you seriously asking me that right now?"

"I just need to know—"

"Yes, it's yours!" The words came out louder than I meant. Somewhere behind me, a wheel of Manchego rolled off the shelf and thudded to the floor. "You were the only person I'd been with in like, a year. The math isn't complicated."

He held up his hands. "Okay. I'm sorry. I just—" He dragged a hand through his hair. "Why didn't you tell me?"

A bitter laugh escaped. "You gave me a fake number, Nick. You ghosted me at the bar. What was I supposed to do, hire a private investigator?"

He winced. "I panicked, okay? We had one night—"

"We had three months," I corrected. "Three months of you saying you wanted something real, that you were tired of hookups, that I was different." My voice shook. "And then the second I finally let you in and told you I had feelings for you, too, you disappeared. After you got what you wanted, of course."

"That's not—" He stopped, jaw working. "It wasn't like that."

"Then what was it like?"

He didn't answer.

The silence stretched. Outside, a tour trolley rattled past, the guide's cheerful voice muffed through the glass.

I sank into one of the bistro chairs near the window, my legs suddenly unreliable. The baby shifted, pressing against my ribs.

Nick sat across from me, elbows on his knees. "Look, I get that I screwed this up. But I'm here now. We can figure it out."

"Figure what out?"

"Whatever you need. Money, support, if you, you know, want to… I can help."

I shook my head. "I don't need your money."

"Tally, come on—"

"I don't need anything from you," I said firmly. "I'm fine."

His eyes swept the shop—the apron, the cheese wheels, the small space that had become my refuge. "Are you? Because it looks like you're working retail while pregnant and living with your brother."

The judgment in his voice made my chest tight.

"I'm building a life here," I said quietly. "I have work. I have friends. I'm figuring it out."

"By yourself."

"I'm not by myself."

"Right." He leaned back, something bitter crossing his face. "So there's someone else."

"That's not what I meant."

"But there is." It wasn't a question.

Before I could answer, the back door banged open.

"Tally, you ready for—"

Charlie stopped mid-sentence.

His eyes landed on Nick, then flicked to me. I saw the moment he put it together—the tension in the air, my white-knuckled grip on the table, the stranger sitting across from me.

"Everything okay?" His voice was calm. Too calm.

Nick stood, extending a hand. "You must be the brother. I'm Nick."

"Charlie," he said flatly, ignoring the hand. "Not the brother."

The silence went sharp.

Charlie crossed the room and stood behind my chair—not touching me, but close enough that I could feel the weight of him. Solid. Steady.

Nick's eyes darted between us, and I watched understanding dawn. "Oh. So you're—"

"A friend," Charlie supplied.

Nick let out a humorless laugh. "Right. Friend. I used to be one of those to her, too." He turned back to me. "This is why you didn't call. You've already moved on."

"No, I did call. You just gave me the wrong number, as I said." I snapped. "And anyway its not like—"

"Looks pretty clear from where I'm standing."

"You don't get to do this," I said, voice shaking. "You don't get to show up after months and act like I owe you an explanation for my life."

Nick's jaw tightened. "I came here to make sure you were okay."

I slammed my palm on the table between us. "I am okay."

"Are you?" He gestured around the shop. "Because this doesn't look okay. This looks like you're hiding in the middle of nowhere, pretending everything's fine when you're about to have a baby alone."

"She's not alone," Charlie said quietly.

Nick's eyes snapped to him. "And who are you, exactly? The rebound? The backup plan?"

"Watch it," Charlie warned.

"I'm just trying to understand how my—" Nick stopped himself. "How the mother of my kid ended up shacking up with some guy in Georgia."

"I'm not shacking up with anyone," I said, standing. "And even if I was, it's none of your business."

"It is if you're pregnant with my child."

"A child you didn't want," I shot back. "And don't even pretend you do because if you didn't want me, then you don't want, or deserve, this."

He flinched. "That's not fair."

"None of this is fair!" My voice cracked. "You don't get to waltz in here and play concerned father after you made it clear you wanted nothing to do with me."

"I'm here now," he said, quieter. "Doesn't that count for something?"

I looked at him—really looked at him. At the man I thought I knew, who turned out to be yet another person who couldn't stay when things got hard.

"No," I said finally. "It doesn't."

He stared at me for a long moment. Then he pulled out a business card and set it on the table. "That's my real number. In case you change your mind."

I didn't touch it.

"But just know that I'm not that guy, Tal," he said, backing toward the door. "I don't know how to be a dad. I have plans—travel, my career. I can't be stuck."

"Then don't be," I said simply. "I'm not asking you to stay."

Something flickered across his face—relief, maybe, mixed with shame.

"I hope it works out," he said. "I really do. I'll be outside waiting for my Uber if you want to talk about this more."

The door chimed as he left and the shop fell silent except for the whirr of the wine cooler. I stood there, hands pressed flat against the table, trying to remember how to breathe.

Charlie crouched beside my chair. "You okay?"

I laughed—sharp, shaky, barely holding together. "Ask me in five years."

"Tally—"

"He found me." My voice broke. "Dig ran into him, and then he just—he found me."

"Dig didn't tell him," Charlie said gently. "He figured it out from your photos. From the work you've been doing."

"Same result."

"No." His hand covered mine. "Dig protected you. He punched the guy. Nick came here anyway because that's who he is—someone who shows up when it's convenient and leaves when it's not."

I wanted to argue, but the truth of it settled in my chest.

"He's gone now," Charlie said firmly. "And he's not coming back."

"How do you know?"

"Because you didn't give him a reason to." He squeezed my hand. "You told him the truth. You didn't need him before, and you don't need him now."

The baby kicked, hard enough that I gasped.

Charlie's eyes dropped to my stomach. "That the baby?"

I nodded, pressing my hand to the spot.

"Strong kid," he said softly.

"Takes after their mom," I managed.

A small smile tugged at his mouth. "Yeah. They do."

We stood there in the quiet, my hand still in his, and slowly—slowly—my breathing evened out.

"Thank you," I whispered. "For being here. For not making me feel like I need to explain anything."

"You don't," he said. "You never do. Not with me."

And somehow, that was exactly what I needed to hear.

CHAPTER SIXTEEN

Charlie

I gently lifted Tally from her chair and helped her start closing up the shop so she could get ready for the elopement. While I restocked the Chablis, she stood in the middle of the floor, staring at nothing, her hand pressed flat against her stomach like she was trying to hold herself together from the outside.

I stayed quiet. Gave her space.

She blinked once, hard, then crossed to the wine barrel where Nick had left his business card. Her hand shook as she picked it up. For a second, I thought she might keep it—tuck it away just in case—but then she tore it in half. Then again. And again. Tiny pieces scattered across the floor before she gathered them up and dropped them in the trash behind the counter.

"I'm fine," she said, voice flat.

She wasn't.

She moved through the shop like she was checking off a mental list— champagne flutes straightened, camera adjusted, bottles lined up with unnecessary precision. Her hands were steady, but I caught the way she kept swallowing hard, the tension climbing up her neck into her jaw.

She wiped the counter twice.

Rearranged the same three cheese wheels.

Her breathing was too controlled. The kind of controlled that meant she was one wrong word away from shattering.

"Tally—"

"I need to finish closing," she cut in, not looking at me. "Hoyt and Charlotte are counting on me. I can't—" Her voice cracked. She cleared her throat. "I just need to focus."

She grabbed her apron strings and tried to untie them. Her fingers fumbled. Once. Twice. She yanked harder, frustrated, and the knot pulled tighter.

"Damn it," she whispered.

I crossed to her, gently batting her hands away. "Let me."

She stood there, arms at her sides, staring at the floor while I worked the knot loose. Her shoulders trembled. She was holding her breath.

"Breathe," I said quietly.

She let out a shaky exhale, and with it came the tears she'd been fighting since Nick walked out. Silent at first, then harder. Her hand came up to cover her mouth, like she could stuff the emotion back in if she tried hard enough.

I pulled the apron free and set it aside. "Come here."

She shook her head. "I don't have time to fall apart. I have to—there's so much to do—"

"Tally."

She looked up at me, eyes red and wet, and I saw it—the exhaustion, the fear, the sheer force of will it was taking to keep moving forward.

I wrapped my arms around her. She resisted for half a second, then collapsed into me, her face pressed against my chest as her whole body shook.

"I've got you," I murmured into her hair. "I'm here."

She cried quietly, fists clutching my shirt like I might disappear if she let go. I held her, one hand on her back, the other cradling her head, and let her get it out.

After a minute—maybe longer—her breathing steadied. She pulled back, wiping her face with the heel of her hand.

"I'm sorry," she whispered. "I don't have time for this."

"You just had your ex show up and tell you he wants nothing to do with your baby," I said. "You're allowed to fall apart."

"But I can't." Her voice cracked again. "Charlotte and Hoyt are getting married in an hour. I have to be there. I have to take photos and make sure everything's perfect and—" She pressed her hands to her face. "I just need to hold it together for a few more hours."

And there it was.

The thing that floored me about her.

She wasn't pretending she was fine. She knew she was wrecked. But she was showing up anyway. For people who needed her. For a baby she was already protecting. For a life she was building one impossible day at a time.

"You don't have to be okay," I said quietly. "You just have to show up. And you're doing that."

She looked up at me, hazel eyes tired but determined. "I just need a minute to cry. To say goodbye to him, I think. I wanted closure, but not like that."

"He's not worth it, darlin'."

She gave a bitter laugh. "No, he's not. I just wish I'd seen that before I fell in love with him."

Everything in me went still.

She'd loved him. And he'd looked her in the eye and walked away.

"Why did you just go stiff?" she asked, studying my face.

I unclenched my jaw. "He rubbed me the wrong way, that's all."

She nodded, stepping out of my arms and squaring her shoulders. "Can you help me finish closing up? The last thing I need is Doyle showing up and finding a bottle out of place."

She was already moving again—grabbing her camera bag, checking the champagne cooler, locking the register. Powering through because that's what she did. That's who she was.

And watching her do it—watching her pull herself together with sheer force of will and show up for people who were counting on her—was the most beautiful, heartbreaking thing I'd ever seen.

I was out the door before I could talk myself out of it.

"Hey, asshole."

Nick's head snapped up. He flinched before I even closed the distance, like he already knew why I was there. Good. I stopped toe to toe with him, close enough that he had to tilt his chin up to meet my eyes.

"Listen to me," I said, my voice low, steady. "You stay away from her. And that baby. For good. Do you understand?"

He let out a careless laugh. "She's your problem now, man. I don't want a thing to do with any of it."

That laugh was the last straw. My fist connected with his jaw before I even thought about it, a clean shot that sent him stumbling back into the stoplight with a grunt.

I didn't chase him. Didn't need to. I just stood there, shoulders squared, breathing easy, because I'd never been more certain about anything in my life.

"I'll take that problem any day," I said. It came out quiet, but it carried. A promise more than a threat.

Then I turned back toward the shop, tossing over my shoulder, "And I mean it. Stay gone."

***

It had started as a scramble. Charlotte and Hoyt were supposed to say their vows in front of the Forsyth Fountain, but a late-afternoon downpour had rolled in with no regard for their plans. By the time we reached the square, the ground was slick, the air holding that clean, heavy scent only Savannah rain leaves behind. Guests huddled under umbrellas, and the fountain, usually a backdrop for tourists, stood nearly alone in the mist.

Tally was the one who saved it. She pulled out her phone and dialed Eunice, asking her if there was a gazebo nearby, covered yet still charming. She didn't hesitate and called for cabs to send us a few blocks over to Whitefield Square. Charlotte and Hoyt loved the idea instantly. Within minutes, they were tucked beneath the white-railed gazebo, flowers and fabric repurposed from the fountain setup, the rain pattering on the roof while they exchanged vows. It felt intimate, almost secret, as if the weather had pushed us into exactly the right place without meaning to.

When the rain eased, we made our way back to Forsyth. The park was nearly empty then, rain scaring away anyone who might be lingering, the fountain framed in that narrow band of golden light you only get before the sun disappears. Pastor Donnelly's ceremony had already wrung tears from all of us, but watching Hoyt and Charlotte cut their cake with her mother close by—blanket tucked over her knees, smiling through every second—was enough to undo the rest. The fountain bubbled steadily behind them, its spray catching the light in a way that made the whole square feel suspended in time. A few passersby slowed at the edges, pausing long enough to take it in, the way you do when you realize you're walking past a rare moment in time.

When, in the middle of an ordinary day in Savannah, you stumble across a love story.

Tally pulled them aside for photos, steadying Charlotte's mother with

132

a light touch so she could stand long enough to kiss her daughter's cheek. She caught it in one frame, the kind of picture that would live on a mantle and draw a tear every time someone walked past it.

A knot rose in my throat. Magnolia would be married soon, and our mother wouldn't be there. Neither would our father. Or our uncle. Just the two of us left to hold each other up through every milestone.

Tally drifted toward the shade of a moss-covered oak, hand settling over her belly as she whispered softly. How a man could walk into her life and ask her not to be the one thing she was meant to be was beyond me. She'd made her choice, hers alone, and the strength in it floored me.

"You all right, darlin'?" I asked, stepping into the shade.

She nodded, wiping her eyes, taking a sip of water. "It's been quite the emotional day." She looked up at me, soft and steady, even after everything. No bitterness. Only the quiet rhythm of being what her child needed most.

"You know, you could call your mom," I said. "You don't have to wait for her to call you."

"I know. And I probably should. Just… not yet. I need to handle this on my own first."

I didn't know the whole story between her and her mother, but I knew enough. And I knew if mine were still alive, she'd be there—lifting Magnolia and me up even when the ground gave way.

"Hey," I said, catching her hand before she walked off. "You're doing this your own way. But you're doing it. You're not hiding, you're not looking for an exit. You're living, every day, for both of you. You should be proud of that."

She moved back toward the fountain. Hoyt was watching Charlotte the way I'd just been watching Tally—like nothing else in the park mattered. I understood that look.

Tally raised her camera as Charlotte and Hoyt cut the cake, Pastor Donnelly grinning beside them. She glanced over her shoulder at me, a smile tugging at her mouth but not quite reaching her eyes. Her lips shaped the words I already knew.

"Thank you," she whispered.

My body didn't get the memo that we were playing it cool. I stayed put, because if I moved, I wasn't stopping at holding her hand.

CHAPTER SEVENTEEN

Tally

The dream was good. Which, in my world, usually meant real life was about to deliver a deeply humiliating plot twist.

Lately, my dreams had been circling one man in particular. Charlie Pruitt. Uninvited. Unavoidable. Showing up night after night as if my brain had conveniently forgotten we were supposed to be keeping things light. Sometimes Lee wandered in too, because even my subconscious knew a hot, guitar-carrying man in tight jeans deserved some mental screen time. And once—deeply, painfully—there was Hoyt, the doorman, wearing nothing but a tool belt and carrying a tray of hot, salty fries with the solemnity of a priest offering communion.

But this morning, it was only Charlie.

His hands found my waist, steady, like he'd always known exactly where they belonged—the sheets bunched around my knees, warm from sleep and the heat of his skin. The weight of him settled beside me, the quiet press of his body close to mine.

The room smelled like him—sawdust, cedar, and earthy undertone that had worked its way into the walls and, apparently, into me.

His voice came low at my ear, lips brushing close, the words blurred but thick with want. A murmur about staying right here, not rushing. Not moving.

His breath coasted down my neck. Desire clenched low in my ribs.

And then he kissed me. Not desperate, not heated—just careful, deliberate. A slow press of his mouth to my forehead that sent everything in me into freefall. My body curled tighter into the dream, clinging to the last trace of him before morning pulled it all away.

I was about to lean into the heat of it, to let my subconscious fully betray me—

"Tally Tater Tot Aden, you better scoot the hell over and make room because your Christmas miracle has ARRIVED!"

I bolted upright with a yelp, half convinced I was still dreaming. But no, there he was. Dig. Wearing a red velvet robe over God knows what, grinning like the lunatic best friend he was, and climbing directly into bed with me like this was any other normal, Wednesday morning.

"Dig?" I blinked, still not convinced he was real. "What? How? What the hell are you doing here?"

"I missed you," he said simply, flopping down beside me and throwing an arm across my middle like I was a damn body pillow. "Also, the weird little mermaid play I'm in—*Siren'd Duty*—got canceled for the weekend because half the cast came down with what we think is food poisoning, but might just be a collective existential crisis over our shared failure to make it under the bright lights of the big city. Either way, I'm here. Surprise!"

Nancy, insulted by being displaced, leapt to the foot of the bed and began tap dancing in protest. Dig scratched her behind the ears, unfazed.

A sound somewhere between a sob and a laugh bubbled up in my throat. I hadn't realized how much I needed him until he was here.

"I was dreaming," I muttered, collapsing back into my pillow. "It was delicious."

"Was it the big guy?" he waggled his eyebrows. "Savannah's resident grump? Tall, bearded, brooding? Name starts with a *Charlie* and ends with *makes you feral in your dreams?*"

I groaned and dragged a pillow over my face.

Dig gasped. "It was. Oh my God, you want to kiss him under the mistletoe and name your baby after him, don't you?"

"I will suffocate you with this pillow," I mumbled. "Also, I'm still mad at you for the whole Nick fiasco. He figured out where I was from my Instagram posts and just... appeared. In the shop."

"Okay, but in my defense," Dig said, patting my stomach gently, "I told you to send me the avocado emoji if he showed up. How can I win favor as your knight in sequined armor if you don't follow protocol?"

"I didn't have time! He just walked in—"

"And now Charlie looks like the hero," Dig interrupted, shaking his head in mock disappointment. "This is what happens when you don't trust the system, Tally."

I stared at him. "Are you seriously making this about you right now?"

"A little bit, yes." He grinned. "But also, tell me everything. What happened?"

"He walked in like he owned the place, asked if the baby was his, offered me money to 'handle the problem.'"

Dig's face went from playful to murder in half a second. "He what?"

"Yeah. So Charlie punched him."

"CHARLIE PUNCHED HIM?" Dig squealed, wriggling across the bed like an overexcited golden retriever. "Oh my God. What's it like to be God's favorite? Two men throwing punches over you? That's practically one of those supermarket paperback novels with the shirtless pirate on the front!"

I rolled my eyes. "It wasn't like that. Nick was being a creep, and Charlie just... handled it."

"He *handled it*," Dig repeated, swooning dramatically. "Listen to yourself. You're in a Hallmark movie and you don't even know it."

"It's not a Hallmark movie. It's my life falling apart in real time."

"Falling apart?" He propped himself up on one elbow, studying me. "Babe, you're literally glowing. You've got a hot guy next door who punches douchebags for you, you're building a whole new life in Savannah, and you're about to have the cutest baby in Georgia. Where's the falling apart?"

I opened my mouth to argue, then closed it. Because when he put it like that...

"Shut up," I muttered.

"Never," he grinned.

Changing the subject, Dig steepled his hands, a playful glint passing over his eyes. "Anyway, I brought snacks, questionable holiday-themed lube I found at the airport gift shop in case I run into that guy from the haunted speakeasy I hooked up with last time I was here, and a new scene from *Siren'd Duty*. Wanna run lines?" He clapped his hands together. "Oh! And you must tell me every single detail regarding the elopement shoot. I need to see those shots of Charlotte and her momma."

Naturally, ten minutes later, Dig was in the middle of an interpretive dance performance of Ursula's monologue—tentacle gestures and all—in the tastefully holiday-decorated living room. Nancy Reagan was howling in chorus, twirling in frantic little circles, and I was on the floor with my phone, snapping photos, half for the memories, half because Dig insisted I *"document his creative genius for future generations."*

I let him carry on, my mind drifting back to the way Charlie had studied me at the elopement. His gaze stayed on me as I moved through the shoot, adjusting a veil, framing a shot, taking a moment to breathe. When he caught my hand, I didn't want him to let go. The thought sent a rush of butterflies through my stomach, though it might have been the baby shifting.

The baby my situationship had asked me to get rid of as if this baby and I weren't already a package deal, no matter what. Charlie seemed to understand that in a way no one else ever had. He didn't flinch, didn't treat me like I was too much to take on. It was all there in the way he looked at me, steady and certain, like he'd already decided he wasn't going anywhere.

Maybe things between us *were* casual. We were just friends. Weren't we?

Doyle padded out in pajama pants, hair sticking up in every direction. He stood at the edge of the living room, blinking slowly like he was trying to decide if he was hallucinating. "What in *God's* name—?"

"Welcome to morning theater, Savannah edition," Dig said, spinning dramatically with a plastic trident he'd borrowed from a wreath hook.

Nancy barked. I cackled. Doyle looked like he had aged six years in two minutes.

Jordan peeked out from the kitchen, wearing a robe and holding a mug of something that smelled suspiciously like Bailey's. "We are *never* going to get through this crisis if you two don't go outside."

"What crisis?" I asked, frowning.

"Hush," Doyle said too quickly. "Go. Do something. Take a walk. Buy olives so you stop stealing them from the shop. I don't care."

My brother's tone sent me on edge. There was definitely more going on between them than they were saying. "Aren't I supposed to be watching my salt?"

"Tally, if you don't get your butt out the door and give us some damn peace, I'm going to start shrieking so loud, someone will put me on Nextdoor. Or worse, the siren will summon Momma."

Jordan shot me a pitiful look. "Just… go, Tally."

Dig was already slipping on his shoes. "Field trip! I wanna see all the places you've been hanging and meet all of your people!"

I didn't have the heart to tell him I was still finding my people here. I was getting closer, inch by inch, but it still felt a little like I was standing on the porch, peeking through the window at everyone else gathered around the table. Some days, the door cracked open. Other days, it stayed shut. Whether the key was in my hand or someone else's remained unclear.

Jordan and Doyle whispered as I grabbed my bag, their voices low and clipped, like I wouldn't notice. Doyle kept glaring at Jordan across the kitchen island, tight-lipped and stiff, his whole body coiled like he was trying to hold it together—or keep the situation from blowing apart. He dried the same mug three times without once looking at me. Jordan, usually the calm one, the peacemaker, pushed scrambled eggs around his plate and kept glancing at the clock.

Whatever was going on, it wasn't nothing.

Ten minutes later, we were in the back of a horse and buggy, driven by Savannah legend Franny Jo Anderson, crawling through the quiet morning streets of Savannah like this was what everyone did on a Wednesday. She hadn't offered a reason or an explanation when she pulled up in front of the building and shouted "Get in!" from under a wide-brimmed velvet hat and waved at a group of tourists with the flourish of a woman who'd been born for the stage.

She was the kind of woman people in town spoke about with a mix of awe and deep, affectionate fear. A retired drama teacher who never quite retired from performing, she'd traded curtain calls for ghost stories and sequins for more sequins. She once told me the only lie she ever tolerated was the one she told herself every year about cutting back on champagne.

She had taken to Dig instantly the last time he came down, clasped his face in her rings-heavy hands, and declared him "one of the good ones." Ever since, she treated him like an honorary grandson. Me? She treated me like cargo that needed protecting. Ever since she found out I was pregnant, she'd made it her mission to keep me off my feet and out of trouble, even if that meant swinging by my building unannounced and ringing the carriage bell until I came outside.

Dig, for his part, was eating it up. He waved to every tourist we passed like he was on a parade float and chatted with Franny Jo like they were old drinking buddies instead of two people who had known each other for maybe a week total.

Franny Jo looked back at us with a wide grin and a single, glittery eyelash attached to one eyelid like a festive bird wing. "Ain't this nice? Just like old times. Remember when I took y'all to that underground roller derby with those vampire people last time you were here, Diggy?"

"Yes," Dig said, dreamily. "It changed me."

We kept rolling through the streets in Franny Jo's open-air buggy, the morning quiet except for the rhythmic clip of hooves and the occasional rattle of the bench beneath us. Wreaths hung from iron balconies, and storefronts blinked with twinkle lights that hadn't bothered shutting off after sunrise. The air was soft and heavy with that stubborn Southern humidity, carrying the smell of pine garland and fried dough from somewhere we couldn't quite see.

Dig sat beside me, fixing the hem of his shorts like he was getting ready for a party instead of a ride to the coffee shop.

"Only a few more weeks until Christmas," he said, voice low, like he didn't want to startle the peace. "Any big plans with the brothers?"

I shrugged. "They're doing brunch with their friends. They haven't invited me yet, but… I don't know. I think baby and I will be parked on the couch, watching reruns and eating pie without Doyle looming over me like a judgmental fridge warden." I gave him a weak smile. "What about you? Please tell me you're staying here."

He shook his head. "I wish, babe. That week's a war zone at Errico's. Sal will have me filleted if I don't show."

I nodded again, turning to watch the Spanish moss ripple in the breeze.

"You know," Dig said gently, voice laced with quiet concern, "You're not as alone as you think. Seems like you and Franny Jo have been thick as thieves lately."

I squinted at a slow-moving herd of tourists shuffling toward the Telfair, clutching glossy pamphlets and lining up neatly for a trolley ride. "She's been taking me to appointments when Doyle or Jordan can't," I said, keeping my tone light. "And I've been helping out on her ghost tours, taking fun pictures for her social media. Just… staying busy."

I kept my eyes on the passing squares, careful to avoid his staring gaze. "Besides, who said I was alone?"

Dig didn't say anything right away, he only sat there—patient, quiet—the way only someone who's seen all your worst days and still shows up can. "Tell me about the elopement! God, I can be so shellfish… I mean selfish," he winked, as I handed him my phone to look through the first photo edits.

"These are so great, Tally," he said quietly. "You pulled all of it together in just a few weeks, too. It's amazing."

"I've been taking a lot more photos lately, too," I said, reaching for my phone to show him the other shots I'd been working on. "Franny Jo hooked me up with this local photographer she knows, and I tagged along on a maternity shoot last week. Nothing major. I mostly held reflectors and fluffed hair. But it felt good. Like I was doing work that made sense again."

Dig's expression softened, the way it always did when I talked about my camera.

"And I've been running Franny Jo's social media, plus the account for this old lady's club here in town, Lee Wilder's mom is the president, or whatever. I keep reaching out to the connections I've made for a permanent gig, but no bites yet."

"See, it's not nothing," Dig said, stretching his arm across the back of the buggy seat. "You've got the eye. You've got heart. And you've got hustle when it counts."

I gave him a look, half amused. "Tell that to my inbox full of polite rejections."

He shrugged. "Maybe they're not supposed to hire you. Maybe you're supposed to go off and do it yourself."

I blinked at him. "What, like start a business?"

"Why not?" he said. "You've got the skill. The camera. A town full of pretty people who love to get married under Spanish moss. And a best friend who is more than willing to model fake engagements if you need portfolio content. Use the elopement session as a blueprint."

That made me laugh. A real one. Small, but real.

For a second, the ache in my chest eased, and there it was—a flicker of warmth, small but stubborn, like hope refusing to take the hint.

***

Our beloved chariot dropped us off at Savannah Coffee Roasters, and we settled in front of the fireplace with a table of charcuterie between us.

Dig, already more than halfway through the plate, looked up at me, wide-eyed. "Why aren't you eating? You love cheese."

I sipped my decaf and let the cozy quiet settle over us. "I can't eat soft cheese, remember? Or deli meat." I lifted my cup and gave it a small wave. "Or real coffee."

"Is this a prison sentence or a pregnancy? I've never been happier to be biologically excluded from the process."

We laughed and fell into an easy stretch of silence, the kind that only existed between people who didn't need to fill space with words. My body was still, but my brain was racing. I reached into my bag and pulled out my phone, tapping a few thoughts into my notes.

What if I started a business of my own? I'd need to save money, which meant more shifts at the wine shop, maybe some extra gigs here and there. The holiday season meant places were hiring. But what exactly would I *do*? Savannah was full of talented photographers. If I wanted to stand out, I'd need more than the desperate wave of hope crashing against my soul.

"So," Dig said, snapping me out of it. "What's going on with you and the burly, very broody guy next door? Aside from the Rated R dreams. And don't say '*nothing*', because I know you, and this feels very *something*."

"Honestly? It's hard to explain. It's gone beyond humiliating run-ins and turned into more of Charlie showing up for me in ways no one else has. I just can't tell yet if it's because he wants to… or because it's the right thing to do."

I could still feel the echo of those moments—his hand steadying me without hesitation, the way his eyes stayed on mine like he was making sure I was really okay. They lingered longer than they should have, enough to leave me wondering what, exactly, we were doing.

"That's not nothing, Tally. That's practically a master class in a guy falling for you, and you're doing that thing where you've got the blinders on again."

I stood and peeled off my sweatshirt, the heat from the fireplace—or maybe whatever nonsense had fallen out of Dig's mouth about Charlie falling for me—finally getting to me. I knotted it low around the swell of my belly, letting my hand settle there, quiet and still. And there it was—that small flicker of pride I didn't always let myself feel. The quiet awe of knowing I was growing a life inside me.

"You really do look beautiful," Dig murmured. He stood and rubbed slow, steady circles over my stomach with both hands, and we stood there, foreheads resting together in front of the fire.

To anyone passing by, we probably looked like the picture of glowing domestic bliss. A happy couple. Dreamy and in love. Planning a baby shower and buying matching Mama and Dada shirts. Not a woman doing this alone with nothing but a hopeful heart and a bottle of Pepcid, and her best friend who could barely remember to eat a vegetable.

But for a moment, I let myself lean into it. Let myself believe it was real. Long enough to quiet the ache.

"Well, if it isn't the cutest couple in Savannah," came a familiar voice behind us.

We both looked up to see Doyle's friends, Sutton and Ryan—Lee's bandmate—heading toward the exit with their arms full of brown paper bags and iced coffees.

Sutton lifted a perfectly arched brow, her gaze flicking from Dig's hands on my belly to the very little space between us. "Didn't know y'all were together," she said. Her tone was light, but there was definitely curiosity tucked inside it.

I opened my mouth to explain, prepared to ramble my way into awkward honesty or pure weirdness—but Dig beat me to it. He grinned and winked, fully committed to the bit.

"Scandalous, right?" he said, pulling me a little closer like we were starring in some sweet, small-town romance and halfway through our press tour.

Sutton let out a quiet laugh, caught off guard. Ryan elbowed her, already focused on unwrapping a cronut from his bag.

"We'll let y'all get back to it," he said as they passed. "You promised me we could make out a little after we grabbed supplies for the party you're catering."

Sutton rolled her eyes and gave us a quick shake of her iced coffee in place of a wave. Then they disappeared through the door, leaving the scent of espresso and sugar behind them.

I turned to Dig, still blinking. "Dig," I muttered, elbowing him. "What the hell was that?"

He shrugged with a little too much satisfaction. "What? You're glowing. I'm supportive. Let them wonder."

I groaned, dragging a hand down my face. "You know that's going to come back and bite me in the ass, right?"

"Oh, absolutely," he said cheerfully. "But at least you looked hot while it happened."

CHAPTER EIGHTEEN

Charlie

The music had found its groove—low, raw, and full of grit, the kind of track that let my hands take over. Lee had dropped off a new batch of demos that morning, and being his built-in listener again gave me rhythm to work to.

I'd propped the doors open to let the December air drift in, cutting through the heat and sawdust that still clung to the studio walls. The light stretched long across the floor, catching on the sculpture I was building for Lee and Ryan's latest album cover—a mess of old metal and broken wood, jagged in places and strangely beautiful in others, which felt about right.

Sweat collected at the back of my neck, and I peeled off my shirt, tossing it over a crate of salvaged parts before bending back over the piece. I liked it best when my arms ached, when my palms picked up splinters, when the weight of what I was making pressed into my shoulders. In the studio, surrounded by half-finished ideas and forgotten tools, I didn't have to answer to anyone or explain the knots in my chest that never quite loosened. I could just be the guy with dust in his lungs and unfinished thoughts.

Then I heard it.

At first, I thought there was a glitch in the track, a weird mechanical chirp that didn't belong. But then it came again, sharp and high and carrying an unmistakable attitude.

Nancy Reagan.

The blur of brown fur tore across the studio before I even had time to turn down the music. She darted past my feet, sniffed around a stack of wood scraps, then zeroed in on a flattened cardboard box and began tearing at it with wild enthusiasm.

I stared at her, still holding the heat gun mid-air. "You've got to be kidding me."

A breathless voice answered from the doorway, and there she was.

Tally stood in the frame, hair piled on top of her head, cheeks flushed, hand on her stomach as if steadying herself from the chase. The sleeves of her sweatshirt hung long past her fingers, and her leggings clung to her legs, dusted with whatever she'd picked up chasing her insane dog around.

"She got out when I took the trash to the alley," she said, trying to sound casual. "She's got a thing for cardboard."

"Of course she does." I nodded toward the box she was currently destroying. "You sure she's not part goat?"

Tally stepped inside, one careful foot in front of the other, and I didn't miss the way her face lost its color as soon as she crossed into the light. Her hand reached out, caught the edge of the bench, and her body swayed ever so slightly, shoulders dipping.

"I'm fine," she said before I could ask, eyes unfocused, voice low. "Just dizzy."

I moved toward her, already setting the heat gun aside, but she waved me off. Still, I kept walking, kept watching, alarm bells going off in my head.

And then her knees buckled.

I caught her before the ground did, lowering us both down to the cool concrete floor. She felt warm and unsteady, her skin too damp, her breathing uneven.

"Tally." I brushed my hand across her forehead. "You're clammy as hell."

Nancy sat beside us, tail flicking against the floor. I reached for my phone, but before I could open Doyle's contact, she stirred, fingers curling around the fabric of my jeans.

"Don't call my brother," she whispered, not opening her eyes. "He'll put me on some kale cleanse and make me meditate through it."

I let out a quiet laugh, part relief, part disbelief. "Fine. But you're letting me carry you upstairs."

"Worst day ever," she muttered, barely above a breath.

"You say that every time you end up on the floor in my studio."

One eye cracked open, a flicker of life returning to her expression. "I'm starting to think you're cursed."

"Or maybe you are." I slid my arms beneath her carefully. "You've got a knack for showing up just in time to keep things interesting."

She didn't answer. Her head tipped against my shoulder as I stood, her weight sinking into me, deciding not to argue this one. Nancy trailed behind us, still chomping on a flap of cardboard, utterly unbothered.

And as I carried her through the open door, her breath soft against my chest, I couldn't stop the thought from rising—one that had been pressing at the edge of my mind for days.

Maybe things weren't so bad after all.

Maybe what I'd been waiting on had already found its way in.

***

She was featherlight, all things considered. Curves, soft and round, her limbs slack against mine, her warmth bleeding through the fabric of her shirt, stirring up thoughts I had no business entertaining. Her breath came in short bursts against my collarbone and I forced my focus on getting her upstairs, not on the way she smelled—bright citrus with a trace of sweetness.

"Tally," I said, brushing her cheek with mine, just enough to coax her back to consciousness. "Come on, now, darlin'. Stay with me."

Her lashes fluttered as if she'd been pulled from a deep dream. "Oh no," she groaned, already beginning to curl inward, trying to disappear from the moment.

"This is very dramatic," I told her, shifting my grip so I wouldn't drop her on the tile. "You know, if you wanted to hang out with me, there were easier ways."

"Kill me," she muttered, her voice hoarse.

"I considered it," I said, moving toward the alley door. "But I figured bringing you to your brother so he could finish the job was more civilized."

She blinked up at me again. Her skin was too pale, her features slack with exhaustion. "I'm sorry, Charlie."

In the hallway, we were met with the sight of Hoyt standing beneath a length of crooked caution tape, clipboard mid-air, expression frozen between panic and apology.

"I'm so sorry, Mr. Pruitt," he said, straightening his tie with one hand and gesturing toward the elevators with the other. "Small hiccup in the system. Should be back up in just a minute or two. Tally, my dear, are you all right?"

"She's fine," I said, not slowing down. "Probably her low blood sugar. She'll be okay."

I didn't mention that she'd collapsed in my arms or that she had the cold sweats and fought my help because she didn't want to seem fragile. I also didn't mention how her fingers had curled into the back of my hair like they knew exactly where to land. I just kept walking.

Hoyt chuckled, completely oblivious. "My Charlotte is as stubborn as a mule, too. Women, huh?"

I didn't answer. I was too focused on how tightly Tally had started to hold on as I approached the stairs.

"You really don't have to do this," she said, her voice barely above a whisper.

"I'm not risking a second tumble because you're too stubborn to ask for help."

"This is so embarrassing."

"For both of us. I'm shirtless and covered in sawdust, and you're melting into my shoulder. We're a mess."

That made her laugh, low and tired. Her head tipped against me, and I adjusted my grip again, climbing steadily.

"Stop squirming," I said as we rounded the third floor.

"Then stop frowning and muttering under your breath," she shot back.

"This is just how my face looks, Tally."

She looked up at me with glassy eyes and said, "Not when you look at me."

I almost tripped up the stairs and took us both down and out.

By the time I reached the penthouse and shouldered the door open, my arms were aching, my back was damp with sweat, and the thoughts in my head were a little too loud. Like the one that kept wondering what it would feel like to carry her into the bedroom and close the door behind us.

I laid her gently on the couch and pulled the throw blanket around her, keeping my hands steady.

Her eyes blinked open, still heavy. "Are you done playing knight in sweaty armor?"

"Just making sure you don't roll off the couch and give me another reason to have to pick you up."

"I was going to sit down."

"Sure, you were. You were about to take a nosedive into the floor."

"You're so annoying."

"You passed out in my arms, Aden. Pretty sure that earns me thirty full minutes of sass-free silence."

She opened her mouth, probably to tell me off again, but Nancy Reagan jumped up beside her, spinning twice before settling in with a huff that suggested she'd been the one carrying someone up five flights of stairs.

I brought Tally a glass of water and set it on the coffee table, trying not to look too long. Trying not to get caught in the way her expression had changed. She looked tired, and not the nap-fix kind, but the sort that lingers behind your eyes. There was a softness in her face now that hadn't been there earlier, and a hollow sort of sadness I recognized too well.

I wanted to reach out to touch her. Whatever was simmering between us—hot and steaming, about to boil over—felt inevitable. I leaned in and brushed the damp curls from her forehead, resting mine against hers for a second. Told myself I was checking for a fever, but the truth was, I wanted to be closer to her. And I didn't want to move from that spot.

"What in the actual hell is going on here?"

Both our heads turned toward the lanai, and the two of us moved apart at the same time, slow and guilty.

Doyle stood in the doorway with a wineglass hanging loose from his fingers, his mouth parted.

Tally, visibly defeated, groaned and threw an arm over her eyes. "God, I wish I were still unconscious."

CHAPTER NINETEEN

Tally

Charlie had gone back downstairs, mumbling about cleaning up the cardboard carnage in the studio. The door clicked behind him, and the apartment fell into that awkward hush that comes after chaos. Paint still clung to my skin, mixed with his scent—warm, steady, a little too easy to miss already.

Doyle hovered near the couch like a worried parent, Jordan paced the living room, and Dig sat cross-legged next to me, his eyes boring a hole into the side of my head.

"Stop staring at me," I whisper-hissed.

He pinched my arm.

"Ouch!"

He snickered. "Well don't scare me like that, ever again!"

"I didn't do it on purpose."

"You literally collapsed," he said, louder now, not bothering to whisper. "In a hot guy's arms. While I was upstairs eating charcuterie. Do you know how tragic that is? I should've been there to document it. You know how I love a dramatic rescue."

"You're insane."

"And *you* have yourself a little boyfriend," he shot back.

Before I could answer, Doyle's voice cut through the room.

"What if you went by yourself and I stayed here?" he murmured to Jordan, though not quietly enough.

Jordan sighed, pinching the bridge of his nose. "She's going to be fine. The doctor said it was orthostatic hypotension—low blood pressure. It happens in the second trimester. She needs fluids and rest. Maybe we—"

"—Find a babysitter," Doyle cut in, throwing a look over his shoulder like I wasn't three feet away on his pristine white couch. "Because that's what we're talking about, right?"

I groaned, grabbing the nearest throw pillow and hurling it in their general direction. It landed with a pathetic flop.

"I can hear you, you know. And I don't need a babysitter."

Dig perked up. "Speaking of babysitters," he said, eyes gleaming, "can we circle back to the real issue here? The very large, very broody man who apparently swept you off your feet, carried you to safety, and saved your life?"

He set down his glass with the flourish of a Broadway actor in the third act. "You know I require more details."

I sighed, pressing the heel of my hand into my forehead. "It wasn't that dramatic."

"That's not what I heard," Dig said. "I heard he was rugged, mysterious, *shirtless*, and he lifted you like you weighed nothing, which—frankly—I find offensive."

My eyes narrowed on him. "Where are you always getting this information from? You *just* got here. Who told you he was shirtless?"

Dig shrugged. "Hoyt, we're practically besties now."

Heat flushed up my neck and spread across my cheeks. Of course, Dig was friends with everyone in the entire city limits already.

"He flat out said that a sweaty, shirtless Charlie, eyes a'blaze with concern over your poor, crumpled, pregnant ass, all but took the stairs three at a time to get you up here as fast as he could. He just keeps piling on those romantic gestures." Dig fanned himself with a hand, offering me a smug smirk. "That was the most action you've had in a while in that dark, cool stairwell. Practically got to second base in your world."

Doyle made a sound somewhere between a cough and a snort.

Jordan rubbed his temples, pacing in front of the couch. He stopped, lowering himself onto the coffee table in front of me. "My mother's not doing well, Tally," he started quietly, looking toward Doyle for reassurance. "My father has asked me to fly home to California to spend some time with her before the holidays. The doctors don't think she has a few months ahead of her."

Tears pooled in the corners of my eyes. I was making everything about me, and here was Jordan—more than a brother-in-law—struggling with this.

"I'm so sorry, Jordy."

He shook his head. "I don't want… sorry, *we* don't want anything to happen to you while we're gone."

I stood up a little too fast and had to catch myself on the side of the couch. "I'll be fine, I promise. Please don't worry about me. Go spend time with your mother."

Jordan exhaled and turned to me. "Tally, I'm sure your brother feels the same, but we truly wouldn't forgive ourselves if something happened to you while we were gone."

"I can function," I said, stung. "I can walk. I can breathe. I can manage my own body."

"You are having some real medical issues right now, Tallulah. Fainting and having my friend carry you up the stairs isn't going to become a daily event," Doyle said flatly. "And the man who caught you is… not known for his bedside manner, but he's reluctantly agreed to check in on you while we're gone."

"Add it to the list of things I didn't sign up for," Charlie said from behind us, calm, a trace of amusement in his voice.

Dig took one look at Charlie as he stepped back into the penthouse and immediately slumped against the couch cushion, mimosa still in hand.

"Aww, you found your shirt," he said, tone mournful. "Such a shame. You were giving sweaty fireman in an emotionally unavailable Jane Austen reboot. I was rooting for you."

I rolled my eyes, but Charlie didn't rise to the bait. He moved quietly into the room, brushing a hand across my shoulders, almost like he was checking to make sure I hadn't vanished. He didn't look at me. Didn't look at anyone, really. And honestly? I preferred that to the overly careful glances I'd been collecting all afternoon, like pity was a party favor.

I *was* fine. A little dizzy. A little overcooked. Maybe riding the tail end of a hormone surge. But fine.

Still, Jordan had launched into a full-blown logistics breakdown. He was leaning against the kitchen island with his laptop open, itinerary half-typed and color-coded.

"Sylvie will be keeping an eye on the shop, so feel free to keep your shifts.

You've got follow-ups scheduled on Tuesday and the following Friday," he said without looking up. "And we already called in groceries, so you shouldn't need to go anywhere."

Charlie pulled his phone from his back pocket, typing quickly while listening closely. His eyes caught mine, and he gave me a sly, half-smile and the quickest blink-and-you'll-miss-it wink. He was equal parts serious and, possibly, enjoying every minute of this.

Because the one thing I'd learned about Charlie Pruitt was that he was always steady. Always there. That quiet, brooding reliability people trusted without needing a reason. And now, apparently, I was going to be living in his orbit for the next few weeks.

Jordan clapped his hands together. "So it's settled. Franny Jo will help with transport if needed. But otherwise, you're staying close to home, resting, and letting Charlie be your bodyguard."

"Bodyguard?" I echoed.

"Roommate. Guard dog. Overqualified babysitter," Jordan said with a smirk.

"You do realize I'm thirty-one, right?"

Dig leaned forward and whispered, "In her condition."

I grabbed another throw pillow and launched it at his head. He caught it one-handed like a baseball pro.

"I'm not fragile," I muttered, trying not to look at Charlie, who was now sipping his beer like he had no plans to get involved.

Jordan, ever the diplomat, offered a tight smile. "We know. But I'd feel a lot better handling one family crisis if I wasn't worried about another happening back here."

I knew what he meant. I saw it in Doyle's face, even if he wasn't saying it out loud. That latest fainting spell had rattled them both.

But the truth was, the idea of being alone had already started to gnaw at me—now it was practically roaring. So maybe this wasn't the worst idea after all.

I cleared my throat. "So…it's just a few weeks?"

Charlie's gaze lingered on mine, steady and unreadable. "Long enough to drive each other crazy," he said. "Short enough that you might still miss me when I'm gone."

CHAPTER TWENTY

Charlie

I was pacing.

Not the productive kind, either. The kind that wore a trench in the floor and left you muttering to yourself like a man possessed. Every few steps, I'd rake both hands through my hair, which only made it stick up more, some kind of wiry auburn warning signal that I was officially losing it.

I dipped a wad of toilet paper into the bucket of gluey cornstarch water I'd mixed up at least two mental breakdowns ago and slapped it onto the canvas spread across the floor.

Behind me, the beer fridge clicked shut. "The male artist, in his natural habitat," Lee said, slipping into a barely-passable Australian accent, "submerges bathroom tissue in ceremonial goo, slaps it with the fury of a jilted marsupial, and paces his enclosure like a lion in emotional captivity."

Sutton choked on her cider and doubled over, her laughter bubbling out in wheezy bursts while Lee kept narrating.

I leaned against the worktable and crossed my arms. Let them laugh. Even pissed off, I liked having them around.

"You okay?" Lee finally asked, swiping a tear from his cheek. "You look like you're about to combust."

"I'm fine," I said.

"You're not fine," Sutton added. "The porcupine hair, the pacing, all signs point to Charlie Pruitt on the verge of a breakdown."

"I'm annoyed," I answered honestly.

"Yeah," Sutton said, dry as ever. "Because, once again, being Mr. Responsible comes back to bite you in the ass."

It wasn't just that. Of course it wasn't. It was everything—stacked too high and shifting under its own weight. Commissioned pieces that needed finishing before the holidays, my sister's slow-motion car crash of a wedding, and now Doyle's pregnant sister camped out in the penthouse while he went off to play the dutiful son-in-law across the country.

I told myself I'd agreed to help because it was the right thing to do. But I also hadn't factored in how close this would put us. How every small thing she did—padding barefoot across the floor, curling into the couch with that stubborn little frown when she thought no one was looking—would get to me. I hadn't planned for carrying her upstairs, or for the way her weight fit against my chest like she belonged there. For the warmth of her skin on mine, or the quiet, uneven breaths that stayed with me long after I laid her down.

And it wasn't the first time I'd imagined carrying her to bed—but it was the first time she'd been close enough to make it feel real.

Doyle would kill me. He'd take a tire iron to my knees and bury me in Bonaventure.

Still, there was no denying she was beautiful. Not in a polished, pageant kind of way. Tally had this rough-edged, real-world beauty that didn't ask for attention so much as dared you to look closer. And the thing was, I couldn't stop looking.

A beautiful woman is like good art. Not because it's perfect, but because it moves you. If you're paying attention, it'll show you exactly how it was made.

To me, that kind of beauty lived in the imperfections—the cracks, the brushstroke someone tried to hide, the mismatched pieces that somehow held together. That's what made it honest. Worth the study.

And she had that. All of it. This sort of impossible strength was tangled up with a vulnerability she didn't try to disguise. She could throw a one-liner across a room and make you laugh out loud—and then turn away fast enough that you missed the flicker of doubt behind her eyes.

And despite all the very loud, very rational reasons I had for keeping my distance, I wanted to know her anyway. Not the curated version she offered everyone else, but the real one. I wanted to know her. Not to fix her. Not to claim her. To *know* her.

I wanted to see which of her flaws made her beautiful.

CHAPTER TWENTY-ONE

Tally

"And don't forget her check-up on the 14th," Doyle fussed, grabbing his bags and dodging a very anxious Nancy Reagan, who was tap dancing around his feet like she sensed there was a major shift occurring. "Make sure she's drinking fluids and keeping her feet up. And no fast food. Tally, really, take care of that baby. They did not ask to have a mother who survives on fries and martini olives."

From the kitchen, Dig called out, "Girl dinner!" before sauntering around the corner in one of Jordan's giant, probably very expensive, plush robes. Jordan tensed by the door.

"And Charlie," Doyle added in a loud whisper, gesturing toward the man standing like a reluctant bodyguard near the living room. "Whatever she says or does, do not hold it against Jordan or me. We love you. I won't let her ruin that for us."

Charlie stood between Doyle and me, his wide, flannel-covered back toward me. I took in his height, the way his long, copper-brushed hair curled slightly around his earlobes. Cedar and something warm wafted toward me and I took a step in his direction before I caught myself.

"Remind me again why Dig can't stay with me?" I asked, a little too casually. "We did fine in New York, just the two of us, since you abandoned us for wine and money and good looks. No offense, Jordan."

Jordan lifted one shoulder, already fighting a grin. "None taken."

Doyle, ever the dramatist, shoved poor Nancy Reagan out of the way to reach for his Louis Vuitton carry-on, then squared his shoulders like he was about to march into battle. "Tallulah, you were living in a fifth-floor walk-up that smelled like lo mein and broken dreams. And might I remind you," he added, his voice climbing as he flung a hand in the general direction of my stomach, "you are now with child and have no plan, no roadmap, and not a single clue how to raise a human."

Dig sashayed across the glossy hardwood floor and threw his leg up in a Rockette's-style kick. "He's not wrong, Tally."

I narrowed my eyes and crossed my arms. "Thanks for the support."

Dig smirked. "Anytime, doll. That's what family's for."

I crossed to Jordan and wrapped my arms around him. "Please call me if you need anything, even if it's just to vent. Especially if Doyle makes this trip all about him."

"You wouldn't hit a pregnant lady, would you, Doyle?" Dig asked, snacking on an olive from his martini. God, I would've sold a kidney for that drink.

My gaze flicked to Charlie, who stood a few feet away, arms loose at his sides, watching the circus unfold with a look I couldn't quite read. Not amused, not annoyed—just... there. Noticing everything. Including me.

Dig tossed back the rest of his cocktail and grabbed his overnight bag, slinging it over one shoulder before sauntering over to press a kiss to my cheek. "I have to go back to New York, Tal," he said, holding my hand like he was about to deliver a eulogy. "We talked about this. Shifts at Errico's, a callback for Clam Number Three in *The Little Mermaid* reimagining, and a situationship I can't let get too stale. You know I require at least three viable options at all times."

Charlie laughed—low and surprised, like it caught him off guard.

"All right, Clam-Boy," Doyle said, already heading for the door. "If you're piggybacking on our Uber, we need to go. Tally, please don't burn my house—or the city—down."

I crossed the room and kissed my brother's cheek. "A girl sets the town gazebo on fire *one time*..."

"Bye, y'all," Charlie said, stepping to my side while the three of them argued and stumbled their way into the elevator, bags dragging behind them.

Dig turned, clicked an imaginary camera at us, and blew me an air kiss as I slammed the door shut.

"Tallulah!" my brother's voice echoed from the descending elevator.

I exhaled, leaning against the door, pressing my palm to my stomach.

"You okay?" Charlie asked, voice low and rough.

I nodded, even though I wasn't totally sure.

He rubbed the back of his neck and sighed. "All right. Well. Guess we'd better figure out how this is gonna work."

I swallowed hard. "Well, I thought I could soften you up a little by baking you a treat. Wait here."

Charlie's eyebrows shot up, but he stayed put, murmuring to Nancy as she pranced around on the marble, proud as only poodles can be when getting attention.

I opened the oven and pulled out the blueberry bake, an exact, well, okay… that's ambitious of me. It *was* supposed to be a replica of the ribbon-winning Blueberry Boyfriend Bake my grandmother, Nonie, had perfected over the years. But without a recipe, I was winging it, and when I set it on the stove it deflated like a balloon.

But while Jordan, Doyle, and Dig were packing, I needed to keep my hands and mind busy, and though I'd maybe baked twice in my whole life, if you count oven-ready pizzas as baking, I wanted to show Charlie that I was appreciative of him and his time.

I grabbed the potholders and took a deep breath. Maybe it tasted better than it looked? I turned the corner from the kitchen into the living room and ran smack into Charlie.

"Are you okay? Wha–" he started, then yelped when the hot dish nicked his forearm. He cursed, good and loud, more from surprise than pain.

"Oh my God!" I squealed as the dish slid from my grip and exploded across the floor in a purple tide.

Charlie glanced from his arm to the bruised-blue splatter across the pristine white floor and loveseat, then to my face. When our eyes met, the scowl he'd been wearing eased.

He moved without hesitation, closing the steps between us and steering me away from the mess as gently as possible. "You look like you did before you passed out," he said. "Can you make it to the couch?"

I, indeed, could not make it to the couch.

***

By the time I came to, I looked like Violet Beauregarde, if she went twelve rounds with Betty Crocker and Betty took the gold. My limbs were trembling, my

159

clothes clung damp to my skin from the cold sweat that washed over me, and the stupid blueberry blast. I couldn't tell if the chill running down my spine was from the cold tile or the creeping realization that perhaps I did need a babysitter after all.

"Come on now, darlin', you're okay," Charlie whispered, his rough hands stroking my forehead and cheeks. "One of the nurses from the OB's office is on the line, she's asking if you still feel dizzy?"

I shook my head and craned my neck to assess the damage. There was blueberry goo everywhere, including all over Nancy since she was snouting around and mashing it into the ground and her chocolate-brown fur.

"Fuck me," I muttered, trying to sit up. Charlie made a sound into the phone that was half laugh, half fond exasperation. "No, ma'am, that was not an invitation," he said, then promised the nurse he'd take me to the ER if anything like that happened again and he'd try to keep me off my feet until my appointment.

"I need to clean myself up," I sighed, looking down at myself.

Charlie helped me to the bathroom, and I tried my best to get it together. The doctor had assured me that this is normal, that it happens, but to take it easy. Probably stress baking over my best friend leaving, my brother's anal attitude, and my brother-in-law in pain over his mother was not the route to go.

But I never knew how to sit still. That was always the way it went with me.

Charlie was crouched in the living room when I emerged, mop in hand, sleeves rolled past his elbows, hair in full rebellion like he'd been dragging his fingers through it for the past half hour. He looked up long enough to register I was there, then went back to scrubbing and muttering to himself.

I lingered in the doorway longer than I meant to, shame and exhaustion tripping over each other. I'd done worse. I'd been worse. But seeing him there—flannel, boots, and all that quiet, easy helpfulness—undid a knot in me I hadn't known was there. For a second, I didn't want to be brave. I wanted to let myself be small, and let someone else carry the weight for once.

And that scared me more than it should have.

"I'm sorry," I said, voice barely bigger than a breath.

Charlie rose to his feet, brushing his palms on his jeans. He kept his gaze down, and I was grateful for it.

"I'm gonna run down and grab a few things from the studio. Will you be all right?"

I nodded, but this time I meant it. My limbs still felt untrustworthy, my stomach was a minefield, and I could hear the echo of my brother's worry and annoyance in every corner of this too-big penthouse. But Charlie had helped me without judgment, with that quiet steadiness that didn't demand anything.

And for reasons I didn't want to dig too deeply into, that made me feel safer than I'd felt in months.

"Please park your behind on the couch and do not move," Charlie said, heading for the door. "So help me God if I come back up here and you're anywhere near the kitchen, your ass is grass, Aden."

I let out the most pathetic laugh as I pressed a hand to my belly, not for comfort, but for clarity. Trying to remind myself what this was all for. Who I was doing it for.

"I'm trying," I whispered. "I really am."

Nancy let out a long, theatrical sigh and rested her blueberry-covered chin on my knee, like she could sense how close I was to crumbling.

I tilted my head back against the back of the couch, letting the silence settle around me. Somewhere under the fatigue and the nausea and the ever-present panic, I could still hear the girl I used to be. The one who dreamed in Technicolor. Who believed in late-night dancing, open windows, and hands that held on when things got hard. Who traveled and searched the world for what she believed could save her, the perfect life—the perfect love.

She didn't feel close. But she wasn't gone.

There was still a part of me that wanted to fight for her. Maybe not with fists raised and a battle cry but with more patience. The kind of strength that came from staying. From trying again. From refusing to let go of the idea that there was a place for me in this world. A space that didn't ask me to shrink or perform or apologize.

A place I'd walk into and recognize—not by its shape or its sound, but by the way it settled in my chest but the way it felt when I finally let myself belong.

A place that felt a lot like home.

CHAPTER TWENTY-TWO

Charlie

I tossed a pair of jeans into my duffle bag, followed by two of the cleanest t-shirts I could find in my laundry rotation, then paused, hand hovering over the drawer. It was supposed to be one night. That was the plan. Long enough to make sure Tally didn't pass out, crack her head open, and bleed all over the pristine penthouse floors. Then, I'd head back to my studio, my apartment, my routine. Check in on her from time to time. Easy.

But instead I was packing like I was moving in. The longer I stood there, the more ridiculous it felt. Tally was an adult, and she probably didn't want me hovering.

But, God help me, I *wanted* to be.

I shut the drawer a little harder than necessary and dragged a hand down my face.

I sighed and turned my attention to my art supplies, twisting the caps on a few acrylics to make sure they wouldn't dry out overnight. The movement felt mechanical—if I kept my hands busy, my brain wouldn't spiral into all the places it was clearly trying to go. I stacked the jars neatly along the edge of the worktable, lined up my brushes, and adjusted the lamp even though it didn't need adjusting—still too much noise rattling around in my head.

My phone buzzed across the table, sliding an inch on the wood before stopping. Sutton's face lit up the screen, grinning like a maniac, her River Rats cap on backward like she was the damn mayor of minor league baseball.

I smirked and tapped answer, propping the phone up against a stack of sketchbooks.

"Charlie Pruitt's Babysitter's Club, at your service."

"Nice," Sutton said, the sound of chopping echoing in the background. "You two are moving in together already? I knew I saw sparks flying."

I rolled my eyes and reached for the phone like I might physically throttle her through it. "I'm not moving in with her. It's just for the night. She's not feeling great. Again."

"Uh-huh." She didn't even try to hide the smugness in her voice as she looked up from her prep work. "So why do you look like you're packing for a cross-country road trip?"

I exhaled hard through my nose. "What if I need extra socks?"

"While you're four floors away from your own apartment?"

I paused, really unsure of what I was even doing in the first place. "What if there's a sock-mergency, and suddenly we need eight pairs of socks?"

"Mm, valid," Sutton said. "This is, after all, from the guy who once reorganized my entire pantry, half-drunk, at two in the morning because you *saw the beginnings of a system failure.*'"

I ignored that and reached for the zipper on my duffel instead. "She really *isn't* feeling well, and even though the doctor assured us it was normal, I don't want to take chances and end up on Doyle's shit list in case something happens to her and I'm out drinking with you idiots."

There was a pause. The sound of chopping stopped.

When Sutton leaned closer to the camera, I could already feel it coming, the slow, surgical look she got when she was about to rip you open and lay all your tender insides out on the table.

"Charlie," she said, sing-songing like she was revving up for a takedown. "I know that look."

"What look?"

She grinned, all teeth. "The furrowed brow. The pacing. The whole emotionally constipated dad-from-a-90s-sitcom vibe. Pretending there is anything more fun in this life than going out to the bars with me and Lee. It's giving 'nervous about catching feelings.'"

"Jesus, Sutton—"

"I'm just saying," she interrupted, holding her hands up in faux surrender. "If you were feeling a little… warm and fuzzy about Savannah's newest houseguest, you should probably know something. I didn't want to tell you the other day because I wasn't sure, but…"

I paused, one foot on the edge of the rug, waiting.

"She's seeing someone."

I blinked. "What?"

"She is," Sutton said, clearly loving every second. "Ryan and I saw her at Savannah Coffee Roasters last week. Some guy was with her—very cozy. Hand on the bump. You know. Real *doting father-to-be* vibes."

My jaw tensed. "Why would I care about that?"

"Oh, I don't know," she said, all fake innocence. "Maybe because you packed like you're moving in with her and haven't unclenched your jaw since she rolled into town? Or maybe it was the phrase… 'The doctor told us it was normal'?"

I didn't respond.

Because the image of Tally with some other guy had lodged itself somewhere deep in my chest, pressing into a spot I hadn't known was sore until she touched it.

Had Nick stayed in town, hiding in the shadows, even after I told him to fuck off? She would have told me, right? Had she met someone since moving here? Or maybe I was wrong. Perhaps she'd been texting someone this whole time, slipping off to call him when she thought no one was paying attention.

The only guy in her orbit was Dig—who preferred men, musicals, and moisturizers in that order—so I hadn't worried.

Not that it mattered. Not that I was keeping tabs. Not that I—

"You're mad," Sutton said, her eyes gleaming now. "Oh my God. You're mad."

"I'm not mad," I snapped, a little too fast.

Sutton clutched her chest like she'd been gifted the greatest Christmas present of all time. "He's *mad*! He's *mad*! I mean, can't say I blame you, Charlie. She is *glowy*."

"I'm going to hang up now," I muttered, reaching for the phone.

"At least you don't have to pack condoms!"

Click.

I stared at the black screen, Sutton's laughter still echoing faintly through the speaker.

***

165

The penthouse was quiet when I let myself in, the kind of heavy stillness that made you feel like you were trespassing, even when you'd been invited.

Well—*invited* might've been a stretch.

Nancy scuttled past my feet with a half-hearted yap, then changed her mind and decided she hated walking more than she hated me, so she collapsed in a judgmental heap by the door.

I set my duffel bag down near the entry, careful not to wake her—Tally, not the dog.

She was curled up on the couch in the living room, one arm slung under her cheek, the other protectively tucked over her bump. The TV was on low, some cooking show humming in the background, and the flickering light from the screen painted her in warm golds and soft shadows.

I stood there for a second, taking her in, silently hoping she hadn't caught any sudden, kitchen-ambitious ideas from the TV.

That should've been my cue to leave. To head straight for the unoccupied guest room, unpack, and act normal. But instead, I walked deeper into the living room, grabbed the throw blanket off the arm of the couch, and gently draped it over her. She stirred, her face scrunching like she was about to wake up, but then she sighed and settled deeper into the cushions.

Cradling her bump as if it were the only thing tethering her to the earth.

I stepped back, scrubbing a hand down my face.

This wasn't my job. I wasn't her anything. I was the guy her brother guilted into keeping an eye on her, a guy who hadn't even wanted to take this on in the first place. And now?

Now I couldn't stop looking.

The kitchen was a mess—mostly in that lived-in way that made it look like someone had been having an ordinary day, and partially because it looked like a toddler had gotten into a fight with a Kitchenaid. The fridge was cracked open enough to cast a sliver of light on the counter, where a jar of olives sat empty beside a spoon and a half-drunk bottle of ginger ale.

"Girl dinner," I muttered, shaking my head.

I cleaned it all up without thinking. I ran the dishes under hot water, wiped down the counter, and shut the fridge. But every few minutes, I found myself glancing back toward the couch.

Was she really seeing someone? Sutton wasn't above a dramatic retelling, but that tone in her voice—that smug little "gotcha"—had rattled me. I wasn't quite sure what to do with it. It wasn't jealousy. It couldn't be.

But the thought of her with someone else, getting cozy, or whatever the hell Sutton had said, somehow set my blood boiling. And, of course, it wasn't implausible. She was a beautiful woman in a new city who was glowing in a way I'd never seen someone glow before, and everyone who stepped into her orbit felt the magnetic pull of being in her presence. Even if, as far as we all knew, she was just passing through.

Maybe whoever this guy was would be the reason she stayed. And maybe if I couldn't have her, I'd still get to keep her around in some way.

I poured myself a bourbon over one giant cube and slid open the lanai doors, stepping into the cool night like it might slap the confusion out of me.

Nancy dragged herself after me, nails ticking across the tile before she collapsed again, this time at my feet like some grumpy little nanny making sure I didn't wander into the living room and wake her charge.

I leaned on the railing, sipping my drink as the sky deepened from peach to plum, the city below glowing as it stretched to wake itself up for the long night ahead. The river bended lazily in the distance, wide and winding, slow as molasses, carrying with it the weight of a hundred stories. Laughter floated up from the cobblestones, tourists chasing ghosts, to-go cups in hand, unaware they were walking through some place sacred. Savannah didn't rush you. She curled her fingers around your wrist, whispered low and lazy in your ear, and taught you how to stay still. How to listen. How to love a city for the way it breathes.

I pulled out my phone and dialed Magnolia. She answered on the third ring, her voice bright and clipped like she was mid-wedding task.

"Charlie Pruitt. If this is another speech about Dane or the wedding, I swear to—"

"It's not." I cut her off before she could get going. "It's about Tally."

There was a pause, the kind that always showed up right after I said the wrong thing.

"What about her?" Magnolia asked, a little softer now.

"So she is seeing someone, isn't she?"

More silence. Then a sound, almost a laugh—but not quite.

"Why?"

"No reason." I looked out across the balcony, down at the city, at the rooftops and windows lit up in quiet defiance, like the world didn't know I was up here bleeding out. "Just wondering what I'm walking into."

She was quiet for a beat longer.

"I don't know, Charlie. But I think you've already walked into it."

I sighed, taking another long pull of my drink. "I just don't want to get hurt, Mags." It was the only time I'd admit it out loud, and I would admit out loud to my sister, and my sister alone. "Nothing's even happened yet, and I feel like the girl's already broken my heart."

"You know, Charlie," Magnolia started, sounding like she was settling in. If I had to guess, she was curling up by the to-go window, waiting for someone, anyone, to stop by. "Maybe you'll get hurt. Maybe you won't. But you know what I guarantee *will* happen?"

Leaning back onto the ledge, I turned my body to face the lanai door. The soft, warm glow of the TV spilled over the couch and across Tally's sleeping body. "What's that?" I asked, voice like gravel.

"You will have done something for yourself, for once, and you could let that be enough."

I didn't have a response for that, so I took another sip, scratched behind Nancy's ears, and let the silence stretch between us like a line I didn't know if I wanted to cross.

***

She slept most of the night on the couch, buried under the blanket I'd pulled over her, Nancy wedged behind her knees. I should've gone to the guest bedroom. Could've stretched out, gotten actual rest. But I didn't. I stayed on the too-small loveseat across from her, stiff and wide awake.

It started as concern. She hadn't looked well. But at some point, the excuse thinned, and I was left with the truth: I didn't want to leave her alone. Not in case she needed water or a trash can. But because I didn't want to be anywhere else.

Arms crossed, eyes closed, I refused to give the thought space. It didn't matter what I wanted. She had enough on her plate. She didn't need someone else hovering. Still, I stayed. Her chest rose and fell with each breath, one arm tucked around her stomach, the other folded beneath her cheek. There was peace in the room—the kind that only shows up when someone feels safe—and I couldn't look away.

By the time I drifted off, ten or fifteen minutes at most, the city outside had settled into that middle of the night softness. What pulled me back wasn't the sound of traffic or the ache in my back. It was her.

I opened my eyes and found her standing in front of me. One half of her face caught the faint glow from the streetlamp, the other shadowed in the quiet. Her arms were crossed, but there was no fire in her expression. She didn't look angry or annoyed. She looked tired in a different way. Guarded, but open.

"You're snoring." She nudged me gently, voice low.

I rubbed a hand across my face and tried to sit up without making it worse. The throw blanket slid into my lap. My shirt was twisted. My neck ached. But she was watching me.

"What are you doing out here?" she asked.

I glanced toward the kitchen and then back at her. I didn't have a good answer. I hadn't meant to stay out here all night. I hadn't planned anything, but I couldn't lie.

"You looked comfortable."

She stepped closer. Her sleeves were pushed up to her elbows, her eyes steady. She reached for my hand, and I let her take it without hesitation. Her fingers curled around mine. There was warmth in her grip, quiet certainty. She guided my hand to her stomach, held it there, and waited.

Then something stirred beneath my palm.

The first flutter was faint, a shift under the skin. I stopped breathing. My heart jumped once, then steadied. The next kick was stronger—a small, insistent pulse pressing against my hand, proof that something real was taking shape beneath the surface.

I brought my other hand up, placing it beside the first. Her skin was warm. Her breathing was shallow. I didn't move. I couldn't.

Her eyes found mine, and neither of us looked away. There was no smirk. No shield. No sarcastic remark held at the ready. Only this moment, suspended in stillness, the air thick with questions neither of us knew how to ask.

She kept her hand on mine, light and steady, as the baby moved beneath it. The silence wasn't awkward or stretched thin. It was full. Her expression softened. Her shoulders dropped. A small curve touched the corner of her mouth, so fleeting I wasn't sure I hadn't imagined it.

Then it happened.

Her gaze shot past me, and the color drained from her face. Whatever calm she'd found a moment ago shattered in an instant.

"Oh my god," she whispered. The sound was softer now, threaded with something wary.

I yanked my hands away and turned toward the hallway, not sure if there was a knife-wielding serial killer on the loose, a ghost materializing from thin air, or, worse, her brother hiding under the shadows, waiting to catch us in the act.

But no. It was far worse.

Nancy Reagan stood frozen at the edge of the carpet. Then, without fanfare or shame, she dropped her rear end to the floor and began scooting across the living room with unhurried determination. That damn dog was dragging her poodle butt across Doyle and Jordan's snow-white, terrifyingly expensive rug with the slow, methodical grace of a creature who knew exactly what she was doing.

And just like that, the spell was broken.

CHAPTER TWENTY-THREE

Tally

I'd stayed in my room long enough.

After one of the most unexpectedly intimate, deeply strange moments of my life, everything had come crashing back to earth thanks to my geriatric poodle dragging her crusty, little ass across the pristine carpet like she was possessed by a demon with a dingleberry.

The two of us, locked in stunned silence, had scrambled to clean it up as fast as humanly possible. Charlie, ever calm in a crisis, muttered about Eunice Wilder—Lee's mother and savior of antique upholstery—probably having a stain removal spell or knowing a guy. I hadn't waited for a follow-up. I bolted to my room and leaned against the door.

Hours later, I was still replaying it.

His hand on my belly, the heat sinking through. The air held still, thick with silence that felt holy.

I hadn't meant to wake him. Hadn't planned to stand there watching him sleep. But he'd looked so... peaceful. And uncomfortable. And there was this unspoken truth in the room—he'd stayed. He could've gone back downstairs, could've crashed in the second guest room, could've done anything but contort himself like a human pretzel on that tiny love seat.

But he hadn't.

When I pressed his hand to my stomach, the prickliness he wore like chainmail melted away. It wasn't the jolt of surprise when the baby kicked, no, but the way his whole body leaned toward mine, drawn to us without even realizing it. It was like some invisible thread was tugging us together. When our foreheads nearly touched, whatever had been brewing between us suddenly felt real.

Now, sitting on the edge of my bed, I pressed a hand to that same spot on my belly, the ghost of his touch still warm against my skin.

It wasn't the baby fluttering this time.

It was me.

That slow, unmistakable bloom of wanting. Of being seen. Of hoping for that one, unreachable thing you didn't think you were allowed to have.

The knock at the door sent me practically hurtling across the room like someone had fired a starter pistol.

"Yeah?" I called—too loud, too fast—already halfway there, my bare feet skimming across the polished floor.

Charlie filled the doorway with that impossible stillness of his, like nothing in the entire world could touch him. Like last night hadn't happened. Like I hadn't placed his hand on my stomach and watched his entire face soften in the dark.

"Hey," he said, rubbing the back of his neck. "I'm heading down to the studio. I've got to finish this piece before Christmas, and I'm already behind."

I could see it—the twitch of his jaw, the tightness around his eyes. Charlie wasn't just stressed. He was pressure personified, like a man who lived with a ticking clock inside his chest and refused to let it skip a single beat.

"You got plans today, or—"

"I'll come down with you," I cut in too quickly. "I told Jordan I'd check in with Sylvie anyway, but otherwise…"

He blinked. For a split second, his face almost—*almost*—lit up. But then his eyes slid past me and landed on Nancy Reagan, who was standing behind me, squinting at him with elderly contempt.

"Yeah," he muttered, "We should probably get her out of here. Carpet cleaners'll be here in an hour. Best if the criminal isn't present at the scene."

"Don't let her hear you say that," I murmured, bending to clip on Nancy's leash. "She knows people."

I took her for a walk through the square, stopping into *Cheese, Please!* to say hi to Sylvie and pretend I wasn't hyper-aware of the man I was about to follow into close quarters. I was trying to tamp down the thing brewing inside me—the part of me that had curled up on the couch before I woke him up and thought, *God help me, maybe I do want this.*

By the time I walked through the front entrance of the studio, my nerves were shot.

It was warm inside, even though the door was cracked open in the back. A low breeze curled in from the alley, but the heat was from the space itself—alive with energy and paint fumes and sawdust and whatever else Charlie used to make the chaos in his mind come alive.

The front half of the studio looked like a gallery curated by someone half-mad and full of genius—trash turned into treasure, light bending across sculptures made of rusted metal and broken glass. But it was the back room that pulled me in, where the edges blurred between creation and comfort. A worn couch. A long worktable. Coffee mugs stacked haphazardly beside paint-splattered rags.

Home, but only if you knew how to look.

Lee's voice drifted in from the speakers—slow and dreamy, a little mournful, the kind of song that slipped under your skin and settled in.

Nancy let out one sharp boof like she was announcing us at a gala, and Charlie looked up from where he was crouched, organizing a stack of sketchbooks.

"Hey, you," he said, voice low, almost easy.

He looked better down here—calmer. Grounded. As if the tension that followed him around like a shadow had finally slipped off his shoulders, the moment he stepped into his world.

"This place looks a lot different when I'm not actively vomiting or unconscious," I said, curling into the corner of the love seat tucked against the back wall.

From here, I could really take it in—the quiet tangle of creation that made up Charlie's space. Layers of paint-splattered rags, dog-eared sketchbooks, old snapshots pinned to the walls without a frame in sight. There were piles of what might've been trash or art, or maybe both, depending on how generous you were feeling. But it felt lived in. Rooted. It was like someone had poured their entire self into the walls.

Charlie huffed out a laugh but didn't turn around, his focus locked on the large canvas stretched along the far wall. It was close to finished—the kind of piece that vibrated with meaning even before you knew what it was about.

I stood and wandered closer, pulled forward as if the thing was magnetic. When I finally caught it in full, I exhaled. "That's Magnolia," I murmured, standing in front of it now, dwarfed by the sheer scale.

The whole piece was her, built out of tiny mosaic portraits—snapshots of family and friends, O'Malley's, the river, sun-drenched porches, and fireworks over Forsyth. Savannah, and everyone who made it home, woven together into the shape of his sister's face.

Tilting my head back, I took in the loops of writing running through it all, winding between the images like a thread. "Are those... song lyrics?"

Charlie didn't look away from what he was doing—tweezing a tiny photo into place with the care of a surgeon—but his voice was soft when he spoke. "Yeah. This one's for Magnolia. Lee commissioned it. It's a Christmas gift."

I frowned a little. "Isn't she marrying his brother?"

He let out a dry laugh, then finally looked at me. There was a flicker of restraint in his eyes, or maybe curiosity he didn't know what to do with. "That she is," he said, placing the photo, a shot of the two of them as kids, right above her collarbone. "But somehow, their love song keeps playing on a loop in this town."

I smiled, hugging my arms across my chest. "Savannah seems to have a thing for complicated love stories."

Charlie walked to his worktable, where hundreds of small photos fanned out across the surface in careful disarray. I followed without thinking, drawn to the table and maybe to him, too. I hovered beside him, letting my fingers brush the edges of old memories I wasn't part of but suddenly wanted to understand.

There was so much history here. In this space. In these pictures. In him.

"Magnolia told me about your uncle when Dig and I were at O'Malley's not long ago," I said, tracing the rim of my water bottle with my thumb. "He owned the bar?"

Charlie chewed on his bottom lip, eyes scanning the table of photos. "Yeah. Our parents died when we were still kids, so our Uncle Cole took us in. We grew up in the apartment above the bar."

He stepped across the room, and I followed again, drawn in without thinking. The way he said *we* made me ache in a way I didn't expect. There was a security there, even in the grief.

"Mags still lives up there," he added.

I snorted. "Seriously? I thought her fiancé was loaded."

Charlie glanced over his shoulder, the corner of his mouth twitching like he was trying not to smile. "You're awfully chatty today. Must be feeling better."

I wanted to make it a joke, toss the moment aside. But all I could think about was his touch—how the room had gone still, how it hadn't felt fleeting at all. "Yeah," I admitted. "I guess I am."

He leaned onto his elbows over the worktable, fixing me with a playful squint. "Okay, then riddle me this, Nancy Drew. Why the hell is that dog named after a First Lady?"

I smirked, gesturing vaguely toward Nancy Reagan, curled into a tight ball and snoring dramatically on the loveseat. "She doesn't give off major Nancy Reagan energy to you?"

"Not even a little," Charlie said, after pretending to study her like a museum piece.

I popped open an iced tea from the mini fridge, that familiar tightness in my chest easing enough to let the moment in. "She was my Nonie's dog. My grandmother."

Charlie looked up, quiet now.

"When Nonie got really sick, she had a fall and had to be moved into a nursing home. Doyle told me our momma was planning to send Nancy to the pound." I twisted the cap tighter on my tea and looked down at the table, the sharp memory of that day still catching at my throat. "Said she was too old, too untrained. That she didn't comply."

Charlie winced.

"The shelter said dogs like her don't get adopted out at that age." I gave a small shrug, like the whole thing still didn't piss me off. "I was back in New York, trying to get some money together before my next trip to Scotland, but instead, I hitchhiked home and picked her up."

His head snapped toward me. "Wait. You *hitchhiked*? For a poodle?"

I laughed, and maybe it was a little unhinged, but I couldn't help it. "Yeah. It sounds wild, I know. But... I know what it's like to be left behind for reasons you don't understand. What it feels like when someone decides you're too much trouble to keep around. I couldn't let that happen to her."

Charlie didn't say anything for a second, the air between us softening into the kind of quiet that said he got it. That he wasn't going to tell me it wasn't that bad or that I should move on.

I looked over at Nancy, the stubborn, crusty little thing. "She's kind of the worst. Smells like socks and corn chips. But I'd do it all over again."

Charlie studied me for a moment. "I knew I was right about you, Tally Aden."

I tilted my head, the corner of my mouth tugging up. "And how's that?"

His voice was low. "You're the one doing the rescuing. Not the one waiting to be saved."

I rolled my eyes, mostly to keep from crying.

I settled back into my spot on the couch while Charlie went back to work, his hands moving with focused precision. Every so often, he paused to glance over at me. "So what happened next?" he asked, trimming a photo down to fit an empty space.

"What do you mean?"

He shrugged. "You hitchhiked, picked up the dog, brought her back to New York—then what? What'd you do with her when you traveled?"

As if she knew we were talking about her, Nancy started chasing her tail, barking at it like she had just discovered it was attached to her body.

"Well," I said, nodding toward the mayhem, "She clearly needs constant supervision, so I stayed in New York."

"So you gave up all your dreams for a poodle?"

It did sound ridiculous. But that was one thing Charlie and I had in common.

"I'd do anything for the people and creatures I love, even if it means rearranging everything. Not everyone gets that kind of love. I didn't, not really. But I do now. Especially now."

"I get it," he said, his eyes locked on mine.

I nodded, then asked, "And what would you do for love? Would you buy a bar? Cancel your plans? Give up your dreams?"

Charlie didn't answer right away. When he finally spoke, it was barely above a whisper. "For me, love itself is the dream."

CHAPTER TWENTY-FOUR

Tally

Nancy Reagan gave me side-eye from her perch on the unmade bed, her snout pressed dramatically into the comforter.

"Oh, don't start," I muttered, brushing mascara across my lashes and trying not to stab myself in the eye. "You're still my baby. I just happen to be carrying another one."

She huffed.

"I mean it." I dropped the mascara wand and crossed the room, crouching beside the bed to scratch behind her ears. "No one's replacing you. You'll always be my crusty firstborn."

Her only response was a suspicious little grunt, but her head tilted enough to lean into the affection. I took it as a win.

I stood again, eyeing myself in the mirror. The dress I'd picked out was nothing special, just soft, floral cotton with a little stretch, but I looked... good. Not in a glowing, ethereal, earth-mama way. But in a *me* way. There was a roundness to my stomach that no longer felt strange or wrong, and my skin had settled into something closer to dewy than haunted.

I'd never tell him this, but perhaps Doyle was right with his suggestion that I adopt a skincare routine.

And maybe it was the dress. Or the sunlight spilling through the curtains, soft and golden. Or it was the way Charlie had looked at me the night before while we moved around the kitchen, tired from a long day in the studio, both of us too worn out to talk much but still sharing small glances—his smirk, the quiet flicker in his eyes, the kind of look that made me feel like we were figuring this out together, even if neither of us knew what *this* was.

But I was more confident and a little steadier in my skin.

In the days since Doyle and Jordan left for California, Charlie and I had fallen into an almost-rhythm. It wasn't seamless, but it held. There were stretches of stillness, edges that didn't quite line up, but somehow it still worked—two people coexisting in a borrowed penthouse with a judgmental poodle and too many unspoken thoughts.

Mornings started slow, with both of us on the lanai. Charlie nursed his coffee in silence, gaze distant, while I picked at a bagel or whatever carb didn't turn my stomach that day. Nancy Reagan made her rounds, eyeing squirrels like they owed her money. Sometimes we'd talk. Sometimes we wouldn't. Either way, it didn't feel uncomfortable or forced. Just... settled.

After breakfast, he'd disappear into the kitchen, wiping down every surface obsessively, and I'd drag my laptop to the couch and pretend to make progress on my life.

I wasn't only scrolling photography boards. I was chasing something murkier. I emailed magazine editors who never wrote back, stalked photo studios in nearby cities, and hunted down internships I was technically overqualified for, but still, no bites. My inbox became a graveyard of polite declines—or worse, nothing at all. Starting over in a creative field was a lot like screaming into the void and hoping someone handed you a camera and a detailed plan.

Still, I tried. Every morning. Because if I didn't, then what?

After that, we'd ride the elevator down in silence, me clutching my water bottle, Charlie clutching whatever shred of sanity he appeared to have left, Nancy Reagan trotting contentedly between us as if she'd appointed herself chaperone, sniffing at the corners of the elevator, making Charlie jumpy. The short walk from the lobby to his studio—barely twenty steps—became a strange kind of ritual. Not romantic. Not even really warm, but quietly consistent.

We hadn't had any other honest, deep conversations. And we hadn't talked at all about that first night, when I let his hands rest on my swollen belly, feeling the life inside me stir in time with the wild, uneven rhythm of my own heart pressed so close to his.

But lately, he'd gone quiet again—focused. The commissioned piece for Lee had him in overdrive, and I didn't blame him—it was massive, complicated work, and he only had a short window to finish it. So sometimes, I stayed out of his way. I'd wander the streets for hours, ducking into shops, nursing iced teas on shaded benches, letting Savannah unfold in pieces. Sometimes I'd walk. Sometimes I'd climb into Franny Jo's carriage like a visiting dignitary and let her narrate the city in her sing-song voice, full of half-truths and tall tales.

Every day taught me a little more—about the city, about Charlie, about how it's possible to drift and still start finding your footing.

At night, I'd retreat to my room like I was supposed to. But more often than not, I'd find myself sneaking out in the middle of the night, the soft patter of my steps drowned out by the hush of the penthouse. I'd steal a glance at him—curled up on that ridiculous loveseat, arms crossed, brow still furrowed, waiting for the next emergency. Even asleep, Charlie Pruitt looked like he was bracing for impact.

What was supposed to be one night had turned into night after night after night…

I tried not to read too much into it. I told myself he was being his typical, dutiful self. Or, maybe, that the penthouse was a little nicer than the studio, and he was enjoying the luxury of Doyle's refined tastes. But some traitorous voice in the back of my mind—the same one that liked to whisper impossible things when the lights were low and I was too tired to fight it—kept nudging at me. Telling me maybe he was still here… for me.

I was still brushing the thought away when I heard his voice echo from across the penthouse, gentle but impatient.

"You ready or what?"

He was pacing again. I could picture it—the tight line of his jaw, the way his arms would cross then drop again when he couldn't settle. I smoothed a hand over my stomach and called back, "Coming!"

Today was a follow-up appointment. A check-in on the little life growing inside me. And maybe the closest I'd come to meeting them, even if it were only through a screen and some fuzzy, grey outlines—a FaceTime with my future.

Charlie was waiting at the elevator. He didn't speak as we rode it down, only nodded and walked ahead, opening the truck door for me. He shut it gently, careful and reserved in that way he always was when he thought I wasn't paying attention.

Sliding into the driver's side, he fastened his seatbelt with a frustrated sigh. He didn't look at me, but there it was—the edge. Not anger, exactly. More like a pot starting to boil.

"Everything okay?" I asked.

He started the truck, one arm slung over the seat as he backed up. His forearm brushed my neck—warm, rough, close enough to short-circuit a few brain cells. Not nausea. Not nerves. Just trouble.

The cab of the truck smelled like paint thinner and old beer—maybe pine sap or sawdust if you leaned in hard enough—and the dash was cluttered with Charlie's brand of lived-in disorder. There was a photo taped to the vanity mirror. The five of them—Charlie, Magnolia, Lee, Sutton, and Dane—grinning in mismatched formalwear, probably from some high school dance or prom they'd stormed together.

I leaned in slightly to get a better look at the grainy photo. "Sutton looks the same."

He glanced at the picture, then returned his eyes to the road, a tight smirk pulling at one corner of his mouth. "Probably because no one's ever stuck around long enough to suck the life out of her."

I didn't laugh. Something about the way he said it felt pointed, even if it wasn't directed at me.

We rolled over the cobblestones in silence for a moment. The truck groaned softly beneath us, the windows fogging slightly from the heat inside versus the chilled December air outside.

"Did something happen?" I asked, carefully. "With your sister? Or Lee?"

He adjusted the gear stick, flicked on his blinker even though no one was around, then shrugged. "Nothing specific. Just... everything." His voice dropped lower. "Dane's in Atlanta, tied up in court until after the new year. And Lee's using the opportunity to—what? Win her back? Even though he's got some maybe-girlfriend here who just left to go back to Nashville for the holidays that he seems to have already forgotten about."

He shook his head. "I don't know what anyone's doing anymore. Magnolia won't tell me anything. Sutton's being weird. And Lee—" he broke off with a grunt, rubbing his hand over his mouth. "I don't know. I feel like everyone's playing a game and I don't get the rules."

I listened, hands folded in my lap. I hadn't heard him say this much in days. Maybe ever. And there was a thread of disappointment or disorientation in his voice that tugged at me.

"You're a good friend, Charlie," I said softly, laying my hand over his where it rested on the shift stick. I meant it as comfort, nothing more. But the contact sparked the inevitable embers flickering between us and he looked over at me, eyes shadowed and unreadable.

Then, as quickly as I'd reached for him, I pulled my hand back. I turned my face toward the window, pretending to be interested in the brick buildings rolling past us.

CHAPTER TWENTY-FIVE

Charlie

The waiting room felt like a test—some twisted endurance challenge designed by the ghost of a midwife with a dark sense of humor. There were too many bodies and not enough chairs, and every surface radiated a quiet, sticky tension. Somewhere behind the check-in desk, Enya hummed faintly from a speaker, clashing spectacularly with the soundtrack of small children wailing in various keys and women moaning and bouncing in their seats, teetering on the verge of giving birth at any moment.

Tally sat next to me, bolt upright, her spine so straight it looked painful. Her hands were folded over her belly, fingers twitching every few seconds. She wasn't breathing like a person who wanted to stay in the room.

To our left, a woman balanced two squirming babies in her lap—both red-faced and wailing, their fists thrashing. And if that wasn't enough, she was clearly pregnant again, her belly rounding out beneath a stretched T-shirt. She bounced her knees in an endless rhythm, eyes glazed with the kind of exhaustion that no amount of sleep could fix, thumbing through her phone, probably looking for an escape route or a portal to another dimension.

Then came the toddler.

Barefoot, dressed in nothing but an oversized t-shirt and a sagging diaper, he wobbled across the carpet like a tiny drunk uncle at a wedding and zeroed in on Tally. He stopped right in front of her, looked up into her face like she was the Virgin Mary herself, and then—without warning—hacked a lung directly into her lap. Before either of us could react, his chubby fingers had latched onto a fistful of her curls with terrifying strength.

There was a cacophony of screeching—hers, then his, then mine, if I'm being honest—as we scrambled to dislodge the kid and return him to his equally horrified mother.

When it was over, Tally didn't say anything. She stared at the exam room door, her eyes wide, mouth parted slightly, like she was seriously considering launching herself out the nearest window.

"You good?" I asked carefully, my voice low. I didn't want to spook her more than she already was.

She didn't look at me. Didn't move. She kept her gaze fixed on the door, hand braced on the waiting room chair, ready to bolt.

"I don't know if I can do this," she whispered.

I turned her toward me, slow and careful, like defusing a bomb with zero training. My hands hovered at her elbows, waiting to see if she'd cry, snap, or both. When her eyes met mine—wide and panicked—I gave her my best version of calm, which was probably closer to *please don't explode on me.*

She recoiled like I'd flashed a knife.

"What is that face?" she hissed, like I'd somehow made it worse.

Immediately, my mouth fell back into its usual, well-worn scowl. "I'm trying to comfort you," I muttered, though it came out more growl than whisper, like my voice didn't know how to operate at bedside-manner volume.

Before she could respond, the door to the exam rooms swung open. A nurse appeared, chart in hand. "Tallulah Aden?"

Her eyes landed on us—on me with my hand still awkwardly cupped around Tally's arm, as if I could physically steady her. There was a faint smile, one of those soft, maternal kinds, and then a glance flicked from Tally to me.

"And will the father be joining you today?" She didn't ask, not exactly. She assumed.

I opened my mouth, ready to explain that I wasn't that guy. That I was the one on puke patrol. The reluctant chauffeur. The last-minute, worst-case scenario babysitter. That I was only here to make sure she didn't collapse or pass out on a street corner.

But then I looked at her and I saw what I wasn't supposed to see. It flashed behind her eyes, just for a breath, but it was enough. Not panic. Not discomfort.

Fear.

The deep, agonizing kind that didn't belong in a room like this, didn't belong on her face, and sure as hell didn't belong in the eyes of someone walking into a doctor's appointment alone.

So I nodded, and the lie slipped out before I even realized I was saying it. "Yeah. I'll go back with her."

Tally turned slowly to look at me, and the fear, the shrill, deer-in-headlights look softened into something much calmer. Something like relief.

***

Tally sat on the edge of the exam table, her posture too straight to be casual, the thin paper gown rustling every time she shifted her weight. It was bunched awkwardly around her thighs, the stark white of it jarring against the golden warmth of her skin. She looked steadier than she had in the waiting room—less like the woman who'd been three seconds from bolting and more like someone working hard to stay upright, one breath at a time.

The room had settled into that particular kind of quiet found only in medical offices, where even the fluorescent lights seemed to buzz with unspoken tension. It wasn't peaceful. It was the kind of stillness that made you feel observed even when no one was looking. I stayed where I'd been for most of this ride— on the periphery. Hands in my pockets, back to the counter, doing everything I could not to intrude.

She didn't look at me, and I didn't press.

A soft knock broke the silence, followed by the click of the door swinging open. The doctor entered with the brisk efficiency of someone who'd said the same things a hundred times already today. She didn't hesitate as she slid onto a rolling stool and came to a smooth stop at the foot of the table, flipping through the chart in her hands.

"You're looking a lot better than the last time I saw you, Tallulah," she said, her tone lighter than the air in the room.

Tally scooted herself back, then reclined against the crinkling table, her eyes flicking to me for the briefest moment before she spoke. "Tally's fine," she said lightly, but there was an edge beneath it. "Tallulah's the girl my mom's still yelling at back in Newnan."

The doctor gave a quick laugh, then lifted the gown. That was my cue to turn my head and fixate on a spot on the far wall—some motivational print about maternal health that I suddenly found fascinating.

"This'll be cold," the doctor warned, and I heard the squelch of gel being applied.

The lights dimmed as a nurse I hadn't even noticed passed behind me and rested a gentle hand on my shoulder. "Come stand over here," she whispered, guiding me closer. "You'll get a better look at the screen."

I moved automatically, careful not to crowd the table or Tally. Her arm was tucked above her head, her breathing slow and shallow, almost comfortable. And then—

The machine hummed, the wand pressed down, and for a moment, all I heard was static. A low, watery whoosh, the kind of sound that lives deep in your ears after a long night out. Then, clear and steady, it came—that rapid rhythm, fast and strong.

Thud-thud-thud-thud-thud.

A heartbeat.

The doctor smiled, small and satisfied, then turned the monitor toward us.

There on the screen was a tiny figure, strange and perfect. It was still a little alien-looking, but it had arms. Ears. Feet. Little hands waved, like it was mid-story. It had a spine. A heartbeat. A center that pulsed steadily and strongly, clearer than I expected.

And those feet. The same ones I'd felt pressing into my palm that night. I could almost feel them again now, shifting, stretching, making their presence known. Right there in front of me.

It was all so very real and unimaginably beautiful.

"Heartbeat sounds great," she murmured, her tone clinical but soft enough to catch me off guard.

Tally's fingers found mine without warning. She didn't grip—only settled there, warm and tentative, then tightened slightly until her palm rested fully against mine. I turned my head enough to meet her eyes.

She was smiling, not wide or certain, but it was there, that upward curve halfway between awe and disbelief. "Now you look like you're the one about to hurl, Pruitt," she whispered, her voice unsteady with nerves she was trying to pass off as sarcasm. "Don't go getting all mushy on me now."

I didn't answer. I let the corner of my mouth pull up in return, my jaw clenched too tight to let anything else slip through.

Because whatever was shifting beneath the surface—whatever had cracked open in me the second that sound filled the room—it was already finding space I hadn't offered, pushing against parts of myself I'd kept locked down for years. And it wasn't going anywhere.

Neither was I.

***

"So let me get this straight," Magnolia said, leaning across the bar at O'Malley's like she was about to hear a murder confession. "She hitchhiked—from New York to Georgia—to rescue that scraggly little poodle she drags around like a designer handbag?"

I took a slow pull from my drink and nodded. "Swear to God. It was her grandmother's dog, and when she found out her momma was going to ditch her, she popped her thumb out and made her way down south."

Sutton clutched her chest. "That is… incredible."

"Y'all know something crazy, too?" I set my drink down. "We went for a walk through the square after her appointment, and she was telling me that one time she tackled a man trying to rob an influencer doing an outfit check video or, I don't know, but she straight up linebacker wrestled him to the ground and got the girl's purse back."

Both of them stared at me, slack-jawed. Magnolia blinked first.

"She's incredible," she breathed.

"She's done so much with her life, too," I added, because apparently I wasn't done. "She's worked at pizza joints, salons, did hair and makeup for some off-Broadway thing Dig was in. She's traveled all over the world, seen the Northern Lights, and the running of the bulls. Stuff we'd never even dream of doing. And, she caught every moment on her camera."

Lee, who'd been half-listening from the next stool, let out a wheezy, full-body laugh that caught the attention of half the bar.

"What?" I asked, defensive but not really annoyed.

He jutted his chin at me, grinning. "Charlie, I've known you since you were a kid. And aside from that weird summer when my momma let you come along on all those estate dumpster dives, I don't think I've ever heard you talk this much in one sitting."

Magnolia pretended to clutch her pearls. "Oh my God, he *is* talking. I didn't even notice until you said something. I was *riveted*."

I rolled my eyes and reached for my drink again, trying to tamp down the smile that was tugging at my mouth.

"She's got stories," I muttered. "And I just happen to like listening to them."

Sutton leaned back in her chair, one eyebrow raised. "Too bad she's got a boyfriend. Otherwise, I'd say Oscar the Grouch here finally met his match."

I didn't flinch or respond. I reached for another slice of pizza and shoved it in my mouth like that might muffle the sting. I'd forgotten all about the supposed boyfriend until Sutton just had to interrupt me and bring it back up.

"Boyfriend?" Lee asked, craning his neck to see Sutton behind me.

"I don't buy it," Magnolia said, her eyes locked on mine. "I think you saw what you wanted to see, Sutty."

Sutton's phone lit up and skidded once across the bar. She glanced at the screen and sighed. "LaMonte needs a warm body to fill in for Katie at the Telfair Ball. Looks like I'm it. Love you, losers."

She kissed the side of my face with an exaggerated smack, wiping pizza grease off my cheek with her sleeve as she bolted out the door in a blur of urgency.

Lee stood, stretching with a dramatic sigh. "Guess I'd better head out too. I'm performing at said ball tonight with Ryan, and we are, how do you say, completely unprepared and wildly unrehearsed. Here's hoping he's not already drunk in a tux somewhere."

Magnolia dismissed him with a flick of her hand, her expression unreadable. She stayed silent, still, watching him back out the door, that damn grin still tugging at his mouth, like she was the only one who could pull that kind of smirk from him. Her fingers curled slightly against the edge of the bar—the only sign she hadn't taken a full breath since he walked in.

It reminded me of when we were kids, back when the two of them first started sneaking around. Making out in the back storage room of O'Malley's, locking themselves in Magnolia's bedroom, and pretending no one noticed.

We'd noticed.

She caught me watching and turned, her expression hardening. "Don't start."

I raised my hands. "Didn't say a word."

"Please. You didn't have to." She cracked open a beer, giving me a look that said she wasn't in the mood for brotherly wisdom. "Besides, you've got your own mess now. How was the appointment, by the way? Everything okay?"

"I think so, she seemed to relax a little after. I think seeing the baby, and maybe having some support there, really helped ease her anxiety."

She stared at me. "You could've said no to all of this, you know," she said pointedly, taking a long pull from the bottle, her voice lighter but not without an edge.

"Are you serious?" I asked, flat. "You've met Doyle. Imagine if I bailed on his sister today or didn't provide around-the-clock updates on her vitamin schedule and if she's doing her prenatal stretches. He'd drown me in a vat of wine in the back of the shop."

"Unfortunately accurate." Magnolia leaned over the bar casually, as if she wasn't about to toss a grenade into the middle of the table.

I grabbed another slice of pizza and focused really hard on the crust.

Magnolia looked wrecked—hair in a messy bun that had lost the battle with gravity hours ago, dark circles blooming under her eyes, and that tight line between her brows that only showed up when the weight of everything got too heavy.

"Never mind me, how are you doing, baby sister?" I asked, softer than I meant to, which always happened with her.

"Don't change the subject." Magnolia popped open the top of the pizza box I'd brought—Vinnie Van GoGo's, of course—and peeled off a slice. "Sutton swears she saw her cuddled up with some guy in front of the fireplace at the coffee shop."

I clenched my jaw. "So I've heard. Sutton needs to mind her damn business."

"And you," I said, jabbing a finger in her direction, "Could stop playing matchmaker and maybe focus on the fact that your fiancé skipped town for Christmas and your ex-boyfriend looks five seconds away from throwing you over his shoulder and disappearing into a dark corner every time he sees you."

"You sure you don't care? Because I know you. I've seen what happens when you try not to catch feelings and fail miserably. You go broody. You get weird."

"I'm not getting weird."

"You are deeply weird right now," she said calmly. "Which is fine. But I think you like her."

"Again, maybe you should focus on your own drama. And trust me, sis, you have plenty of it."

Magnolia raised an eyebrow. "I'd love to pass the drama baton, thank you very much. You haven't dated in *years*, and you certainly haven't been this twitchy since that girl from SCAD ghosted you mid-sculpture."

I rolled my eyes. "I've dated, Mags. Don't be ridiculous."

She gave me a long, unimpressed look. "Charlie, you and I were two minutes away from becoming the Southern Gothic version of *Grey Gardens*—just two emotionally stunted siblings holed up in a crumbling bar, talking to our dead relatives and scaring off tourists."

I groaned, dragging a hand down my face. "Oh, please, Magnolia. Really rich coming from someone who finally has a boyfriend after years of swearing off men because her first love broke her heart—and now she's swatting said first love away like a gnat who won't leave her alone, but she secretly *loves* it."

Magnolia had the nerve to smirk. "Again, I would love to volley the drama."

"There's no drama," I muttered, reaching for another slice of pizza—my fourth, maybe fifth, I'd lost track. Emotional damage was apparently carb-fueled tonight.

"I don't even know what it is with her," I went on, quieter now. "She's just... whenever she's around, suddenly my skin feels too tight. Like I'm breaking out in hives, or I can't breathe right."

Magnolia narrowed her eyes, catching it before I could stop myself. "Charlie—"

"You'd think I'd be used to that by now," I added quickly, trying to cover, waving a hand between us. "I've spent my entire life sharing oxygen with you."

From inside the bar, it probably came off as a joke. A sarcastic jab between siblings. But from the open to-go window, where a certain poodle had just barked loud enough to turn heads, it landed like a punch to the gut.

Magnolia turned toward the sound, squinting through the glass. "Oh. Oh, my God. Was that—"

I was already on my feet, barstool screeching backward across the floor as I lunged for the door.

"Tally!"

She was already halfway down the sidewalk, her shoulders rigid, Nancy Reagan trotting furiously beside her like she, too, was deeply offended. A fine mist had started to fall in soft, silvery threads that caught in the streetlights, and by the time I caught sight of her face, she looked washed out. Blank in a way that made my stomach lurch.

She didn't turn around until I called her name again. When she did, her expression didn't crack.

"Not sure why you're chasing after me if you don't like me," she said flatly. "Wouldn't want you to break out in hives just standing beside me."

The words hit me like a sucker punch, and my throat tightened. "You weren't supposed to hear that."

"Well," she said, tucking a piece of hair behind her ear with fingers that weren't quite steady, "I did. Loud and clear. So—thanks for the clarity."

"Tally, wait. I didn't mean—"

"Yes, you did." Her voice wasn't angry. It wasn't raised. But it was steady in that way that meant she was holding in what she really wanted to say. "You meant every word. And it's fine. You can relax. I don't want to be your problem. I never did."

I stepped forward, useless. "Tally—"

She exhaled, one slow breath that cracked between us like thunder. Then she looked at me—really looked—and it felt like standing dead center in a storm I hadn't seen coming.

It was the look I'd dreaded since the moment I met her. That sharp, unflinching way she saw people, the same way she did behind her camera lens. And now, she'd found it in me—the thing I'd buried so deep I thought no one could touch it. That beneath all the steady, reliable armor was a man bluffing his way through, desperate for the world not to notice he had no idea what the hell he was doing.

"You're doing my brother a favor." Her voice wavered, then steadied. "And I thought… I don't know what I thought. I guess I let myself believe all the little moments meant more than they did. But now I get it. Message received."

The rain picked up, gentle but persistent, flattening her curls and darkening the hem of her dress. Nancy Reagan gave a single bark, judgy and unimpressed, before they both turned and walked away, shoulders high, spine straight, dignity fully intact.

And I didn't chase her.

Because maybe this time—whether I meant it that way or not—I'd earned the walk away.

CHAPTER TWENTY-SIX

Tally

The rain had started soft, barely a breath against my skin—as if the sky couldn't decide if it wanted to cry or not. Kind of like how *I* couldn't decide if I wanted to cry or not. But a few blocks from O'Malley's, it made up its mind. The mist turned to a steady, warm drizzle, slicking the cobblestones beneath my feet, painting the streetlights in hazy halos, and muffling the city's usual chatter into a gentle hum.

I didn't run. I didn't pull up my hood. I walked.

It felt like the city was exhaling with me, and maybe I could loosen my grip on everything—the shame, the panic, the tightness behind my ribs—and exist. For a minute. For a block. For as long as I needed.

Nighttime in Savannah was when the real charm broke through the bustle. She was older, quieter, alive in a way that didn't need to shout through the iridescent glaze of the moon. Gas lanterns flickered beside chipped bricks, casting golden halos that danced along the wet pavement. The Spanish moss above me swayed in slow motion, like it was watching me from above, patient and unbothered. A cargo ship groaned in the distance, its whistle breaking the stillness.

I turned down a side street without thinking, Nancy padding beside me like a soggy, judgmental cloud. She stopped to sniff a fire hydrant with the gravitas of someone solving a cold case, then looked up at me with sullen chocolate-brown eyes.

"I know," I murmured, brushing damp hair from my eyes. "I was an idiot. I shouldn't have stormed off like that."

But it wasn't about Charlie. It wasn't what I'd overheard. It was everything. The weight of not belonging. Of being the one who always showed up too late, with too much baggage and not enough answers. I'd spent most of my life being a visitor. A layover in someone else's story. Never the destination.

And yet… here.

Here, even angry and embarrassed and soaking wet, a spark of hope uncoiled inside me. Like maybe this place didn't care about my past. Maybe it only cared that I kept showing up.

I stopped in front of a bakery with fogged-up windows, the warm glow inside casting silhouettes of someone folding dough, dusting flour from their apron. Across the street, two college kids ducked under a tiny umbrella, laughing like it didn't matter that they were already soaked. A group of older tourists shuffled past a ghost tour guide with a cane and a top hat, who looked like he'd been pulled straight from a Dickens novel. And they were all… here. Living, moving forward.

For the first time since landing in Savannah, I wasn't watching from the sidelines. Maybe I was already part of the story. Maybe this was the start. It was messy and imperfect, sure, but finally, there were words on the page.

Nancy Reagan gave a little sneeze beside me, shaking the water from her wiry curls, and I crouched to scratch behind her ears.

"I think we might be falling in love with this place," I whispered.

She sneezed again, which felt like a yes.

The poodle paused to sniff at what I was sure was some other dog's disgusting pile in the grass while I slowed my steps, one hand resting on the curve of my belly. My dress clung to my skin, damp and a little chilled, but I didn't mind. It grounded me in the moment—this strange, in-between moment where I wasn't quite the girl I used to be and not yet the woman I hoped I'd become.

I kept seeing Charlie's face. The way his mouth twitched when he was trying not to smile. The way his voice dropped low whenever he said anything kind and tried to pass it off as an insult. The way he stood there, looking torn between staying silent and fighting for what he didn't want to admit he cared about.

He'd said he didn't like me. That being around me gave him hives.

And yet… he'd carried me up five flights of stairs. Cleaned up after me. Took me to my appointment, eyes filled with wonder at the life growing inside me. Slept on a too-small couch to make sure I wouldn't wake up alone.

That didn't seem like someone who didn't care. That seemed like someone who didn't know how to do it.

And what was worse—I kept noticing all of it. I kept letting it get to me.

That little softness in his voice. His hands hovering near my back when he thought I might trip. The way his eyes found me when he didn't think I'd notice—frustration and awe tangled together, like I was a puzzle he couldn't solve but couldn't stop trying to.

It was infuriating. And comforting. And confusing.

I stopped at Whitefield Square, the white gazebo where Charlotte and Hoyt said their vows was cold and slick with rain, but offering a necessary shelter from the drizzle. The benches were slightly damp, but I sat anyway, my dog curling up beside my feet, and I tipped my head back to look at the thick canopy of moss above me. The branches swayed in the breeze, heavy with water and history.

What the hell was happening to me?

Savannah was getting under my skin. Charlie was getting under my skin. And I wasn't sure which scared me more.

All I'd ever wanted was to belong somewhere. To be seen and accepted and not just tolerated. And maybe it was starting to happen here, in a city I barely knew, with a man who looked at me like I was fire and he didn't mind the burn.

I let out a shaky breath and rubbed a hand over my belly.

"We're in trouble, little one."

Nancy groaned softly, shifting closer, and I smiled faintly.

We stayed like that until the rain lightened, until the silence stopped feeling lonely and started to feel like peace.

And when the rain started up again, and the tall, iron street lights cast a soft glow over the quiet square, the city didn't feel so big anymore. It felt close and familiar, a place that I might be able to hold onto if I stopped running long enough to try.

CHAPTER TWENTY-SEVEN

Charlie

The rain had started coming down harder, and she was still nowhere to be found. I moved through the penthouse like a storm myself—back and forth, trying to keep calm, trying to reason through it—but every pass in front of the kitchen counter made it worse. Her phone sat there, useless and infuriating, vibrating now and then with the buzz of another unanswered call or ignored message, as if she might somehow reach through the air and grab it. As if she wasn't already out there somewhere, alone.

MAGNOLIA: *any word?*
SUTTON: *doyle's gonna murder you if you lost his sister, ya big dumb idiot*
LEE: *ryan & i are free—want us to check this side of town?*
CHARLIE: *no, don't. you'll just get soaked. I'll head out.*
DOYLE: *YOU LOST MY SISTER?!?! WTF CHARLIE*
MAGNOLIA: *shit. wrong group chat*

I slammed my phone down next to hers and let out a string of quiet curses. The clatter of the two devices knocked hers enough to light up the screen—and there it was.

A poodle-shaped tracker pulsing on a map.

Nancy Reagan. She had a damn GPS on the dog. I grabbed both phones and zoomed in. The little poodle icon had stopped moving—settled somewhere in Whitefield Square.

CHARLIE: *found her.*

I didn't even bother with the truck. Just took off on foot, dodging pedestrians and slick patches of cobblestone, barely registering the sound of horns or the taste of rain slicking down my face. I couldn't risk the delay of getting it out of the garage or wading through Hoyt's weather commentary and useless small talk. My only goal was distance—closing the one-mile gap between my studio and Whitefield Square.

I ran harder than I had in years.

Each step pressed the weight deeper into my chest—fear, guilt, frustration. But underneath it, a seed of hopefulness had begun to bloom. A slow, reluctant, dangerous vine.

I told myself it was about keeping her safe. That she ran because of me—because I said too much, or not enough. Because I was the one who always had to make it right, who fixed broken things even if I wasn't the one who broke them and especially if it was me wielding the hammer. It's what I do. But the more I moved—heart pounding, lungs burning—the more the excuses began to unravel.

This wasn't about duty. This wasn't about Doyle or my sister or all the eyes that were on me watching me unravel at the seams. This wasn't even about the damn poodle.

I wanted her near me. I wanted *her.*

And the realization hit with such force that it nearly stopped me in my tracks. But the square was ahead, the white gazebo rising out of the darkness like a castle in a fever dream, glowing under the dull yellow wash of a lamplight. I slowed my pace—not because I wasn't desperate to see her, but because I didn't want to barrel in like a man unhinged. I didn't want her to see how out of breath I was, how hard I'd run just to get to her.

Just to be near her.

But then—screw it. I picked up speed again.

Nancy Reagan saw me first, all scraggly fur and righteous indignation, hopping around in demented circles, half barking, half growling, her own personal brand of greeting. She lunged, then froze, as if trying to decide whether to bite me or throw me a parade.

Tally stood suddenly, eyes scanning the square. Her hair was damp and

curling around her face, and her clothes clung in all the places that made it difficult for me to form a single coherent thought.

And I probably looked like I'd come out of the sea—soaked to the skin,
hair dripping, chest heaving from the run. She took a step toward me and froze.

"Charlie—"

But I didn't let her say anything else.

I climbed the steps of the gazebo and stopped in front of her, the rain
pounding against the roof overhead, the air thick with tension and the scent of
warm pavement and wild winter storm.

I was angry. But not at her. I was angry with myself. Frustrated, and
fractured at how deeply I'd gotten tangled up in this without even realizing it. At
how deeply I'd gotten tangled up in this *woman*. At how scared I was to admit
what I was feeling for her.

She looked up at me then, lip trembling slightly, a little breathless, hair
sticking to her temple, and I couldn't take it anymore.

I didn't ask. I didn't speak. I reached for her, inch by inch, leaving space
for her to pull away.

She didn't.

My hand found the slope of her jaw, fingers trembling enough to betray
me. She didn't pull away. If anything, she leaned in. The pad of my thumb traced
her cheekbone, slow and reverent, and for one suspended breath, she let her eyes
fall closed. Like we'd finally caught up to the moment that had been waiting for
us all along.

I took it all in. Every rain-slicked eyelash, every freckle softened by the
wet streetlamp glow, every rise and fall of her breath as she stood perfectly still,
letting me hold her in the quiet. Her eyes fluttered open again—wide, uncertain,
bright-hazel eyes full of questions neither of us dared to ask.

And then I dipped my head. Not to kiss her. Not yet. But close enough
that our foreheads touched, damp skin pressed together, both of us breathing in
the same tight pocket of air. Her breath caught. Mine was already lost. My other
hand slid to her waist, steadying us both, and still, we didn't speak.

She was shaking slightly. Or maybe I was.

She tilted her chin up a fraction, barely noticeable unless you were looking for it. But I was looking—God, I'd been looking—and that was all it took.

I closed the distance.

The kiss started gently, hesitant at first, like a thread pulling tight between us. But then she sighed—soft and broken—and the sound unraveled every bit of restraint I had left.

I pulled back just far enough to study her face, chest heaving, searching for the faintest sign that she didn't want this—that she didn't want *me*. That she didn't need me the way I needed her, in the way a soul needs a body, an artist needs a muse. But all I found was light. Mischief. That *don't you dare stop* gleam that knocked the breath clean out of me. And that was all it took.

My mouth found hers again, harder this time, the kind of kiss that left no air between us. My fingers slipped into her damp hair, the heat of her skin searing through me. She gripped my shirt like she needed to anchor herself, and I let go of every wall, every warning, every bit of control I'd been clinging to.

It wasn't neat. It wasn't careful.

It was heat and rain and the wild, aching truth of two people who'd been circling the same fire for far too long.

And when she kissed me back—really kissed me, hungry and sure—I forgot every reason I wasn't supposed to be here. Forgot every rule I'd written for myself. Every wall I'd spent years holding up.

She was the storm.

And I walked straight into it.

CHAPTER TWENTY-EIGHT

Tally

His hands were warm, sliding into my hair, anchoring me right where I was, and it was almost too much. Not the kiss—no, that part was perfect—but everything wrapped inside it. The tenderness buried under all that control, the way his breath hitched when mine did, like we were caught in the same rhythm.

The weight of everything unsaid pressed between us—two months of near-misses and small disasters, of learning each other's edges and soft spots, of Charlie showing up in every way that mattered without ever being asked. It was all there: in the lingering looks, the arguments that weren't really about what they seemed, in every *almost* that had burned itself into my skin.

And now it lived in this—the slide of his mouth against mine, the firm hold of his hand at the back of my neck, the unspoken certainty that this had always been coming. We'd finally stopped pretending we could fight it.

And I let him kiss me the way you do when you're trying to find life in another person's touch—not because I trusted him not to hurt me, not completely, but because, for once, I trusted myself. Trusted that what I felt wasn't a mistake or a hormonal blur or an accident of timing. It was real. It was happening.

His mouth was gentle and unhurried, but there was tension beneath it, a held breath in his chest that trembled under my hands. When I pressed my fingers to the front of his shirt, his exhale moved through me, slow and shuddering.

Everything inside me cracked open with that sound.

His voice came low and rough, worn thin at the edges. "I thought I'd lost you. I'm so sorry, Tally, I—"

I shook my head, trying to knock myself out of whatever spell that kiss had cast. Because my feelings were still hurt. And Charlie had been the one who hurt them.

But the way he looked at me then—that wasn't performance. That wasn't panic. That was someone stripped bare. That was someone telling the truth with more than just his mouth. His hands hadn't moved from my waist, and I hadn't pulled away. Because in his arms, everything felt… aligned. Solid. Like I'd finally slotted into the space that had always been carved out for me, even if neither of us had known it until now.

And maybe that was foolish. Perhaps I was about to look back on this and wince.

Wouldn't be the first time.

"Did you mean it?" I asked. The words tasted bitter. "What you said. Back at the bar."

His hand rose again, gently. Two fingers brushed the edge of my lips, tracing the shape like a memory he didn't want to forget, his thumb pausing at the corner of my mouth like it hurt to let go.

"You're not going to love this, but—on the surface? Yeah. I meant it."

I jerked back, but his hands found my waist again, holding me in place— not possessive, only sure.

"No—Tally, listen. You make me feel like I'm going to break out in hives. But not because you annoy me." He exhaled, clearly flustered. "I mean—okay, you do irritate me sometimes, but that's not the point."

I blinked up at him, dumbfounded. "So… you kissed me because I give you a rash?"

Charlie groaned, tilting his head back. "God, I'm so bad at this."

"No argument here," I muttered.

"I said something stupid. I know that," he said, quieter now, almost a confession. "Because the truth is—being around you these few months has messed with my head. I don't do unpredictability. I don't like it when things change. But then you showed up and… now I'm making sure my studio fridge is stocked with iced tea and olives. I'm freaking my friends out because I'm talking about something other than art they don't understand, and the concept of reclamation as a means to recycle. I'm losing sleep on a too-small couch just in case you need me in the middle of the night."

He paused, his eyes searching mine.

"You make me nervous, Tally. In the kind of way that keeps me up at night, wondering what else I could get you to say—what other sounds I could pull from you—just by putting my mouth on you." He closed the little space I'd created between us, head dipping down so his lips grazed my ear. "You have no idea what you do to me, darlin'."

A grin tugged at my mouth before I could stop it. "Charlie Pruitt," I said, leaning in, "You've got a crush on me."

His hands finally dropped from my waist, long enough for him to rake a hand through his rain-dark curls, plastered to his forehead. The scowl was gone, replaced by mischief and certainty—an expression that made it very clear he knew exactly what he was doing.

"Yes, Tally Aden," he said, stepping in so close his breath mingled with mine. "I've got a wicked crush on you."

And then he kissed me again, deeper this time, unapologetically. No hesitation. Only heat, and rain, and the hum of a new spark curling to life between us.

The kind that felt an awful lot like falling.

***

Fresh out of the shower, my hair still damp and curling at the ends, I was wrapped in one of Jordan's oversized robes, dabbing moisturizer under my eyes when Dig's name lit up my phone.

I answered on the second ring, propping him against the sink.

Dig, in full crab regalia, rhinestones glittering across his forehead, sitting under the fluorescent lights of what looked like a high school auditorium dressing room, squealed as he appeared on screen. The claws on his costume twitched every time he moved.

"I heard there was kissing," he said without so much as a hello. "Gazebo. Rain. Emotional carnage. Tell me everything."

I groaned. "You called me two hours ago and I replayed the whole thing. Twice."

"Yes, and this is a follow-up. A debrief. A necessary encore. Tally, we are building a scrapbook here."

He broke into song immediately, belting at full volume, *"I am sixteen going on seventeen—blessèd by the Lordddd—"*

"Okay no," I said, dragging a hand down my face as I crossed the room and climbed into bed. "You are not allowed to *Sound of Music* me right now."

"Sorry, I'm in a heightened emotional state and only Rogers and Hammerstein can anchor me back to the earth," he said, still humming, waving a bejeweled claw. "But in all fairness, so are you."

I bit the inside of my cheek, trying not to smile, even as the memory crept in.

The kiss. The walk back. The way Charlie had slipped his hand into mine like it was second nature—his grip firm, thumb brushing along my knuckles in a quiet kind of reassurance. In his other hand, he held Nancy Reagan's leash, her old-lady trot perfectly matching the stillness between us. We didn't talk, only walked through hushed, rain-slick streets that shimmered under the low spill of the streetlamps until we reached the penthouse. He opened the door, waited until I was upstairs and behind the bathroom door, before retreating to the other guest room like nothing had happened.

Except it had.

"I think I might be in trouble," I said finally.

Dig leaned closer to the screen, eyes gleaming. "What kind of trouble?"

"The falling for someone who's sleeping twenty feet away from me and holding my dog's leash kind."

He pressed both claws to his chest. "Sweet baby Jesus in a Target nativity set, it's happening."

A soft knock at the door jolted both Dig and me from our giggle haze, his bedazzled crab antennae bouncing like they were reacting to the sudden shift in energy.

"I'll let you go," he whispered, eyes glinting with mischief. "I'd say wear protection, but you can't get more pregnant, so…"

"Oh my God, goodbye." I jabbed at the screen, hanging up mid-cackle, and launched the phone onto the bed. "Come in!"

Why was I shouting?

The door eased open, and there he was.

Charlie stood leaning against the frame, damp curls pushed back from his forehead, arms crossed over his chest. He'd showered—fresh skin, flushed cheeks, a clean t-shirt clinging to his torso. A faint trail of cedar and pine trailed behind him, mingling with the scent of my lavender lotion, and it made the air in the room tilt.

"Hey, you," he said, voice low and lazy, like we'd slipped into a moment that belonged only to us. His eyes swept over me—bathrobe, bare feet, probably mascara smudged under one eye—but there was no judgment in them. Just awareness and a whispered kind of adoration.

My breath caught. Because all of a sudden, words were hard. And that had never happened to me before. Not once.

He chuckled softly under his breath, his lips twitching as if he knew exactly what he was doing to me. "Come on," he said, tipping his chin toward the hallway. "I set up some snacks. I thought we could watch a movie or something."

Or something.

I nodded, mumbled a word in the shape of a "yeah," then shut the door and scrambled to change, preparing for what felt like a date but was most definitely, probably, not a date.

A few minutes later, in soft leggings and one of Doyle's stolen cashmere sweaters that I refused to return, I stepped into the main room—and stopped short.

The living room had been transformed.

Short, stout candles lined the windowsill and coffee table, flickering low and golden. The TV was paused on the opening screen of *The Princess Bride.* And in the middle of it all, Charlie had assembled what could only be described as a miracle.

A takeout spread worthy of saints and hormonal women alike.

French fries from four different restaurants were arranged in mismatched bowls on the coffee table, still steaming, sprinkled with sea salt and pepper and a dash of what smelled suspiciously truffle-y. Next to them, three kinds of pickles—dill, bread and butter, and a weird spicy variety I loved from the shop—were set out like appetizers at a five-star deli. And sitting proudly at the center was a Shirley Temple in a highball glass, garnished with not one but *seven* maraschino cherries skewered on a cocktail sword.

I turned to find him already watching me, a dish towel slung over one shoulder, his eyes impossibly soft but intense enough to knock the wind from my lungs.

"You said you've been craving fries and pickles, so I figured we'd do a taste test." His voice was casual, but the way he looked at me wasn't. It was heavy.

Hungry, in the kind of way that wasn't about food.

I crossed to the couch slowly, afraid that if I moved too fast, I'd spook whatever magic had settled into this room.

"This is…" I swallowed. "Charlie, this is *so much.*"

He shrugged, grabbing the remote, eyes still tracking me as we both took our seats. "Yeah, well. You deserve good things."

I sat, stunned and silent for a beat, watching the candlelight flicker over his profile. Watching him see me—really *see* me—in a way no one had for a very long time. Maybe not ever.

Nancy Reagan trotted in from the guest bedroom and made herself a little nest between us on the couch with a sigh so dramatic it could've won her an Emmy.

Charlie laughed under his breath, passed me a plate of fries, and asked, "You ready?"

CHAPTER TWENTY-NINE

Charlie

A soft snore stirred me awake—sharp, wheezy, unmistakably canine—
and it took me a second to remember where I was. The candles were still burning
low across the windowsill, casting slow, warm shadows across the living room.
The TV screen had frozen on the credits, some long forgotten names glowing
white on black.

I eased back and glanced toward the sound.

Tally was curled on the couch, one arm folded beneath her, the other
resting over the small rise of her stomach. Her legs tucked in, her body turned
inward, as if she could protect what she loved by keeping it close. Nancy Reagan
slept in a ball at her feet, snoring with the kind of raspy determination only an
old poodle could muster.

I should've woken her and told her to move to the bed to get some proper
rest. But instead I sat there, watching her sleep in the flickering candlelight, caught
in a silence that felt too sacred to break.

It was strange what a handful of days could do. How we had teetered on
the edge of this for months, and now it was finally here, and nothing in the world
felt more comfortable than this moment between us.

She'd swept into my life like a tornado, shaking the foundation that I'd
been so proud to stand so firmly on, knocking down the walls that I'd spent so
long trying to keep up, keeping everyone in my life tucked safe inside.

Tally Aden didn't just rattle those walls. She made me want to knock them
down and look at all the parts of myself I'd kept sealed off, too busy taking care of
everyone else to wonder if I even liked the life I'd built for myself.

She wasn't fixing me. That wasn't her job. But somehow, in her messy, relentless way, she was changing my heart, one day at a time.

I could have watched her sleep all night, but the thought made me sound a little less like a man teetering on the verge of falling for this woman and a little more like a serial killer, so I gently nudged her awake.

"Why don't you lie in bed, baby girl?" I said as she stirred, my voice still rough from sleep. She blinked up at me, slow and sweet, the corner of her mouth curling toward a smile. Her sweater hung loose off one shoulder, and everything about her in that moment—rumpled, flushed, impossibly soft—pulled at my chest.

"It's pretty late," I added, half hoping she'd take the hint, half terrified she might.

Tally stretched, arms overhead, her hand brushing against mine before dropping into her lap. When she met my gaze, I saw it. That shadow of desire—unspoken, but clear as day. A beat of silence settled between us, heavy with this impossible thing we kept circling, never quite brave enough to touch.

Then she nodded, quietly. "Yeah. Okay."

She stood, gave me one last glance that should've been illegal, and padded down the hall with Nancy trailing behind her, tail swishing like she knew she'd won her mother all to herself.

I stood there for a second too long in the stillness, then turned, blew out the last of the candles, and lowered myself onto the too-small loveseat that had already wrecked the left side of my body that week.

She wasn't even in the room anymore, and I still felt the echo of her—her laugh, her breath on my neck from earlier, her hand in mine as we walked home. I closed my eyes and saw her smile, the way she'd looked at me under that damn gazebo, rain clinging to her lashes.

The cushions were lumpy, the expensive—probably cashmere—throw blanket barely covered my chest, and the streetlight outside was flickering maddeningly, casting a disco ball–like stream of light over the living room. But the worst part—the absolute worst part—was knowing she was right down the hall, tucked into bed, that soft, delicate sweater wrapped around her in a way that I wanted to be. And I couldn't stop imagining what it would feel like to crawl in beside her, to pull her close, and pretend we had more than this borrowed, strange moment between us.

***

Before the sky even thought about lighting, I was already up, elbow-deep in Doyle and Jordan's junk drawer, sorting things that didn't need sorting. The acrylic containers were already lined up like a showroom display, but I rearranged them anyway—tape rolls by size, post-its by color family, pens laid out in neat rows, even though I was pretty sure half of them didn't actually work.

It didn't do a damn thing to calm me down.

I was halfway through debating whether to alphabetize the spice rack or kick open her door and show her, in great detail, what other fun things my mouth could do, when I heard the faint click of claws on tile. Nancy entered first, her nails tapping out a disapproving rhythm, as if she could read my thoughts. Tally followed a few seconds later, hair shoved into a messy knot, one sleeve falling off her shoulder, eyes still puffy from sleep.

She didn't say anything as she stood there watching me crouched over a drawer, every nerve on edge, trying to remember why I cared so damn much.

And then her expression eased, barely enough to notice. Not a smile, not even softness really—just a little looser around the edges. Whatever it was made her look less like she was already halfway out the door. For the first time since she got here, it felt like she wasn't passing through anymore.

But whatever that moment was, it flashed and vanished.

"Doyle'll be back soon," she said, heading to the fridge like this was any other morning. "Guess that means you'll be off the hook. What'll you do with yourself once I'm out of your hair and everything goes back to normal?"

She said it breezily, but tension ran beneath the words. A thread pulled tight, waiting to snap. She was daring me to open my mouth, to admit I didn't want her to leave.

I squared my shoulders, bracing myself with a hand on the counter. When she looked at me again, her gaze lingered for a heartbeat on my chest, and the look she gave me this time wasn't quite teasing. It had teeth.

And because I'm a dumbass, I opened my mouth and said the worst possible thing.

"Don't you have a boyfriend?"

Her expression froze long enough to register the hit. Then she blinked and reached for a glass like I hadn't just punched her with my insecurity.

"Pretty sure everyone knows what happened when Nick showed up here a few weeks ago," she said. "So, no. No boyfriend."

"Right." My voice came out rougher than I meant it. "So then, there's not someone here, in Savannah? That you went to coffee with not that long ago."

She stopped mid-motion, the glass in her hand barely hanging on. "Come again?"

"At Savannah Coffee Roasters. Sutton said you were… canoodling. With someone."

Her stare went flat. Then she barked out a laugh so loud it bounced off the marble backsplash.

"Canoodling? Jesus, Charlie. That was Dig. We were having one of those bestie moments in front of the fireplace, and Sutton happened to walk by. But, no, definitely not canoodling. Unless you count having to listen to Dig recite a monologue about a misbehaving crawfish as foreplay."

I dragged a hand across the back of my neck, still standing there like I'd forgotten how conversation worked. Idiot didn't even begin to cover it.

Tally had almost reached the lanai before she stopped. She turned slowly, arms folded tight across her chest, mouth set in that unreadable way she had when she was either about to tear me apart or crack a joke.

"So let me get this straight," she said, voice calm but with an edge enough to slice me clean. "You chased me through the streets in the rain, kissed me under a gazebo like we were starring in a Nicholas Sparks fever dream, spent half the night looking at me like you were trying to crawl in my pants and set up shop there—and *that whole time*, you thought I had a boyfriend?"

I opened my mouth. Not a single word made it out.

She didn't look mad. Not exactly. She looked amused. Dangerous.

"You ever think to just, I don't know, *ask me?*"

I blinked. "Guess I didn't want the answer."

She let that hang there for a second, tilting her head like she was trying to figure out what part of me was most emotionally constipated.

Then she grinned. Slow. Familiar. A little smug.

"You've got it bad," she said, already stepping backward through the open door. "And trust me—I can smell that sort of thing from a mile away."

She wasn't wrong.

I followed her out onto the patio, the tile warm from the morning sun. The light caught her in a way that made her look almost otherworldly—hair haloed, the river spread out behind her, the Talmadge Bridge standing tall in the distance. She rested one hand on the curve of her belly, fingers curling there like it was the most natural thing in the world, her gaze fixed on the horizon as if it might give her the answer to some question she hadn't asked out loud. I wanted to be the one with a camera in that moment, wanted to catch her exactly like this, so I could look at it later and remember the ache in my chest.

"Would you think me forward if I asked a question?"

She didn't look away from the water. "You've asked me a lot of questions, Charlie. What's so different about this one?"

I came to stand beside her, leaning my elbows on the railing. "Do you plan on staying? In Savannah, I mean."

Her eyes stayed on the river. The silence stretched long enough that I wondered if she'd answer at all. When she finally turned toward me, it was slow, deliberate.

"I have a problem… staying places."

I let out a short laugh. "Care to elaborate?"

She crossed to the iron chair and sank into it, the sun sliding across her face. "I don't know. I guess I've always thought that when I found where I'm supposed to be, I'd know it. Like everything would somehow click into place, and I'd be home."

I sat down next to her, my arm brushing the back of her chair. "I can't say I get that. I was born eighteen miles from here and never really left. My whole life is here. Everyone I love is here. Savannah's as much a part of me as I am of it."

She set her hand in mine, light and tentative, and looked down at the swell of her stomach. "I've never felt that before. But it's all so different now."

I knew what she meant in ways she probably didn't expect because the thing that was different for her was changing me, too, in ways I hadn't planned for.

"I thought Nick was different," she said, her gaze flicking toward me like she was checking for signs I might pull away. I didn't move. I wanted to hear her out. "But before him, I'd fallen in love in Australia—hard. The kind you don't bounce back from quickly. He wanted the wild, table-dancing version of me, the one who stayed out all night. But I got tired of that. I wanted something

211

more… steady."

Her voice trailed, and she smoothed her hand over her thigh. "When I went back to New York, Nick and I became friends first. I guess I didn't realize he was more of a rebound than anything real. Or that he was telling me what I wanted to hear to get what he wanted. He got it, and then… well, you know the rest."

I studied her, the light shifting on her face, the small set of her jaw. "So he didn't see the real you. He saw the version you let him see."

She tilted her head toward the river again, the bridge holding steady in the distance. "Most people start out loving the wild version of me. But eventually, they want less. Or more. And then they try to change me into the person they wanted all along. Like they just… settled with me."

Without thinking, I reached up and brushed a tear from her cheek. "Only a fool would call it settling with you, Tal."

She gave me a smile that didn't quite reach her eyes, and I gave her one back anyway.

"I see you, Tally," I said, my voice low, careful. "You keep asking for someone to love you, but don't you see? You are love. You smile at strangers. You wave to babies. You cry when old couples walk by holding hands. You whisper prayers when an ambulance passes. You cheer for people, even when they don't cheer for you. You make space for those who feel like there's no room left in the world for them at all."

Her eyes blinked, holding mine, and I could see it land—like she was letting herself hear it, really hear it.

"Can I tell you a secret, Charlie?" Her voice was quiet, almost unsure. "I think motherhood is going to change me more than anyone or anything else ever could. And that scares the shit out of me."

It might change her. Or it could take the wild parts of her and shape them into the best kind of mother this baby could ever have. But she was already changing, rooting herself into this city, into this life, whether she knew it or not. We were all watering her in our own ways, little by little.

"They'll never be bored, that's for sure," she sighed.

And right then, I hoped I never would be either.

CHAPTER THIRTY

Tally

We'd been at the studio all day. Charlie was hunched over the final stretch of Magnolia's portrait, brush moving in short, precise strokes while his t-shirt pulled just enough across his back to make it criminally hard to concentrate. I was curled up on the loveseat, laptop open in front of me, pretending to care about editing Hoyt and Charlotte's wedding album, but really, I was watching him. Watching the way his hand hovered before it landed, the way his jaw flexed when he was focused.

We hadn't kissed again, but the space between us had gone tight. Electric. Every glance stretched too long. Every brush past each other in the narrow studio hallway felt like it could tip us over the edge. And maybe it was the hormones, or the hours of silence humming like a live wire, but eventually I couldn't take it anymore.

"Let's walk the dog," I'd said—casual, breezy, like I wasn't moments from crawling out of my skin.

Charlie barely looked up. "She's asleep."

"But she loves a good sunset," I'd lied. "And besides, it's good for the joints."

Before I could change my mind, I was texting Franny Jo. I needed air. Motion. An industrial sized fan to cool the flush climbing up my neck.

Franny Jo pulled up in a horse-drawn sleigh that looked like Santa threw up on it. String lights blinked along the frame, candy canes dangled from the railings, and the whole thing smelled faintly of cinnamon and horse manure. She handed Charlie a dented thermos with a warning about sipping slow—"It's from the good batch"—and passed me a chilled bottle of water with a wink, like she didn't just hand him a one-way ticket to blackout moonshine island.

"The usual spot, Tal?" Franny Jo asked, glancing over her shoulder with a look that was equal parts curiosity and suspicion as she clocked Charlie beside me.

The carriage crept through the sleepy, sun-warmed squares of Savannah, the horse's hooves echoing against brick and stone. I leaned back against the cushioned bench and let myself take it in. Every moss-lined street looked different that day, the way everything does when you're sitting beside someone who changes how you see things.

Savannah had already made its case, curling under my skin and asking me to stay.

And who was I to say no?

But after that kiss in the rain, it wasn't only the city holding on to me.

It was him.

And I wanted him to ask me to stay.

He'd been the one to bring it up, to ask if I saw myself in Savannah for more than a moment. And when he asked, I'd opened my heart in ways I wasn't used to—letting him see the cracked, dented parts of the woman who'd spent too much time falling in love while quietly falling apart.

Charlie had asked if I was going to stay, but he'd never asked me *to* stay. And no, I didn't need a man to decide my place in the world. But if he wanted me here, I wanted to hear it from him.

Beside me, Charlie unscrewed the lid of the thermos and took a cautious sip. He gagged instantly, coughing as he tried to pass it off with a weak thumbs-up that fooled no one.

Franny Jo cackled. "Careful, sugar. That stuff'll grow hair on your kneecaps."

Charlie wheezed. "Pretty sure I'm good on knee hair, thanks."

She grinned and gave me a knowing look. At the base of River Street, she pulled the carriage up to the curb and winked. "See you next week for those Instabook shots, right, Tal?"

Charlie stepped down first, then turned and held his hand out to me. I reached for him before I could think, my fingers sliding into his like they'd always belonged there. The city buzzed around us—the clop of hooves, the far-off rush of the river—but all I could register was his hand closing around mine. His thumb swept over my knuckles, slow and deliberate, a touch that seemed to say more than either of us had figured out how to put into words.

When I landed on the cobblestones, he didn't let go right away. We stood there, too close, the December light catching in his eyes, making them burn darker and warmer all at once. The air between us felt thin, threaded tight with everything we hadn't said.

"It's called Instagram, Franny. And yes—if my captor approves," I managed, still holding his gaze.

The corner of his mouth lifted. Maybe a question. Maybe an answer. Maybe the thing I'd been waiting to hear all along.

And then the horse behind us let out a truly biblical pile of steaming shit, breaking the moment clean in half. We both laughed, and with that, the spell was gone.

"Okay, I'm not really sure if you're joking or if you're actually under duress." Franny Jo shot Charlie a sideways glance. "But I'll leave you two to figure it out along the banks of the river. I've got poop to scoop."

We walked River Street with Nancy Reagan leading the charge, her leash slack in Charlie's free hand. His other hand had found mine somewhere between the cobblestones and the waterfront—no announcement, no hesitation, only his fingers threading through mine while cargo ships drifted past in the distance.

The evening light turned everything copper and soft. Tourists shuffled by with to-go cups and cameras. A street performer played something jazzy on a sax that echoed off the brick buildings. Nancy stopped to investigate every iron bench and lamppost, and neither of us rushed her.

We crawled up the cobblestone ramp from the river to the bustling street above, winding our way through the squares until we reached Broughton Street.

"Leopold's?" Charlie asked, nodding toward the crowd spilling out onto the sidewalk up ahead.

"Obviously."

The line wrapped around the corner—families with strollers, college kids in SCAD sweatshirts, a bachelor party wearing matching elf hats. It was December, barely sixty degrees, and somehow every human in the greater metropolitan area had decided tonight was the night for ice cream.

"Is this a thing?" I asked, watching a woman in a puffer jacket order three sundaes. "Ice cream in winter?"

"Leopold's is always a thing," Charlie said, stepping up behind an older couple debating butter pecan versus rum raisin with the intensity of a hostage negotiation. "Tourists don't care about the weather. Hell, half of them probably think this *is* summer. Probably warmer here than wherever they came from."

I laughed, and he squeezed my hand.

We shuffled forward in increments. Nancy sat between us, panting dramatically, performing her best impression of a dog on the verge of collapse. A little girl in a tutu crouched down to pet her, and Nancy—despite being a known terrorist—leaned into it like she'd been starved for affection her entire life.

"She's a con artist," Charlie muttered.

"She's a professional," I corrected.

By the time we made it to the counter, I'd already changed my order three times. Charlie got a single scoop of salted caramel in a cup, because of course he did—practical, contained, no risk of dripping. I got a banana split loaded with hot fudge, whipped cream, and enough toppings to require structural engineering.

"You're gonna regret that," he said as we stepped back onto the street.

"Probably."

But I didn't. We strolled toward Monterey Square, weaving through the evening foot traffic, Nancy trotting between us like she'd orchestrated the whole thing. I ate my ice cream too fast, and Charlie kept glancing over, half-amused, half-concerned I was going to choke.

When we hit the square, the light had shifted again—deeper now, the kind of gold that made everything look like a painting. The Mercer House loomed ahead, wrapped in tasteful garland and bows. Charlie steered us toward a bench, and I sank into it without thinking, pulling my legs up under me.

He sat beside me. Not on the opposite end. Right beside me, close enough that our knees touched.

And it didn't feel new. It felt like something we'd been doing for years. He leaned over and took a spoonful of my banana split, eyes on mine the whole time as if daring me to stop him. He shot me a playful wink as he licked the spoon clean.

"Not what it used to be, back in the day," Charlie said, nodding toward the sprawling mansion. A streak of whipped cream clung to the corner of his lip, and it took everything in me not to lean over and lick it off. Slowly.

"Jim Williams used to throw insane parties around Christmas," he continued, totally unaware of the internal meltdown I was having beside him. "Or so I've heard. I was too young to remember."

I forced myself to look away from the sweet cream slinking down his beard and up at the house instead. "Does anyone still live there? It looks like the kind of place that's definitely haunted."

"It's a museum now," he said, leaning back into the bench with a little grunt. We were both crammed into the right side of it, even though the left side had a perfectly good seat just waiting for him. "Magnolia, Lee, and I broke in there once when we were kids. We wanted to see if the ghost stories were true."

I whipped my head toward him. I didn't need a mirror to know my eyes were wild. "And? Were they?"

He grinned, eyes crinkling from the sun. "Not haunted by ghosts. Cats, though. Dozens of 'em. Lee's mom was working on the restoration at the time. She's an antiquarian."

I squinted. "I thought she just made that title up and threw parties all the time. That's a real job?"

"For her, yeah."

I snorted and looked back at the house, dragging my spoon through a streak of fudge. "Dig and I used to charge people fifty bucks to do séances in their rent-controlled Upper East Side apartments. Rich old ghosts are the chattiest— probably because they're used to having people listen to their nonsense."

Charlie's laugh melted into me. I didn't hear it often, but when I did, it curled around the edges of my chest and warmed some aching part of me I didn't know had gone cold.

"I'm not breaking into Mercer House again, if that's where this is going."

"It's not," I said, pointing to a row of houses off the square. "I'm asking you to break into that one. The blue one. That's the most haunted house on this street."

He turned toward me fully, and his arm, already draped across the back of the bench, dropped slightly so that his fingers brushed the bare part of my arm. I didn't move. I couldn't. His touch was light, casual, but a slow current buzzed beneath my skin, steady and unrelenting.

"And how exactly would you know that little tidbit from all the way over here?" he asked.

I shrugged, trying to look nonchalant even though my insides were doing cartwheels. "I just know these things. Call it intuition."

He huffed. "A séance would not be good for your blood pressure. Wouldn't want to go breaking any more of Doyle's rules."

I leaned into his side, nudging him with my shoulder. "He didn't say anything about séances. He said to watch my salt intake, try not to pass out, and stay hydrated. That's it."

"And that you need to eat actual food. Don't forget the gourmet meals I've been making."

"Oh, yes. Chef Charlie's signature dish: unseasoned air-fried chicken that disintegrates on contact. So far, we've ruined the carpet and the air fryer. Doyle's going to kill us."

He let out a deep, mock-offended sigh. "You wound me."

I glanced up at him. His arm was still behind me, fingers resting lightly on my shoulder now, thumb moving in slow, lazy strokes that made me forget whatever smart remark I'd been about to deliver.

And I knew if I turned to face him fully, if I leaned in even a little, he'd kiss me again, just like he had the night before in the rain. Maybe slower, deeper this time.

But I didn't. And neither did he.

Instead, we sat in the stillness of the park, watching the shadows lengthen as the twinkle of the Christmas lights winked around the square and on the porches of the homes surrounding it. His thumb kept brushing against my shoulder, steady as breath. His knee pressed into mine, grounding me. And for once, I didn't feel the need to fill the space between us with chatter.

I liked this side of Charlie. Studio-dwelling, rule-following, emotionally constipated Charlie was great. But this version—the one laughing beside me, ice cream melted into his beard, letting his arm linger without overthinking it, letting his presence say what he wouldn't—this was the one I was falling for.

And that scared me more than any haunted house ever could.

Charlie flicked a piece of banana from his jeans, then tipped his head my way, eyes bright. "You still want your séance?"

I turned to look at him, brows raised.

"I mean," he shrugged, a grin tugging at the corner of his mouth, "I do happen to know a bar that's been around long enough to have its own ghosts."

I narrowed my eyes. "Are you offering to break into O'Malley's?"

"Not break in," he said innocently. "I have a key. And access to the good candles."

I laughed, letting the sound slip out before I could hold it in. "You're gonna bring a Ouija board, too, I suppose?"

"Nope," he said, standing and offering me his hand. "Just you, me, and whatever spirits still linger in the woodwork. Who knows—maybe they've got something to say."

My fingers slid into his. His touch wasn't urgent or teasing now—only steady. The kind that made it really, really hard to remember how I'd ever lived without it.

"Let's go raise the dead," I said.

CHAPTER THIRTY-ONE

Charlie

"You just have to pretend like we broke in. We're not actually committing a felony," I said, leaning against the bar, staring down two of the most unimpressed women in Chatham County.

Sutton raised an eyebrow as she popped open a bottle of red wine and poured herself a glass. "You sound like a man who's about to get himself arrested trying to impress a girl."

Magnolia stood behind the bar, casually flipping through her phone like this conversation wasn't even worth her full attention. "But you have a key," she said flatly.

"He knows he has a key, Magnolia. That's not the point," Sutton chimed in, chin propped in her hand, already halfway to plotting. "This isn't about logistics. It's about *romance*."

"It's not about anything," I said quickly. "She's waiting outside with the dog, and I figured, you know, make it fun. Something different."

"Something borderline criminal," Magnolia muttered.

"She's got this whole séance thing she wants to do," I said, ignoring the way my voice dropped when I mentioned her. "Ghosts and energy and all that stuff she was into in New York."

"And you, big bad skeptic, are willingly playing along?" Sutton leaned back, narrowed her eyes. "She must really have you spun out."

I cleared my throat and looked at the wall.

"She doesn't have a boyfriend, by the way," I added casually, though it landed with all the grace of a cymbal crash in a library.

Sutton's face lit up. "Oh? And how do you know that tidbit, huh?"

"She said so. This morning."

Magnolia didn't even look up from the glass of wine Sutton had handed her. "Sounds like she has one now."

I pushed off the bar. "All right, I'm leaving. Can you two just, I don't know, go upstairs and make your giant pitchers of margaritas while you pretend not to stalk people on Instagram and watch bad reality TV."

Sutton grinned and raised her glass in mock salute. "Tell her hi from us. And good luck summoning spirits and pretending you're not completely smitten."

"Try and have fun, Charlie. Don't ruin her night by being… yourself," Magnolia called after me.

I stepped out the front door and made my way around the block and into the alley, and there she was—holding the leash, Nancy Reagan circling her ankles in distracted, wiry loops. Her cheeks were flushed from the cold or the anticipation or both, and the second she saw me, she grinned.

"Did you get approval from the board?" she asked, nodding toward the building.

"What do you mean, I was just making sure the place was empty," I said, hiding the keys in my back pocket. "Do you want spooky or subtle?"

"Oh, spooky, obviously."

I unlocked the service door, pretending like I was jimmying it open, and held it open for her.

She stopped in the doorway, lifted her chin. "Look who's casually doing a B&E now."

"What are you, a cop?"

***

I couldn't tell if I was nervous because the last time I broke into a historic building I'd nearly shit my pants after being "attacked" by a cat tangled in a painter's drape… or because I was standing alone in the dark with the girl I wanted more than anything in this world—and whatever comes after.

I led her over to the front table, the one closest to the stage, and hurried behind the bar to grab supplies, even though I had no idea what I needed.

"Salt?" I muttered under my breath.

"A Shirley Temple, please," she said, sliding onto the barstool beside me. "No salt. But go heavy on the cherries."

I gave her a look, but caught hers in return—wide-eyed and bright, her chin propped on one hand, legs swinging beneath her stool like she was waiting for a lollipop instead of a mocktail. It disarmed me, that mix of ease and sweetness, the way the moment hung between awkward flirting and what felt real. We must've looked ridiculous, both of us wearing crooked smiles, quietly stunned that we'd landed here together.

It had been years since anything had reached me like this. Years since I'd even let it. Yet here we were, sitting at an empty bar in the middle of the night, the air still carrying the tail end of a joke we hadn't bothered to finish. I couldn't remember the last time I'd laughed this hard, or when a conversation had flowed so easily it didn't need a reason to keep going.

Being around her made me feel like there was magic in the world again, the way you feel when you're a little kid and the most wild, unimaginable things seem possible and real. I'd spent so long tightening every screw in my world, keeping everything locked down and predictable. But with her, I didn't need the usual blueprint. Somehow, the chaos didn't feel threatening. It felt like an invitation.

She didn't quiet the noise in my head. She didn't fix anything or play pretend. But she made it bearable to sit in the mess, to stop trying to fix it all for once, and just be. And in that stillness, I found the magic I hadn't realized I was missing.

Not safety. Not order.

Her.

"You want to kiss me again, don't you, Charlie Pruitt?"

Her voice was low and grainy, the lightness from earlier gone. What replaced it was hungrier. There was a pull in her eyes, slow and deliberate, the kind of gaze that didn't ask for anything outright but left no room for confusion. She wasn't teasing. She was daring me.

I slid the drink down the bar, watching her fingers curl around the glass. Then I vaulted the thick stretch of mahogany between us in one smooth motion. She barely had time to react before my hand found the back of her neck, the other threading through the ends of her hair. I tilted her chin toward me until our eyes locked.

"You tell me," I murmured, voice rougher than I meant it to be. "Is that what you want?"

A sharp thud from the back of the bar made both of us flinch, and I loosened my grip, letting the strands of her hair slip from my fingers.

She smiled, slow and knowing, her palm gliding along the inside of my forearm before she hopped off the stool. Her gaze lingered a second longer, heavy with promise.

"Come on," she said, backing toward the darkened corner of the bar. "Let's go raise the dead."

***

"I can't believe I'm doing this."

"Can't believe it, or don't want to believe it?" Tally asked, arranging a mess of crystals she yanked from her bag and a shaker of salt I'd found behind the bar, like we were one candle away from summoning a coven.

"I can't believe I'm indulging this nonsense," I muttered, dropping her drink on the table and folding my arms like I was guarding what little dignity I had left.

She wagged a finger at me. "Careful with that negativity, Pruitt. Spirits can smell bad attitudes."

I sighed, though it came out more like a laugh. "Jesus. Let's just get this over with."

She didn't even flinch as she lit the candle like it was the most serious thing she'd done all day. "Okay," she said, settling in. "You ready?"

"No."

Her eyebrow arched, the corner of her mouth twitching. She pointed to the seat across from her. I stared at it like it might bite, then finally dropped into it, arms still locked tight across my chest.

"First things first," she said, sprinkling salt in a neat circle like she was seasoning a pot roast.

I sneezed so hard I nearly blew the candle out.

She gasped, grabbing it before it toppled off the table. "Do you have any respect for the dead?"

"I have allergies. What even *is* that?"

She held up the salt shaker, squinting at the label. "It's margarita salt. With Tajín, you goof."

"It was all I could find."

"You're trying to ward off spirits with cocktail seasoning?" She gave me

224

a look sharp enough to cut, then set it down and spread her hands, palms up.

"Now put your hands in mine."

I blinked. "You're serious?"

Her fingers wiggled in invitation. "It's part of the ritual."

I hesitated long enough for her brow to arch and that smug little smirk to form—like she already knew I'd cave.

And, of course, I did.

She slid her hand into mine without hesitation, her fingers tracing the ridges and rises of the calluses on my palm. I'd held her hand before, felt the weight of it, small but steady, but this was different—intentional, almost reverent.

And now I knew she didn't have a boyfriend. Knew the only thing standing in the way was *this*—this charged, impossible pull stretched tight between us, like it had been waiting for one of us to finally say the word.

It had almost been easier when I thought it couldn't go anywhere. When I could pin it on timing, or circumstance, or her maybe-boyfriend, or the fact that we were both living on borrowed time. But now? Now there was nothing standing between us. And that thought lodged itself in a place I didn't have defenses for. Because if this thing between us wasn't a temporary distraction from the chaos— then it mattered. Way more than I was ready to admit.

Her thumb gently brushed over my knuckles, and I didn't pull away.

I didn't *want* to.

Because the second I touched her, everything else slipped out of focus. The bar. The candles. The Tajín-laced salt. Her ridiculous setup. It all blurred at the edges.

All I could register was *her*.

Her hand rested against mine, warm and deliberate, her thumb tracing an absent path over my wrist. The steadiness of it anchored me. She didn't make a joke or pull away; she stayed there, focused, her fingers tightening slightly as if to remind me she was still with me.

And I sat there, pretending I wasn't already falling headfirst into a place I had no map to navigate and no tools to help me climb out of it.

She closed her eyes. "Oh great spirits, we call upon you tonight with open hearts and open minds—"

I didn't hear the rest. Not really. I should've been listening. I should've been mocking her, like I planned. I should've kept my head on straight. But all I could think about was how badly I wanted to kiss the corner of her mouth when she said my name. Not for the bit. Not for the drama. Not even because she was beautiful—though God, she was.

I wanted to kiss her because that empty crevice inside me felt a hell of a lot less barren when she looked at me like I wasn't the guy stuck babysitting the mess she'd dragged in with her.

She didn't flinch when I got quiet. Didn't try to fix it. She stayed close.

And now here she was, sitting across from me, her hands in mine, trusting me with this weird little moment. Maybe it was nothing more than a game to her—a night of make-believe in a bar that wasn't even open.

But for me? It was the first time in longer than I could admit that I didn't want to be anywhere else.

That invisible string yanked at me again, the same pull that had me leaning closer, closing the space between us before I could think better of it. Through one squinted eye, she caught it and cut me a look that landed like a warning.

"What are you doing?" she whisper-hissed.

A laugh rumbled out of me. I wasn't even sure myself. I was just trying to get close, I guess. And if she hadn't caught me, there was a very real chance I might've lifted her straight out of her seat and onto the damn table.

Instead, my hand found her cheek, then drifted to her chin, my thumb catching on her lower lip. She breathed out a quiet, toe-curling sound that stole every bit of air from the room. Eyes still closed. Still pretending she was focused on the séance. But I knew better. I had her—right there in that soft, electric pull of wanting.

That same hand drifted under the table, resting across her lap, draped in one of those tight, low-cut dresses she insisted on wearing as if they weren't designed to ruin me. I half-expected her to slap my hand away. But she didn't.

She ran her tongue over her bottom lip, then tugged it between her teeth. And that? That was all the permission I needed.

I eased my hand beneath the hem of her dress, eyes locked on the rise and fall of her chest as it started to quicken. Her skin was soft, warm, thighs parting ever so slightly as my fingers brushed exactly where I'd wanted to be since the second our lips crashed together.

She let her head fall back and made a sound that might've turned me feral—

Had a loud bang not split the air, sharp as shattered glass.

We both jolted, hearts in our throats.

But even that wasn't enough to break the spell of my hands on her. "What the hell was that?" I asked.

We turned toward the hallway as another clatter echoed through the dark.

Nancy Reagan went ballistic—barking, spinning, full-blown poodle meltdown. She scrambled across the floor like someone had opened the gates to the seventh circle of hell.

"Nope," I said, backing away. "Nope. I'm out."

Tally grabbed my sleeve. "Wait—"

A gust of wind rattled the liquor bottles behind the bar. The candle flickered, then went out. Nancy howled and tried to climb a barstool, legs flailing like a deranged circus act. A crash sounded from the back room.

We both jumped. The table nearly flipped. "This has never actually worked for me before," she whispered.

Towering over her, I shot her an alarmed look. "You mean to tell me that you think this actually worked?"

For a beat, we froze and stared at each other. Another rustle toward the back of the bar had her shooting to her feet, too. Then I shook my head slowly. "Don't even try to explain that."

Tally opened her mouth like she might. Then closed it again.

Silence settled around us, and I caught her face half-lit by the streetlamp outside. Her gaze flicked to mine, steady, searching. It wasn't fear, not exactly. But whatever was in her expression kept me rooted in place when every other instinct said *run*.

And then the hallway door creaked open, letting in a sliver of light from the street.

"OOOOoooooOOOoooo—!"

A thud echoed throughout the bar, followed by the scrape of a chair leg and a burst of muffled laughter.

"Shit, I tripped on my sheet!" Magnolia stage-whispered, her voice carried on the rustle of fabric.

Sutton's unmistakable wheeze-laugh cut through the dark, the kind of laugh that made you want to join in even if you didn't know the joke.

"Why are we whispering?" Sutton managed between gasps. "They already know we're ghosts!"

More stumbling. More laughter. "OH MY GOD, I'M GONNA PEE!"

We both turned just as Magnolia came barreling into the room, swallowed up in a white sheet that clung and twisted around her like she'd lost a fight with a haunted laundry basket. Her hair stuck out in a dozen directions, eyes wide and unblinking, and whatever she was going for, it definitely wasn't ghostly restraint.

Sutton stumbled in behind her, hiccuping laughter spilling out of her as she clutched the trailing edge of Magnolia's sheet—more like it was dragging her along than the other way around. The two of them looked less like spirits and more like drunk bridesmaids who'd wandered off from a bachelorette party and decided to haunt the bar out of pure spite.

I reached for the nearest thing within arm's length—the salt—and lobbed it across the room.

Nancy went nuclear, barking like we were under a full-blown attack.

Magnolia yelped and pitched forward, hitting the floor with a hollow thud that rattled the floorboards. Sutton tripped over her, both of them collapsing into a heap of tangled fabric and limbs, shrieking with laughter until they could barely breathe.

I froze, caught somewhere between laughing and bolting for the door. Across from me, Tally's shoulders shook with silent laughter, her cheeks flushed, her eyes wide and glinting in the dim light. And for a moment—long enough for me to feel it in my chest—I swore she was going to kiss me again.

But then Magnolia groaned from the floor, flinging an arm over her face. "Well? Did we scare the spirits out of you or what?"

I let out a slow breath and tore my eyes away from Tally. "I don't know about the spirits," I said. "But I think the mood is officially dead."

CHAPTER THIRTY-TWO

Tally

I'd spent most of the morning reminding myself that a bit of space would be good for me. Good for both of us. Just because Charlie had been all over me the night before didn't mean I had to melt into him every time he came within a foot of my personal space. Which was harder than it sounded, because apparently, Charlie had decided my personal space didn't exist.

He'd been brushing past me in the kitchen, his hand skimming my hip when he reached for the coffee—standing behind me at the counter with his palm flat against the small of my back, leaning in to grab the sugar when there was plenty of room to go around the other way. At one point, he came up behind me while I was rinsing dishes and pressed a kiss to my shoulder like it was the most natural thing in the world.

It was maddening. And addictive.

I tried to focus on reorganizing the stack of cookbooks Sutton had dropped by, telling myself I wasn't going to read into it. But every time I turned around, he was there—close enough that I could smell the faint mix of sawdust and soap on his skin. Close enough that my pulse jumped, right before my brain chimed in with a reminder that this was a terrible idea.

"You're quiet today," he said from behind me, his voice low enough to brush the back of my neck. "Everything okay?"

"Mm-hm." My voice came out a little too high. "Totally fine."

He smiled like he didn't believe me and reached past me to grab a mug, his chest brushing my shoulder. "Thought we could go through those boxes Magnolia sent up from the bar. Might be something we can use to make this place less… oatmeal chic."

I looked up at him, trying for casual, even though my whole body was leaning toward him on instinct. "Yeah. That could be fun."

What I didn't say was that if he kept touching me like that, we weren't going to get any decorating done at all.

***

Charlie's merry little experiment had backfired spectacularly.

He moved through the penthouse like he did everything else—casual and utterly unaware of the slow torture he was inflicting under the faint glint of Christmas lights. It was not the distraction I'd been hoping for, and, if anything, it made things worse.

The low hum of a jazzed-up holiday classic drifted through the room while I stood there, fists clenched around a ball of tangled lights, trying not to picture him unwrapping me one inch at a time.

I needed to get a grip.

"What's your plan for Christmas?" I asked, even though I already knew. I'd asked before—more than once.

He didn't seem to mind the repetition. "Maggie and I stay up all night, kind of a dare now. Started as waiting up for Santa when we were kids. Now we bet on who'll fall asleep first. Loser owes the other one a free pass to cover for the other at a Eunice Wilder function—no questions asked."

He stretched up to drape a garland across the fireplace mantle, and I focused way too hard on the movement of his arms, the way his shirt lifted slightly, enough to flash the waistband of his jeans.

"I can't stay over this year, though," he added. "I've got to drop Lee's piece off at the bar before Magnolia wakes up. So I'll probably head out early."

There was a flat, indifferent shift in his voice. Things were changing for him. For Magnolia. For all of us.

"We're doing brunch on Christmas Eve too," he added after a moment, adjusting a stray branch on the tree. "Magnolia mentioned pancakes and mimosas, which means it's going to be a three-course affair. I'm sure your brother'll let you tag along."

"Ha," I said, winding a strand of lights around the mantle garland he'd just hung. "Yeah, I'm sure he'll continue locking me up in this penthouse tower like some knocked-up Rapunzel. Far away from the rest of the kingdom."

Charlie glanced at me under the rim of his baseball cap but didn't push. He turned back to the tree, removing the sleek, impersonal gray ornaments from its branches and replacing them, one by one, with hand-painted oyster shells. They were delicate, flecked with faded pastels, initials still visible where someone had traced them in careful script.

"He's not trying to punish you," Charlie said eventually. "Everyone likes you. You've been here long enough to see that."

I shifted around the lights, keeping my eyes on my hands. "Right. That's why I'm still in time-out."

"You're not in time-out."

"I'm certainly not invited anywhere."

He exhaled, stepping back to survey the tree. "Doyle's just trying to protect you. That's his go-to move when he's worried." He turned back toward me. "And besides, there's really been nowhere *to* go. In case you haven't noticed, we've been sitting up here night after night watching *Golden Girls* reruns."

I didn't respond. Because he wasn't wrong, but it still stung. My brother used to be the one shouting my name the loudest, dragging me into the center of things, reminding people I was worth paying attention to. Now he avoided eye contact during dinner and acted like I might combust if left unsupervised for more than ten minutes.

Charlie must've sensed it, the shift in my mood, because he added, "You're not an outsider, Tally. Not to me."

My hand froze mid-air, the string of lights tangled around my wrist. Charlie didn't turn around; he kept carefully sorting through the ornaments, the muscles in his back shifting beneath the thin fabric of his shirt—deliberate and steady, as if he hadn't said the one thing I'd been waiting to hear all week.

The soft crackle of the Christmas station droned through the speakers. The scent of pine, gingerbread, and warm sugar cookies wafted through the air. The realness and the coziness of it all was making me crack.

I turned back to the tree, blinking against the sting behind my eyes. I tried to pretend I was focused on a rogue bulb or an uneven ribbon, but really, I needed a second to get my pulse under control.

Being wanted wasn't new. But this kind of wanted—gentle, no strings—was.

In the end, the living room was a beautiful, chaotic mess. Lights sprawled unevenly across the mantle, paper snowflakes stuck to the windows like a kindergarten classroom. Seashells, hand-painted by Charlie and Magnolia's momma when they were kids, now nestle in the tree between soft white bulbs and leftover garland from the bar. The coffee table was covered in tangled tinsel and half-finished mocktails.

It looked like Buddy the Elf had been left unsupervised in a vintage Sears catalog.

And I loved it.

My phone vibrated on the table and I lifted the screen to check the message. "Oh my God," I said, turning the message toward Charlie. "Pastor Donnelly just booked another wedding, and he wants me to come with him to take the photos."

Charlie grabbed my phone and quickly scanned the message, putting it back down on the table to lift me, ever so gently, to spin me around in a circle. I was buzzing. This was really happening, and I had another shot at getting my foot in the proverbial door here in Savannah.

He set me back down, then ran his fingers through my hair, cupping my face.

"Did you read the whole message?" he asked, eyes bright. "They're looking for someone to bake a cake, rustle up some last-minute flowers, and uncork something bubbly."

I shook my head, stepping out of Charlie's embrace, the magic draining from the room. "Shit, I don't even know where to start."

A catlike grin stretched over Charlie's face, wide and full of mischief, but beneath it all there was a thread of wild, unapologetic belief. In me.

"Darlin', you *just* did this for Hoyt. You know a chef, one of the most well-connected women in this city who orders more flowers per year than I'm sure the funeral homes do." He stopped, closing the space between us yet again, wrapping his arms around my waist this time. "And not only do you know a bartender, but need I remind you, you have access to thousands of dollars worth of fancy bubbles right downstairs."

Charlie's gaze locked onto mine, and he brushed a wad of curls out of my face, watching me closely. "He also said, if this works out, maybe this could turn into a permanent thing for both of you."

Could I really do this? Could I really take this opportunity and run with it, instead of running from it? I didn't want that life anymore, I didn't want my heart or my legs to send me packing and running away from here. Away from *this*.

And then it crept in—the ache of it all. Not loud or sudden, but slow and sneaky, settling behind my ribs like it planned to stay awhile. The grief wasn't about lost cities, missed chances, or the life I left behind. It was for all the years I spent trying not to want things. For every time I shrugged and laughed it off when really, I wanted to be seen. Picked. *Kept.*

Not for a project. Not for my potential. For me.

And now, somehow, I was standing barefoot in a borrowed penthouse, wrapping discount lights around a fake tree and thinking about what it might feel like to stay. Not pass through. Not stall out. *Stay.* With these people. With him.

Not in some perfect, Pinterest-worthy fantasy. In the real mess. The kind of life I spent my whole life believing I wasn't allowed to have.

Charlie moved across the room, the clinking of ice in glass pulling me out of the spiral. He poured his bourbon, slid cherries into my Shirley, and stood for a long beat, watching the tree.

Then, without looking at me, he said, "Come outside with me. We should celebrate. Plan. I don't know, but this deserves extra cherries and some fresh air."

He didn't wait for me to answer, only gathered both glasses and headed for the lanai doors, the soft sound of his bare feet against the floor pulling me after him..

I sat beside him under the twinkle lights he'd strung along the railing, their glow soft and steady against the dark. The river moved below us, slow and unhurried, catching the light in little ripples. Somewhere down the street, music drifted up from a bar, faint and warm like it had been playing forever.

I'd brought out one of the boxes Magnolia sent from the bar—odds and ends she figured I could use—and somewhere between flipping through old Savannah wedding photos and sipping my Shirley, the conversation drifted somewhere deeper.

One frame held a photo of a couple kissing in Whitefield Square, rain misting around them in a halo of light. Almost identical to the shot I'd taken of Hoyt and Charlotte on their wedding day. I could still see Charlotte's face that morning—crestfallen when the fountain was out of the question, and then alight again when we found the gazebo. By the time the rain let up, she told me it had been the wedding of her dreams.

I'd made that happen. Moved the pieces, kept it all standing, turned disappointment into a day they'd remember forever. I could do that again.

"You could make this a real thing," Charlie said, nodding toward the stack of frames at my feet. "The elopements. The photos. The planning and the pivoting. You've got the eye for it. People would eat that up here."

It startled me how much I wanted to believe him. How much I wanted to picture myself doing exactly that—turning this half-formed idea into a business that could actually keep me here. For the first time in months, the thought of staying somewhere didn't feel like a trap. It felt…possible.

I didn't speak right away. My fingers followed the worn groove of the frame, my thoughts leaping ahead to what a life here could mean. Not work. Not a place to sleep. A home. My home.

When I finally looked over, Charlie was watching me, his arm stretched along the back of my chair, close enough that the heat of him sank into my skin. A quiet spark lit his eyes, the kind that made it clear I wasn't the only one imagining what else might be possible.

And that was the moment I knew. Things weren't just falling into place with the business. They were falling into place with him, too.

The thought made my pulse kick, followed fast by the old, familiar warning in my chest. The one that told me to run before it all got too good, too complicated, before it fell apart and took me with it.

I forced a smile and set the frame down. "Guess I'll have to start taking it seriously, then."

Charlie's mouth curved, easy and a little dangerous. "Guess you will."

A stillness passed between us, and we were growing more and more comfortable in those moments together. The ones where we didn't have to say anything, we only had to exist, side by side, no conversation or pretenses or anything but each other's company settling between us.

"I have something for you," he said, breaking the quiet between us. His voice was gentle but certain, like he'd been holding the words in his mouth for a while. "It's an early Christmas gift. It's not anything big. Just something I—"

"You didn't have to," I cut in, already shaking my head. "Charlie, it's not—"

He brought our joined hands to his mouth again, brushing soft kisses across my knuckles until the rest of the words evaporated from my throat. "Tally River Aden, will you for once in your life hush your mouth and let someone do something nice for you?"

I bit my lip, smiling despite the tears already welling behind my eyes.

Still holding hands, we slipped back indoors and walked over to the tree, the poor thing barely staying upright under the weight of seashells, lights, and about five too many strands of garland. We sat on the floor, cross-legged and facing each other beneath the drooping branches.

Charlie handed me a small, neatly wrapped package. The brown paper was covered in doodles and stickers, scribbles in his messy handwriting, and tiny ink stamps pressed into the corners. It looked homemade, but not rushed—thoughtful in a way that made its way across my chest in a warm and sweet bloom.

As I kept searching the wrapping, tears pooling in my eyes, I saw scraps of my time here. A torn napkin from Leopold's. A ticket stub from Winter Gala. A receipt from the McDonald's window. The corner of a coaster from O'Malley's. Each one taped down with care, turning the ordinary into a treasure worth saving.

"I don't even want to open this," I whispered, staring down at it. My voice cracked on the last word.

Charlie reached over and took the package from my hands, opening it slowly, carefully, treating the wrapping as part of the gift. It was.

"I just didn't want you to forget any of it," he said. His fingers traced the edge of the paper, reverent. He pulled the tape off the corners gently. "Actually, you kind of have Lee to thank for this. I suppose this is loosely based on his idea for Maggie's portrait."

"All of these little moments with you…" He paused, eyes still on the frame. "They've meant the world to me."

Housed in a delicate, gold frame was a sketch of me. Barefoot, windswept, standing at the edge of the river. The sunset behind me cast everything in amber and rose. The faint curve of my belly visible beneath my dress. And behind me, distant but steady, The Waving Girl.

Charlie's voice broke through the silence, barely above a whisper, but steady all the same. "Especially this moment here."

A single, full tear slipped from the corner of my eye and cut a slow trail across my cheek.

It overwhelmed me—the tenderness of his gift, the way he'd sketched me not as a mess of jagged edges or wild mistakes, but as someone worth seeing. As someone worth remembering. The kind of person who might deserve to stay.

I touched the glass frame again, unable to look away from that quiet moment he'd captured. It was everything I hadn't dared to hope for—proof that someone saw me, really saw me. The ache beneath the jokes. The hunger to belong. Not only for me, but for the baby I was carrying. I'd spent so long pretending I didn't care where I landed, and here I was, sitting under a crooked Christmas tree in my brother's penthouse, hoping with everything in me that I'd finally found home.

Charlie reached out, thumb grazing the tear from my cheek, his hand lingering ther with enough pressure to steady me. I tilted my face toward him, drawn like a magnet, and met his gaze.

And I fell.

No resistance left in me. No hesitation. No armor. Only me—open and raw and ready—because how in the hell could I not love Charlie Pruitt?

The man who handed me silence when I needed peace, who carried me without question and kissed me without regret. The man who looked at me and saw more than a disaster trying to find her footing—someone worthy of being chosen.

"I have a gift for you after all," I whispered, voice trembling. I reached for the hand resting against my cheek and brought it to my chest, over my heart, holding it there like a promise. "It's yours, if you want it. Just… promise me you won't break it."

His brows drew together, an unreadable emotion flickering across his face. Then he nodded, solemn and sure. "Never."

Charlie reached up, tugged the bill of his cap forward, then spun it around so it sat backward on his head. It was such a simple move—casual, thoughtless—but it knocked the air out of me like he'd just changed the rules of the game.

And then he dropped to one knee in front of me, and that was it. Game over.

His hands found my hips, steady and unhurried, before sliding to rest against the curve of my bump. He looked up, his thumbs moving in slow, absent circles, his eyes locked on mine like he was waiting—for me to push him away, for me to run, for anything but what I actually did.

I stayed. Breath caught, heart somersaulting, knees weak in a way that had nothing to do with pregnancy and everything to do with the man on his knees before me. Charlie Pruitt—backward cap, rough hands gentled on my hips—like he was kneeling at an altar he hadn't even realized he'd built until this moment.

He looked up at me, eyes so green they caught every scrap of me and held it there. And in that reflection, I saw her—the woman he saw. The one falling, faster than she meant to, for the man who made it impossible not to.

"You giving me your heart," he said, his voice low and gruff, "Is the greatest gift I've ever gotten. The only thing I would've wished for this Christmas."

My throat tightened. Whatever walls I thought I had left didn't stand a chance.

His palm stayed pressed to my heart as he leaned in, brushing his lips against my fingers with a reverence I hadn't been ready for.

My fingers left his lips and curled into his shirt, clinging as he pushed to his feet with slow, deliberate grace until he stood over me—taller now, broader, filling every inch of space around me like there wasn't enough air for both of us.

His mouth met mine, a breath released after days of holding back. His restraint gave way, his need finding mine in all the places we'd pretended didn't exist.

And still, he kissed me again. And again. And again. Like he needed to memorize everything—the shape of my mouth, the sound I made when he tugged at my lower lip, the way my body leaned into his like it had been waiting for this exact kind of touch all along.

Still holding me close, he stood, lifting me off the floor in one smooth motion. I wrapped my arms around his neck as he carried me down the hallway. Past the tree. Past the ornaments and scattered wrapping paper. The lights behind us twinkled against the windows, casting soft, amber reflections that danced across the walls.

He nudged the door open with his foot, setting me down only once we were inside.

Nancy let out one short, scandalized bark from the living room, and Charlie reached behind him, shutting the door.

And the rest of the world fell away while I let Charlie Pruitt undress the truth of me—piece by piece, until there was nothing left but the part of me that had somehow always belonged to him.

CHAPTER THIRTY-THREE

Charlie

Something wet and warm shoved straight up my nostril woke me out of a deep, glorious sleep.

It wasn't exactly the way I'd imagined my morning going, especially after the night we'd had. I'd fallen asleep with Tally curled into me, soft and spent, her leg hooked over mine, one arm flung across my chest. Her breath, slow and steady, had kept time with mine until I'd finally drifted off, high on whatever the hell kind of alchemy had happened between us.

But now? The alchemy had teeth and smelled vaguely of liver treats.

"What the—" I blinked against the pale morning light and wiped my face, groggy and disoriented. Nancy Reagan stared back at me, eyes wild, tongue still out like she hadn't just assaulted my sinus cavity.

I groaned and rolled onto my side.

She was still there.

Curled toward the middle of the bed, one arm tucked under her cheek, the other flung across the pillow I'd abandoned. Her curls were a tangled halo across the sheets, catching the morning light in soft brown streaks. Lips parted. One knee hitched up like she'd been ready to bolt mid-dream. She looked peaceful. Beautiful. But even in sleep, she carried that quiet storm with her—brewing beneath the surface, ready to tear through the room the second she opened her eyes.

I exhaled, slow and careful. Stupid how much I already missed her, even with her right there.

I sank back into the mattress for a second, trying to hold onto it all—the way she'd looked under the glow of those lights, her laugh balanced somewhere between reckless and shy, the way her fingers had curled in my hair like she never wanted to let go—the way she'd handed me her heart and trusted me not to screw it up.

And I stayed there on my knees, in front of her—my queen, in every way that mattered—vowing I'd do everything in my power not to.

Even if that meant sharing a bed with her dog, who clearly had no sense of boundaries and needed a bath in the worst possible way.

"Alright, Reagan. Message received," I muttered, giving her a half-hearted pat. She sneezed in my face.

I was starting to drift again, hand lazily resting on the curve of Tally's hip, when the front door swung open.

Loudly.

Nancy Reagan launched off the end of the bed like she'd been shot out of a cannon, barking so hard her front paws left the floor. Tally jolted awake with a gasp, half sitting up and dragging the sheet over her chest as I blinked toward the door in sleepy confusion.

"I swear to God, Jordan, if she broke any of my vintage crystal Baccarat ornaments, I will strangle her, pregnant or not." Doyle's voice boomed through the penthouse, all smug cheer and early morning audacity. "Surprise, sis! We're home early."

Jordan was quieter, trying to smooth things over with some sort of yoga breathing that was loud enough to hear behind closed doors. "Let's not judge until we see all of it. Inhale peace, exhale expectation."

"Oh, I'm inhaling something, alright," Doyle grumbled. "What the hell is that smell? Is that spray paint?"

Tally hissed through her teeth and flopped back against the pillow. "Tell me that's not my brother."

"It's your brother," I said, resigned, throwing an arm across my eyes as footsteps echoed down the hallway.

Dig's voice rang out a moment later, far too enthusiastic for someone who probably hadn't slept in two days. "Helloooooo! Did Santa come early, or is that just the scent of sin and sugar cookies?"

And then the bedroom door creaked open.

I sat up as Doyle stepped inside and froze. His gaze darted from the twinkle light explosion in the living room behind him to the sight of me, shirtless in bed beside his naked, definitely-not-just-visiting sister.

There was a beat of silence—a long, painful one.

"So… the worst part is not that you two are in bed together. The worst part is that it looks like a coked-out Christmas elf blacked out in here and had a nervous breakdown with a Bedazzler."

"You did, indeed, smell spray paint," Jordan muttered from the hallway.

Tally let out a strangled laugh and pulled the sheet higher.

Dig, bless his heart, flopped down on the other side of her, completely unbothered by the situation or the state of undress. "Aw, you started without me."

Nancy barked harder, leaping onto the bed and ricocheting off to pounce on Jordan and Doyle, her nails clicking wildly against the wood floors as Doyle tried his best to keep the dog off of his perfectly creased, white linen pants.

I closed my eyes, sighed, and said the only thing I could.

"Merry damn Christmas."

***

Doyle, Jordan, and Dig had me cornered—shirtless—in the kitchen, while Tally hid in the bathroom under the guise of taking a long, hot shower. At this point, she was well past the acceptable timeline of a post-coital rinse and creeping into definite *avoidance* territory.

Not that I could blame her.

She wasn't just hiding from her brother, her best friend, and her brother-in-law. She was hiding from me.

Because last night had changed everything.

The tension we'd been winding tighter between us for months had finally come undone, and it wasn't the physical relief that had wrecked me—it was everything else. The way her fingers threaded into my hair like she'd been waiting her whole life to hold on. The sound of her laughing quietly in the dark when I cracked a joke that wasn't even that funny. The way she whispered my name like a prayer, over and over until she felt that release too—more than once. Not like I was counting or anything.

I'd felt all of it. Not only through my hands but under my skin, buried deep in a place I'd tried to keep locked up. And I couldn't stop replaying it or wondering how the hell I was supposed to go back to pretending it hadn't happened.

"Charlie," Doyle snapped. "It's one thing to screw my sister in my bed.

241

It's another to stand there, half naked, clearly replaying it in your head, while you drift off in my damn kitchen."

I coughed and adjusted the waistband of my pajama pants. "Sorry. Just—uh…"

Dig laughed, arms crossed over his chest like he was trying *really* hard to appear tough. "I may come off as the Betty White of the gays here, but don't get it twisted. I've been doing chorus-line squats for a month straight. I could Rockette your ass into the next ZIP code if you so much as bruise her heart."

Jordan grumbled under his breath and busied himself pouring mimosas.

I leaned back a little and looked down at the only creature in the room not actively threatening me. "I would *never* hurt your mother, Nance," I murmured to the poodle, who blinked back at me with zero faith.

"It's not you we're worried about," Jordan said mildly, handing me a champagne flute. "It's Tally. You never know when she's gonna get that look in her eye and decide she's done here. That she needs to run. Somewhere else. Someone else."

Dig drained his glass and topped it off with champagne only, not a drop of juice. "Honestly, I thought she'd end up back in New York with me. We could raise the baby together, have a perfect lavender marriage, and co-parent the next Broadway prodigy. It'd be *fabulous*."

Doyle snorted. "I figured she'd run back to Momma by now."

I groaned, dragging a hand down my face. "What if she stayed?"

That shut them up for exactly two seconds. And then they all laughed in unison, a joke that I wasn't a part of rising in the kitchen and blanketing the group of us.

"Tally?" Doyle scoffed. "In *Savannah*? With *you*? A stable, responsible man who's hardly ever left Savannah and has the organizational skills of an Eagle Scout?"

"Wild," Jordan added.

"Bold," Dig said, nodding.

I rolled my eyes at all of them. "This is why she is caught in a constant state of fight or flight, you guys. She doesn't think anyone believes in her enough."

I told them everything about our weeks together. The conversations we'd had, how she worked so diligently to find what she'd been searching for, and what had landed in her lap was so fucking perfect for her.

"She's got an Excel spreadsheet and everything. She's fucking smart. And fucking determined. You all should stop making her the damn punch line of every single joke."

"The thing is, Charlie," Doyle started, voice locked low and gaze on mine. "It's not funny," Doyle said, his voice low. "Not when we've seen her come up with grand ideas and then… poof." He made a little explosion with his hands.

I was about to fire back when I caught movement from the corner of my eye.

A flash of hair and a shadow disappearing down the hall.

CHAPTER THIRTY-FOUR

Charlie

"You got laid. Holy *shit*. You got *laid*," Lee whispered conspiratorially the next morning as we helped Magnolia set up for Christmas Eve brunch.

I was exhausted—half from staying up all night finishing the piece for Magnolia, the other half from not sleeping at all once I moved back into my studio. It wasn't her fault, or, hell, maybe it was. But I couldn't shut my brain off. I kept replaying that night, over and over. Her soft, beautiful face. The way she looked at me when I touched her, the sounds I knew I'd be able to drag out of her, given the chance. The way she whispered my name in the dark like a prayer.

Now, Lee was grinning at me with the smug satisfaction of a man who *knew*.

I cleared my throat. "What makes you think that?"

He tilted his head, amused. "Because you, my friend, are smiling at absolutely nothing."

I tried to wipe the grin off my face, busying my hands with napkins screen printed with holly and, for some reason, a Santa-hat-wearing Pickle the cat. But I couldn't help it. The smile kept creeping back, slow and uninvited, planted there by some unseen hand the moment she walked into my life—and it bloomed the way only she could make happen, changing me so irrevocably that I knew I'd never be the same.

Lee didn't press as he kept working beside me, quieter than usual. And when I met his eyes again, I saw it. That faraway, aching look I'd come to recognize.

He was leaving right after the New Year. A secret I'd only been trusted with, and the grief was already taking root as it had over ten years ago. The familiar ache of knowing he wouldn't be around day after day was starting to overshadow

245

the warmth I'd been feeling all morning. We'd only just gotten him back, and now he was slipping away under the guise of what he considered doing the right thing.

He'd walk away, again, to let my sister have the life he believed she had chosen. One that didn't include him.

"You don't have to go, you know," I said, smoothing a wrinkled napkin too many times. "Just because she didn't pick you doesn't mean there's not a life here worth staying for. A family."

Lee exhaled, laying down a gold-rimmed charger with more care than necessary. "I've thought about that. But it's not just that I love your sister, Charlie. I *need* her. She's part of my story. Has been since I was a kid. And if I can't have that story here with her, I don't want to pretend I'm living some other version of it."

I swallowed hard. "What about the rest of us?"

He smiled, but there was no joy behind it. "Y'all figured it out without me the first time. Look at this place. You've made a family. Built a real life. All I've done is come in and light a match."

"Ha. You sound like Tally."

That got him. He glanced up, scanning the room, then turned back toward me. "Speaking of, is she coming today?"

I shook my head, watching Doyle and Jordan laugh with Magnolia in the corner, throwing the occasional sideways glance at Lee. "I told her about it," I admitted. "Mentioned the brunch. But I never actually… invited her. I figured Doyle might, and when he didn't—"

Lee gave me a look that bordered on exasperation. Then he clapped a hand on my back. "You know you could've just flat-out asked her yourself, right? She's your girl, Charlie. She should be sitting here. Next to you."

My girl.

The words lodged in my chest, heavy as hell. And he was right. She should've been here. I'd pictured it more times than I wanted to admit—her curled hair, flushed cheeks, rolling her eyes at Sutton, stealing bites off my plate like she owned the place. Like she belonged here.

But that was the problem, wasn't it? I wanted it too much.

"She should be here," I muttered, mostly to myself, flinging another napkin onto the table with a little too much force.

Lee tilted his head. "Then why isn't she?"

I didn't answer right away. I kept dutifully folding, pressing the corners together like I could smooth the tightness in my chest right along with the linen.

"Fuck, I screwed up," I said finally, low enough he had to lean in to hear. "I told her about brunch. I just… never actually said, '*Come with me.*' And now it feels like she probably thinks I didn't want her here."

Lee didn't say a word. He gave me space to find it on my own—the thing I'd been circling around for weeks. With him, the words always came easy, everything spilling out before I had time to second-guess it. But with Tally, it wasn't that simple. The hesitation ran deeper, rooted somewhere I couldn't talk my way past, proof that some things get harder to share when the person in front of you matters too damn much.

"I've spent months telling myself not to fall for her. And then last night—" I shook my head. "Everything changed. Now it's all I can think about. But Tally… she's had enough people pull her in too fast and then vanish just as quickly. She's always been the one who feels first, feels harder—and it's burned her every time. This time, it's me. I'm the one who's fallen first. And if I push too much, it won't matter how much I mean it—she'll feel cornered, and I'll lose her before we've even started."

"I know she's not the type to stay in one place too long," Lee said quietly, "but she doesn't strike me as the type to run from the truth."

"No, not the truth," I agreed. "But she might run from pressure. From someone trying to write her next chapter before she's ready."

I glanced toward Magnolia, laughing with Doyle and Jordan, unaware that a part of me had just come undone. "If I'm not careful, I'll let my heart get ahead of my common sense. And then she'll go, and I'll still be here—picking up the pieces of what could've been."

"How would you know if you don't give it a chance?" Lee asked, watching me closely.

"It's not just her I want, Lee. It's the life she's building. Her and the baby. I don't want to be some story she tells over a cocktail with Dig one day—I want to write the whole damn book with her. But what if she doesn't want that with me? What if every step is complicated because I'm not the baby's father? Because I have to figure out how to love and protect someone I didn't help create, without overstepping, without screwing it up before it even begins?"

Lee nodded, placing the last fork with the kind of precision only a Wilder could manage. Nothing out of place, every detail perfect.

"You should text her," he said finally, stepping back to survey the table.

I glanced toward Magnolia, laughing with Doyle and Jordan, her engagement ring catching the light. On the surface, everything looked perfect—like Tally had seemed at first. But I knew better. I'd seen how fast things could go sideways, how easily a polished smile could hide the cracks.

"You don't think it's too late?"

Lee's gaze lifted from me to my sister. "It's never too late."

I pulled out my phone. Typed. Deleted. Typed again, deleted again. Finally, I hit send on quick note, hoping it read like an invitation instead of a plea.

CHARLIE: The only thing missing from brunch is a beautiful woman who doesn't know how to bake but sure does know how to kiss. You should come, but leave the baked goods at home.

See? Honest. Not needy.

The undeniable truth settled in, louder than any craving or instinct—I wanted her. Needed her.

My gaze slid back to my sister, showing off floral designs to Jordan and Doyle, smiling as she did, though a trace of hesitation lingered beneath it. She was already getting tangled up in all the *somethings*—borrowed, blue, and new—and I was still trying to hold onto the pieces of her I had left.

Could I do both? Could I keep my sister safe and still give in to what I wanted for myself?

What if protecting Magnolia meant keeping my heart on a leash?

***

Magnolia was in the kitchen, balancing a bottle of white between her thighs and propping her phone up against the sugar jar, FaceTiming with Sutton as she stirred the garlic butter for the mashed potatoes. I was supposed to be queuing up *Meet Me in St. Louis*, like I did every year, but my thumb hovered over the remote, frozen.

Because I wasn't really here, not the way I usually was.

The apartment above O'Malley's was cozy in the way my sister always managed since I'd moved out. Candlelight flickered from her windowsills. There was a pie cooling on the stove and the whole place smelled like nutmeg and browned butter and the faint pine from the tree Lee dragged in two weeks ago, the one he'd insisted on decorating with all the ornaments we made in elementary school, glitter peeling off them like dead skin, and the ones our Momma had had painted before she'd passed. Every inch of the place radiated warmth. Tradition. Home.

And yet, I kept thinking about the girl who wasn't here.

What she was doing. If she'd eaten. If she was warm enough. If she'd been lying in bed all afternoon, staring at the ceiling, wondering why she wasn't included. Or if she'd put on a brave face and distracted herself by making a mess in the kitchen, eating olives straight out of the jar with her fingers, irritating the perfect cadence of her brother's world by simply existing.

She hadn't texted me back. No surprise there. Still, the thought of sitting through that brunch without storming out, tossing her over my shoulder, and dragging her to O'Malley's—claiming her, claiming us in front of everyone—was eating me alive.

Maybe she needed space. Perhaps she was in a knock-down, drag-out fight with Doyle. Maybe she knew I was with my sister, and that this might be the last time we'd carry out this decades-old tradition together.

"Charlie," Magnolia called, glancing over her shoulder with a smile. "You're up. Hit play. We've only got until the timer goes off."

I stood, careful not to get too close to the Christmas tree where Pickle was perched halfway up like a furry gargoyle, tail twitching, eyes locked on me as if daring me to ruin her holiday. She batted a paw in my direction when I passed.

I cleared my throat and pressed the button. The screen filled with the soft, vintage glow of old film stock as Judy Garland's voice crooned gently through the room. I settled into my spot on the couch and grabbed my wine glass from the coffee table, where Magnolia had dropped it off.

"This really isn't a Christmas movie," I said, because that was my line. I didn't even think about it anymore. It tumbled out, muscle memory from thirty-some-odd December 24ths.

"It was Momma's favorite," she said, walking in and collapsing next to me on the couch, tucking her feet under my thigh. "And *Have Yourself a Merry*

Little Christmas' made her cry every year. Don't you remember?"

I nodded and sipped. But my mind was still five blocks away in a penthouse that smelled like citrus shampoo and clean laundry, where twinkle lights hung half-heartedly from curtain rods and where a wild girl with wild curls had built herself a Christmas out of scraps.

I wondered if she'd thought about showing up today. Wondered if Doyle had stopped her, or if she'd talked herself out of it before she even reached for the door.

She was good at that—convincing herself she didn't belong, before anyone else got the chance to do it for her.

But this time, we'd all proved her right by not asking her to come along. She'd given me her heart and asked me not to break it, and I wasted no time being the asshole she thought I was at the start.

I stayed quiet the rest of the movie, watching Magnolia mouth the words under her breath, her rapid blinking during Judy's song as she tried, like she always had, not to let me see the emotion swelling in her eyes.

When the credits rolled, she leaned her head against my shoulder. "Can't believe you're ditching me this year."

"I've got a delivery in the morning." I tipped back the last of my drink. "Commissioned piece. Big one. Hard to miss."

She didn't move right away, and the air between us tightened with her disappointment.

"That's okay," she said eventually. "Who wants to have a sleepover with their baby sister anyway?"

I looked down at her and smiled, even though I knew it didn't quite reach my eyes.

"Me," I said. "Always."

***

It was past midnight when I stepped outside. Savannah was quiet—the kind of hush that only settled in on holidays, when everyone was inside with full bellies of Christmas dinner and wine, and the city exhaled for once.

I walked.

No destination in mind but burdened with the need to move. My breath fogged in front of me, and the fairy lights strung between gas lamps made the brick sidewalks shine. I passed Lafayette Square, then Monterey. At Whitefield, I slowed.

The gazebo stood in the center, familiar and still. I stepped inside and sat down on the bench, stretching my arms across the back of it, letting the cold bite into my fingers.

This was the part I didn't know how to do.

I could build furniture out of scraps. Rewire the lighting at O'Malley's with one trip to Lowe's and a twelve-pack. I could keep Magnolia afloat through a broken heart and a collapsing business. I could survive hell and come back smiling.

But love? Love was different. There wasn't a tool for that. No blueprint. No instruction manual. Only the risk of putting your heart in someone else's hands and praying they wouldn't drop it. And I had no idea how to hand mine to Tally without losing her in the process.

I didn't want to scare her. Didn't want to put one more weight on her shoulders when she already had enough to carry. I didn't want to reach for it too soon and ruin what we'd found—this rare, slow-burn thing we'd built between bickering and bourbon and her throwing up on my shoes.

But I loved her.

God, I loved her.

I loved her laugh, and her messy curls, and the way she still said y'all even when she was pretending to be too sophisticated for this place—the part of her stint in New York still so ingrained in her soul. I loved how hard she tried to act unaffected when I walked into a room. How she softened when she didn't think anyone was looking. How she lit up when she looked at Nancy Reagan, or the baby on the ultrasound.

She didn't see herself clearly. But I did. And I didn't know how to hand her that truth without making her run.

I sat there a while longer, breathing in the cold and listening to the sound of the city settling into bed. Somewhere off in the distance, a church bell rang.

I stood and shoved my hands into my coat pockets. My boots scuffed the floorboards as I left.

As always, I had shit to do.

***

Back at the studio, I opened the door and was met with the smell of cedar and sawdust, along with the faintest trace of her perfume—citrusy and floral, but not overpowering. My chest ached.

The piece for Magnolia was already wrapped and leaning against the wall. Lee was coming by in a few hours, and if I thought I could muster it, I'd get a few hours of sleep.

But first, I sat down on the loveseat where she'd once curled up and fallen asleep. The very spot where she had spent hours sitting there, watching me, figuring me out in a way no one else had ever bothered to. Where she told me all of her stories, and I listened with all the intensity of someone hearing their favorite song for the first time. I ran a hand down my face and exhaled.

I didn't know what tomorrow would bring.

But I knew one thing for sure—Tally River Aden had gotten under my skin. Into my blood. She'd worked her way into the softest, most guarded parts of me. And the truth was, I'd already fallen. Harder than I planned.

It scared the hell out of me, because I'd seen what happened when people mistook the rush of new love for something unbreakable. Magnolia and Dane had started with fireworks, too, and now the fallout was simmering right in front of me. Tally had her own history of crashes, the kind that left you wary of anything that felt too good to be real.

And here I was, standing on that same edge, wondering if saying out loud what sat between us would make it real—or send her running.

Because wanting her wasn't the problem. It was deciding if I could have her without losing everything else.

CHAPTER THIRTY-FIVE

Tally

The penthouse was too quiet. And it wasn't the kind where it felt peaceful and you could curl up and watch old Christmas movies on the couch. It felt punishing.

I'd spent the last ten minutes pacing barefoot across the cold marble floors, one hand on my lower back and the other gripping a half-empty glass of ginger ale, pretending not to care that I hadn't been invited to a brunch that happened hours ago.

I didn't even know who I was mad at. Doyle, for not inviting me? Myself, for assuming I'd be included? Or Charlie. Maybe, especially, Charlie.

I'd spent the day with Dig, and while that helped ease the pain slightly, I was now up burning the midnight oil and wearing a tread into the floors from all of my incessant pacing. And no matter how hard I'd tried, I couldn't stop the thoughts from wandering back to Charlie.

I reread the text again. And again. And again.

CHARLIE: *The only thing missing from brunch is a beautiful woman who doesn't know how to bake but sure does know how to kiss. You should come, but leave the baked goods at home…*

I stared at it until the screen dimmed, then set the phone back down. Cute. Honest. Maybe even sweet. But it had come too late. Hours too late.

If I meant something to him—if I really mattered—I wouldn't have had to wait for an afterthought text.

He'd made me feel welcome, warm, wanted. He let me into his space, fed me, took care of me, gave me the most soul-altering sex of my life—and now here I was, alone on Christmas Eve in the world's most beige penthouse, the sparkle from my festive Bedazzling fading into the corners. Unclaimed. Forgotten. Too much and not enough at the same time.

I kept pacing, arms crossed tight over my chest. The tree we'd decorated together sparkled mockingly in the corner—droopy branches, handmade ornaments, a fever dream of tinsel and oyster shells. The whole place smelled like real pine, nutmeg, and the sweet whiff of cookies Charlie had baked and left out on the counter. It should've felt cozy. Magical, even.

Instead, it felt like a stage I'd already been booed off of. And, of course, my brother was in the front row, booing the loudest of them all.

Snippets of the fight with Doyle kept flicking through my head, the way you can't stop pressing on a bruise. His voice rising, mine matching it, both of us circling the same tired points: why I hadn't been invited to brunch. How I'd "turned the penthouse into a Christmas craft-store explosion." How my "messes" weren't cute anymore. And then, the part that stung the most—watching him pull out his phone, muttering about calling our mother.

He hadn't, of course, it was a vague threat. But what he did say, the part stuck on loop like a broken record, was louder than anything else in my head:

"You know what, Tally. Momma and Daddy would be better off handling this than Jordan and me right now. We've got too much going on, and at this point, you need more support than we can give."

I'd laughed it off at the time, tossed out a snarky comment like armor. But the echo of it followed me now, every word making me question my place here all over again.

What if this wasn't where I belonged? What if this was another wrong detour on the map I'd been drawing wrong for years? I had no idea.

I drifted toward the window and pressed a hand to the glass, staring out across the river. Everything was still and peaceful as Savannah rested her head, waiting for Santa to arrive and the bright possibility only Christmas morning brings. But there it was, crashing into me like a wave—the old, familiar itch to pack a bag and run. To get in front of the rejection before it hits me.

Only this time, I wasn't sure if I wanted to go… or if it was a habit. The reflex of a girl who'd spent her life leaving before she was left. Before I started a business, it failed. Before I built a home here for the baby, and regretted it. Before Charlie saw all of me—the real me—and decided he couldn't love the fragmented pieces.

All I knew was that I desperately, unabashedly wanted someone to ask me to stay.

My breath fogged the glass as I leaned closer, forehead pressed against the cool pane. I didn't know how long I stood there, watching the world move quietly without me. Beyond these walls, families gathered. Lights sparkled across the water. And here I was, waiting for someone—anyone—to say it: *Don't go.*

When no one did, I turned away from the window.

I padded toward the kitchen, bare feet brushing against the cold tile. There was still a trace of glitter on the counter from the ornaments Charlie had made, and my stomach gave a tiny, hopeful twist at the thought of him. Not the version who held me in his arms and whispered sweet, racy promises in my ear, but the man underneath it all. The one that he tried too hard to keep buried inside. Not the reliable guy with the tattoos and the muscles and the sister he felt like he needed to save. The one who was talented, an artist with his hands on the canvas and on my body, which he painted with kisses and whispers and faint traces of his fingers that knew exactly where to touch and what to do. The one who, if I really sat back and thought about it, wasn't ever trying to save me. Since the first moment he met me, he'd been trying to coexist alongside me.

I glanced toward the elevator.

Then I changed my mind.

Instead, I slipped through the back door and tiptoed down the narrow service stairwell, one hand on my belly and the other skimming the railing. My body knew the way before my brain caught up, like it had already decided where I needed to be.

I didn't knock when I reached the studio; instead, I eased the door open and slipped inside. The lamp on his worktable cast a low, golden glow across the room, softening the edges of everything it touched.

Charlie Pruitt stood barefoot and shirtless, tattoos winding over his skin like art upon art, a pair of worn jeans slung low on his hips. His dark auburn curls were damp and unruly, as if he'd just run a hand through them in thought—or frustration. A massive sheet of sketch paper was taped to the far wall, and his fingers, smudged with charcoal, moved quick and sure across its surface.

The Waving Girl.

My throat tightened.

"You know, for someone so bad at breaking and entering," Charlie said without turning, his voice a soft rasp, "You sure make a habit of it."

He turned then, setting the charcoal down on the stool beside him. The lamplight caught the edge of his jaw and the curve of his mouth. His eyes landed on me—standing barefoot by the door, in nothing but one of his t-shirts he'd left upstairs.

The softness in his expression melted away, replaced by a heavier heat that settled between us. He took a step closer, slow enough for the boards beneath him to protest.

His eyes traced the length of me, lingering, returning to my face with a kind of hunger he didn't bother to hide. His jaw tensed, the only betrayal of what he was trying not to say.

"Lucky for you," he said, voice lower then, rougher, "I've stopped locking the door."

I didn't speak. I couldn't. My chest was too tight, my heart thudding loud enough I swore it echoed off the studio walls. Maybe I didn't need him to ask me to stay. Perhaps the words would never find their way to my heart. But maybe our hands would once again say all the things we'd left unsaid between us.

He crossed the room with careful steps, eyes locked on mine, searching for hesitation.

There wasn't any, not tonight.

I reached for him first, pressing my hands to his chest, warm and solid under my palms. And then he kissed me.

It wasn't tentative or slow this time. It was desperate. Familiar. Deep. A kiss that knew everything we'd been through to get here and didn't give a damn about anything but *this*.

His hands gripped my waist, pulling me against him, and my fingers curled into his shoulders, anchoring myself there, in the only place I wanted to be.

When he pulled back, his breath caught. "Tell me you're sure. Tell me you want this. You want me again."

"I've never been more sure of anything," I whispered.

His mouth found mine once more, softer now, more reverent, and then we were moving. He guided me back toward the hallway where I knew his narrow bed sat tucked behind the curtain, our bodies brushing furniture and canvases as we went, our lips never leaving one another's.

I tugged at the waistband of his jeans, and he peeled the shirt from my body, a slow lift of the fabric that inched carefully across my body, sending sparks of desire coursing through my veins.

We fell into the mattress in a tangle of limbs and want, the whole world narrowing down to the weight of his body, the heat of his skin, the way his hand found my belly, eyes searching mine with a hold that felt dangerously close to hope. That this moment—this fragile, impossible moment between the two of us and the shadow of the three we could become—changed things.

And it did. God, it did. I knew I'd carry it with me long after the sheets cooled, long after his voice faded from the quiet corners of my memory. This wasn't just another night. It was an ache I'd feel forever. A mark I'd never be free of, even if I tried.

We moved in sync this time. No rush. No frantic edge. Only that quiet, consuming tenderness that made every kiss, every whispered breath of my name, feel like both a promise and a farewell.

There was no doubt anymore. I loved him. Completely. Recklessly. Irrevocably.

And maybe that was the problem. Love wasn't enough to anchor me to this shore.

We stayed tangled, skin slick and breathing uneven, the room so still it felt like even the Christmas lights outside were holding their glow for us. He didn't speak, and neither did I. We didn't need to.

He'd fallen asleep with one arm tucked under his head and the other curled around me, his hand resting over my belly in a way that wasn't protective but possessive, like he already saw the two of us as his to claim.

I wanted to stay in that moment. Goddamnit, I wanted to. To let myself believe I'd finally landed somewhere solid. That this bed, this man, this city could be mine.

But my mind wouldn't stop. It never did. Doyle's words still rang in my ears—too loud, too messy, too much for him and Jordan to manage. He'd as good as told me to go home, to let our parents "handle" me. And maybe he was right.

On my doorstep were three things that would alter the course of my life.

A child who deserved a mother who could give them stability without flinching.

A business, still nothing more than scribbled plans and favors from strangers.

And a man—this man—who I knew would lay his life down for me and this baby without a second thought.

But what if I couldn't be the woman who stayed? What if I broke under the weight of all three?

Because that's where I always got it wrong, things would land in my hands and, instead of holding on, I'd open my palm, watch them scatter, and call it fate. I'd tell myself I was better off. Safer. Alone.

Lying there, wrapped in the warmth of everything I swore I wanted, that old reflex stirred—the instinct to run before anyone could change their mind about me. To leave before rejection had the chance to arrive.

Only this time, it wasn't me running.

This time, I was being asked to go.

And the cruelest part?

Even knowing that, a part of me still wanted to stay.

My gaze drifted over the inked lines on his skin—Magnolia's flower curling across his shoulder, a guitar pressed gently against it, a tiny chef's knife tucked in for Sutton, roots and clocks filling the spaces, bright paint splashed through it all. His family, his history, his art—stitched into him, carried with him every day.

I lay there, syncing each breath with his, my heart aching in time with his chest. He'd given me more than I ever expected—kindness, softness, a place to land. But Charlie Pruitt never belonged to me alone. He belonged to his sister, to this city, to everyone he'd ever held together when it would've been easier to let it all fall apart. I loved him too much to be the thing that finally broke him.

And yet leaving felt impossible.

My fingers traced his arm, memorizing the scar by his elbow, the twitch of his pinky as he drifted deeper, the strength that steadied me in ways I didn't even know I needed. I wanted him with everything I had. But wanting wasn't the same as staying. Not for me. Not yet.

I slipped from the bed, breath caught when he reached for me in his sleep, hand curling into the space I'd left behind. It almost undid me.

At the doorway, I turned back, my fingers curled tight around the frame. Everything in me screamed to stay. To climb back into bed beside him. To stop running. To stop giving up on myself.

He didn't stir, only lay there with his hand still resting in the space I'd left behind. A wet laugh rose in my throat. "Of course you'd sleep through my dramatic exit, you giant oak of a man."

I closed my eyes and whispered softly, "Goodbye, Charlie Pruitt. Thank you for loving the broken, jagged pieces of me."

And I knew then, in the deepest part of me, that I'd spend my life on the bank of my own river—not the girl who waved to bring others joy, but the one the world romanticized. The woman forever flagging down passing ships, hoping one of them might finally bring the man she loved back to shore to carry her home.

CHAPTER THIRTY-SIX

Charlie

By the time I made it back to River Street, the sky had turned that soft, inky blue that only showed up when the world was still hungover from too much wine and too much hope the night before.

I pushed open the lobby door, juggling coffees and tote bags full of gifts. I hadn't planned on spending my Christmas Day in the penthouse, but I couldn't help myself. I didn't have much, Lord knows I never did, but I'd raided the bar at O'Malley's and snagged a couple nice bottles of bourbon for Jordan and Doyle, a dram of that peach liqueur I knew Dig liked, and Magnolia's bougiest unopened can of maraschino cherries for my girl.

The piece for Magnolia had been delivered hours before the sun came up. Lee had stayed behind, setting up his guitar with some grand plan to play downstairs under the dim glow of the stage lights, hoping the sound would drift up the stairs and pull my sister down to see what was going on. One last attempt to win her back under the guise of a grand gesture. The one thing Lee was forever good at.

I wished him luck as I slipped out, watching him fiddle with the lights and retune his guitar, muttering to himself about everything needing to be perfect.

But Magnolia didn't need perfection. She only needed him. Not that either of those two idiots knew that yet.

I should've stayed behind to help. Should've hung around, kept him company, steadied his nerves. But my thoughts kept drifting back to the one place I couldn't seem to stop circling. The one person who had unpacked her mess in my heart and, I'd hoped, would take up permanent residence there.

She hadn't been there when I woke up. I'd reached for her instinctively, hand skimming across cool sheets and nothing else. At first, I told myself she probably couldn't sleep, that she might've wandered up to the penthouse for her morning prenatal vitamins. Or maybe she wanted to sneak back up before Doyle woke up and scolded her. Or, worse, Nancy woke up and thought she was abandoned.

"Morning, Hoyt," I said with a jolly wave.

Hoyt met my unusual reaction with a half-hearted laugh. "You certainly look chipper this morning, Mr. Pruitt."

I hit the button for the elevator and shrugged. "Christmas magic, maybe. Has Tally been down to walk Nancy yet this morning?"

Hoyt frowned and lowered his eyes, pretending to fiddle with the notes on his desk. "Not yet, sir. Still a little early for Miss Aden and Miss Reagan."

"Fair enough. Merry Christmas, Hoyt. Tell the same to Charlotte, please."

As the elevator doors glided shut, I heard Hoyt call out, "Merry Christmas to you, too, Charlie."

I shook off the odd tone in his voice and the fact that, for the first time in years since he'd worked the door, he'd used my first name. Tried to ignore the gnawing in my gut, that steady, relentless warning that nothing about this was right.

I moved quietly through the penthouse, setting the coffees down on the counter and slipping the bag of gifts underneath the tree, clearly suffering under the weight of the ornamental pressure. The lights were still on, blinking softly.

"Tal?" I called out, gently, in case she had fallen back to sleep in her room.

Nothing.

Her bedroom door was cracked open, but not wanting to disturb her, I stood there a second, listening for the tap of Nancy's feet, the rustle of a blanket, her voice calling back. But all I got in return was silence and the faint hum of the fridge kicking on.

Still half-hopeful, I took a minute to tidy up the penthouse and the small messes on the counter left over from whatever they'd gotten into the night before. I needed purpose, I needed to keep my hands busy so I didn't spiral. So I didn't read too hard into the fact that I'd all but broken in the house, and Nancy didn't greet me in her usual manner of unhinged self-defense poodle.

I opened the cabinet to pull out her tin of food, thinking that maybe the sound of kibble would raise the dog from slumber, and I'd know, for sure, Tally was behind the door sleeping peacefully, waiting for me to join her.

Jordan sauntered out of his room looking like a man who had just returned from war. His hair was a mess, and he had deep, dark circles under his eyes. He wouldn't look at me and crossed the room to try to coax the lazy tree back into an upright position.

"Where is she?" I asked, barely recognizing my own voice. It cracked straight down the middle.

Doyle walked out next, a heavy sigh escaping his body when he saw me standing, dumbfounded, in the middle of the living room. The place felt crowded with the memory of her, but empty in every way that mattered. The hook where her coat had hung was bare, the pink leash by the door was gone, and the faintest trace of her perfume lingered in the air, already starting to fade.

"She's gone," he said.

I blinked. "What do you mean, gone?"

Jordan straightened, pressing his palms flat on his thighs before dusting invisible lint from his sweater. "She and Dig left this morning. Packed their things and slipped out before either of us woke up."

"No note. No call," Doyle added, his voice tight. "She's not answering her phone. Just gone."

My stomach dropped. That familiar twist deep in my chest clawed its way up my throat.

"I thought maybe she'd just gone out," Jordan said, more to himself than to me. "For a coffee run, or a walk by the river. Maybe down to see you. Something. But her stuff's gone. The room's empty."

"She took everything?" My voice pitched. It was too loud. I didn't care. "Did something happen?"

Doyle finally turned, cheeks flushed, jaw tight with whatever he was trying not to say.

"I told her I needed some time to figure things out," he said, barely above a whisper. "I didn't mean pack up and disappear."

He couldn't meet my eyes; his hand went to the back of his neck, fingers worrying at the skin while he stared at the floor, like the answer might be hiding somewhere in the grout.

I leaned against the doorframe, trying to catch my breath. "You told her you needed to figure things out? Jesus, Doyle."

He didn't flinch, only kept rubbing the back of his neck, shoulders hunched under the weight of it.

"What was I supposed to do?" he snapped, louder this time. "Jordan's mom is so sick, and I need to be focusing on my business and my husband. And my sister shows up, throws our life off-balance, and I'm just supposed to pretend I can handle it all?" He motioned around the room as the remnants of her presence were quietly erased, the beige walls reclaiming themselves. "Look at this place, Charlie. It's been chaos since she got here. I'm not saying it's her fault, but…" His voice cracked a little. "I've been hanging on by a thread."

"No," I said, stepping toward him. "You're supposed to show up for your sister. You're supposed to open the door and say, 'I'm glad you're here, make yourself at home,' no matter what. That's what family does."

"She was never going to stay," he said, softer now. "You and I both know that. And I didn't tell her to go, but I didn't exactly make it easy for her to stay, either."

The words landed heavy between us, impossible to move past.

"So where is she, then?" I started pacing, hands running through my hair. "Where would she go?"

Jordan and Doyle shared a look, and Jordan let out a sigh so loud his entire body seemed to sink with it. "There's a chance Doyle suggested Dig drop her off back in Newnan. With their mother."

I stared at him. "You told her to go back to your mother. The one who ripped her to shreds every chance she got. That's what you thought was best?"

Doyle's jaw worked, guilt bleeding through in the twitch of his mouth.

"She needed direction. She needed—"

"She needed you," I cut in, my voice climbing. "She needed you to say, 'You're not a burden. I want you here.' Instead, you treated her like some squatter in your pristine penthouse—the one you dragged her to, by the way. You think folding her laundry and ordering Korean skin care makes you a big brother? She needed someone to believe in her, Doyle."

For a second, I could see her there—on the couch, that ridiculous dog in her lap, smiling at me while I rearranged things in the living room that didn't need rearranging, just to give myself a reason to be close to her. The ache that followed hit deep; I didn't know when I'd see that again.

I stepped past Jordan, the words still burning in my throat. I didn't know much, but I knew this: being family meant showing up. It meant staying. It meant proving, over and over, that when everything else fell apart, you were still there.

I stomped through the quiet streets of Savannah, my boots hitting the pavement a little harder than necessary. The whole city was still and soft under a layer of Christmas calm—shops shuttered, restaurant windows dark, the only sound the rustle of wind through the trees and the occasional honk of a far-off car.

Magnolia always closed the bar on Christmas. She said the ghosts of our past deserved a little peace and quiet one day a year. But I needed a drink—and more than that, I needed somewhere to breathe. So I keyed myself in.

The lights were low inside O'Malley's. The old wood floors creaked under my weight, and that familiar mix of whiskey and stale stout clung to the air— warm, lived-in. The kind of scent that wrapped around your ribs and squeezed.

My eyes landed on the far wall. The portrait I'd made for my sister hung there like a promise. Photographs, lyrics, layers of memory stitched together in acrylic and ink. I'd poured everything into that damn thing. My love for her. My hope. The part of me that knew she needed to see herself the way we all saw her—strong, steady, brave.

But beneath it, hunched on the floor, surrounded by shattered glass, was Magnolia.

She was crumpled like a discarded napkin, knees pulled tight to her chest, sobbing into her lap. Her red curls clung to her damp cheeks, and her shoulders shook with every breath she tried to hold in and failed.

My stomach dropped.

"Magnolia." My voice caught as I moved fast, dropping to my knees beside her. "What happened? Who did this?"

I already knew. Hell, I'd known for weeks. But I needed her to say it out loud.

Her mouth opened, but no words came—only a broken whimper. She looked up at me, her eyes swollen and red.

"Lee's leaving. After New Year's Eve."

I swallowed hard.

"And Dane…" She couldn't even say it. She didn't have to.

I pulled her into my arms, holding her like I used to when she was little and the world felt too big and cruel. My hands trembled as I stroked her hair, the scent of her floral shampoo nearly undoing me. She felt so small in that moment, far too small for all the weight she carried.

I hated him. I hated Dane Wilder with every bone in my body, and I hated that she'd been the last to see him for who he really was.

We stayed there for a while, my arms locked around her, the only sound was the soft clink of broken glass settling around us. I was already plotting the slowest, most painful way to make him disappear when she whispered, "You have to let it go."

I didn't answer.

"If you don't…" she started, "I can't lose the bar, Charlie. I can't. It's the last thing holding us to our family. It's all we have left." Her voice cracked on that last word.

I looked around the room—the garland sagging over the bar, the wreath made of bottle caps and ribbon, the old neon sign flickering behind the counter. This wasn't just a bar. It was Sunday afternoons, broken hearts, birthday shots, and stories passed down over whiskey and song. It was everything we'd managed to hold together after everything we'd lost. It was the only real thing left.

And she was right. All we had left was each other. A couple of stubborn orphans with bruised-up hearts and a bar full of memories, trying to keep the pieces from falling apart. And somewhere along the way, we'd picked up a few more. Sutton. Jordan. Doyle, even. Lee. And now Tally.

A mismatched, chaotic, sometimes infuriating group of people who had somehow become ours. Not by blood. But by choice. By showing up. By loving each other, even when it got hard. And this place was where we called home.

I glanced down at Magnolia, still tucked against my chest. I had to be there for her. No matter what.

She was the one person in this world who had never walked away from me. And I couldn't walk away from her—not now. Not ever.

Even if it meant letting go of the girl I'd finally let myself fall for. Even if it meant saying goodbye before I was ready.

Because being a brother—being *her* brother—would always come first.

Maybe some people were destined to end up with the wrong person, and others were meant to make sure they didn't lose themselves in the process.

And for the first time in years, the weight of that truth settled in my chest. Not as a burden, but as a choice. One I'd make again and again.

No matter how much it broke me.

***

A few hours—and a few pints—later, Magnolia and I had the bar somewhat cleaned up as Christmas movies flickered on the TV above the shelves. Not exactly the Christmas either of us had hoped for, but we had each other. And for now, that felt like enough.

Sutton showed up first, ditching her early-morning private catering gig a few hours early. Her new situationship, as she'd officially deemed it, trailed in shortly after. Ryan was hot on her heels, clutching a sprig of mistletoe like it might double as a romantic weapon.

"That's not gonna end well," I muttered, nodding toward a half-drunk Ryan weaving through the tables like a toddler at a wedding.

"No," Magnolia said, not even trying to sugarcoat it. She sat in her usual spot on the far side of the bar, by the takeout window, even though we wouldn't see a single patron today. "It certainly is not. Speaking of doomed romance—here comes Jordan and Doyle. You think maybe—"

"She's not coming," I cut in, sharper than I intended. I shot her a look, and to her credit, she took the hint—for now. Magnolia Pruitt never dropped a subject in her whole damn life. I was buying myself five minutes, tops.

Jordan entered the bar with a hint of a smile, but Doyle looked like a kid getting dragged into church on Sunday—head low, shoulders tight, and about ten seconds from bolting.

I didn't move. I wasn't about to throw punches, but I wasn't getting up to hug him, either.

"Merry Christmas, y'all." Jordan nudged Doyle toward me until they stopped at the bar. "Doyle's got something he wants to say," he said, eyes flicking to Magnolia and Sutton. "In private."

I led him to the back office and shut the door behind us.

Glass still glittered faintly in the corners of the room, though someone had half-heartedly tried to sweep it up. A half-drunk bottle of whiskey slumped on Magnolia's desk, surrounded by torn-up photos and crumpled bridal magazines.

The whole place looked like a heart had exploded, and no one had dared clean up the mess properly.

I dragged in a breath and let it out slowly. My sister had begged me not to kill Dane. *Especially* not on Christmas.

"Have a seat," I said, taking the chair behind Magnolia's desk. Doyle didn't sit.

He stood by the edge of Magnolia's desk, arms crossed over his chest. He looked more like a boy than a man—flushed, raw, and strung too tight. The version of Doyle I'd never met before but was all too familiar with now, thanks to all of Tally's stories.

"I'm sorry I gave her the impression she should leave," he finally said.

I didn't respond.

"I just thought… maybe she'd be better off figuring things out in Newnan. I didn't mean for her to disappear. I didn't mean—" His voice cracked. "I was angry. And I was scared."

"Of what?" My voice came out rough, scraping at the edge of the word.

He scrubbed a hand over his jaw. "Of her. Of the way she drags me back into who I used to be. I couldn't wait to see her again after California, but the closer it got, the more I dreaded it. I didn't want to… regress."

"Regress?" I barked out a laugh.

"Yes, Charlie. Regress." His eyes flashed. "I've worked my ass off to be a different person. And she's still—God, she's still *her*. Wild, reckless, magnetic. And part of me envies the hell out of it."

I pushed back my chair, the legs scraping against the floor.

"She's always been the bright one," he said, breathless now. "I was the good kid, the clean one—the one who followed the rules. But I always wanted to be her. And then I realized her kind of freedom made me anxious. Maybe it wasn't anxiety at all. Maybe it was just… me stuck in her shadow."

He dragged a hand through his hair, finally unspooling. "Even Dig—he was my best friend first. But she's the one who *got* him. They speak the same language: fast, impulsive, half a joke, half a cry for help. And I hated that sometimes. That they were so in sync, while I was always two steps behind."

In front of me was the man I'd known for years, the one who never let you see a wrinkle in his clothes or a hair out of place. That was his light. A light that was unique only to him. A good friend, a good husband, a successful business owner.

"I guess, as brothers, we can kind of see ourselves as inverted reflections of our sisters." I leaned up against the bookshelf, steadying myself, the emotion of the day finally settling into my bones. "We don't all burn the same way, Doyle. Doesn't mean you're not bright, too. You just light up a different room."

The silence stretched between us.

"Charlie," Doyle said, finally. "She really loves you. I can tell. She's never looked safer, or so at ease, around anyone like she looked when she was around you."

I kept my eyes locked on the floor in front of me.

Doyle's voice wavered. "You were the only one who believed in her. In her elopement business dreams, and in her photography. Even in her ability to really knock this motherhood thing out of the park. She told me last night, when I found her crying in the bathroom. She said, 'Charlie looks at me like he sees who I could be… not who I've been.' And I didn't have a damn thing to say, because I knew she was right."

My hands balled into fists.

"Maybe," I muttered, "She just needed someone to believe in her so completely, so deeply, that she finally dared to believe in herself."

"And it should've been me," Doyle whispered. "But goddamnit, I'm so glad it was you."

I looked around the office—at the shattered things. The color that was draining out of my own sister's life. The way I was doing nothing to stop it. The way I was watching her walk away from the things she loved, too.

"You should've invited her to brunch," I said.

"So should you."

He wasn't wrong. And that made it worse.

"I'm sorry, Charlie," he said after a long pause, his voice cracking again. "The hotheaded, hot mess side of me really took the reins. I guess I'm more like my sister than I thought."

That made me smile—just a little.

Sutton knocked once and let herself in, eyeing the wreckage like a detective at a crime scene. Doyle took the cue to slip out, quietly excusing himself from the emotional fallout we'd dragged into the light.

I'd forgive him, of course. Not that day, or maybe not the next, but that's what friends do. If someone trusts you enough to show you who they are at their lowest, that's true bravery. And that's not something to step over. That's when you grab their hand and help pull them back up.

And I had a feeling Doyle would need that soon—when the weight of pushing his sister out the door finally settled in.

"Wow," she said, stepping over a busted picture frame. "Didn't think you'd actually knock Doyle around, but honestly, everything's surprising me lately."

I motioned to the scattered glass and mangled bridal magazines. "Wasn't me. If I'd done it, he'd have a black eye on that unnaturally pretty face of his."

We shared a dry laugh—exhausted, brittle at the edges.

"Fucking Dane," she muttered, crouching to collect a chunk of torn cardstock that used to be part of a centerpiece design.

"Fucking Dane, indeed."

She stood and leaned against the desk, her eyes flicking across my face, taking inventory of the damage there, too.

"You know," she said carefully, "Magnolia's not the only one who's hurting."

I didn't respond.

Sutton folded her arms, letting the silence stretch a little. "Charlie, you've been the dependable one since we were kids. Steady as hell. Always fixing everyone else's mess before you even look at your own."

My eyes stung, but I didn't blink.

She stepped a little closer. "But what do you need? Right now. Not your sister, not your friends—*you*."

I shook my head. "Does it matter?"

"It does," she said, quiet but firm. "We all just heard you give Doyle hell for not being there for Tally, and now Magnolia's sitting at the bar, probably replaying whatever happened in here while listening to the world's saddest Christmas album on repeat. You wanna be everyone's anchor, but eventually even anchors rust out."

She didn't say it to hurt me. She said it because she meant it.

"And maybe… maybe Tally didn't leave because she was running for once in her life," Sutton added. "Maybe she left because she didn't want to get in your way. Of being exactly who you've always been. The guy she knew you wouldn't give up being. The guy who stays behind."

My throat felt too tight to answer.

She leaned over the desk, careful to avoid the spray of glass peppering the desktop, and touched my arm lightly. "Your sister needs you right now. But so does someone else. And the question is… who do *you* need?"

Then, without waiting for a reply, she walked to the door, pausing with her hand on the frame. "Think about it, Charlie. Just don't take too long. People, especially the people worth fighting for, won't wait forever."

When she left, the quiet was deafening.

I looked around the room—the broken glass, the deflated decorations, the chaos Magnolia had been trying to clean up alone.

And I thought, not for the first time that day, or the first time in my life:

My sister needs me.

CHAPTER THIRTY-SEVEN

Tally

The house I grew up in had always been too big. Too many rooms, too many formal sitting areas nobody actually sat in, too many framed photos of political handshakes and ribbon cuttings and Christmas cards from state senators we'd never actually met. It echoed, even when it was full, especially now, when it wasn't.

I'd been holed up in my childhood bedroom for days, staring at my old bulletin board like it might suddenly come alive and offer me advice. The poster above my bed still read "LIVE LAUGH LOVE" in glittery cursive, but even the glitter seemed tired. I was not living, or laughing, or loving. I was rotting in bed, crying and pretending I didn't care about the guy who was five hours away, probably sitting in his studio, already moved on without me.

Dig's face filled the screen of my phone, too close and way too sparkly. "Do I look like an appropriate amount of slutty?" he asked, adjusting the collar on a rhinestone-studded jacket that looked like it cost more than my rent back in Brooklyn. "Because it's a 'regrets only' kind of party tonight."

I managed a half-smile. "You look like the Times Square Ball."

"I'm hoping it's flashy enough to get the attention of someone who wants to watch *my* balls drop if you catch my drift."

I wrinkled my nose. "Ew."

"What's going on with you? You look like you're trapped in a horror movie about emotional repression and bad lighting. And you're not laughing at any of my jokes."

I flopped back on the bed with a groan. "Welcome to Newnan. Population: me, a very judgmental dog, and the Mayor of Passive-Aggressivetown."

"Nancy?" he asked, offended.

273

Nancy whined from her spot by the door, pacing with the urgency of someone who had just remembered where they buried a bone. I sighed. "Speaking of, I think she has to pee. Which means I have to venture into the Wilds of Parental Disappointment. Pray for me."

Dig leaned closer, his tone softening. "Has Charlie called?"

I shook my head once. "No."

He didn't push, only offered that soft, sad smile he'd perfected after years of watching me fall apart in slow motion. "Happy New Year, Tally. Go make some noise."

But I did quite the opposite as I tiptoed my way down the elongated, winding staircase that led to the front foyer. I tried to be as quiet as possible so that my mother, wherever she was lurking in the halls of this home, didn't hear me and start accosting me with a million questions.

Coming back to my hometown with my tail between my legs was one thing. Coming home pregnant, single, and jobless was another. And my mother, as she did, was using this as the kerosene she poured on the already outrageous blaze that was her disappointment in me.

Somehow, I had managed to successfully and stealthily waddle my way out of the double front doors and onto the hilly street, taking Nancy on a softly lit stroll through my childhood neighborhood. I also treated her to a montage of all the historical hotspots.

"And under that tree is where Doyle smoked his first cigarette and blamed it on me. And over there, on the Davis' swing set, is where he told me it was him and me forever. Us against the world. Rat-faced liar…"

Nancy whimpered in agreement, trotting along ahead of me. She seemed spooked, and who could blame her? We left lazy, sleepy Savannah for this cookie-cutter, Stepford cul-de-sac.

As quietly as we could, we stretched open the front doors and tiptoed back through the foyer, but overhead lights flicked on like spotlights in a damn prison yard, and my mother ascended down the stairs like the warden herself.

"Tallulah," she hissed. "You'll wake the whole neighborhood up with that yapping dog."

I rolled my eyes. "Settle down, *your honor*. You and I both know the dog didn't make a single noise. You just hate her for no good reason." I scooped the poodle up in my arms and stared my mother down. She used to scare me, but not anymore. "You'll have to turn the gas up a little higher to drag me into your narcissistic, crazy alternate reality."

A flat smile settled on her lips. But my father appeared from the direction of the kitchen, breaking the staredown contest between us, wielding a plate of peach cobbler loaded with ice cream.

"I didn't miss this at all," he said, shaking his head as he made his way up the stairs.

My mother flicked her wrist toward me. "At all hours of the night, Hollis. Out traipsing the neighborhood like a lost soul—with that yappy mutt and that disgrace of a belly. What if someone saw her?"

Hollis Aden, the first gentleman himself and steadfastly used to being agreeable to his wife, Mayor Vivianne Aden, shook his head as he passed her on the stairwell. "Whatever you say, Vivi."

I groaned, staring up at both of them. "Shouldn't you two be off at some New Year's party? Isn't it bad for your image that you haven't left the house since I got home?"

"Now let's make one thing perfectly clear, Tallulah," my mother's voice boomed through the massive house. "Your father and I are embarrassed enough as it is that you would show your face here, in this town, with *that* child who belongs to God knows who in your stomach. To go to a party? To be asked questions about why you are here in this town in the condition you are in? I'd never get reelected again. You fool."

She turned on her heel, following my father up the stairs. "And don't forget—you're a guest in this house. This is no longer your *home*."

***

I sulked back into the bedroom, which was a virtual time machine to my past. Not a hair out of place since I left at 18.

Same white, wrought iron bedframe. Same floral wallpaper curling at the corners from too many steamy summers. It was the same stiff white carpet that looked clean but felt like walking on needles. Same crippling defeat after a showdown with my mother in the foyer.

I crawled into bed and curled onto my side, facing the muted television where Times Square glittered in grainy, hyperreal joy. Nancy Reagan was snuggled against my stomach, her tiny snores keeping rhythm with the soft thump of baby Aden's kicks. I held them both like lifelines.

My thumb hovered over my phone, the weight of it suddenly enormous.

Was he watching this, too? Or was he back at the studio—shirt half-unbuttoned, charcoal on his hands from his latest sketch, Sutton's voice bouncing off the walls while he pretended not to listen? Maybe he was at the bar, stealing a laugh with Magnolia or teasing Lee about their relentless on again off again tryst. Or were they having a party? Was my brother there?

Maybe it didn't matter where he was. Maybe what mattered was that he was still exactly who he'd always been—steady, dependable, good. And maybe—just maybe—he wasn't thinking about me at all.

But my God, I was thinking of him.

I missed the way he held me—not like I was breakable, or already broken and needed to be fixed—but like he was anchoring me to a place I didn't even realize I'd been searching for. A place that felt steady. A place that felt like mine.

I missed his hands, always warm, always steady, never hesitant. The way they found the parts of me I wasn't sure how to love yet, and touched them like they were already worthy. Like he'd known all along that I deserved to be held gently.

I missed his scent—cedarwood soap and paint thinner, threaded with something warm that clung to my skin long after he was gone. It lingered on my clothes, in the sheets, in the air itself. The kind of thing that made a room feel occupied even when it wasn't.

And Lord above, I missed his laugh. Not the big, easy one he tossed to his friends like spare change. The other one. The one that barely made a sound. The one that slipped out when he thought no one was listening—the one he only ever gave to me.

I blinked back the sting of tears and typed it out before I could change my mind.

TALLY: *Happy New Year.*

Sent.

Delivered.

No response.

The crowd on screen erupted, a thousand voices counting down all at once as the volume on the TV climbed—ten, nine, eight…

I turned it up a little more and let it fill the space.

Seven, six, five…

I kissed my hand and laid it gently over my stomach.

Four, three, two…

"Happy New Year, baby Aden," I whispered. "I can't wait to meet you this year."

One.

The screen exploded with confetti. Music blared, people kissed, and fireworks lit up the world. And I stayed where I was, in a house that had never really been home, holding tight to the only things I hadn't already lost.

CHAPTER THIRTY-EIGHT

Charlie

My phone was vibrating somewhere beneath me. Or maybe it was inside my skull—hard to tell with the hangover roaring through my temples like a freight train.

I groaned, blindly groping for it among the crumpled throw blanket and empty water glass beside the couch. The screen lit up, too bright for my burning eyes. I squinted, swiped up with a shaky thumb, and there it was.

TALLY: *Happy New Year.*

From *her.*

For a second, I thought maybe it was the whiskey from the night before staging its final act. But no—my heart was pounding, hard and fast and splintering in my chest.

She'd thought of me.

And I was still thinking of her. Always.

My thumb hovered over the screen, ready to fire off something back—anything, even a dumb joke to keep the thread alive—when the phone buzzed again. Same number. Not her.

I frowned, rubbed the heel of my hand into my eye socket, the hangover grit of sleep and whiskey dragging at me. Then I answered. "Yeah?" My voice came out wrecked, rough with more than sleep.

"Charlie—hey, it's Taylor. From the shop across from O'Malley's. I've been trying to reach you—"

Something in her tone pulled me upright. "What's wrong?"

"There's a fire," she said, breath ragged. "At the bar. It's bad. The street's full of smoke, man. You need to get down here."

For a second, I couldn't move. Couldn't breathe. Then the words hit, and I was already scrambling—feet on the floor, searching for shoes, keys, anything.

"O'Malley's?" My voice cracked on the name.

"They think it started in the back. I don't know how bad it is yet, but the fire trucks are on the way. Just—hurry."

She hung up, and I ran to my truck, fumbling to get the keys in the ignition, my whole body shaking while I tried to process what was happening with the ever-spinning, ever-tilting world around me.

The sirens were already wailing down Whitaker by the time I skidded onto the block, tires squealing as I threw the truck into park in the middle of the street. I spotted it before anything else—the smoke, thick and choking, curling up from behind the bar and catching in the glow of sirens.

But I didn't stop to gawk because Magnolia was up there, somewhere.

I bolted across the sidewalk, heart pounding harder than it had all night, and shouldered the bar door open with a crack, my keys still stuck in the ignition of the truck. I didn't have time to go back. Every second counted as I finally beat the old, crooked door open, the bell giving one sad jingle as it tumbled to the ground with a shimmering crash.

"Mags!" I bellowed. "Magnolia!"

Flames hadn't reached the main barroom yet, but smoke was crawling along the ceiling like something alive. I barely registered the overturned stools, the flicker of Christmas lights still blinking along the back shelves. There were still empty glasses and shrapnel from the party that night, napkins and paper confetti still peppered across every surface.

I ran, legs moving on instinct, straight through the barroom and toward the back stairwell. The metal handle of the door scorched my palm, but I didn't stop. I shoved it open and took the stairs three at a time, yelling her name again.

"Mags! Answer me!"

The apartment door gave way with a single hard kick. I tore through the rooms, coughing through the haze, checking every corner, every closet, behind the damn shower curtain. "Magnolia!" My voice cracked. "Come on, dammit—"

She wasn't there.

She had to be downstairs. In the office. Or the green room. Maybe she'd fallen asleep on the couch again after another one of those too-late nights. Maybe—

I didn't let myself finish the thought.

I raced back down the stairs, two at a time, but pulled up short when I saw a small, trembling ball of fur in the corner landing of the stairwell.

"Jesus," I whimpered.

Pickle. My sister's savage, asshole cat was wide-eyed and silent for the first time in her chaos-fueled existence, her matted tail curled tight to her body.

I crouched and scooped her up, and for once in her feral, hellcat life, she didn't claw my face off. She pressed her tiny body against my chest and let out the saddest, tiniest meow I'd ever heard.

"Good girl," I said, my voice barely there.

Then I ran again.

The fire had already overtaken the back rooms by the time I stumbled out of the stairwell and into the barroom again, Pickle still pressed to my chest. The smoke was thick now, black and choking. I could barely see through it, but I staggered forward anyway, hand outstretched toward the greenroom door.

It wouldn't budge.

The heat behind it was unbearable. The second my hand closed around the knob, the heat lashed up my arm, and I recoiled, eyes burning, lungs heaving.

"Mags!" I tried again, slamming my shoulder into the door.

Nothing.

Panic tore through me like the flames eating through our walls. I turned toward the office—managed to shove the door open enough to see that it was already gone. Flames clawed up the walls like a demon out of hell. The couch was ablaze. The metal desk was the only thing left standing. If she were in there—

No.

I backed out, Pickle whimpering against my chest, her body shaking like mine. I had to get her out. I could drop her off outside and go back in. I'd find my sister. I'd drag her out if I had to. I'd—

Something caught my eye through the smoke.

The portrait. The one I made for her. Moments and memories, tangled and vivid, spilling across the surface like the past come to life. It had fallen off the wall, resting on its side beneath the flickering light of a melted sconce.

I grabbed it on instinct, dragging it behind me as I stumbled through the dark, coughing, the smoke screaming in my ears and in my lungs.

The front door was still lying on its side, and I stumbled over it. The cold air hit me like a slap, and I ran, depositing Pickle into the bed of my truck with the softest apology I'd ever whispered in my life, begging her not to move or run away. She blinked up at me, dazed and silent. I propped the painting against the side of the truck like it was the last holy thing in the world.

And I turned to go back in.

But I didn't make it.

"Sir! Get back!" A firefighter caught me around the chest as I hit the sidewalk.

"No—my sister's still in there!" I fought, twisted, screamed. "I have to— she's still—"

"You can't go in," another shouted. "The second floor's collapsing!"

I looked up.

The windows above the bar buckled inward with a groan, and then—crash.

The roof caved. Wood splintered. Smoke roared.

And with it… all of it.

Magnolia.

My sister.

My whole damn world.

I dropped to my knees, hands clutching at my hair, eyes wild. The street tilted under me. My lungs refused to work. My throat tore open on a scream I didn't even feel coming.

I was alone.

For the first time in my life, I was really, truly alone.

***

I sat in the back of the ambulance, the scratchy wool blanket doing nothing to stop the shaking. Pickle was pressed against my chest, wrapped up in my hoodie like a burrito of trauma. Her ears twitched at every siren wail, but she didn't move otherwise—only blinked up at me, weirdly calm for a creature who normally tried to murder me with her bare claws.

"Who would've thought, huh?" My voice broke. I swiped at my face with the back of my hand, snot and ash and tears smeared across my skin. "In the end, it's just me and you, kid."

I tried to laugh, but it came out like a sob. My whole body folded inward as I clutched the damn cat tighter. I couldn't stop crying. Couldn't stop seeing it—that second floor crashing in. Couldn't stop hearing the fire roar like it was alive and taking everything I loved with it.

A red blur whizzed past the paramedics, and before I could blink, the screaming started.

"My bar! That's my bar!" Magnolia's voice tore through the smoke. "Oh my god—my cat! Please, someone, my cat's still in there!"

She latched onto the nearest firefighter, shaking his arm like she could drag him inside with her, hair flying every which way, eyes blown wide with panic.

I shot to my feet so fast that Pickle nearly tumbled out of my arms. "Magnolia?"

Her eyes snapped to mine.

She froze.

I froze.

And then we were moving—crashing together halfway like neither of us could stand another second apart. I dropped the cat—she let out a noise of pure betrayal but didn't budge—and wrapped her up tighter than I'd ever held anyone in my life.

"You're alive," I rasped, my face buried in her curls.

"So are you," she whispered, her voice shredded from smoke and screaming.

"I thought I lost you. I thought I was..." The rest broke apart in my throat.

We clung to each other in the freezing night, smoke still clawing at the sky behind us, the bar smoldering at our backs, the world still on fire—but she was here. And so was I.

Lee came sprinting up from the far side of the block—barefoot, half-dressed, all panic and purpose. His curls were smashed flat on one side, like he'd rolled straight out of bed and hadn't stopped running since.

His hand found the small of Magnolia's back the second he reached her, steadying her where she clung to me. She softened under his touch, her trembling easing as she turned toward him. For a heartbeat, her eyes lifted to his, and something unspoken passed between them before she folded into his chest.

"Where's my brother?" he demanded, voice rough.

Before I could answer, Pickle came launching out of nowhere and scrambled up Lee's bare chest like a feral mountain climber with claws.

"Jesus Christ," he hissed, catching her awkwardly. "This cat has nine lives and no boundaries."

He glanced up at me over the cat's fur, his expression flickering—relief first, then fury, then raw concern. He passed Pickle back into my arms, gentler than I expected.

"Charlie. Where's Dane? Magnolia said she left him in the office when she…" His voice trailed, eyes snapping back to her before he forced the words out. "Before she came to see me."

I shook my head, still holding onto Magnolia's arm like she might slip straight back into the flames if I let go, completely ignoring the bomb he'd just dropped. "I don't know, Lee. I tried. I tried looking downstairs, but the smoke—it was too thick."

The words scraped out of my throat like gravel. My voice cracked again, and this time, I didn't stop the tears. "I found Pickle in the stairwell between the bar and the apartment. I thought—" I pulled Magnolia tighter and said, again, "I thought you were dead. I thought I was alone. I thought you left me."

Magnolia made a broken sound in her throat and hugged me back with everything she had.

Lee stood there, grief and confusion twisting his face, his arms hanging useless at his sides. For once, he had no words, no easy quip—only that haunted look in his eyes that said he understood. We'd all lost something big.

Maybe not each other, but something.

The wind cut sharply across the street, smoke still curling up from the wreckage as the fire crews battled the last of the stubborn flames. The sirens had quieted, but the crackle of ruin still echoed in every corner of my mind.

Eunice and Vance Wilder came rushing up in pajamas and tightly wrapped robes, faces drawn with worry. They didn't speak at first, only pulled each of us close, as if they could somehow shield us from what we'd already seen.

In hushed tones, Eunice took Magnolia aside, her voice low. Vance did the same with Lee, his hand firm on his son's shoulder, nodding as if already forming a plan—whether to rebuild the bar, find Dane, or simply figure out how to keep us all standing.

"Y'all come on back to the house," Vance said after a beat, loud enough for all of us to hear.

I looked to Magnolia, needing her cue. Her eyes were flat, her shoulders slumped, the fight gone out of her. She gave the barest shake of her head.

"All right," I said. "The fire chief wants to talk to us anyway."

She didn't argue as she stared back at the crumbling shell of the bar like she was watching a funeral.

As the Wilders led us to their car, I turned for one last look.

O'Malley's stood in ruin—smoke curling from the remnants of the collapsed second floor, windows blackened, the old neon sign hanging sideways like it, too, had given up. The whole place looked like the life had been sucked out of it—like it had been sucked out of my sister.

It wasn't only a bar. It was where my momma was born. This is where I said goodbye to my parents, where I climbed the narrow stairs to that stifling little apartment and tried to piece together a life after everything fell apart.

And now, watching it burn, it felt like everything had fallen apart all over again.

Like maybe the life had been sucked out of me, too.

CHAPTER THIRTY-NINE

Tally

It was freezing in Newnan, the kind of cold that bit through your gloves and stung your lungs a little when you breathed in too fast.

I wasn't sure what I was doing in town, other than trying not to go completely stir-crazy in my parents' mausoleum of a house. The McMansion, as Dig had so lovingly dubbed it years ago, had too many rooms and not enough warmth. My bedroom might've been a tomb to my youth, but nothing else in that house made me feel like I belonged. Not anymore. Maybe not ever.

I passed the square and slowed, the giant glittering New Year's display still half up in the plaza. Most of the folks were at work, or enjoying the last few, blissful days of their holiday break, but a young couple sat huddled on a bench, wrapped in matching scarves, bouncing a squishy, wide-eyed baby on their knees. Every time the baby squealed, they'd look at each other and laugh, really, truly *laugh*, like being parents was the funniest, best thing that had ever happened to them.

And I stood there like a creeper, watching.

It hit me harder than I expected. Not jealousy. Not even regret. But a sharp ache for what I'd never really had, but still wanted the chance to make right.

I bought a hot chocolate from the café on the corner, even though it was more whipped cream than anything, and wandered toward the gazebo at the far end of the park. It had been rebuilt since the infamous ride-on mower incident of my youth, and the freshly painted white wood gleamed against the gray sky.

I sat carefully on the bench, both hands wrapped around my cup, the warm cardboard pressed to my ribs.

Nancy Reagan curled up at my feet, her fluffy head on my boots.

"Okay, baby Aden," I said softly, pressing a palm over the curve of my

287

belly. "Here's the deal."

My breath came out in a little cloud. The wind rushed past the gazebo, rattling the tiny lights still strung up from the holidays.

"I don't know what the hell I'm doing. But I'm gonna figure it out. Not because of your dad, or your grandparents, or whatever the universe thinks it's got planned for us." I blinked up at the sky. "Because of *you*. Because you deserve to be somebody's everything. And I'm gonna be that person. Messy, dramatic, broke... but yours. Always yours."

A tear slid down my cheek, but I didn't wipe it away.

"I'm gonna be the kind of mom who dances in the kitchen with you. Who reads every book you love, even the weird ones with the scratchy textures. Who teaches you how to be soft and brave and loud and kind. And when you fall—because you will—I'll be right there, steadying you. Just like I'm trying to steady myself now."

I paused, pressing the cup to my lips. It tasted like fake cocoa powder. But it was warm.

"I love you already, kid. That's the thing no one ever tells you. You fall in love with someone who hasn't even arrived yet. And it changes everything."

Nancy let out a huff, as if she agreed.

"I don't need a man to do this. I don't need a plan. I just need you. And we're gonna be okay."

I leaned back, letting the quiet settle in, the sound of distant traffic and the sleepy hum of the town brushing against my ears. The baby gave a little kick under my hand.

I reached for my phone and opened the search bar, my thumb hovering midair like it needed permission to hope again.

Elopement planning in Georgia.

It felt a little ridiculous—like searching for lightning in a bottle while standing in the middle of a thunderstorm—but I scrolled anyway.

There were a few photographers in Atlanta, an officiant service based two counties over, and even a traveling pop-up chapel out of Macon that looked like it hadn't updated its website since 2014. None of it matched what I'd started to build in Savannah. There were no bar owners or cake-baking friends, no studio lights or vintage squares strung with fairy lights—but that didn't mean I couldn't find a version of it here. Something quieter, maybe. Something mine.

The seed was small, but it was there, pushing against something solid, something that might finally hold.

Down the path, the baby squealed again, and both parents laughed without hesitation—loud and open and full of love that didn't care who heard it. I stood for a minute longer watching them, letting the moment soften me.

Then, before I could second-guess myself, I stepped out of the gazebo and called over, "Mind if I take y'all's photo?"

The woman blinked at me in surprise, then offered a smile that made me feel like maybe I wasn't a stranger after all. "Sure!"

I pulled my camera, which I carried like a lifeline, from my bag and began to shoot. The way the light curved around their shoulders, how the baby's tiny hand clung to the edge of his dad's coat, how the mother's eyes never left her child for more than a second at a time.

It was love, right there in the middle of an ordinary day. Messy and loud and completely unposed. But real. Beautiful.

We exchanged information. I promised to edit the photos and send them along, and they thanked me like I'd captured a memory instead of a few snapshots.

I kept walking after that, making my way back through the square with Nancy Reagan trotting beside me. The town was still quiet, tucked somewhere between New Year's haze and January's slow unraveling.

A florist with a half-lit window. A bakery that smelled like warm vanilla. A dusty bridal shop with a paper sign taped crookedly to the glass. I paused at each one—not because they held answers, but because they felt like possibilities.

Outside the old courthouse, I stopped to take a few shots of the building's weathered charm. A couple stood nearby, trying to take a selfie with trembling hands, all bundled up and laughing about the angle.

I waited until they lowered their phones, then stepped forward.

"Want me to take one for you?" I asked. "I can edit it a bit and send it back to you—if you don't mind helping me out with a few practice poses."

The woman's eyes lit up. "We just got engaged!"

A spark kicked up in my chest—unexpected, but welcome after weeks of feeling flat. "Congratulations," I said, smiling for real this time. "If you like what you see, I'd love to do a full engagement session. On the house."

They nodded, already posing again, and I adjusted my settings, letting the camera do what it always did best—focus on what mattered.

Because here's the thing about photography—and Lord knows I've been chasing the light with a lens in my hand since I was a kid—there's beauty in the moments no one's trying to make perfect. There's magic in the small stuff. The ordinary. The overlooked.

A couple on a bench. A baby's laugh. A memory slipping through your fingers long enough to make you ache for it.

A fleeting moment with someone who was only in your life for a heartbeat, but somehow changed everything.

There's even joy tucked inside the grief of losing someone you love—because at the end of the day, the simple, aching truth is this: you got to *love*.

And loving Charlie Pruitt—however fleeting, however tangled in grief—was the most beautiful thing I'd ever done.

***

By the time I got home, the joy I'd felt earlier had started to wear thin.

Dig had called to check in, his voice still echoing in my ears—asking if I'd heard anything from Savannah.

I hadn't.

And the silence was starting to feel like an answer. One I didn't want.

I hung up and stared at the ceiling of my childhood bedroom, one hand resting on the gentle rise of my stomach. Nancy Reagan was curled up beside me, already snoring like the world wasn't quietly shifting underneath us. I wanted to believe it was all in my head—that the space between me and the people in Savannah was just geography, not something more profound. But when you've been left before, it doesn't take much time to start calling it abandonment.

I needed to get out of that room, so I grabbed my laptop to work on the edits of the photos I'd taken earlier, hoping the change of scenery would snap me out of the funk I was feeling.

Downstairs, the house was too quiet in that eerie, tiptoeing way it always was. Like it was holding its breath, waiting for someone to explode. My mother was still at City Hall, bossing people into resolutions they never asked for, which meant I had a window of peace. All I wanted was a snack, maybe a glass of my dad's overly sweet iced tea, and five minutes where I didn't feel like a stranger in my own life.

I found him in the kitchen, his back to me, rummaging through the fridge.

"Please tell me there's leftover banana pudding," I said.

He looked up, startled, then smiled that soft, worn-out smile of his. "I think you polished it off."

"Sounds about right. Sorry, I startled you."

"Just not used to sharing the house much anymore. Your momma's always out and about." He grabbed a pitcher and poured two glasses of tea. "You look tired."

"I *am* tired." I took my tea to the table, setting my things down. "But I feel good today. I've been working on some photography stuff. I got to shoot a few photos—wanna see?"

We sat at the kitchen table—me on the left like always, as if muscle memory had carried me right back to the only spot that ever felt like mine in this house.

Dad leaned over my shoulder, watching me scroll through the shots, tweaking the warmth, editing out parking signs, stray elbows, anything that pulled focus from the people I wanted to highlight.

"These are great," he said, rubbing my shoulder. "You've always had an eye. I'm surprised you never pursued this full-time."

I shrugged. "Not for lack of trying, but maybe I should've tried harder. I guess I needed someone to believe in me before I could start betting on myself."

He sat across from me, folding his hands. "I've been meaning to talk to you. Ever since that fight you and your momma had the other day…"

I didn't say anything.

"You know, we always laid a gentle hand on your brother," he said carefully. "Because we knew the world might be cruel to him, just for being who he is. We tried to armor him with love—so much that if anyone ever tried to hurt him with their words, it would bounce right off."

I let out a dry laugh. "Yeah. Great plan. You just created a self-righteous little tyrant."

He chuckled, then nodded, the smile falling away. "You… you never needed that kind of handholding, Tallulah. You came into this world strong. Fierce. Unapologetic."

I looked at him. "Is that the truth? Or just a nice way to explain away neglect?" He didn't flinch.

"What you felt in this house, growing up… it wasn't okay. I can see that now. But that doesn't mean you were supposed to float through life without purpose."

"That doesn't excuse the years I felt like y'all were ignoring me. And it sure as hell doesn't excuse Momma chipping away at me until I barely recognized who I was." My voice didn't shake. "I only got tough because I had to. Because this house demanded it. And that's not a legacy I plan to pass on."

I eased to my feet, balancing my laptop in one hand, the other instinctively settling over my belly.

"You might be trying to apologize right now, Daddy—and maybe some part of me hears it. But you don't need to. You should be proud of me. Not because I've got a fancy job or a penthouse view—because I don't. But because I *know* who I am now. And I'm proud as hell of the woman sitting in this kitchen."

Later that night, the house was still quiet aside from the low hum of the TV downstairs when my father knocked softly, his head poking through the doorway like he didn't want to risk too much.

"I'm not interested in continuing this conversation," I muttered, not looking up from my phone. "I said what I said."

Daddy chuckled, easing into the room and sitting on the edge of my bed. "As you always do, Tallulah." He motioned toward the hallway. "I brought some things down from the attic. You might not believe it, but your momma saved all your baby clothes. Said maybe one day you'd want them for your own."

I held his gaze for a moment, then carefully pushed myself off the bed and followed him out. Boxes were lined up in the hallway, some half-open, full of soft blankets, tiny shoes, and hand-me-down toys. All arranged so neatly it nearly broke me.

"There's a crib and a rocking chair, too. Still up there," he added. "And, well… we've got plenty of room, if you needed it."

The hope in his voice landed like a punch. It was the first time I'd seen it—how much he *wanted* to be someone I could count on. And maybe he didn't know how to say it outright, but he was trying. Trying in the only way he knew how.

Was it too late for me to accept that? Too late to believe I was still worthy of someone showing up?

"Can I think about it?" I asked, lifting a mint green sweater from the top of one box. It was soft and hand-knit, with tiny booties to match. I rested it on my stomach. "I think this might be just your size, kid," I whispered.

Daddy reached out and patted my back. "No rush. Take your time." He started down the hallway, then paused. "Was your momma's idea, by the way."

I recoiled like the sweater had grown fangs. "Ew, no. Never mind then."

He grinned. "Thought that might ruin it for you."

Before he disappeared around the corner, he looked back. "You know... I don't know much. But I figure if someone shows up—" he gestured toward the boxes, "—trying to be better, trying to do right... maybe you meet them where they are. Maybe you get to know the version of them they're trying to be."

I stared at him, unsure if we were still talking about him or me or even Momma anymore.

Then he added, with a smile so dry it could start a fire, "And I'm guessing you haven't driven a John Deere into a gazebo lately, bottle of whiskey in one hand, Spice Girls blasting full volume?"

I coughed out a laugh. "Can't say that I have."

"Right," he said. "Well, then. Goodnight, Tallulah."

CHAPTER FORTY

Charlie

The pencil scratched across the page in uneven lines, the graphite smudging under my palm. I blinked at what I'd created—if you could call it that. A few misshapen circles. A half-hearted horizon line. The beginnings of an installation I'd been dreaming of, misplaced, discarded items brought together to create something meaningful. But it wasn't anything.

I crumpled the page and tossed it to the corner, where a mountain of other false starts had already claimed squatters' rights—another failure, right on schedule.

The studio felt less like home these days and more like a prison. Maybe that was because I had nowhere to go. The bar was gone. Magnolia barely spoke. And Dane—Jesus. Hours before the fire, she'd walked in on him tangled up with Kasey, one of Magnolia's bartenders, in the O'Malley's office. The one person she trusted to help her keep the place running had been screwing the man who was supposed to love her.

She ended it right there, ring off, voice shaking, Kasey slinking out like the world's worst scarlet letter. And then the fire started. Hours later, O'Malley's was nothing but smoke and ash.

Nobody'd caught Dane yet. He and Kasey were on the run—some pathetic knockoff of Bonnie and Clyde, if Bonnie had a fake tan and Clyde wore boat shoes.

I didn't even have the energy to be surprised. Of course, Dane would leave wreckage in his wake and walk away clean. That was his talent—the mess burned, and he kept moving.

I stood, stretching my back, and walked the few steps into the small bedroom tucked off to the side. It wasn't anything fancy—just a full-sized bed, an overloaded bookshelf, and a lamp that flickered like it was in mourning too. But on the far wall, I'd hung the unfinished sketch.

Her.

The Waving Girl statue in the distance. The curve of the river. And her—silhouetted against it all, her hand resting gently on her bump, eyes fixed on the horizon beyond the frame. A replica of the one I'd given to Tally, or it was supposed to be.

It should've been beautiful. It *was* beautiful. But I couldn't finish it.

Not because I didn't know how. But because we didn't.

We didn't finish.

I ran a hand over my jaw, letting my eyes trace the outline I'd drawn so many times I could still see it when I closed them. She was right there and completely out of reach, like every goddamn thing in my life.

The only person who ever made me feel like a part of *something real* left without a word in the middle of the night. And I couldn't even blame her.

I didn't bother brushing the charcoal off my hands. I changed my shirt, shoved on a clean pair of jeans, and grabbed my keys off the hook by the door—anything to get out of that damn studio.

Jones Street was quiet in that old-money way—dignified, expensive, and a little smug about it. I used to hate walking past those houses as a kid, with their gas lanterns flickering and their manicured window boxes that never seemed to wilt. The Wilder place sat halfway down the block—a wide wraparound porch, two perfect rocking chairs, and a front door painted a red that was definitely chosen by someone with generational wealth and a flair for design. It was the kind of house that said *we've been here for a long time, and we'll be here long after you're gone.*

Back then, it made me feel like I didn't belong.

Now... it felt like another kind of home. Not because I'd earned it, exactly, but because Eunice Wilder never once made me feel like I had to.

I was halfway up the steps when the door swung open.

"Well, Lord, have mercy. Charlie Pruitt, you look like you've been through hell."

I almost smiled. Eunice stood in the doorway in a soft cardigan and jeans, her bare feet tucked into slippers, and a glass of iced tea in her hand, like she wasn't expecting company but not surprised to see me. That was the thing about Eunice—she always made you feel like you were *exactly* who she was hoping to see.

"Don't think hell has me on their guest list just yet," I said, scrubbing a hand over my face.

She stepped aside and drew me into the kitchen. "Come on in, my dear. Have one of Sutton's scones, a glass of my sun tea, and tell me what's working that restless mind of yours."

Before we reached the breakfast nook, she pulled me into a long hug—warm and steady, the way she used to do when Magnolia and I camped out there as kids. Back then, Eunice Wilder never treated us like the rag-tag orphans trailing after her son; she treated us like family. No matter what had happened that past week—or who might have struck the match—I knew that part of her hadn't changed.

We settled at the nook beneath the window, and I stared out over the sprawling yard. The azaleas weren't in bloom yet, but they would be soon. Spring would come dancing into Savannah like it did, announcing itself with a trumpet of greenery and vines, blooms and bugs, humidity and brine drifting in off the bustling river.

Eunice set out an entire spread—scones, tiny cucumber sandwiches, lemon bars—because a snack in her kitchen always turned into high tea. She sat across from me, hands folded.

"I'd like to ask how Magnolia's doing," she said gently, "But I don't want to pry if she would rather I not know, given the circumstances."

I filled a plate—there was no refusing food in her house—then rested my elbows on the table. "She's keeping to herself. Any news on Dane?"

Eunice shook her head. "None, sweetheart. Not a whisper."

I picked at my plate, a sudden wave of unease washing over me at the thought of him, still out there, still a threat to my sister. Because, truth be told, if she weren't with Lee that night, she would be dead. The memory of the fire, the way the smoke filled my lungs so quickly, and the waves of flames flickered furiously, eating away at the walls of my childhood home, suddenly started playing on a loop in my mind. I couldn't stop the images. I couldn't stop remembering how, for a flicker of a moment, I thought that I wasn't just an orphan but truly alone, that Magnolia was gone.

"How are you holding up, Charlie?" Eunice said, pulling me from the memory. "You look tired." I had to laugh. What a nice, southernly way to say I looked like shit. I probably did. I rubbed the back of my neck and leaned back on my side of the booth. "Tired is a good word, I suppose. I haven't slept since…"

Since the fire. Since Tally left. Hell, since the day she bulldozed into my life.

Eunice poured more tea. "Before Lee drove back to Nashville, he mentioned you were seeing someone. Was it Tally? You two were getting along quite well every time I bumped into y'all."

"I wouldn't call it that," I said. There weren't words for what Tally had become to me; she'd felt less like a girlfriend and more like a missing piece I'd never known I'd lost. "It's over now. She's gone."

I stared out the window, searching the brittle lawn for answers.

Eunice's voice cut through the quiet. "You've always flown guard for Magnolia, Charlie, but have you thought that spending all your strength shielding her might keep you from finding your own sky?"

"What's that supposed to mean?"

"She'll carve her path, stubborn or not. You can't steer it for her, and you can't stay ground-tethered forever waiting to catch her. You can't find your own way in this world, Charlie, if you keep focusing on clipping your sister's wings."

I traced a circle on my saucer. "She's all I've got."

"Maybe," Eunice said, "but she's not all you are." She reached across the table and squeezed my hand. "It's time to let yourself want a life that's yours."

Her words sat heavy and painfully true in the hush between us. I didn't answer; I didn't have to. She gave my fingers one last press, then released me to my thoughts, the untouched scone sitting on my plate, and the first hint of purpose stirring in my chest.

But what could I do?

She was gone.

"Sutton said you wanted to talk to me about something?"

She nodded, a tip of her lip letting me know she was welcome to changing the subject, only if I was. "I did. I wanted to pick your brain about giving Magnolia what would have been her wedding gift."

"It better not be a bar," I deadpanned.

She shook her head. "We wouldn't, actually, be giving it to her. She would have to pay us back. And it's not a bar. It's an empty canvas for whatever she might dream up on her own."

"On her own," I parrotted.

Eunice sighed and reached back over the table. "Yes, Charlie. On her own."

***

Later that night, despite the traitorous way it felt to be sitting on another worn barstool, elbows planted on a different slab of sticky, beer-slicked mahogany, I joined a few of my friends for a drink at The Irish Immigrant Pub. It was the first time the four of us—Jordan, Doyle, Sutton, and me—had all been together since the fire.

Magnolia, under the guise of reviewing insurance documents, had locked herself in my studio with a stack of paperwork and a white-knuckled grip on control. None of us had the heart—or maybe the guts—to stop her. Not yet. Because we all knew she needed to do this now. She needed to believe there was a plan, a next step. But soon, I'd have to intervene. Or would I? Eunice Wilder's voice kept circling back: *You can't find your own way in this world, Charlie, if you keep focusing on clipping your sister's wings.*

Maybe I didn't have to fix everything for Magnolia. Maybe, just maybe, I could trust that she'd find her own way through. And, especially what Eunice had brought to me earlier in the day, a secret I couldn't reveal yet, she'd forge her way back to solid ground. But, she would have to do it on her own.

"What a dump," Doyle muttered, squinting around the bar like he'd walked into a health hazard. "I've drank in some real shitholes, but this one has both character *and* mildew."

"Pretty sure the wallpaper's just beer residue that evolved into its own ecosystem," Sutton added, pulling her sweater tighter and making a face at the menu.

"It's not O'Malley's," Jordan said under his breath.

That quiet landed like a stone in the middle of the table. We all looked down for a second too long.

"No," I said. "It's not. But it's what we've got tonight."

"On the plus side," Doyle offered, lifting his glass and giving me a weary side-eye, "Charlie hasn't punched anyone yet, so that's something."

"There's still time," I muttered loud enough to remind him that I hadn't

299

forgotten who drove his sister out of town.

"Can't blame him," Sutton said. "His whole life just caught fire. Literally. And he's dealing with it by sitting here, drinking this—" she took a sip and grimaced, "—swamp water pretending to be a stout."

We sat for a while, talking like people do when nothing's normal but they desperately want it to be. Lee's upcoming tour. Whether we should mark Magnolia's would-be wedding date with an impromptu picnic or just take her the hell out of town to get away from it all. Planning the next art show at *Cheese, Please!*. Sutton debating whether she should break up with Ryan for calling her his "main bitch" instead of his girlfriend.

"You know," she said after a few more pints, loosening into her seat, "you and Tally never labeled it. You just… went off vibes."

I scoffed into my beer. "Yeah. And look how that turned out."

Doyle met my eyes over the table. A question hung there. Did he know? What happened between Tally and me was more than a fling? That I lay awake most nights, staring at the unfinished sketch of her by the river—the twin to the one I gave her on Christmas—forever incomplete, like the way she left me.

Sutton yawned four times in ten minutes before finally standing. "Time to go home to my super fun roommate, who's definitely not listening to Lee's latest single while plotting the total demise of this entire city."

"Don't forget your new pet," I said, kissing her cheek. "Give my girl Pickle a kiss for me."

"She only likes you now because you saved her life. Give it time. She'll be back to shredding your ankles and swatting at the back of your head."

Jordan and Doyle exchanged a pointed look as Jordan pushed back his chair. "I should head out too. See you at home, love." He kissed Doyle's head, and before I could ask why they weren't leaving together, Doyle waved toward the bar.

"One more round."

I raised an eyebrow. "Are you really sticking around, or planning to Irish exit once the bartender stops making eye contact?"

"I'm not the one who ghosted on Christmas," Doyle said, drumming his fingers on the rim of his glass. "But sure. Let's pretend *I'm* the flaky sibling."

"That was low," I said. "Even for you."

We sat with that. The jukebox flipped to a slow and bluesy tune. The kind of song that makes you miss someone who's not dead but might as well be—roughly 290 miles away. Not that I was counting.

"I'm sorry," he said, not looking at me. "For a lot of things."

"I know."

Silence passed between us like a puck sliding across ice. But it wasn't awkward. It was too old friends trying to figure it out.

"Wanna go in on a soft pretzel?" Doyle asked, dead serious. "You look like you need the carbs."

I huffed out a laugh. "Yeah, alright. But I'm getting the cheese cup. And you're buying."

As the server dropped the pretzel, Doyle stiffened in his seat.

"It's not exactly *Cheese, Please!* caliber," I said, biting in. "But we're drunk, and it's edible. Now's not the time to be a diva."

He shook his head and reached into his messenger bag, pulling out a worn envelope—edges soft, creased, like he'd been carrying it around for weeks. "I found this in her room," he said, sliding it across the sticky table. "I've been struggling with when to give it to you. And probably not for the reason you think."

My gaze bounced between him and the envelope like it might explode.

"I don't know what she says," he added, nodding toward it. "Didn't open it. I wanted to, because I'm nosey. But I was afraid she'd say…"

The anger came fast, hot up my neck. "Just spit it out."

"Okay, fine." He took a huge gulp of cider and slammed his glass down. "I'm afraid she's gonna tell you to fuck off. That she didn't love you. Because shutting people out is her go-to defense. And I know you've got a lot going on, and I didn't want to make it worse and—"

I held up a hand. "You should've given it to me when you found it. No matter what it says. You've been a shitty friend lately, Doyle. And I'm trying—really trying—to give you grace. But it's getting harder every time we do this."

"You're right. I have been a shitty friend. And a shitty brother." He stood, grabbing his bag and one last piece of pretzel. "I've got things to work on, and so do you. Let that be our New Year's resolution."

I frowned.

"To be better," he said, stepping back. "For the people who love us. That includes being a little less selfish for me… and a little *more* selfish for you."

CHAPTER FORTY-ONE

Tally

Sitting in the nursery, Nancy snoring at my feet, I couldn't stop thinking about Savannah. I couldn't stop thinking about Charlie, of course, but being in my childhood home, in the rooms where Doyle and I were a power unit, forged so tightly together by the chaos of our mother's moods and shifting affections, I missed my original person. I missed my goddamn brother, despite how we left things, despite that he, solely, was the reason for my broken heart.

The nursery was starting to come together. For once in my thirty-one years, Momma and I actually agreed on something—we'd painted the room a soft mint green. My old crib and her old rocking chair looked downright quaint against the white rug. Daddy had even hung up some photos from my own nursery days, framed like relics.

And on the side table next to the rocker sat the watercolor Charlie made me. Me and The Waving Girl.

"That's me and you, kid," I whispered to my belly as I lowered myself into the chair. "It's the only picture of the two of us so far."

The thought hit like a lightning bolt—not only had Charlie had captured the sheer loneliness of being Tally River Aden, but something else, too.

He'd seen this version of me. Tally River Aden, the mother. And he'd loved her anyway. Loved us anyway, even though this baby wasn't his.

Nancy Reagan groaned from her blanket nest on the floor, shooting me a look like even she was over this pity party. I knelt, ran my fingers through the scruff behind her ears, and sighed.

"You think I'm overreacting?" I asked her softly. "Or not enough?"

She huffed and flopped dramatically onto her side.

"Yeah. That's fair."

I settled back into the rocking chair, one hand on my belly, the other reaching for my phone. Doyle was the first person I'd called when I, in a blurry haze of wine drunkenness, realized I was pregnant, and I'd envisioned us doing this together. Me, the doting mother I always needed, him, the uncle that would sweep in with presents and terrible jokes, the one who'd teach her to be fearless. I decided to be the bigger person.

Doyle answered on the second ring.

"Is it time, is the baby coming? I can get on a plane right now, Tal, I swear to God—"

Aha, so he didn't hate me.

"No," I sighed, and I could practically hear him deflate on the other end. "It's not time. I just... I'm sitting in your old room, which is the baby's nursery now, by the way, and I'm remembering all the times we used to sit in here late at night, telling each other secrets and making plans together. And I..."

"I'm sorry, Tal." His voice cracked, and that's how I knew he meant it. "I should have never done this to you. You should be here... especially now."

I sat up straighter, sending Nancy into a half-awake frenzy of indignant snorts. The tone of his voice wasn't laced with apology. It was laced with concern, the kind that made my stomach drop.

"What happened?"

"There was a fire and—"

"Is Charlie okay?" The words came out loud and panicked. My free hand flew to my belly like I was covering the baby's little ears.

Doyle sighed, long and heavy. "He's fine. Shaken up, but fine. O'Malley's burned down on New Year's Eve. The whole place, Tal. It's just... gone."

I couldn't breathe. O'Malley's. The place where I got to actually talk to Magnolia, for the first time, and it was like meeting with an old friend. The bar where Charlie and I had one hysterical yet somehow intimate night. How important that building was not only to the Pruitts', but to Savannah's history, as well.

"The fire department's still investigating," Doyle continued, and I could hear him moving around, probably packing up wine orders, keeping his hands busy during a difficult conversation. "But Dane is suspect number one. Charlie's been at the station giving statements, dealing with insurance, trying to figure out what the hell comes next. Everyone's been rallying around him and Magnolia, but it's bad. Really bad."

"Wait, it was Dane? Like Magnolia's fiancé, Dane?"

"Turns out he was having a full-blown affair with Kasey—the bartender. They ran off into the night and haven't been seen since." Doyle's voice tightened. "But that's not even the worst of it. He forged Cole Pruitt's death certificate—Charlie and Magnolia's uncle—and never filed the real one. Which means Dane technically still holds the majority share of the Wilder family trust. So when Cole died, the payout from his life insurance went straight to Dane." He exhaled, frustrated. "There's more, but honestly, Tally, I don't want to stress you out right now."

But I was already spiraling. Charlie had lost O'Malley's. The bar his uncle left to Magnolia, the place they'd both grown up in, where their whole lives lived in the grain of the wood and the stories etched into every barstool. And Magnolia—God, Magnolia had lost everything. Her bar, her fiancé, probably her sense of trust in anyone or anything.

And Charlie, sweet Charlie who took care of everyone, who'd probably spent the last however many days holding his sister together while his own heart broke, dealing with police and insurance adjusters and the wreckage of the only home he'd ever really known.

And the loss of me, walking away in the middle of the night.

"He's been taking care of Magnolia, hasn't he?" I asked quietly.

"Of course he has. You know Charlie."

I did. I knew him so well it physically hurt. Knew that he'd put everyone else first, that he'd swallow his own grief to make sure his sister didn't drown in hers. That he'd probably barely slept, barely eaten, but kept moving because that's what Charlie Pruitt did when the people he loved needed him.

And I wasn't there. I was here, pregnant with another man's baby, too proud or too scared to pick up the phone.

"I should come back. I should be with him." The words tumbled out before I could stop them. I thought of them all, huddled around each other trying to work through this moment, how many ways Charlie had been there for me when my world fell apart, and... he should have called to tell me. Shouldn't he?

"Did you give him my letter?" I asked, the words catching in my throat.

Doyle hesitated, releasing what sounded like a long-held sigh. "There's just… a lot going on right now. It might not have been the right moment."

"Yeah," I whispered, though my chest squeezed. "I get that."

But I didn't. Not really. When was it ever the right moment? When was anything in our lives ever simple or easy?

"I am really sorry, Tally. I'm going to come for a few days when you have the baby. Just me. I can't ever make up to you what I put you through, but I can start by trying to make things right, for you and the baby."

My throat closed up. "I love you, Doyle."

"I love you too, Tal."

After we hung up, I sat there in the golden morning light, Nancy's snores resuming their steady rhythm, and felt the tears sliding hot down my cheeks. Magnolia's bar had burned down. Not only her bar—their family's legacy, her inheritance, the place where we'd fallen in love over spilled margarita salt and late-night confessions, where he'd first looked at me like I was something precious instead of something broken. And he hadn't called. Doyle hadn't given him my letter. And I was here, hundreds of miles away, growing another man's baby while Charlie's entire world collapsed around him, while he held his sister together and faced down the wreckage alone.

My eyes drifted back to the watercolor on the side table. The Waving Girl, forever frozen in her gesture of goodbye or hello or maybe both at once. Charlie had painted me as her, pregnant and alone, waiting for someone who might never come back. Had he known, even then, that this was who we were? Two people who loved each other, one of them carrying someone else's child, separated by hurt and pride and terrible timing?

I picked up my phone, his contact still saved under "Charlie 🖤" because I'd been too stubborn or too hopeful to change it. My thumb hovered over his name. One call. That's all it would take. I could tell him I was sorry, that I didn't care about the letter or the timing or any of it—I needed to hear his voice. I could tell him that I wanted to be there, wanted to help him rebuild, wanted to be part of his life even if mine was messy and complicated.

But what if he didn't answer? What if he did, and his voice was cold, indifferent, too exhausted from holding Magnolia together to have anything left for me and this baby that wasn't even his? What if the fire had burned away whatever feelings he'd had, and now all that was left was ash and the memory of what we could have been?

I set the phone down and pressed both palms against my stomach, feeling the baby shift beneath my hands. Maybe letting go was the kindest thing I could do for both of us. Maybe love wasn't always about holding on. Sometimes it was about knowing when to let the ashes settle.

***

Momma had agreed—after Daddy's gentle nudging—to attend a few therapy sessions with me. To keep the peace, he'd said, but I knew it was more than that. He knew, and I knew, that as soon as I could, I'd run again, taking the baby with me, and they'd never have a relationship with them.

The sessions were awkward at first—me picking at a tissue while Momma sat stiff in her chair, arms crossed, saying all the right things with that tight, polite smile she'd perfected for the cameras. But by the third one, her attitude started to shift. Maybe it was the way the therapist didn't flinch when I said the hard parts out loud. Or maybe Momma ran out of energy to perform.

I found her in the kitchen, leaning against the counter with her phone face down beside her and a mug of coffee cradled in both hands. An unreadable look sat on her face, but over the last few days—and a few mother-daughter therapy sessions—she'd started to soften toward me. And, frankly, she didn't scare me anymore.

I knew how easy it was to love a child. Even one I hadn't met yet. Whatever resentment Momma carried—that was hers to reckon with. I'd carried it for her long enough. Maybe that's what changed between us. Perhaps she sensed I'd finally ripped that power right out of her hands.

She leaned against the counter while I rummaged through the pantry for a snack that was vaguely healthy yet didn't taste like cardboard. Now that I had my power back, maybe they'd even let me pick out the groceries.

Then, quietly, she slid a piece of paper across the counter.

I stared down at it—a flyer.

Single Moms Meet-Up

Tuesdays at 9

Newnan Carnegie Library.

Free coffee. No judgment.

"You should go, Tallulah," she said, her voice lower, gentler. "I could come with you, if you want. I'll clear my calendar."

I blinked, unsure if I'd heard her right. "You'd do that?"

"I would."

A splinter of sadness I didn't know I'd been carrying cracked open in me. It wasn't a grand gesture. But it was a start. The kind of thing I used to fantasize about when I was younger, before I learned to stop hoping for it.

She gave a soft, practiced smile, collected her mug, and disappeared down the hall toward her office.

Not even a full second later, Daddy came barreling through the back door like he'd returned from a mission.

"Am I hearing correctly from your brother that you don't have a baby registry?" he asked, like I'd confessed to a federal crime. "You're nearly there, girl—we should at least go into town and pick out a few things."

"I didn't think I needed one," I said, still staring at the flyer. "I wasn't sure anyone would even..."

"Nonsense," he said, already grabbing his keys. "We should throw you a shower. We'll do it here."

From the hallway, Momma called out, "I'll add it to the calendar."

The mayor of Newnan, Georgia, publicly throwing her unwed pregnant daughter a baby shower. Six months ago, that would've been unthinkable. Six weeks ago, even. But here we were.

I was still processing that when something else clicked. "Wait a second— you talked to Doyle?"

Daddy tossed me my coat and purse from the mudroom hook. "He says hello. And that he's glad you're doing just fine here."

I made myself ask it. "Did he say anything else? About... anyone in Savannah?"

He paused, giving me a long look. "He did say something odd. Maybe you can figure it out. He said, '*Tell my sister I did the right thing.*'"

CHAPTER FORTY-TWO

Charlie

I'd been staring at the damn letter for three days, moving it around the studio like a cursed object. Hiding it under paint rags, tucking it behind half-finished canvases like that would stop me from reaching for it. Time and time again, I found my hand resting on the seam of the tab, itching to open it.

What if all it said was to leave her alone?

Would she really write that out? Wasn't her silence enough? That one generic *Happy New Year* text had done the job just fine.

What if it said it meant nothing to her?

But worse—what if it said it meant *everything?*

I shook my head, pushing back the thought. If she wanted to be here, she would be. Sitting by my side, helping me figure out how to piece together the melted, scorched wreckage of Magnolia's portrait.

I hadn't even told Mags I'd saved it yet. I stopped by Eunice's last week to see if she knew anyone who could restore damage like this, but no luck. Now all I had was a half-melted, ash-streaked version of my sister glaring back at me—and no one to bounce ideas off of.

I groaned and dropped onto the nearest stool, scrubbing a hand down my face. This was loneliness. Not being alone, but loneliness in its most distilled, raw form.

There were people around all the time. Jordan and Doyle were upstairs. Mags was down the street. Sutton was on her way over. Lee was a phone call away.

But the loneliness? It was a living, breathing thing pacing these uneven floors right alongside me.

And loneliness, someone once told me, makes people do the most unbelievable things.

"Jesus, you look like you're about to run into traffic. And could you please, for the love of God, put on a shirt?"

Sutton stood in the front gallery, flanked between the wine-bottle and hubcap Bird Girl statue and an old piping spool I'd turned into a side table. More art. More junk. More unfinished projects.

I shook my head, like that could dislodge the weight of everything. I'd lived a meaningful life before her. I could do it again.

And maybe this time, I wouldn't waste it chasing demons that didn't belong to me.

I grabbed the to-go bag from Sutton and motioned for her to sit. I started plating our food in silence.

"Are you gonna talk to me at all?" she asked, flopping into the seat across from mine. "Or is this one of your signature brooding episodes that I'm the lucky guest of tonight?"

I grunted.

"Noted," she muttered, popping up to grab drinks from the fridge.

We ate. Or rather, *I* ate in silence. Sutton yammered on about Magnolia finding out Dane hadn't canceled their honeymoon and how Magnolia thought it'd be *fun* if the two of them went to Ireland together.

The old me would've had a full-blown panic attack about that. My baby sister leaving the country while her arson-happy ex-fiancé was still on the loose?

But the new me—the me trying to listen to Eunice Wilder and be a person with *boundaries*— and a heart that was beating erratically out of my chest at the thought of the piece of paper sitting on the workbench behind us, only had one thing to say.

"She left me a letter."

***

Charlie,

I never planned to become the Waving Girl.

I'd always felt a quiet kinship with her, sure. But now here I am—standing on a shoreline you can't see, scarf in the air, hoping that one day a boat carrying a broad-shouldered artist might cut through the fog and dock beside me. Whether you read this an hour after I'm gone or a year from now, I'll still be waiting.

I already miss you. I missed you before I was even brave enough to admit you were mine to miss.

I miss sitting in the studio with you, watching you work, immersed in the rhythm of doing what you love. I miss the way you grumbled when Nancy claimed half your pillow or barked at you like you were a threat, but you let her stay anyway. I miss waking up to find you stretched out on that far-too-expensive loveseat, pretending you hadn't been listening for my footsteps.

I miss the way you looked at me when what was bubbling beneath the surface finally broke through. After weeks of circling it, how your hands felt on me, whether in the heat of intimacy or in those quiet moments when you'd just rest a steady palm on my back, grounding me without a word.

I'm sorry I ran.

Fear was the only reason, and it isn't noble. I was terrified that the second I believed in this—believed in you—you'd be the one to let go. And I've fallen too many times to survive another drop. So I left first.

That doesn't mean it didn't matter. It means it mattered too much.

I loved you so quickly, I didn't realize I'd handed you every jagged piece of me until you were holding them like they'd always belonged together. And maybe that scared me most of all. Because I didn't think I deserved that kind of love.

But I'm trying now.

Not for a relationship. Not even for redemption. For this baby.

I want to build something steady, solid as a bridge in a storm. A safe place where my child will never have to wonder if the ground will hold. I want to be the kind of mother who can't be knocked down, but is still the softest place to land.

If love finds us after that—if it finds me—then maybe the tides will carry you to our shore.

I won't ask for forgiveness. But if someday you find yourself reaching across the water, looking for the woman waving her white flag on a Savannah bank...

Know that I won't be waving out of loneliness or regret.

I'll be waving because I believe you'll see me.

And if that day never comes—know this. Every kiss, every grin you tried to hide behind that beard, every late-night confession on a couch too small for what we felt. It was real.

I'll raise this baby with the courage I found in your eyes.

The courage taught me that I might be worth loving.
And if you come ashore…
You'll find us waiting.
Not broken pieces. But something whole.
Always waving,
Tally

CHAPTER FORTY-THREE

Charlie

Magnolia handed the letter back to me with both hands, like it was sacred. Or dangerous. Maybe both.

"Wow," was all she said. Her voice barely carried above the rustle of the trees.

"Exactly," Sutton muttered, beginning her fifth lap around the bench like a caged animal. "And exactly why we are still sitting on this bench in this damn square in Savannah and not jetting down the highway on our way to Newnan is beyond me."

I didn't respond. I couldn't. The letter sat in my lap, my thumb rubbing across the spot where Tally had signed her name. *Always waving.*

"You're gonna need to do something eventually, Charlie," Sutton said, spinning on her heel and pointing at me. "Because sitting here looking like a heartbroken Labrador isn't a strategy."

"I'm thinking," I said, though it sounded like a lie even to me.

Magnolia let out a quiet sigh, her eyes still fixed on the little fountain in the center of the square.

"Do you really think she wants to hear from me?" I asked. "That she meant any of that?"

Sutton threw her hands up. "God, men are exhausting. That letter was practically a love song and a GPS coordinate."

"She's not wrong," Magnolia said, finally looking at me. "Tally doesn't throw words around like that unless she means them. You know that."

I shook my head. "It's not that simple."

"It never is," Magnolia said gently. "But hard doesn't mean wrong."

Sutton flopped down onto the bench beside me, exasperated. "You love her. She clearly loves you. There's a baby involved. What the hell are you waiting for?"

I stared down at the letter again, trying to make sense of the mess in my chest. I wanted to go. I *did*. But what if I'd already missed my chance?

"She's not waving because she's lonely," Magnolia said, her voice soft. "She's waving because she believes you'll see her. Don't prove her wrong."

I turned toward my sister. Quiet, sad eyes and a crumpled frame sat next to me. She was destroyed, too. Our lives were upended. The romances, the fire, the bar, gone forever. She needed me.

I needed her, too.

"You need me here, Magnolia, I…"

She shook her head, placing a gentle hand on my arm. "I don't *need* you, Charlie. I like having you around because you're not only my brother, but you're my best friend, too. But I do not need you to fix me."

Looking back out over the square, Magnolia took another deep breath, arms crossed tight over her chest like she was holding something in. Or maybe keeping something safe.

"Tally doesn't need you to fix her, either, you know," she said, voice steady. "She just needs you to stand beside her. Not in front of her. Not behind. Beside. Do you get the difference?"

Sutton and I groaned in unison.

"You two are insufferable," Sutton muttered, pushing off the bench. "We should be in the truck speeding down I-75. But yes, please, continue being wise and poetic, Magnolia."

Magnolia smirked but didn't take her eyes off the fountain. "The point is, Charlie… you've spent your whole life trying to hold things together. Me. Uncle Cole. The bar. Everyone but yourself. And maybe it's time to stop."

I opened my mouth to argue, but she beat me to it.

"I'll be okay," she said, finally turning back to me. "Really. I've got Sutton. Our friends. This wild, ridiculous life I somehow still love—even though a big part of it just went up in flames. I want you to go live yours. Find your family. Build it. Be in it. And one day, when we've both got the love we deserve, we can come back together. Not to fix what broke. But to celebrate what we built."

A knot lodged in my throat. I swallowed hard, trying to push it down, but it stayed right there—grit and hope all mixed together.

"We'll still be us," she said, her voice quieter now. "Just… bigger."

CHAPTER FORTY-FOUR

Tally

The baby registry gun made a satisfying little *beep* each time I pointed it at something ridiculous, which apparently gave me the unhinged confidence to zap everything in sight.

"This?" I asked, aiming it at a miniature baby robe with bear ears.

"Obviously," Daddy said, pushing the cart like it was a parade float. "Every baby needs a robe. With ears."

Beep.

"What about this?" I asked, holding up a wipe warmer with deeply skeptical eyes. "Do I need this? I mean, I'm a child of the nineties. I was raised on cold wet wipes and internalized shame, and look how I turned out."

Daddy gave me a once-over and winced. "Scan the butt wipe warmer, sweetheart."

Beep.

The next aisle was full of things I hadn't even known existed—pacifier sanitizers, vibrating bouncers, a plush giraffe that claimed to teach emotional regulation. Emotional regulation! I was thirty-one and barely qualified.

"You're going a little feral with that thing," Daddy noted as I aimed the scanner like I was hunting for sport. "I love it."

"It's not just a baby registry," I said. "It's retail therapy with a side of delusion."

He laughed, the sound light and unguarded in a way I hadn't heard in a while. "You needed this. Something to look forward to. Something real."

I nodded, emotion catching in my throat before I could answer.

After one more lap through the store—and one regrettable incident where, giggling like a maniac, I tried to scan a store employee's barcode badge to "see what would happen"—Daddy suggested we get some lunch. I agreed, hunger finally catching up with me after a morning of impulse scanning and light emotional unraveling.

We were halfway to the restaurant when I stopped cold.

No.

No way.

It couldn't be.

But there he was, clear as day, standing in the center of the rebuilt gazebo downtown, hands in the pockets of his jacket, head tilted like he was trying to memorize the architecture and beam length. Tall. Broad-shouldered. Viking-level red hair catching the winter light. Sam Heughan could *never*. My lungs forgot how to work.

"Daddy," I whispered.

"Yes, darlin'?"

I didn't answer.

Because the man I'd written a love letter to—the man I'd practically dared to come after me—was standing dead center in the heart of Newnan, Georgia, in the exact spot where he knew I'd find him.

Always waving.

And, finally, he'd come ashore.

"I'll meet you at home," I muttered to Daddy, eyes locked on the gazebo, and the man I loved, one foot inching off the curb.

"How will you get home? Where are you—oh," he said, squinting. "Is that him?"

I nodded, finally turning back toward my father.

He gave a soft, knowing smile. "Go on, doll. I'll see you at home."

As I crossed the street, one cautious step at a time, the thought hit me like a sucker punch to the ribs.

Home.

What a strange word.

It wasn't that big, sterile house I'd grown up in, all echoey halls and pristine carpets. It wasn't Doyle's posh penthouse with its spa-like details and overly plush furniture. It wasn't New York City, or Australia, Los Angeles, or the coast of New England—none of them ever quite fitting the way I'd hoped they would.

Home was standing in front of me, in the rebuilt gazebo, with that unreadable expression on his face, as I climbed the three small steps that separated us.

We stood there in the hush that settles over a small-town square once the holiday magic dies down. No music from the bandstand. No chatter spilling from the diner across the street. Just a lone car easing past and the wind shifting through the winter-bare oaks.

I'd imagined this moment a hundred times. Charlie would read my letter, cross every mile between us, and find me somehow stronger. Stitched up, but with enough to let him fully in.

I wasn't even sure if I was there yet, if I was ready, but he was already here, filling the doorway of the folly—copper curls, steady eyes. And I had no script for that.

"We really do have a thing for gazebos, huh?" The words slipped out before I could stop them.

A slow, reluctant grin tipped one corner of his mouth, the rare kind that actually reached his eyes and made the corners crinkle like warm, worn leather. "Seems we do."

He stepped closer, boots scuffing the old pine boards. He took my hand, wove our fingers together, and pressed them gently over my heart. "You gave me this once," he said, "And made me promise not to break it. And I'm a man of my word."

My throat tightened. I lifted a shoulder, half shrug, half shield. "I don't know if I'm whole enough to love you back the way you deserve. I'm a wreck, Charlie. I come with baggage and a baby and a raggedy poodle and, well, Dig."

He gave a quiet huff, almost a laugh. "You think I don't know that? I counted every piece before I got in the truck, Tally. The baggage. The sequin-covered best friend. The hurricane that you are."

He paused, untangled our fingers, and rested his hand over my stomach. "And this, Tally. I especially want this. With you."

I opened my mouth, but he closed the last inch between us first. Running a gentle hand over my cheek, cupping the back of my neck, and tilting my face toward his. His gaze locked on mine, eyes watching my lips in the way one does when they've kissed you before, and, God help them, they want to do it again.

"That letter of yours?" His voice dropped low. "It wasn't a goodbye. It was a map. And it led me straight here."

He slid his fingers between mine again, sure and steady.

"You're not broken pieces, Tal. You're a work in progress. So am I. We can sand the edges together, one day at a time."

The cold air stung my eyes. I blinked hard. "What if I wave you in, and tomorrow I panic and run again?"

"Love isn't always pretty, Tally." His voice was quiet, but every word landed like it had been etched into my ribs. "It's never going to be this picture-perfect thing you imagined. It's not candlelit dinners and grand gestures every day. Most of the time, it's having someone by your side when you need them most. It's being there on the good days and the awful ones. When a parent's in the hospital. When you're sitting in silence next to a hospice bed. When you're standing in a delivery room, too afraid to ask the questions out loud. Or when you're holding your breath and your baby's being placed in your arms for the very first time."

He took a step closer, eyes blazing. "Love is driving five hours in my dead uncle's busted truck because I had to tell you—without a single shadow of a doubt—that I'm that man, Tally. I'm the one who will hold your hand through every storm. The good. The bad. The heartbreaking. I am that guy."

He paused, breath catching.

"Let it be me."

We stood still, breathless, like the world might split straight down the middle if we moved too fast.

His voice cracked. "I used to think I was the one who took broken things and made them beautiful. That was my story. But then you showed up. You took the mess of me, the broken edges, the scattered pieces, and somehow you made it make sense. You didn't just fix me, Tally. You reminded me I was *worth* fixing."

He took one last step, close enough for his warmth to spill into the space between us as our bodies pressed together. "You made me believe that someone like you could love someone like me."

We stood there, hearts thudding.

I couldn't take it anymore. I gave Charlie the only answer I had in that moment.

I kissed him.

Soft at first. Quiet. Then firmer, fuller. Packed with every promise we had made, and broken, and would make and break again.

I didn't know much about life. Hell, I didn't know much about anything at all. But I did know that maybe the secret isn't being perfect. Perhaps it's not the right job, or the right house, or the right partner on paper.

Maybe the secret to a long, beautiful, heartbreaking, worth-it kind of life is finding the person who sees you at your absolute worst and doesn't flinch. The one who doesn't try to fix it and sits beside you in the mess and holds your hand through it.

Maybe the real magic is in finding someone who will chart a course straight to you, even when you've built every roadblock you can think of.

And when they finally arrive, breathless and stubborn and sure…

I didn't need the river to bring Charlie Pruitt ashore; he'd found his way all on his own.

And this time, I let him stay.

EPILOGUE

Charlie

Libby was double-fisting chunks of her smash cake and showing no signs of slowing down.

She sat in the grass under the playground shade structure, a paper crown crooked on her head, cheeks flushed pink from the heat and attention, hot pink frosting smeared in the crevices of her neck and the chubby little folds of her arms.

It's not every day that the princess of the family turns one year old, and Liberty Savannah Pruitt was making quite the show of it.

Tally hovered nearby, chatting with a group of moms she'd met through the inn's new community brunch series, one hand holding a half-eaten mini quiche, the other clutching Nancy's leash, the leash getting yanked and jerked every time she lunged for the discarded pieces of cake being flung in the grass.

Dig crouched down in front of Libby, snapping a thousand photos of her dressed in tulle, frosting, and pearls. "Smile for your favorite uncle, my little star," he cooed. Libby paid him no mind as she kept digging her fingers into the soft sponge of the cake and squealing from the excitement, or the sugar.

Across the lawn, Sutton finally let herself collapse into a folding chair, heels kicked off, a glass of champagne in one hand and a plastic tiara perched firmly on her head. "I am officially off-duty," she announced. "If anyone even whispers about cheese boards, I'm throwing myself into the fountain."

Lee raised his glass in salute. "To Sutton. Patron saint of baked goods and breakdowns." He crossed the grassy patch and leaned down to wipe frosting off of Libby's cheeks. "Our beautiful girl, look at you go."

"Back off, Lee," Dig said, hopping up and elbowing between Jordan and Doyle. "It's clear I'm already the favorite uncle. I already have her listening to

Funny Girl and learning stage cues. She'll want to move to New York City with Uncle Diggy in no time."

Doyle rolled his eyes. "Please, she's wearing a Tiffany bracelet that I bought her. If anyone's winning this, it's me."

Jordan, watching the exchange from a patch of shade near the tree line, barely looked up from his drink. "They're both idiots. I'm the cool one," he said loud enough for me to hear. "Who do you think she's going to call when all of you drive her out of her mind?"

I gave a quiet nod, adjusting Libby's paper crown where it had slipped down over her eyes. "Noted."

Vivianne and Hollis Aden lingered on the edge of the lawn with Eunice and Vance, their voices soft over the hum of distant laughter and the clink of dessert plates. I gave Vivi a small wave, and she returned it with a tight-lipped smile that didn't quite reach her eyes. She'd warm up to me eventually, and I'd do whatever it took—especially knowing how desperately she was trying to repair things with her daughter. With the woman I loved.

Hollis, on the other hand, looked like he'd stumbled into a candy shop and refused to leave. Wide grin, frosting smeared across his cheeks, a half-eaten cupcake in one hand and a chocolate-dusted cookie in the other. Eunice gave a slight wince, and I had to fight the urge to grin at the scene.

Maybe the four socialites weren't destined for bridge marathons or polite tea parties, but it was a start.

Magnolia was stretched out on a picnic blanket near the food table, one hand resting lightly on her belly. Lee hovered close, trying to pretend he wasn't checking her water bottle every five minutes.

"You're worse than my doctor," she muttered without looking up. "I'm already peeing every thirty seconds as is."

"And yet you married me," he replied, popping a grape in his mouth.

"Regret is a slow burn."

Ryan stood off to the side with a cupcake in hand, smiling faintly but not saying much. He caught my eye, nodded once, then looked away.

I settled onto the grass beside Libby, who handed me a soggy piece of cake like it was a priceless artifact, eyes full of joy and wonder. I took it without a word, heart full in a way I hadn't expected. I used to think happiness was loud.

Something that crashed in with fireworks and confessions. But today felt quiet. Steady. Real.

Libby looked up at me with her mother's hazel eyes and said, clear as day, "Dada."

The entire group turned.

Tally froze, her hand mid-air as she wildly gestured during her conversation.

I blinked, unsure I'd heard her right.

Libby, proud and sticky, said it again.

"Dada."

The world didn't stop. Music still played. Glasses still clinked. A dog barked somewhere behind us.

But something in me did.

I was a dad.

And this was my family.

***

After packing up the mess from Libby's first birthday and sending every-one back to Maggie O'Malley's—the inn and public house my sister now owned outright—we loaded up the stroller. Tally and I had spent the last year renting a room in the back carriage house of the inn, saving every penny, dodging a very pregnant Magnolia's hormonal outbursts, and quietly building something that felt a lot like a life.

Tally had worked her ass off. Long days, late nights, camera always slung over her shoulder. And after enough courthouse ceremonies, pop-up weddings in the squares, and one memorable beach elopement where the ring bearer dropped the rings in the ocean, she'd finally done it. She'd saved enough to launch her own company: *Marry Me, Savannah*—a one-stop shop for wildly romantic, slightly chaotic, deeply heartfelt elopements. She ran it out of the inn, of course, alongside my sister, who helped with the lodging accommodations, and Sutton, who baked all the wedding cakes. We were still Pruitts at heart, never quite able to spend that much time apart from one another.

We were walking Libby through Lafayette Square, her legs kicking under a pink blanket, Nancy Reagan trotting beside us in a rhinestone leash Sutton had insisted on buying her, when we passed a house with wraparound porch, the railing lined with flowering vines in soft bloom. A single, swinging sign hung from the side of the staircase.

Open House.

"Wanna check it out?"

Tally blinked at me. "Charlie. I just opened a business. We can't afford a house."

But we could.

Because that steel drum she threw up in the night we met? It led to thirty commissions. Apparently, divorced women love cathartic art. Their friends did too. And their lawyers. And their therapists. Word spread, and I'd worked steadily ever since. I hadn't just scraped by. I'd saved. I'd planned.

"I wanna peek inside," I said casually, pushing the stroller toward the steps. "Libby's fighting her nap anyway. No idea where she gets this stubborn streak from."

"Probably her auntie Magnolia," Tally muttered, but she followed me up the porch.

Inside, the air carried the sharp tang of fresh paint, mingling with the faint, comforting scent of old wood. The fireplace looked as if it had always belonged here, framed by built-in bookshelves that held nothing yet promised everything. Tall windows let in a soft, golden light that pooled across the wide-plank floors, which groaned softly under her weight as she moved through the space. She lingered in the kitchen, letting her fingers brush over the smooth marble counters, then leaned slightly toward the window, watching the backyard stretch out beyond the glass.

"There's a swing set," she whispered. Then, "Wow—look. A carriage house."

"It would make a great studio," I said, already picturing where I'd put my tools.

She wandered deeper into the house, her eyes tracing the way the old-world details met modern touches—the carved trim running into sleek door frames, the soft light catching on brass fixtures. The air seemed to hum with quiet possibility. But when she stepped into the primary bedroom at the back, something about the space made her pause, rooted to the spot.

There, leaning against the wall, was the sketch. The twin to the one she kept beside her rocking chair. Her silhouette stretched against the river, her bump rounded beneath a flowy dress, the Waving Girl statue standing quietly in the distance. She reached out, fingers brushing the edge with care. "Oh my god, Charlie," she whispered. "You finished it… wait, what did you do?"

"It needs a frame," I said, bouncing Libby on my hip as she grabbed a handful of my hair, tiny fingers tugging and pulling with all the determination only a toddler could manage. "But we can handle that once we get the rest of our stuff in here."

Tally turned to me, her eyes soft and shining, reflecting every late night, every fight, every storm we'd weathered that brought us to this shore. Together. The room felt impossibly still around us, like the house itself was holding its breath.

I kissed Libby's cheek, inhaling the faint scent of her baby shampoo and cake frosting, then met my wife's gaze.

"I love you girls," I whispered, my chest full, the words small but heavy with everything we'd endured to get here. "Welcome home."

THE END

ACKNOWLEDGEMENTS

To say I've been completely blown away by the support I've received since turning what was once a quiet dream into a reality—becoming a published author—is an understatement. Every single person who has read *Our Song*, chatted with me about all things bookish, or begged for the next story, I hope you know how much I love you for it. You've truly, irrevocably changed my life. I hope you love this story as much as the first one.

There are two people I owe this entire career to: my kids, Declan and Everly. The way you've become my biggest fans—telling your friends and teachers about my book and even convincing a few of them to buy it (looking at you, D-Man)—completely blows me away. Your patience when Mom needs to "just finish one more chapter," and your willingness to come along to every event, have shown me that this isn't just my dream—it's ours. I've never been prouder to share it with you.

One day, when you're old enough to read this story, I want you to know that the way Tally feels about Libby from the very start is exactly how I've always felt about you. Becoming a mom is the greatest gift I've ever been given, and it's changed me in every way that matters. I love you beyond measure and am endlessly proud of the people you're becoming.

James—so much of this book comes straight from our own story. The wedding, our gazebo, the girl who runs when things get hard, and the man who loves her through it. But most of all, it's about the quiet strength of partnership— the way Charlie steps up for Tally, even when the baby isn't his. You should be so proud of this family we've built and the father you are. Thank you for standing by me through every chapter of this journey. I couldn't have made it here without you.

Dad, you share every post, tell everyone who gets in your car to read my book, and never stop cheering me on. I've dedicated this one to you because I want you to know that even when we think we don't always get it right, the proof that we sometimes do is reflected in the lives of our children—and the love we poured into them. I'm proud to be your daughter, just as I know you're proud to be my dad.

To my family—thank you for your endless love and encouragement. What a year this has been. From Southie to Florida and beyond, I feel the love and I'm thankful for you all.

To my friends and neighbors who have become family, I'm so lucky to have you beside me through every wild, joyful moment of this journey. Thank you for the laughter, the hugs, the support, and for showing up every single time. Tara, Josh, Rebecca, Vern, Adriana, Gretchen, Adam, Fetle, Rocky, Stacy, Nicole, Quincy, Tiffany, Krislyn, Deanne, Bryanna, Andi, Amy, Julia, Rylee, Dawn, Kim—and everyone else who's come to my events or cheered me on from the sidelines—I'm so grateful for each of you.

Megan, thank you for reading every single version of this story a thousand times over and for making sure I get it right. Remember, life goes on—and so do we. There is strength in this story, one that reflects moving on when you feel like you've been left behind, and I hope you know that your story isn't finished yet. I love you endlessly.

Anita, you're fired as my assistant but never as my friend. Thank you for reading this book a million times, talking me off ledges, and for every blurry photo and video. Still fired, though! Love you anyway.

To Alissa DeGregorio—the best cover artist ever—thank you for your patience and unbelievable talent. How you put up with my shenanigans is anyone's guess but I am so grateful for you. Your talent remains unmatched, and I hope you know that.

Sam McDaniel—thank you for your keen eye, your insight, and for helping shape this story into something I'm so proud of.

Sylvie—spelled your name right *and* got you a job at *Cheese, Please!*. You're welcome. I will never forget you strolling through the bookshop doors at my first solo signing and the relief I felt at having one of my "people" there. Your support throughout this all has kept me going and I want you to never, ever forget that you are the kind of friend people dream of having, and I am so glad you are one of mine.

To the bookstore owners and friends who've put my books on your shelves and my face in front of readers—thank you for believing in me. I am eternally grateful for the opportunity to be a featured author in your spaces.

To my beta readers and sounding boards—Stephanie, Emily V, Emily G, Allison, Colleen, Ashley, and Shannon—thank you for helping this book find its best version. For those of you who had to talk me off several ledges… I owe you a drink. Or two. Stephanie, I probably owe you about five.

Dave—the hype hasn't gone unnoticed. The fact that you became a pastor in this story feels pretty fitting, giving our behavior in our twenties. Love you, friend. Kristy, thank you for keeping us all connected. We love you.

To the readers, thank you for taking a chance on me. The love, support, and kindness you've shown have meant more than I can ever say. This year has been unforgettable, and I can't wait to see what lies beyond.

To Nonie, the true-blue love of my life, I know you have spent the last year smiling down on me and helping me remember that I was born for this. I wish you could have seen what I've done, what I've built, who I have finally become. But it's not lost on me that you walk beside me on this journey and that I carry you with me, always.

And lastly, always, to my mom. Your love of reading and storytelling shaped me into who I am today. You would have loved this one, Momma—I just know it. Keep sending me signs. I see them, and I feel you everywhere. I love you.

All my love, always,

KH

ABOUT THE AUTHOR

Kelly Hennelly writes romantic comedies filled with heart, humor, and a dash of Southern chaos. Her *Savannah Sweethearts* series brings the charm of the South to life with stories about second chances, found family, and the kind of love that feels both messy and meant to be.

A South Boston native now living in Florida, Kelly has a deep love for beaches, bourbon, and beautiful sentences. She spends her days juggling writing, motherhood, and far too many cups of coffee. When she's not dreaming up fictional love stories, she's living her favorite one with her husband, James, and their two kids, Declan and Everly—plus a few unruly pets who think they run the house.

You can find her on social media @authorkellyhennelly, usually talking about all things bookish—and her latest crush on one of her own fictional men.

Also By Kelly Hennelly

The Savannah Sweetheart Series
Our Song
Let It Be Me

www.ingramcontent.com/pod-product-compliance
Lightning Source LLC
Chambersburg PA
CBHW021021310726
48969CB00006B/1482